The Devil's Cocktail

Slough Library Services

Please return this book on or before the
date shown on your receipt.

To renew go to:
Website: **www.slough.gov.uk/libraries**
Phone: **01753 533166**

D1419891

30130503673259

ALSO BY ALEXANDER WILSON
FROM CLIPPER LARGE PRINT

The Mystery of Tunnel 51

The Devil's Cocktail

Alexander Wilson

W F HOWES LTD

This large print edition published in 2016 by
W F Howes Ltd
Unit 5, St George's House, Rearsby Business Park,
Gaddesby Lane, Rearsby, Leicester LE7 4YH

1 3 5 7 9 10 8 6 4 2

First published in the United Kingdom in 1928
by Longmans, Green and Co

Copyright © The Alexander Wilson Estate, 1928

The right of Alexander Wilson to be identified
as the author of this work has been asserted by him
in accordance with the Copyright, Designs and
Patents Act, 1988.

All rights reserved

A CIP catalogue record for this book is available
from the British Library

ISBN 978 1 51002 387 1

Typeset by Palimpsest Book Production Limited,
Falkirk, Stirlingshire

Printed and bound in Great Britain
by TJ International Ltd, Padstow, Cornwall

Slough Libraries

Barcode 30130503673259		
Supplier W.F.Howes	Date 07-Mar-2016	
	Price £19.50	

CONTENTS

CHAPTER 1

AN ADVERTISEMENT

The famous chief of the British Intelligence Department leant back in his chair, and looked thoughtful. The pattering of the rain on his office window, and the subdued noise of the traffic in the street below appeared to have a soothing effect upon him, and to be conducive to deep reflection, for he sat without movement for nearly ten minutes. At length he looked at his companion, and taking a pipe from his pocket proceeded to fill it from a pouch which lay on his desk.

'It may be a waste of time and the loss of a good man for a considerable period,' he said, when his pipe was going to his satisfaction, 'but I have decided to send Shannon to India.'

The fair-haired, good-looking man, seated on the opposite side of the desk, nodded.

'In what capacity will he go out?' he asked.

For answer the other handed him a copy of *The Times* opened at the advertisement page, and indicated a paragraph in the appointments' column.

'Shannon appears to have all the qualifications necessary for the post,' he said, 'and really nothing could be more ideal for our purpose.'

'But this is for three years!' exclaimed the almost equally renowned Deputy Chief. 'Surely you don't intend him to be out there all that time?'

'Why not? In three years a lot may be accomplished, and I want a lot to be done. On the other hand, of course, Shannon may fail, but we must risk that.'

'I don't think he will fail. He is a pretty good fellow, and as keen as mustard. But do you think it is any good sending him to take up a position like this where he'll be tied down most of the year?'

'Yes; he'll be right on the spot in Lahore, and besides he will, no doubt, have endless opportunities for getting about to other districts during the vacations, and they get pretty lengthy ones in the colleges in India. Altogether I don't think anything could have suited our purpose better than this.' He tapped the paper, which his companion had handed back to him. 'It remains now for him to be appointed.'

'Yes; and that is not going to be easy. Probably there will be a host of applications.'

'No doubt, but with his qualifications, and the references we can give him, he should get the job.' He rang a bell on his desk. 'He ought to be in the building somewhere – I'll have him in at once.'

A secretary appeared.

'Find out if Captain Shannon is here,' said the Chief, 'and if so send him up to me!'

'Very well, sir,' said the secretary, and departed. After a few minutes there was a knock, and, in response to the Chief's invitation to enter, a young man came into the room, and stood respectfully by the door.

'You sent for me, sir?' he enquired.

'Yes! Sit down, and help yourself to a cigarette!'

The young man did as he was bidden. The Chief regarded him seriously for a moment, then:

'You made rather a name for yourself at Oxford, didn't you? Got a fellowship and half a dozen other things?' he asked.

The other smiled.

'I didn't do badly, sir,' he replied.

'And you had a double "Blue", which is a great advantage in an appointment of the nature I am going to put before you, Shannon.'

The faintest look of surprise passed across the young man's face.

'Altogether you are eminently suitable to take up the Chair of English Literature at a university college,' went on the Chief, 'and so I wish you to apply at once for this post.'

He handed *The Times* to Shannon, and showed him the advertisement in question. Without attempting to conceal his interest, the latter read the following:

A Professor of English Literature is required for Sheranwala College, University of Northern India, Lahore, at a salary of Rupees 500-50-1000, for a period of three years. Applicants must be graduates of an

3

English University and preference will be given to one who is a sportsman. Apply with copies of testimonials, references, etc., to Mahommed Abdullah, C.I.E., Savoy Hotel, Strand, London.

Captain Shannon read the advertisement twice before handing the paper back, and it was a very astonished young man who looked to his Chief for enlightenment. The latter smiled, and knocked out the ashes of his pipe into an ashtray.

'I want you to get that post, Shannon,' he said, 'you'll probably find it most congenial.'

'You have your reasons, sir?' said the other.

'I have! Very little is done in this department without a reason. Now listen carefully to what I have to say!' He rose from his chair and strolled across the room to the fireplace, where he stood with his back resting against the mantelpiece, and confronted the young officer.

'India is a strange country,' he said, 'and there are things going on there which this country knows nothing about. The time has come, however, when Great Britain must be cognisant of all that occurs, in order not only to safeguard herself, but also to ensure the safety of the Indian Empire. As you are aware, my colleague and I practically succeeded last year in routing out the Bolshevik element in India, but from information received, I believe that representatives of the Russian Soviet have recommenced their activities. Apart from that there is an

4

undercurrent of unrest and distrust and various latent disorders which must be inquired into. Lahore appears to be the centre of the trouble, and it is to Lahore that I wish you to go. India possesses a very fine police force, but there is no Intelligence Department worth the name. In taking up the appointment of Professor of English Literature in this college, you will have endless opportunities to get to the bottom of things. Nobody will suspect that you are a member of the Secret Service – nobody must suspect! Something is going on, and I want you to find out what that something is. You have a big job before you, and it will require infinite tact, patience and resource. I have chosen you because of your knowledge of Hindustani, and because I have found you to be a reliable man. You have no time to think the matter over; your application for this appointment must go in today – either accept or refuse! Which is it to be?'

Captain Shannon looked at his Chief with sparkling eyes. This was an opportunity for which he had longed ever since he had joined the Intelligence Service. Without the slightest sign of hesitation, he spoke.

'Of course I accept, sir!' he said.

'Good,' said the Chief nonchalantly, and returned to his seat at the desk. 'Now you had better write your application at once, and in order to ensure your getting the post, you must have a splendid list of referees. No doubt you can get any number from your college, and so on. Add to them these three—'

He mentioned three names which were household words in England. 'I'll see that these gentlemen respond without any suspicion arising that you are a member of the Intelligence Department. And now you had better get busy at once. Remember that if you are appointed, you are in no way to neglect your duty to your employers, but, of course, your first responsibility will be to us.'

He rose, and held out his hand. Captain Shannon grasped it eagerly.

'I'm jolly grateful to you for giving me this chance, sir,' he said boyishly.

'Well, make the most of it! A lot depends upon you; perhaps more than any of us can say at present. The main thing now is to get the post; everything will be done to help you, and before you sail we shall have a further interview at which all details will be discussed, and your final instructions given to you.'

The Deputy Chief walked with Shannon to the door.

'You *must* get the post!' he said. 'We are relying on you more than we have ever relied upon anybody before. If you succeed in the job that has been assigned to you, you are a made man, if you fail—' He shrugged his shoulders, and held out his hand.

'I shall not fail, sir,' said Shannon, and departed.

CHAPTER 2

WHITE LIES

Hugh Shannon lost no time in applying for the post of Professor of English Literature of Sheranwala College in Lahore. He was a modest young man, and he found it rather difficult to do himself justice without appearing to be, as he put it, 'a conceited idiot.' However, he had a duty to perform, and he did it. The letter of application, with copies of his testimonials – and he had many – was duly despatched. Thereafter he spent two days of anxiety, wondering if he would receive a reply.

Captain Shannon had had a short though distinguished career in the Indian Army, and had left it to take up a post in the Foreign Office, whence he had been attached to the Intelligence Department. He had quickly come under the notice of the astute Chief, who had given him duties which required great resource and tact to carry out, as well as a masterly knowledge of languages. Thus, in two years, he had become one of the most trusted men in the service, and gave promise of rising very rapidly in his chosen profession.

At this time about thirty years of age, he was a

splendidly built specimen of English manhood. Nearly six feet in height, he looked shorter on account of his breadth of shoulder and powerful frame. He was not handsome, but his clean-shaven face, with its humorous mouth, steely grey eyes, determined chin and high forehead, surmounted by a mass of curly brown hair, gave him an attractive appearance, which appealed very much to most people he met. Added to this he possessed a happy-go-lucky nature, a great love for sport of all descriptions, a fearless dispo-sition, and a fondness for getting to the bottom of things; and, therefore, in the Secret Service he had discovered the one job which attracted him above all others. Both parents being dead, he and an only sister lived in a small flat opposite Kensington Gardens, where they were in the midst of a wide circle of friends.

On the morning of the third day after he had sent off his letter of application, he was seated at breakfast with his morning newspaper propped up in front of him. His sister, who had been to a dance the night before, was late in making her appearance, and he had nearly finished his meal when at last she came in.

'Oh, you pig!' she exclaimed by way of greeting. 'You might have waited for me.'

'My dear girl,' he replied, as he arranged her chair for her, 'I am a busy man, and there is a certain matter of daily bread to be earned.'

'Daily bread!' she scoffed. 'Why we have enough

money between us to live perfectly happily, and in spite of that you delude yourself into imagining that you are keeping us on the paltry £500 a year the Foreign Office pay you.'

He smiled.

'Would you have me loaf my way through life, Joan?'

'No; but I cannot understand what you find to do in that musty old office. Now if they made you a King's Messenger there would be some sense in it. I think there must be something mysterious about your work. Sometimes you appear to have nothing to do, and at other times you disappear for weeks on end, and when you come back you are frightfully vague about where you have been, and what you have been doing. You've become a most unsatisfactory person lately, Hugh.'

She poured herself out some coffee, while he sat back in his chair, and watched her. Very few people were aware of Hugh Shannon's real position, and even his sister thought he was merely an ornamental member of the staff at the Foreign Office, though occasionally she wondered why he was so often called upon to make sudden journeys out of England.

'I wish you had stopped in the Army,' she went on, 'I should love to have lived in India for a few years, and kept house for you, and now I shall probably never have the opportunity.'

'You may,' he said quietly; 'in fact there is quite a possibility.'

She jumped up in her excitement.

'Oh, Hugh, do you really mean that? Are you going back to the Army?'

He shook his head.

'No; but I have applied for a post in a college out there.'

She stared at him in astonishment.

'You've what?' she demanded. 'What sort of a post?'

'Professor of English Literature,' he said with a half-defiant note in his voice.

She continued to gaze at him in amazement for a minute or two, and then burst into peal after peal of such infectious laughter that he was compelled to join in with her.

'Do you really mean that, Hugh?' she asked, when her merriment had subsided.

'Of course!'

'But, my dear brother,' she said, with the air of a mother gently chiding her child, 'don't you realise that to become a professor of literature one must devote years and years to study? Besides you don't look like one.'

'Why not?'

'All the professors I ever knew were old and wore glasses and sniffed – you don't, and you're not old. You'd have to be absent-minded too, and you're the very opposite to that.'

'Well, I've applied for the job anyway, and if there's any chance of my obtaining it, I should get a letter today or tomorrow appointing an interview.'

'But, dear,' she said, 'that will mean your leaving the Foreign Office, and I thought you were very happy there.'

'So I am, but this post rather appeals to me – and I'd like to get back to India for a few years.'

She was silent for a little while.

'I don't think I have ever been so surprised in my life,' she said, at last. 'Fancy you, a born soldier, devoting yourself to the teaching of literature. I don't know that I like the idea much, though I want to go to India. You'll take me with you, of course?' she asked.

'I haven't got the job yet,' he said.

'Oh you'll get it. You always get everything you set out for.'

'Thank you!' He rose and bowed with mock gratitude.

'But, Hugh dear, won't you be awfully bored?'

'Not a bit. You see they lay particular stress upon requiring a sportsman, so there should be some fun.'

'That makes a big difference,' she nodded. 'The fact that they want a sportsman makes the whole proposition infinitely more attractive.'

At that moment the maid brought in some letters on a salver. Hugh took them, and handing three or four to his sister, glanced quickly at the rest. One, bearing the superscription in an unknown hand, he rapidly tore open, extracted the single sheet of notepaper it contained and looked at the address.

'Ah!' he ejaculated, and Joan glanced across at him eagerly.

'Is it the one?' she asked.

He nodded. The letter was addressed from the Savoy Hotel.

> *Dear Sir,*
> *I am very much interested in your application for the post of Professor of English Literature. I may say that you appear to be the type of man required. Will you be good enough to call at the above address on Wednesday afternoon at three o'clock?*
> *Yours faithfully,*
> *Mahommed Abdullah*

With a sigh of relief Hugh handed the letter to Joan.

'I think I'll get it,' he said.

She read the note and handed it back.

'Hugh, you are an astonishing person,' she said. 'It certainly looks as though I shall have to see about getting an outfit ready for the tropics.'

He smiled as he rose from the table.

'You are determined to come?' he asked.

'Of course! How on earth could you get on without me? You'd be lost!'

'I believe I would,' he said gently, as he bent and kissed her, and then strolled out of the room.

Joan sat gazing at her plate for some time, with a very thoughtful expression on her face. She presented an exquisite picture of young womanhood as she sat there, with the rays of the early morning sun streaming through the wide-open window and shining on the chestnut glory of her shingled hair. She was seven years her brother's junior and, unlike him, was rather small. Her eyes were almost unnaturally large and of a deep blue colour; her mouth was small and delicately shaped, and when she smiled could be seen a most perfect set of pearly white teeth; her nose was daintily set upon a face with the healthy complexion of the outdoor girl. But what impressed one most was the beauty of her hands and feet, which had caused several artists to go into raptures of admiration. Joan Shannon was a girl who was adored by hundreds, but she had never had a love affair, all her affection being given to her big, burly brother, whom she loved and admired as very few sisters do.

Presently she rose and, crossing to the window, looked out on to the park.

'I wonder why Hugh is so keen on going to India,' she murmured. 'I don't believe he has given up his work at the Foreign Office, he is too fond of it.' She sighed. 'I wish I knew what is behind it all.'

CHAPTER 3

AN INTERVIEW AND A CHASE

Prompt to the minute, Hugh walked into the Savoy Hotel, and asked to see Mr Mahommed Abdullah. Apparently he was expected, for he was at once directed to a lounge, where a dark-visaged man of rather less than medium height, dressed in a suit of some grey material, rose from the depths of an armchair to greet him. Obviously an Indian, the man appeared to be about fifty years of age, his hair was thinning on top and grey at the temples, while he had a slight stoop, which seemed to denote the scholar. In fact his whole bearing was that of a man who had devoted a great part of his life to study. He greeted Hugh with great politeness and, taking him by the arm, led him to a chair which he pulled up close to his own.

'I am very glad to make your acquaintance, Captain Shannon,' he said, as he sank into his seat, 'and I congratulate you on your punctuality. Being a very busy man, I am naturally jealous of every wasted moment. I still have to interview four applicants for this post before six o'clock.'

'Then you have had a good many replies to your advertisement?' inquired Hugh.

14

'Sixty-eight to be exact,' replied the other, who spoke perfect English, without any trace of accent. 'Of course a good many were unsuitable, but I have arranged to interview ten; you are the sixth.'

'I hope you have not decided upon your man yet,' smiled Hugh.

'I have not! To be quite honest your application was the one which impressed me more than any others, and I hope that you will eventually be my choice.'

'That is entirely in your hands, sir.'

Abdullah bowed.

'I must tell you the circumstances,' he said. 'Sheranwala College, which is a Muslim institution affiliated to the University of Northern India, has not been upholding Mahommedan traditions. The governing body has, therefore, invited me to return to India, and take over the Principalship in the hope that I may be able to raise the College to the position it once held. For some time I hesitated, as I had fully made up my mind to settle down in this country for good. However, I was eventually persuaded to accept. I have been empowered to engage a first-class Englishman as Professor of English, and thus my advertisement. I may tell you that I desire the man I select to act as vice principal and in fact to be my right hand man and general aide-de-camp. The salary is not large, of course, and I fear that most Englishmen would find it difficult to live on 500 rupees a month – Are you married?'

'No; but I have a sister who will accompany me if I am selected.'

'H'm! You have no private means, I suppose?'

'I have enough to keep us, but it seems to me, sir, that in making an appointment of this nature, the authorities should be willing to pay an adequate salary.'

'I quite agree with you, and I think I can promise to persuade them to make an increase, which will more than meet your needs. Now for your qualifications . . .'

For the next twenty minutes Abdullah was engaged in questioning Hugh closely about his school and college career, during which the latter discovered that the new Principal of Sheranwala College was a man of very deep learning. He had taken his Master of Arts degree at Cambridge, was a barrister, a retired financial commissioner, and an eminent economist. At the end of the interview Shannon had acquired a deep respect for the quiet-mannered little man, who had proved himself such an adept in questioning him.

'Well I must say, Captain Shannon,' remarked Abdullah, 'that you meet our requirements in every respect, and I am now practically certain that you will be my choice, but, of course, you understand that I cannot say definitely until I have interviewed the remaining candidates.'

'Certainly,' replied Hugh.

'In the event of your being appointed, a sum of seventy pounds will be placed at your disposal for travelling expenses. I am afraid that we cannot very well make any allowance for your sister.'

'No, I suppose not,' said Hugh. 'It is hardly to be expected, is it?'

A few minutes later they parted, Abdullah escorting Hugh to the door of the lounge, where they shook hands. The latter made his way out of the hotel, and, declining the offer of a taxi driver to take him 'anywhere', he strolled westwards feeling rather perturbed than otherwise at the success which seemed about to crown his application.

In spite of his high academical qualifications, it struck him that he was hardly the man to attempt to lecture on English literature to a collection of Muslim youths, when all his instincts, all his ambitions, were centred on his own job. However, it was the Chief's wish and, after all, the appointment as a professor in a college was only a means to an end, and a very great and responsible end as far as Hugh was concerned. He looked forward to his work in India, but it was to his own particular work under the Intelligence Department, not the superficial duties of a member of the staff of Sheranwala College.

He had reached Trafalgar Square, and was turning in the direction of Whitehall, when he almost bumped into a little, sallow-faced man, with shifty eyes and a nose of a decidedly Semitic cast. With a muttered curse the little man skipped out of his way and dived across the road, but with an exclamation of surprise Hugh had recognised him, and without hesitation followed him. The Jew, with the activity of an eel, headed for St Martin's Lane. Shannon, being big and burly, found it more difficult to get along, but he made fairly rapid headway, much to the resentment of the people he unceremoniously bundled out of his path. The chase went on past the Coliseum, then with a malignant backward glance, the little man turned into a small tea shop. Hugh was only a few seconds behind him, but when he entered the shop there was not a sign of his quarry, the place being occupied only by a couple of tired-looking waitresses, a man with a badly shaved jaw, obviously one of the many down-at-heel actors, who infest that part of London, and a fat old woman, just as obviously up from the country.

Hugh dashed by the tea room, and ran up a dingy flight of stairs. He found two or three offices, whose occupants stared at him in surprise, but to his enquiries they all declared that they had not seen anybody even resembling the man he was after. The same negative result awaited him on the other two floors and although he made a careful search – much to the indignation of the people he met, who naturally resented his headlong intrusion into their privacy – he was compelled to descend to the ground floor a puzzled and disappointed man.

'Did you see a little, dark man – a Jew – enter this building?' he asked the waitresses.

18

One of them giggled, while the other looked him up and down in a supercilious manner.

'Do you think we have time to see everybody who comes in that door?' she asked.

Hugh grinned.

'No, I suppose not,' he said, 'still you might have noticed him.'

'Well, we didn't, so there!' she snapped.

'Pardon me, sir!' said a deep voice, and Hugh swung round to confront the actor-looking person who, with a spoon in one hand and a piece of bread in the other, rose majestically to his feet. 'I may say that I saw a rather insignificant specimen of the genus man,' went on this individual. 'He rushed by that door as though he were being chased.' He indicated the direction in a lordly manner with the piece of bread.

'Thanks!' said Hugh. He turned again to the waitresses. 'Where does that passage lead to?' he asked.

'Down to the kitchen, if you want to know,' replied the supercilious one.

Hugh ran along the passage, and was about to turn down the stairs, when he noticed a wide-open window. He looked out on to a dirty little yard enclosed by a low brick wall, and groaned. His man had obviously gone that way; had climbed over the wall and disappeared down a lane, which Hugh knew must be somewhere about there, and which went down past Charing Cross Hospital.

'Hang it all!' he muttered. 'What a fool I was to let him get away.'

He retraced his steps and, entering the tea room, ordered some tea and toast.

'The least I can do after causing you this bother,' he said, 'is to sample your tea.'

'Trying to be funny?' asked the snappy waitress.

'No,' replied Hugh; 'merely polite.'

She snorted, and went to give his order.

'Sir,' said the actor, 'I fear you have failed in your quest. If I am not mistaken you are a detective in chase of a notorious criminal.'

'Something like that,' said Hugh cheerfully.

'May I enquire who it was that you were after?'

'Only one of the most dangerous men in London.' And thereafter Hugh refused to be drawn further.

He drank his tea and ate his toast, watched by the occupants of the room with awe. Even the girl whose object in life seemed to be to treat others as rudely as she could, appeared almost to form a respect for him, though she remarked that her brother was a proper policeman and she could not see what they wanted to have these gentlemen upstarts in the force for.

Hugh bowed solemnly before taking his departure.

'I am sorry I am such an upstart,' he remarked with mock humility. 'Please try to think a little better of me!'

Thereupon he gave her a tip, which made her blink, and strolled out of the shop. A tall, thin man, smartly clad in a brown suit, was standing on the curb. As Hugh came out he turned and, putting his arm through the other's, strolled along with him.

'Hallo, Spencer!' exclaimed Shannon. 'Where did you spring from and why the affection?'

'I saw you dive into that place as though you were chasing the devil,' replied Detective Inspector Spencer of the Special Branch of New Scotland Yard, 'so I waited for results.'

'There are no results,' said Hugh sadly. 'I lost my man. It wasn't the devil either, though it was one of his most dangerous myrmidons.'

'You intrigue me!' murmured Spencer.

'It was Kamper!'

The detective stood still and looked solemnly at Hugh.

'Are you sure?' he demanded.

'Certain! I chased him from Trafalgar Square. The worst of it is that he almost bumped into me there, and if I hadn't been daydreaming, I would have had him.'

'Moral: don't daydream!' said Spencer. 'But I can't think how the little blighter got back to England. Why we saw him snugly off for Russia on board the *Druid* only ten days ago.'

'Nevertheless he is back.'

They walked on together, each deep in his own thoughts.

'Why didn't you nab him in that building?' asked Spencer suddenly.

Hugh hesitated a moment before replying, then:

'I searched the top of the place, where I naturally thought he had gone—'

'While he ran straight on I suppose, climbed through a window, over a wall, and dropped into Somers Lane!'

'How do you know?'

'This district is a pretty open book to me. I wish I had been with you, or had followed you in.'

'I wish you had. No use searching the lane I suppose?'

'Not a bit. Kamper is in a taxi by now, tearing down towards the East End. Well, we know he's back, and that's something. I'll get straight down to the Yard, and warn them. Coming that way?'

Hugh nodded, and the two strolled down Whitehall. They parted near the Foreign Office, Hugh turning into the building which housed the mighty organisation of the department, which most people did not know existed, the British Secret Service, while Spencer continued on his way to Scotland Yard.

The Inspector went straight to his own office, and sat down before his desk.

'I wonder how the devil Kamper came back,' he muttered, 'and why?'

CHAPTER 4

CONFIDENCES

Two days later Hugh received a long letter from Mahommed Abdullah appointing him to the post of Professor of English Literature of Sheranwala College, and asking him to make arrangements to leave for India as soon as possible. Abdullah himself was leaving practically at once, and hoped that Captain Shannon would not be long behind him. He added that a sum of seventy pounds would be immediately placed to Hugh's credit in Grindlay's Bank, and expressed his satisfaction that he would have the assistance of such an able man to help him build up the fortunes of Muslim education in Northern India.

Hugh passed the letter across to Joan with a smile. She read it with great seriousness, and then looked at her brother.

'I suppose I must congratulate you, Hugh,' she said; 'but please tell me why you are doing this!'

'I have already told you that I want to get back to India, and this job rather appealed to me.'

'Is there no other reason?'

He hesitated a moment before replying.

'No!' he said.

She regarded him searchingly.

'You are not telling me the truth,' she said seriously. 'I don't see why you shouldn't take me into your confidence: it cannot be because you are ashamed of something.'

He smiled across the breakfast table at her.

'I can't understand why you should think I have any other reasons,' he said. 'You say yourself that I cannot find anything to do at the Foreign Office. Isn't it likely that I want to go somewhere, where I *shall* find something to do?'

She rose, and, coming round to his side of the table, put her hands on his shoulders.

'I suppose you have your reasons,' she said, 'and perhaps you cannot divulge them, even to me. But I want to know that you are doing nothing to be ashamed of.'

He stood up and looked straight into her eyes.

'No, Joan,' he said; 'there is no shame attached to what I am going to do – rather the reverse.'

'Well, I won't be inquisitive any more,' she declared. 'Now I suppose I must commence to get ready my outfit. What are you going to do?'

'There is so much that I really don't know where to begin,' he said. 'I must write first of all and accept the appointment, then I shall have to explain things at the Foreign Office, order my kit, collect the money from Grindlays, and – oh, a host of other things, including the booking of our passage.'

'When shall we leave?'

'The end of next week, if you can be ready by then, and we can get a boat.'

'Oh, dear! What terribly short notice! Still I'll see what can be done.'

She ran off, and in five minutes had turned the usually well-ordered flat into a scene of bustle. Hugh went out, and jumping into a taxi was driven to Whitehall. He found that the Deputy Chief had already arrived, and he asked for an interview, which was immediately granted.

Major Brien was standing on the hearthrug of his cosy office, when Hugh entered.

'Morning, Shannon!' he nodded. 'Sit down! Everything fixed up, I suppose?'

'Yes, sir!' said Hugh. 'I received the letter appointing me this morning.' He handed it to the other, who read it through without any comment, before passing it back.

'Well, there is nothing to delay you, is there?' he asked.

'No, sir!'

'When do you think you can get away?'

'By the end of next week, if I am lucky enough to get a couple of berths.'

'Why a couple?'

'My sister is coming with me, sir.'

'Oh, is she? I'm glad to hear that, Shannon. If I were you, though, I should not take her into my confidence more than is absolutely necessary. I am sure that Miss Shannon is entirely reliable, but in a case like this the fewer in the know the better.'

'She hasn't the vaguest idea what the real reason for my taking this appointment is. As a matter of fact, sir, she does not even know that I am in the Secret Service.'

'What!' said Major Brien in astonishment. 'Have you never told her?'

'No, sir!'

'Well, you're a funny fellow! And you think she does not know?'

'I'm sure of it!'

The Deputy Chief smiled.

'If I were you,' he said after a pause, 'I should tell her. Something is bound to happen sooner or later which will rouse her suspicions, and ignorance is rather apt to breed unhappiness, more especially as I know you are very attached to each other.'

'I let her think that I was still at the Foreign Office, sir. I thought it better not to tell her that I was attached to this department.'

'How has she regarded your sudden disappearances from home?'

'She has always thought that I went away on some duty connected with the Foreign Office.'

Major Brien shook his head.

'Not good enough,' he remarked. 'No; I think you should tell her – You don't want to go into details, of course, and in the present case just let her know that your work in India is partly connected with the Intelligence Department and that is all. You'll have her full confidence and trust

26

then, and you may find that a day will come when her woman's wit may be of great use to you. I never did believe in being too secretive, and I know the Chief's ideas are the same as mine.'

'I have always acted on the saying, sir, that a little knowledge is a dangerous thing.'

'No knowledge at all is sometimes apt to be more dangerous. There is another reason, too, why it is necessary that she should know a little. Sir Leonard has decided to send out Cousins with you.'

Hugh looked surprised.

'Won't that rather give things away?' he asked.

'Not a bit! Why should it? Isn't it very natural that your valet who has been with you for years should accompany you, especially as you prefer having an English servant to an Indian?'

Hugh appeared more astonished than ever.

'Cousins my valet!' he exclaimed, and then grinned. 'By Jove!' he said. 'I am dense. But though I shall like having him with me, surely the fact of a professor with an English valet will cause comment. Five hundred rupees a month won't keep my sister and myself, let alone an English servant.'

'Oh, that's all right,' said Major Brien. 'You let Abdullah know that you have private means, didn't you?'

Hugh nodded.

'Very well then, that is explained. Of course you did not want to take Cousins with you, but the devoted fellow pleaded so hard that you couldn't very well refuse him. Later on you'll grumble a bit before people out there at the extra expense, and Cousins will be accepted as a matter of course. Naturally there will be people who will scoff at your soft-heartedness and call you a young fool, but *que voulez-vous*!'

He shrugged his shoulders, and Hugh laughed.

'The whole thing sounds rather like a joke,' said the latter.

'There's no joke about it,' said Major Brien. 'You will have two duties to perform – one to your college, and one to us, and neither must be neglected. You must not in any way let your professorial work slide because we have taken advantage of a rather unique opportunity to send you out. Yours is going to be a difficult task, I'm afraid. Be careful not to fall between the two stools.'

'Shall I have to stay out for the three years mentioned in that advertisement, sir?'

'Your work might keep you all that time. If we want you back, no doubt we shall be able to arrange for your release. Now about Kamper. Are you quite sure that you saw him the other day?'

'Positive, sir! If I had been quicker I would have caught him.'

'It's a pity you didn't. There must be some further activity pending, since he has returned. If you were not going abroad I would put you on to it; as it is, Maddison is already engaged with Spencer in searching for him. He knows you, of course?'

'Very well, sir!'

'Well, let us hope that he won't discover that you are off to India. If he does, your job will be rendered a hundred times more difficult.'

'How can he find out?'

'How do these Russian spies find out anything?' said Major Brien bitterly. 'Their system is so well organised that, in spite of all our efforts, they are almost as active as ever. Well, I won't detain you any longer. No doubt you will be fully engaged preparing for your journey for the next few days. Don't come near these offices any more! The Chief himself will see you at his house, and give you his final instructions before you sail.'

'When am I to call there, sir?' asked Hugh, rising from his chair.

'He'll ring you up, and let you know. I don't suppose I shall see you again myself, so I wish you goodbye, and the best of luck.'

He held out his hand, and Hugh grasped it firmly, as he thanked him for his wishes.

'Remember!' said the Deputy Chief. 'We rely upon you!'

Hugh was driven rapidly homeward, and burst in upon his sister, as she was directing the removal of trunks, boxes and suitcases from the box room to the garden, where they were to be aired. He put his arm in hers, and took her along to his own particular den. Placing an armchair for her, he put her into it, and then started to fill his pipe.

'Why this?' she asked.

'I want to tell you something,' he replied.

'Be quick about it then, for I am terribly busy, and I warn you that you will only get monosyllables out of me for the next week. Have you booked the berths?'

'Not yet!'

'If you don't hurry you won't get any. This is the rush season, isn't it?'

'An hour or so won't make any difference. Listen, Joan! I have been talking to Major Brien for the last hour.'

'Do you mean that awfully nice man, who is so famous in the Intelligence Department?'

He nodded.

'Yes! You've met him once or twice, haven't you?'

'You know I have at the Foreign Office "at 'home's" and parties. I adore Mrs Brien – But what have you been talking to him about. Surely you haven't been trying to get into the Secret Service now, have you?'

He grinned.

'I have an awful confession to make, old girl,' he said.

'Then you have?'

'I have been in the Secret Service for quite a long time—'

She looked at him in astonishment.

'Is that true, Hugh?'

'Absolutely! Now you know why I have been rather secretive on occasions.'

There was a pause for a full minute before she spoke, then:

'But how perfectly amazing!' she said. 'My Hugh a Secret Service man. And are you actually working under that wonderful Sir Leonard Wallace?'

'I am!'

'Oh, Hugh! Why didn't you tell me before?'

'Well, you see dear, I thought it wiser to keep quiet about it. This morning Major Brien rather made me see that I ought to tell you, in case misunderstandings ever arose between us.'

She caught hold of his arm, and pressed it.

'Misunderstandings could never arise between us, dear old boy,' she said. 'I have suspected something for a long time, but couldn't exactly place my suspicions. I am glad Major Brien made you tell me. Would you never have told me if he hadn't suggested it?'

'I don't think so!'

'Didn't you trust me then?'

'Of course! Only you see—'

'You felt so important and so secretive that you wanted to keep it to yourself! I suppose you have been going into all sorts of dangers, and I didn't know. Hugh, that was rather unkind of you, wasn't it? We have never had any secrets from each other before.'

'I know, Joan; but this was rather different, wasn't it?'

'How long have you been in the Secret Service?' she asked, ignoring his question.

'Nearly two years!'

'Two years! And I never guessed!' She looked at him with admiration. 'You must be cleverer than I thought,' she said.

'Thank you!' he said, bowing.

'Then you are not going to India as a professor?'

'I am – very much so! You saw my appointment. I shall take up the job as professor, and, I hope, do everything that is required of me. At the same time I have a mission from the Intelligence Department.'

'How exciting! What is it?'

'I cannot tell you any more, Joan. You must be satisfied with what I have told you.'

'Of course I am. I'll never question you in any way, and you shall tell me just as much, or just as little as you like for the future.'

'That's sporting of you, dear. You must be very careful never to give away by word or sign that I am not altogether what I seem.'

'Of course not!' she replied indignantly.

'One of our men is coming out with us to help me. He is an awfully good fellow and you'll like him once you get used to him.'

'Is he very difficult then?'

'No; but he takes a lot of understanding. He has been my valet for a good many years, and I hadn't the heart to leave him behind, when he pleaded to come, in spite of the expense.'

She stared at him with wide-open eyes.

'Hugh, what are you talking about?'

He grinned.

'That is the tale for other people,' he said, 'and we shall have to get it so much into our minds that we'll believe it ourselves.'

'How thrilling it all sounds!' she said with sparkling eyes.

'Forget the thrills, dear! Remember that I am a dry-as-dust professor of English Literature from now on!'

'I'll remember,' she said, rising to her feet. 'And now Mr Professor, run away and book our passage – I am getting anxious in case we have to wait for weeks.'

Hugh departed to do her bidding, while she returned to the maids in the box room. On the way she stopped to look at herself in a mirror.

'What a revelation!' she murmured. 'Perhaps in time I may find myself acting as assistant to Hugh. Joan Shannon, of His Majesty's Intelligence Department, sounds rather nice!'

CHAPTER 5

ENTER COUSINS

For several days Hugh Shannon's flat in West Kensington was a scene of turmoil. Boxes, dressing-cases, trunks and suitcases littered every room and overflowed into the passages. Joan kept her two maids working at such high pressure that, in a remarkably short space of time, the flat was dismantled. She herself worked tremendously hard and never slacked, and Hugh became a veritable handy-man. Then order began to grow out of chaos, clothes were gradually packed away, and, at last, three days before the boat was due to sail, the inmates of the flat started to breathe easily once more.

Hugh had managed to get two very good berths on a mail boat, the *Ispahan*. He was very lucky, for the berths had originally been booked, strangely enough, by a man and his sister, who had been compelled to cancel them at the last moment, owing to some family bereavement. He had obtained a passport for Joan – he, of course, already had one himself – and had had a last interview with the Chief, who had given him final and careful instructions about his work in India.

34

Thus it was that in the evening of the day, when all the heavy packing was at length complete, he sat down and sighed with relief.

'Thank goodness, that's done!' he said. 'Joan, I never knew you were such a slave driver!'

'Well, you shouldn't give one such short notice,' she retorted. 'Maud and Alice have been bricks, and I'd like to take them with me.'

He nodded.

'They have worked hard,' he said; 'and as for you – you've been wonderful!'

'Thank you!' she replied with perfect composure. 'I think I have! At all events I have done something which you did not think of.'

'What's that?' he asked.

'I found all your old books on English literature, and I've packed them in a trunk labelled "Wanted on Voyage". You must be pretty rusty after all these years, and you'll be able to refresh your memory on the way out.'

'By jove! I never thought of that! You're splendid!'

'I rather think I am! Let us go out and have a gay evening. We haven't had one together for some time, and I have no engagements tonight, have you?'

'No!' he said. 'That's rather a good notion. I daresay I'll find an evening suit somewhere.'

'And with a little luck I might find a frock which hasn't been packed. Hurry up, Hugh! I'll be dressed first.'

'You won't!' he declared. Then the doorbell rang.

'If that is any of our sorrowing friends,' said Joan, 'I'll scream!'

Presently one of the maids knocked, and entered the room. She looked as though she had received the surprise of her life.

'Please, Miss,' she said, 'there is a man at the door, who says he is Captain Shannon's valet. I told him that Captain Shannon hasn't got a valet, and all he said was "go and tell your master I've come".'

'What is his name, Alice?' asked Joan.

'Why it's old Cousins, of course,' almost shouted Hugh. 'He was my man for years, Alice, and he's come back. Tell him to come along in!'

Alice departed, still with a look of surprise on her face.

'Hugh,' said Joan severely, 'when did you learn to tell fibs with such ease?'

'I really am getting positively awful,' he grinned. 'I'll have to put the brake on, or it will become chronic.'

And then Joan sat straight up and stared. She had been very carefully brought up, but even carefully brought up young ladies are too surprised to remember their manners sometimes. Joan was very much surprised.

A most remarkable individual entered the room and, seeing her, bowed almost double. Not more than five feet in height, the newcomer had the figure of a boy of fourteen, but his face was so wrinkled that he might have been anything between

36

thirty-five and sixty years of age. As a matter of fact he was forty-three. He was clad in a perfectly fitting blue serge suit, neat collar and tie, patent leather boots and spats. Over his left arm lay a beautifully folded raincoat, and in his right hand a dark grey Stetson hat. Altogether he looked as though he had stepped out of a band-box.

Having completed his bow he straightened himself and glanced whimsically from Joan to Hugh and back again, and Joan found herself looking into a pair of the brightest eyes she had ever seen. They were a deep brown, but so sharp that they fascinated her, and it was almost with an effort that she drew her eyes from his, but the next moment she was looking at his mouth. Perhaps this was the most inviting part of his face. It was full of such humorous curves that involuntarily she smiled. He smiled too, and at once his face was a mass of the most extraordinary creases, each one of which appeared to be grinning at her. This was too much for Joan; her sense of humour got the better of her, and she broke into a peal of laughter. The little man laughed too, and the absurdity of the situation so tickled Hugh that he was compelled to join in, with the result that for some seconds the room resounded with their merriment. Alice stood at the door in astonishment, but she also found it impossible to control her laughter, and stuffing a handkerchief into her mouth, she hastened to the kitchen, where she collapsed into a chair, much to Maud's alarm.

'O-oh!' gasped Joan, as soon as she had regained control of herself. 'I'm awfully sorry.'

She blushed with embarrassment.

'Not at all,' replied the little man. 'A most charming introduction I'm sure. There is nothing more conducive to friendship than laughter. Doctor Johnson says that—'

'Never mind Doctor Johnson, Cousins,' interrupted Hugh. 'This is my sister! Joan, this is Cousins, my valet who has pleaded so hard to come to India with me!'

Joan held out her hand, which Cousins took with the air of a cavalier of the seventeenth century.

'I am very glad to meet you, Mr Cousins!' said Joan, smiling. 'I am sure you are the ideal valet.'

'Ideal is not descriptive enough, Miss Shannon,' he replied. 'There never was, and never will be, such a valet as I. "Clothes maketh the man" is the basis of my religion; you'll be astonished at the difference in your brother, after I have taken him in hand.'

'I'll punch your head if you interfere with me, Cousins,' said Hugh; 'that is, more than is necessary for appearances' sake.'

'When I undertake a job, sir, I do it properly. You haven't a word to say in the matter.'

Hugh looked helplessly at his sister.

'I'm in for a lively time, Joan,' he said.

'Not at all,' put in Cousins. 'You are about to enter the most triumphant period of your life; that

38

is, since I left your service. We mustn't forget that I have been your valet for years – I've merely been away for a year or so looking after a dying relative.' He looked at Joan. 'How long have you had your maid, Miss?' he queried.

'Maud has been with us for eighteen months,' she answered, 'and Alice for just over a year.'

'Then twenty months ago I went away to nurse my dying uncle – he was most inconsiderate and took far too long to die. But here I am back again, sir, and I refuse to leave you any more.'

Joan laughed.

'You are rather callous about your poor uncle,' she said. He shrugged his shoulders in a manner almost French.

'He left me far less in his will than I expected. As Marcus Aurelius says—'

'What are you going to do now?' interrupted Hugh hastily.

Cousins raised his eyebrows slightly.

'Stay here until we sail, of course,' he announced.

'But, my dear chap, the place is dismantled,' expostulated Hugh.

'Don't worry about me,' said the little man. 'I will fit in like a piece in a jigsaw puzzle. All my heavy stuff has already gone to the docks – I have merely brought a portmanteau here. As Gladstone said in 1887—'

Hugh again interrupted him.

'Everybody knows what Gladstone said in 1887,' he remarked.

'But you don't know what he said about port-manteaux,' said Cousins solemnly.

'And I don't want to. What I want to know is, have you booked your berth?'

'Certainly! It was very slack of my employer to forget his man when booking the passage, but your letter and ten crisp five pound notes did the trick, and I am the proud possessor of an upper berth, second class in the RMS *Ispahan*.'

'Good!' said Hugh. 'And now you must excuse us, as we are going to dine out, and do a theatre, and we are already rather late.'

Cousins spread out his hands.

'I'll find the kitchen and the pretty little maid who let me in,' he replied. 'But first of all I'd better come and tie your bow for you!'

'You dare!' returned Hugh, and he and Joan went off to dress.

Cousins repaired to the hall, picked up his port-manteau and found his way to the kitchen. Thereafter there were periods of silence punctuated by bursts of laughter from that direction. Hugh smiled at his reflection in the glass, as he was tying his bow.

'My valet is going to make life very bearable in India,' he murmured.

A couple of hours later Joan settled herself comfortably in her stall at the Winter Garden Theatre. The curtain had not yet gone up.

'What an extraordinary man Mr Cousins is,' she remarked. 'Do you know, Hugh, I felt most awfully guilty for laughing at him, but he passed it off almost as though it were a compliment.'

'That is Cousins' way,' said Hugh. 'He is a very good fellow, but, as I told you, he takes a lot of understanding.'

'He doesn't look a bit like a Secret Service man,' she declared. 'He would probably have made a fortune on the stage as a comedian.'

'And yet,' said Hugh, 'he is one of the cleverest men in the service. He has been everywhere almost, and speaks six languages fluently. If you could get him to talk about himself he would tell you some of the most amazing things. He stands high in the confidence of Sir Leonard Wallace, and it is rather a compliment to me that he has been selected to accompany me to India.'

'I am sure I am going to like him,' said Joan. 'The difficulty will be to know when to take him seriously.'

'Very few people know when to do that. But when he starts quoting from poets or philosophers or scientists, stop him, or you'll have reams of stuff poured into your bewildered head. Really, I don't think there is any branch of the arts or sciences with which Cousins is not familiar.'

The curtain rose at that juncture and Joan turned her attention to the popular musical show which had captivated all London.

CHAPTER 6

A FANCY DRESS DANCE

The *Ispahan* ploughed her way through the waters of the Mediterranean. She had taken on the majority of her passengers at Marseilles, and now, two days out from that port, she was approaching the Straits of Messina and people who had hitherto held themselves aloof were beginning to greet each other as old acquaintances.

Hugh Shannon, with great seriousness of purpose: had settled down to read over once more his many books on English literature in order to brush up his memory on the subject in which he had specialised at Oxford. Joan, on the other hand, devoted herself heart and soul to the amusements of boardship life, and very quickly became the leader of most of the activities of the first saloon. At first she and Hugh had considered travelling overland to Marseilles, and taking the boat on from there, but Joan had such a love for the sea that she preferred joining the ship at Gravesend and going the whole way on the bosom of the ocean, and thus it was decided. Cousins, who had very little liking for the Bay of Biscay, pleaded to be allowed to join at Marseilles, and he came aboard and reported himself at that port, almost before the vessel had tied up.

There was the usual conglomeration of passengers that is to be found on any ship travelling to India in the busy season. Indians returning from a trip to Europe, full of their own importance and stuffed full of platitudes; Indian Army officers and their wives, whose holiday at home for a few short months had given them a fresh lease of healthful life; members of the Indian Civil Service, who appeared to regard themselves almost as the Lord's anointed and treated all others with the patronising manner peculiar to their service; young bank clerks, thinking themselves mighty important fellows and embryo builders of empire railway officials; police officials; forestry officials – all were there, and Hugh in his spare moments found himself watching these others and getting any amount of quiet fun from their peacock mannerisms.

Joan was a wise little lady, in spite of her youth and inexperience, and she soon began to find a great deal of humour in what she described as the plethora of artificiality that existed around her. However, she found several young girls, and one or two young men, who were almost as natural and simple as herself, and with these she organised games, dances, and musical evenings which were very enjoyable, and helped to pass the time pleasantly.

The peculiar laxity of conduct that always exists on an ocean liner at first discomforted her, but not being a little prude she entered whole-heartedly into everything, and was the life and soul of the ship. Of course most of the men fell in love with her, some seriously, some because men on board ship seem to consider it a necessary adjunct to existence; others, and these were the most dangerous, from an habitual belief that a pretty woman was a natural prey and that they themselves were irresistible to the fair sex.

Soon after leaving Marseilles, one of these latter attached himself to Joan almost with a sense of proprietorship. He carried her rugs and books, saw that her chair was placed in the best part of the deck, pointed out the interesting sights on the way, with the experience of a man who had made the journey several times before, and generally made himself officiously useful. At first Joan was merely amused; then as she noticed that he endeavoured to keep all others away from her, she began to get annoyed.

On the morning on which the ship entered the Straits of Messina, he came up to her as she was sitting at breakfast.

'Good morning, Miss Shannon,' he said blandly. 'I have obtained the captain's permission to take you on the fore deck as we go through the Straits. You will have a splendid view there.'

'Thank you,' she replied coldly; 'but I have already arranged to go there with my brother.'

The other was taken aback for a moment, and he turned and looked at Hugh, who was regarding him with amusement.

'You had previously obtained the captain's permission, I presume?' he asked.

'It wasn't necessary,' said Hugh. 'The chief officer told us that the passengers could go on the fore deck if they wished to do so. Your efforts to get the captain's permission were very kind, Hudson, but unnecessary.'

'I was naturally thinking of Miss Shannon's pleasure,' said Hudson stiffly.

'Nice of you,' drawled Hugh; 'still I am quite capable of looking after that, thanks!'

Without another word the other turned, and walked away.

'I seem to have upset the fellow,' said Hugh. 'Who is he anyway? I know his name and that is all!'

'He is a very important man,' said a delicate-looking little lady on the other side of the table. 'I believe he is in the secretariat at Lahore, and draws a salary of two thousand rupees a month.'

'I wish he wasn't stationed at Lahore,' sighed Joan. 'I suppose he'll be calling on us.'

'Let him!' said Hugh cheerfully. 'We'll put Cousins on to him if he does.'

The great ship entered the Straits at half-speed. On one side towered the mountains overlooking the town of Messina, terminating in Etna which, at a height of over ten thousand feet, could be

45

seen dominating the surroundings. On the other side were the gentle slopes of Calabria with the white walls of Reggio glistening in the morning sunshine. Joan thought that she had seldom seen anything more beautiful. A thin spiral of smoke could be observed rising from the volcano, and a white cloud hung just below the crater. Everything seemed so calm and peaceful that it was difficult to imagine that an eruption from Etna had ever cast havoc, sorrow and death on that peaceful district. Small boats with happy-looking natives in them, rocked gently in the swell caused by the passing of the huge liner, and in one were three Sicilians with guitars, who sang gloriously as they glided by. Just ahead a ferry passed with the train which ran from Rome to Palermo.

Joan gazed with entranced eyes, and when they were well through the Straits she insisted upon Hugh taking her to the stern of the ship, so that she could still feast her eyes on the beauties which nature had so lavishly spread before her. Messina was out of sight and Etna a cloud in the distance before, with one last look at Cape Spartivento, she turned with a sigh to her brother.

'Isn't it perfectly beautiful, Hugh?' she said. 'I shall never forget that scene as long as I live.'

'"A thing of beauty is a joy for ever – it's loveliness increases, it will never pass into nothingness",' quoted a voice behind them, and turning they beheld Cousins, still as spick and span as ever.

'Good morning, Miss Shannon,' he said. 'I am glad to see you have an appreciation of beauty.'

'Very few people have not, Mr Cousins,' she replied.

'For the Lord's sake, don't call me "mister"! It is not usual for a young lady to call her brother's valet by such a title.'

'I'm sorry, I quite forgot!' she smiled.

'Please don't! Besides I hope I may be allowed to act as your servant, as well as your brother's. From signs I have seen you may find me necessary.'

'What do you mean?' demanded Hugh.

'Very little at present. But, as I say, there are signs.'

'I wish you'd make yourself clearer.'

'Nothing could be clearer than me! I am one of those blunt, plain, honest fellows, of whom Jane Austen spoke when she said—'

'I'm not interested in what Jane Austen said at present,' interrupted Hugh. 'What I want to know is—'

'And what I want to know,' interrupted Cousins, in his turn, 'is – why did you change your tie? I put out a blue one for you which exactly matched the colour of the Mediterranean, and here are you wearing a hideous gold and black tie, which makes one seasick to look at it.'

'Why those are my college colours,' said Hugh indignantly.

'Then all I can say is your college has the most

47

reprehensible taste – *exceptis excipiendis*. You'll forgive the Latin tag, Miss Shannon,' he added apologetically. 'I got it from the back of a dictionary.'

She laughed.

'Please tell me why you think I want looking after!' she said seriously.

He dropped his voice.

'Don't be too free with Hudson!' he said. 'Will you require me before lunch, sir?' he asked in a louder tone.

'No!' said Hugh. 'But I—'

'Then I'll leave you as I have some pressing to do.'

And raising his cap politely he sauntered off. Joan laughed.

'I somehow can't imagine Cousins pressing clothes, can you?' she asked.

Hugh shrugged his shoulders.

'I'd like to know what he means by not being free with Hudson,' he said, as they made their way back to the first-class deck.

That night there was a fancy dress dance, and great was the excitement among the young people in preparing their costumes, and conjecturing what their companions were going to wear. Joan insisted upon Hugh dressing up for the occasion, and despite his assertion that professors were not so undignified, she procured a monk's habit from somewhere, and insisted that he should wear it. Grumbling that he had grown too old for such frivolities, he was escorted to his cabin by a couple

48

of his sister's young male friends, who had promised to help him put on the sombre-looking
garment. However, Cousins was there and he took
charge of the proceedings. He bundled the high-
spirited youngsters out, declaring that he was quite
able to see to his master's costuming himself.

'Look here, Cousins!' said Hugh. 'You've been
avoiding me all day, and I want to know what
you've got against Hudson. Come on, out with it!'

The ideal valet rubbed his chin thoughtfully.

'I suppose I rather presumed,' he said, 'but that
fellow nearly got into the clutches of the police
while he was at home.'

'In what way?'

'Interfering with young girls in Hyde Park and
various other places. I believe he was warned on
two or three occasions.'

'The deuce he was!' exclaimed Hugh. 'I'll tell
my sister to keep clear of him. Not that she needs
any such warning – she has taken a dislike to him,
and is quite capable of looking after herself.'

'"There's many a slip 'twixt the cup and the
lip",' quoted Cousins.

'Oh, yes, I know,' said Hugh irritably; '"and a
stitch in time saves nine"! For the Lord's sake,
Cousins, give me a rest from your eternal
quotations!'

'Very well, sir,' said Cousins deferentially. 'Now
may I help you into your monkly habit! I think a
little touch of white powder on your cheeks to give
you the requisite "no fish on Friday" pallor would

be an artistic touch, or perhaps you would prefer a little rouge to denote the jolly friar.'

'Don't be a bigger fool than you can help,' growled Hugh.

When he reached the dining-saloon, he found that Joan had been invited to another table, and so he was compelled to put off his warning until later. It was a gala night on the ship and the saloon looked quite gay with its decorations of artificial flowers, flags and palms. There was a regular riot of colour and the scene was very animated. Cavaliers sat next to ladies of the court of Louis XIV; dairy-maids giggled at cowboys; monks laughed with nuns; soldiers, halberdiers, archers, knights, dusky Nubians, Turks, gondoliers, pierrots, pierrettes, maritanas, nursing sisters, all were there, and the majority of the costumes had been supplied by the barber. Truly a ship's barber is a versatile man.

Hugh looked at the scene with interest and, as he put it to himself, felt young again. Presently he discovered that he was sitting next to a lady dressed as a butterfly. For a moment he did not recognise her, then his heart sank. She was a young woman who had embarked at Gravesend, and had tried her best ever since to flirt with him. She had pale blue eyes, the lashes of which were always artifi-cially darkened, eyebrows which received the same treatment, a rather well-shaped nose, lips which transferred their colour regularly to the cigarettes she smoked, and bright, fair hair – the brightness having a suspicion of peroxide about it.

Hugh looked and groaned inwardly. She smiled at him dazzlingly.

'I have invited myself to your table, Professor Shannon,' she simpered. 'I hope you are very pleased.'

'Oh, delighted!' he lied.

'You are going to be very nice to me this evening, are you not? You have neglected me shamefully lately.'

'Sorry!' he murmured. 'I've been busy!'

'Yes, I know, and I forgive you,' she said handsomely. 'You very brainy people always are immersed in books.'

'I'm afraid I am not very brainy,' he said.

'Oh, how modest!' she smiled. 'I have found out all about you.'

'The deuce you have!' exclaimed Hugh, and then added hastily, 'I beg your pardon!'

At that moment the wine steward paused by their side. She looked invitingly at Hugh, and as in duty-bound he asked what she would drink.

'I don't think we can do less than drink champagne on an occasion like this, do you?' she asked coyly.

He ordered the champagne.

By the end of dinner Hugh was in a state of nerves. In order to get rid of her, he made an excuse that he had to go to his cabin, whereupon she smiled at him.

'I must go and get a shawl,' she said. 'Shall I wait for you at the head of the saloon gangway?'

'Yes, do!' said poor Hugh, and escaped below.

He sat down on his settee, and swore. Cousins came in quietly.

'Why the language?' he inquired.

'A female whom I loathe, has attached herself to me, and I can't get away from her.'

Cousins chuckled.

'That's bad!' he said. 'Why not dodge her?'

'I'm going to try, but I doubt if I'll succeed.'

'Have you warned your sister to be careful of Hudson yet?'

'No; I haven't seen her.'

'Well, try and find her! Tonight is one of those lax nights when men like Hudson enjoy themselves!'

'I'd like to see him try to enjoy himself at the expense of Joan!' growled Hugh.

A few minutes later he went up on deck by another stairway, but to his dismay his butterfly lady was there awaiting him.

'You naughty man,' she said. 'I meant the top of the saloon gangway, not this one. However, I saw you pass along below and so here I am.'

'I made a mistake,' muttered Hugh lamely.

His discomfiture was complete when, a little later, a pretty girl dressed as a Spanish dancer came up and stopped to whisper—

'I expected you to be my dancing partner tonight, and you've deserted me.' And she passed on.

She was a girl Hugh really admired, and his spirits fell to zero as he saw her disappear on the arm of another man. He cheered up a bit when he saw Joan talking animatedly to a young cavalier, a youth who was one of the nicest fellows on the boat. Of Hudson there was no sign whatever.

Joan had a perfectly glorious evening. She danced until she could dance no longer. Somewhat to her surprise Hudson, who was dressed as Caesar Borgia, only asked her for one dance, and then left her with the man she had chosen as her dancing partner. She felt a little piqued at first, but thinking the matter over she decided that he was annoyed on account of the slight that had been put upon him in the morning. She was rather surprised, therefore, at one o'clock, when enthusiasm was beginning to wane, to find him at her side requesting her for just one more dance.

'I really couldn't, Mr Hudson,' she said. 'You should have come before.'

'There were so many,' he said, 'that I hesitated to intrude.'

'What do you mean?' she asked indignantly.

'Please don't misunderstand me!' he pleaded. 'Honestly I couldn't very well butt in, could I?'

She smiled.

'I don't see why not. Others butted in, as you call it.'

'I was afraid I might be *de trop*.'

'Don't be silly!' she retorted.

'And you can't spare just one dance now?'

'I'm so tired,' she said.

'Well, let us go on the other deck and watch the moon. It's a glorious night!'

For a moment she hesitated, then smiled.

'It would be rather nice to sit in the moonlight and rest,' she said.

She took his arm, and they went up to the next deck. Then he led her to the gangway that ascended to the boat deck. She stopped.

'Why go up there?' she asked. 'Our chairs are here, and we've quite a nice view.'

'But the awning spoils it,' he said. 'That is why so many people have gone on the boat deck.'

Her innate distrust of the man was dissipated by the announcement that some of the passengers were on the upper deck; with a little nod, she accompanied him up the gangway. Then a sudden doubt assailed her – there was nobody to be seen.

'Where is everybody?' she asked.

He smiled, and his smile, in the moonlight, looked a little gross, she thought.

'I suppose most of them are behind the boats,' he said.

'I think I'd rather go down, Mr Hudson,' she said.

'Oh, I say! Stay a little while! Look how glorious it is up here.'

It was beautiful. A full moon held sway in the sky – such a moon as one can only see in the Mediterranean, and in the tropics. Everything was almost as bright as day, and a great ray of moonlight stretched across the water, and shimmered and danced in a manner to delight any lover of beauty. Joan felt that she was being silly, the sheer

54

love of beauty conquered her, and she went on with Hudson to a snug little corner between two boats where, strangely enough, two deck chairs were placed.

'Some kind people have left their chairs here,' he said. 'Let us take advantage of their kindness, shall we?'

The name on both the chairs was Armitage, and with a little sigh of content she sank into one. He sat in the other. For ten minutes neither spoke, and inwardly Joan began to reproach herself for being unkind to her companion.

'Isn't this glorious?' she said at last.

'Glorious isn't the word,' he replied. 'On such a night as this one feels how wonderful the world is, and how we puny mortals, time after time, by our silly little acts, sully the magnificent creation of God.'

She looked at him in surprise.

'Oh, Mr Hudson,' she said, 'I had no idea that beauty influenced you so.'

'Beauty always influences me, Miss Shannon,' he said, and there was a note full of deep meaning in his voice.

She laughed a little nervously.

'I think we had better go down now,' she said.

And then, in a moment, his arms were round her, and she felt his hot breath on her cheek. With a little cry she struggled to free herself, but he held her so tightly that she could hardly move.

'I love you, Joan,' he said. 'I have loved you ever

since I first saw you, and I want you as I have never wanted a woman before.'

'Let me go! Let me go!' she panted.

'Not until you have come into my arms and kissed me,' he said hoarsely. 'I must have you. You madden me by your aloofness – I will have you!'

He drew her, struggling fiercely, towards him. She fought like a little tigress, but he was a powerful man, and her efforts made no impression on him.

'I'll scream until everybody on the ship hears,' she gasped, 'if you don't let me go at once.'

'You won't!' he ground out, and put a hand over her mouth. 'Listen to me!' he went on. 'I know very well your brother is not altogether what he seems. He plays the professor every well, but he is also – something else. My silence depends upon you. If you say a word about what has happened here tonight, or if you refuse to do what I desire you to do, I will ruin him. Don't make a mistake! I mean what I say – I love you and I want you, and I am going to have you!'

He released her, and she fell back into her seat a frightened, sobbing, pale-faced little figure.

'And now,' said a gentle voice behind them, 'perhaps you have finished your threats, and will permit Miss Shannon to depart!'

Hudson swung round with an oath, and Joan looked up with a cry of thankfulness. Cousins, his face in the moonlight appearing to be more grotesquely creased than ever, was standing calmly between the two boats.

'I am sorry I let this go so far, Miss Shannon,' he went on apologetically, 'but I wanted to know what threat this fellow was going to hold over you. Get down below as quickly as you can, and send your brother to me!'

Joan rose, and departed instantly. Hudson made an attempt to stop her, but he caught the gleam of a wicked-looking little revolver in Cousins' hand, and drew back.

'Who the devil are you?' he demanded in a voice in which fright and rage were equally blended.

'Shakespeare had a very apt reply to that question, and I might also quote a certain passage of Zola's,' said the little man, 'but I won't – it's too long! Let me merely state that I am a gentleman's gentleman!'

CHAPTER 7

AN ENCOUNTER WITH HUDSON

Hugh spent a very unpleasant evening. His butterfly lady never let him out of her sight, and when other men came to her and asked for a dance, which was not very often, she always told them that Professor Shannon was her partner, and that she had no dances to spare. Hugh put the best face possible on the situation. The courtesy with which he always treated the opposite sex prevented him from divulging what was in his mind, and so, a martyr to his own chivalry, he struggled along somehow. She made several attempts to get him to sit out dances with her, but he managed to avoid that until sometime after midnight, when she declared that she could dance no more, and asked him to take her to the upper deck.

'Wouldn't it be better if we sat here and watched the others dancing?' he suggested rather lamely.

'It's much too hot,' she replied; 'besides we should be horribly in the way.'

'I'm afraid you'll find it very cold up there,' he said, 'especially after getting so hot dancing.'

'Cold on a lovely night like this!' she exclaimed. 'What nonsense! Besides I have my shawl with me.'

'But you might get a chill!'

'Never! Anyway I'll risk it!'

So Hugh gave up the unequal struggle, and escorted her to the promenade deck above. There he found two chairs, and she sank into hers with a little sigh. With great reluctance he followed suit, and for some minutes there was silence.

'How quiet you are,' she murmured at last; 'and what a long way your chair is from mine! Won't you bring it a little closer?'

He had no option, but to obey her wish. As he rose she pulled the chair up to hers until the two were touching.

'That's better!' she said. 'Now we can talk without being overheard.'

'We are not likely to say anything which we don't want others to hear,' he said, rather bluntly, as he once more sat down.

'Of course not! Still it is not always nice to know that someone else can hear everything one says.'

There was another pause, broken by a sigh from the girl. 'Isn't it perfectly delightful up here?' she murmured.

'It is a tophole night,' he said grudgingly.

'I have enjoyed myself, thanks to you,' she said, 'and this is an ideal termination to a splendid evening, don't you think so?'

'Of course!' he assented, with the voice of a mourner at a funeral.

'I am so glad you agree.' Again she sighed.

Presently her hand strayed carelessly over the arm of his chair, and he looked at it in apprehension. At that moment he almost wished that the ship would strike a rock, in order that he might be released from the embarrassment of her company. Never in all his life had he been in such a predicament, and he had not the vaguest idea how to escape. Hugh Shannon had had less to do with the opposite sex than most young men; he had always been more or less content with the society of his sister, and two short and uninspiring love affairs were the sum total of his essays into the realms of Cupid. He felt quite unable, therefore, to cope with this altogether unexpected *contretemps*, and he had a dreadful feeling that this ultra-modern young woman might end by forcing him to marry her by some means or other.

'Your name is Hugh, is it not?' she inquired.

'Yes,' he said.

'I rather like it. We are such – friends' – He shivered at the pause – 'that it seems absurd to call you Professor Shannon every time I speak to you. Professor, too, sounds terribly formal, so I am going to call you "Hugh", may I?'

'Of course!' he gulped.

'And you must call me "Olive". Do you like my name?'

'I think it's splendid,' he said heroically.

'Do you really? I'm so glad, because I never did

60

like it very much myself. Now I *shall* like it!' she added softly.

Her hand touched his, and somehow he found her fingers resting in his grasp. He held them as though they were some particularly dangerous explosives.

She looked at him and smiled.

'You are a naughty boy!' she said playfully. 'Why are you holding my hand?'

The coolness of the question took his breath away. Hastily he withdrew his hand.

'I am sorry,' he stammered.

'Don't be silly!' she said. 'I was only teasing. You can hold it just as tightly as you like!'

This time she put her hand right into his, and stretched the other one across, apparently to keep it company.

'Do you know I never let young men do this,' she declared, 'but you are so different, aren't you? I feel so thoroughly safe with you, and though we have been together for such a short time, it is as though we have always known each other.'

'Er – yes!' muttered Hugh.

'What a man of few words you are! But I like you to be like that. It proves that you are so genuine, Hugh!'

A moment later she had snuggled up to him, and Hugh found her head resting on his shoulder. He moved uneasily, and beads of perspiration broke out on his forehead. For a few minutes she did not speak, then:

'Isn't it wonderful?' she said. 'When two people

feel as we do, there is no necessity for words at all, is there? I suppose it is because heart speaks to heart! I am so happy – dear!'

'What the devil am I to do?' muttered Hugh to himself. 'This is going a little too far!'

'Hugh!' she said suddenly. 'You are quite happy too, aren't you?'

'Oh – er – of course!' he said with an inward shudder.

'Then, if you are a very good boy, you may – kiss me, just once!'

And then there came an interruption.

Joan appeared behind them. For a moment she stared in surprise, but her mind was too full of other things to be very concerned with the sight of her brother and a girl in apparently such intimate juxtaposition.

'Hugh,' she said, 'I want you! I've been looking for you everywhere. Please come!'

Hugh sprang to his feet with alacrity, and his companion looked round with annoyance, then smiled.

'I am afraid you have found us out, Joan dear,' she said.

Joan regarded her coldly. She had not spoken more than two or three times to the other, and she resented the familiarity. She took Hugh by the arm and led him away, the other girl calling out that she would wait for him. As soon as they were out of hearing, Shannon stopped and mopped his brow with a handkerchief.

'Thank God you came, Joan!' he said. 'Goodness knows what would have happened, if you hadn't.'

He looked so full of distress that for a moment Joan forgot her own troubles.

'Weren't you – weren't you making love to her?' she asked.

'Of course not,' he said indignantly. 'I can't bear the sight of the woman!' And he proceeded to explain how she had taken possession of him all the evening and ended by behaving as though she had made up her mind to marry him.

'The creature!' exclaimed Joan, when his recital had come to an end. 'I'll teach her that she can't play about with my brother like that. But what a fool you were to allow her to do it!'

'What could I do?' asked Hugh helplessly.

'Poor old boy,' she smiled. 'You are too good-natured. I can see that I shall have to watch over you.'

And then her own trouble returned to her, and she gasped out the story of her treatment by Hudson, his threat and Cousins' urgent request to her to send Hugh up to him. Hugh stiffened with horror and rage.

'Where is he?' he asked in an ominously quiet voice.

'On the boat deck! I think Mr Cousins is keeping him there with a revolver.'

'Good old Cousins!' exclaimed Hugh, and he started towards the gangway. She caught hold of his arm.

'Be careful!' he said. 'He knows all about you, and if you are very severe, he'll probably give you away.'

'I don't care if he does,' declared Hugh. 'He is not going to insult my sister, and get off scot free.'

'But remember, Hugh, you are not your own master, and a lot may depend upon your behaviour in this affair.'

'All right, dear,' he said. 'You go to bed! I won't do anything rash.'

He left her, and ran up the gangway to the boat deck. He found Hudson sitting in one of the deck chairs, while Cousins leant on the back of the other, aimlessly swinging a revolver to and fro. At the sound of his approach the latter turned lazily round.

'I'm glad you've come, sir,' he remarked. 'I found this – er – gentleman molesting Miss Shannon.'

'So I have heard!' said Hugh through clenched teeth.

He took hold of the vacant chair, and threw it aside. Hudson started to his feet, and for a moment the two men faced each other.

'What have you to say for yourself, you black-guard!' cried Hugh, in a voice that shook with rage, despite his efforts to control it.

'Of course, you want to be very theatrical and all that,' sneered Hudson, but there was an unmistakable look of fear in his eyes. 'I warn you, though, that if you molest me in any way, I'll tell everybody what I know about you, and put a stop to your little game in India, whatever it is.'

For answer Hugh caught him by the throat and threw him across the deck with such force that he crashed into a stanchion and fell.

'You cur! You contemptible cur!' he roared.

Cousins caught him by the arm.

'Be careful!' he whispered. 'He might be a dangerous man, and he certainly knows something. Better find out what it is!'

Hugh turned aside with a groan.

'God help me!' he said. 'Fancy having to talk to a skunk like that, when all my instincts are to give him the thrashing he deserves!'

'It can't be helped,' said Cousins.

Hudson rose to his feet, and stood trembling with rage.

'I'll get even with you for that, Shannon!' he said.

'Come here!' said Hugh. 'You and I are going to talk this over, though I might tell you that my inclinations are to knock all the filth out of your dirty body.'

'I have no desire to talk to you at all,' replied Hudson, and turned towards the gangway.

'If you don't come back, I'll go to the captain of the ship at once.'

The other hesitated, then came slowly back.

'Look here!' he said. 'I don't know why you are behaving like this. I admit that I treated your sister rather badly, but I love her, and I am afraid my love got the better of me; but my intentions were perfectly honourable.'

'Your intentions honourable!' sneered Hugh with the utmost contempt. 'Why there isn't a vestige of honour in you. You're an out and out cad!'

'Of course, if you take it like that, it's no use my defending myself!' He shrugged his shoulders.

'Not the slightest bit of good. I've guessed what you are for a long time. I blame myself for not looking after my sister better. Why it's a sacrilege to talk of her to such a thing as you.'

'I ask her forgiveness and yours, Shannon. I forgot myself and am thoroughly ashamed. I can only plead as an excuse that I honestly love her.'

'If you mention her again,' threatened Hugh, 'I won't be responsible for my actions.'

Hudson shrugged his shoulders again and if the look of grief on his face was insincere, it was very well done.

'I want to know,' continued Hugh, 'what you meant by saying that I was not what I seemed, and telling my sister that if she didn't fall in with your foul wishes you would ruin me?'

'Need we go into that? I tell you I am thoroughly ashamed of all I said and did!'

'Answer my question!'

'Well, if you will have it, I happened to be in London one day with a friend of mine who is in the Foreign Office, when you passed. He pointed you out to me as a prominent member of the Intelligence Department. When I saw you on board, and recognised you, I naturally guessed that you were not going to India merely as a professor. I presume also that if your real profession became public property, your mission would be ruined. Of course my threat was only uttered in the heat of the moment – I would naturally never say a word that might do you harm. I am quite candid in saying that I don't like you personally, but I am an Englishman, and I would not do anything that might prove disastrous, or even awkward, no matter what my private resentment against an individual might be.'

Hugh looked him up and down for a moment, not troubling to hide the contempt with which he still regarded him.

'Since you know so much, Hudson,' he said, 'it may interest you also to know that I have been a failure in the Intelligence Department, and have had to resign. That is why I am going out to India as a professor to take up the line I specialised in. I am signing a contract for three years. Common sense will tell you that I would not do that if I were going out on Secret Service business. I don't know why I am telling you this except to show you how perfectly useless your threats were. I should imagine that even you, contemptible as you are, have enough sense of duty to your country and your own position in India to know that if I were still in the Secret Service, it were better to keep the matter quiet for fear of rousing suspicion and distrust in the present troubled state of the country. As it is I am no longer an agent of the service, so it doesn't make any difference.'

Hudson looked at him searchingly for a moment.

'I've been a fool and a rotter. Will you forgive me, Shannon?'

'Leave my sister alone, and I'll say no more. Interfere with her in any way, or attempt to speak to her on this ship, or anywhere else you may see her, and God help you! That's all I have to say.'

He turned his back, and walked to the other side of the deck. Hudson watched him for a moment, and then looked at Cousins.

'Your master is very severe,' he said. 'I really must congratulate him on having such a faithful watchdog as you. At the same time you might tell him that it would be as well to have me as a friend in Lahore. I am not without influence, and Sheranwala College is a pretty poor place.'

'It has the merit of novelty about it, sir,' said Cousins, 'and novelty has a somewhat magic touch. You know what Keats says – "Magic casements opening on the foam – Of perilous seas in fairy lands forlorn".'

Hudson opened his mouth to speak, changed his mind and, turning abruptly, went below.

Cousins strolled across and joined Hugh.

'Our friend will bear watching,' he said. 'Your explanation was very convincing, but – You know what Rousseau said when—'

'No, I don't! And I don't want to know!' snapped

68

Hugh. 'It seems to me that I am making a mess of everything.'

'It isn't your fault that he recognised you. That is sheer bad luck, and part of the dangerous game we have to play.'

'It isn't only that,' groaned Hugh. 'There is a female downstairs who has stuck to me like a leech all the evening. She has put her hands in mine, rested her head on my shoulder, and even invited me to— to kiss her. Hang it all! I shouldn't be surprised if she takes it for granted that I am engaged to marry her.'

Cousins stared at him, and then chuckled softly.

'"Bid me love, and I will give a loving heart to thee",' he quoted. 'How well Herrick understood these things!'

'Blow Herrick, and you, too!' growled Hugh, and going cautiously down below, he managed to reach his cabin without being waylaid.

Whether it was through the machinations of Joan or Cousins, or both, Hugh could not tell, but for the remainder of the time before Port Said was reached, he was not bothered by his butterfly lady, as he still thought of her. Once he caught her looking at him in the most reproachful manner, and trembled for the time when Port Said should be left behind, and he no longer able to avoid her.

He told Joan what had occurred between Hudson and himself, and she was rather inclined to forgive the former than otherwise. Nothing was seen of him previous to their reaching the Egyptian port.

It was reported that he was confined to his cabin with an attack of malaria.

The *Ispahan* drew into Port Said early in the morning, and taking care to avoid Olive – whose surname was Gregson, by the way – Hugh and Joan went ashore as soon as possible, and had quite a good time. Once they saw Hudson, but he took care to keep out of their way, and once they caught sight of Cousins strolling along as though he owned the place, with a brand-new white topee perched rakishly on his head. They returned to the ship just before she sailed, loaded with parcels, most of which they did not want.

Hugh went to his cabin to have a wash as the *Ispahan* was getting under way. He had not been there long before Cousins came in, looking unusually serious for him. He closed the cabin door mysteriously before he spoke.

'Hudson met a friend of his, and had quite a long chat in one of those small drinking places behind *Simon Artz*,' he announced. 'Who do you think the friend was?'

'Dunno,' mumbled Hugh, from the midst of soapy bubbles.

'Kamper!'

CHAPTER 8

IN WHICH OSCAR J. MILES
BUTTS IN

Cousins' announcement gave Hugh such a shock that for a moment he appeared to have lost the power of movement. He just stood and glared at the other. Then he turned suddenly to the wash basin, dived his face into the water and, emerging with a gasp, proceeded to use a towel with great vigour.

'Now,' he said; 'what do you mean by trying to put the wind up me in that outrageous fashion?'

'I made no attempt to put the wind up you,' replied Cousins. 'I was simply stating a plain, unvarnished fact.'

'Do you seriously mean that you saw Kamper – in Port Said?'

The little man nodded.

'But how in the name of all that's wonderful did he get there?'

'Boat!' said Cousins laconically.

'I wasn't supposing that he had walked,' said Hugh, with heavy sarcasm. 'What I'd like to know is, when did he leave England and how? The police and Secret Service were looking for him, and he couldn't have got away without being spotted.'

'Yet he is in Port Said! It doesn't matter so much to us how he got away, as why he is there, and what he is up to.'

Hugh nodded gloomily.

'What an ass I was not to catch him when I had the chance. He may have found out all about our trip to India and be following us.'

'I don't think there is much doubt that he knows a good deal about us, if not all. At any rate Hudson will have put him wise to what he might previously only have guessed at.'

'Good Lord, yes! I had forgotten Hudson. I can hardly credit, though, that that fellow, bad as he is, is in with Kamper's lot. Are you sure it was he?'

'Positive!'

Hugh groaned.

'Why didn't I throw him overboard the other night!' he muttered.

'It was a shock to me,' said Cousins. 'I saw Hudson walking along as though he did not want to be seen, so I stalked him. I watched him go into that drinking den, and followed him in – luckily I was able to hide behind a partition. Kamper was waiting for him and they retired to a corner together.'

'You didn't hear what was said?'

'No, unfortunately. I was not able to get near enough.'

'So, before we ever start our work in India, our arrival will be known to the whole of the Russian circle there. What wretched luck!'

Cousins shrugged his shoulders.

'It is all in the game,' he said. 'Anyhow we start with one advantage. We know that Hudson is connected with them in some way. I think it is likely that Kamper is also going to India, probably on some tramp steamer. I took the precaution of sending a cable in code to headquarters telling them of his presence in Port Said and asking them to give instructions for him to be watched for in India.'

'Good man! It may do the trick!'

'It may not,' replied Cousins doubtfully. 'He is much too cute to be caught like that. He's a wretched-looking specimen, but he has the devil's own ingenuity. Just reflect – we extradite him to Russia under guard; ten days later he is back in London; he disappears again, and three weeks after that turns up in Port Said. He'll take some catching now. I wish I had had time to find out whether he was on a boat, or stopping in Port Said.'

For some time there was silence. Hugh sat on the edge of his bunk and tried to think things out; Cousins strolled to the port-hole and gazed at the passing scene. The ship was just entering the Suez Canal.

'Of all the desolate places in the world,' he said, 'commend me to the Suez Canal. And yet even those weeds growing on the bank conjure up pleasant memories – memories of hours spent in weeding my four by six garden at home – "To me the meanest flower that blows can give Thoughts that do often lie too deep for tears". In case you don't recognise that, it's a bit of Wordsworth!'

'What are we to do about Hudson?' demanded Hugh abruptly.

Cousins turned, and looked at him reproachfully. 'Have you no artistic soul?' he asked. 'What connection can Hudson have with Wordsworth?'

'Get your four by six mind fixed on Hudson for a few minutes, and answer my question!'

'My *garden* is four by six,' replied Cousins, 'I was not talking about my mind. That is more likely to be six by four,' he added reflectively. 'However, returning to Hudson with great reluctance, I think that the only thing we can do is to keep a good watch on him now, and in India.'

'We can't very well have him arrested when we reach Bombay, I suppose!' said Hugh regretfully.

'Of course not! No evidence against him. But on the other hand by keeping him under surveillance he might lead us to the very object of our journey.'

'There's something in that,' admitted Hugh.

'There's a good deal in it. He doesn't know that we suspect his connection with Kamper, and so "*finis coronat opus!*"'

'Is that also from the back of a dictionary?' asked Hugh.

Cousins wrinkled up his face in thought.

'I'm afraid it must be,' he said.

Hugh laughed.

'Run away!' he said. 'I am going to find Joan and gaze on the desolation you spoke about.'

'Go, my son! And be careful never to give Hudson the slightest inkling that you know he is anything more than an Indian Civil Servant, and a blighter. I have an interview with the laundry man about a shirt that was returned without a button. As Epictetus remarked at Hierapolis—'

But Hugh had gone.

'He seems to know me,' muttered Cousins, and with that cryptic remark he went off to find his laundry man.

Hugh made his way to the promenade deck, and had a narrow escape of falling into the clutches of Miss Gregson, who was talking to an elderly man near the head of the gangway. However Joan, who evidently had been waiting for him, darted across and, taking his arm led him to the ship's side. She was immensely interested in everything she saw, and to her the Suez Canal was anything but a scene of desolation.

'Oh, Hugh,' she said, 'it's wonderful to travel, isn't it? I could spend my life just journeying round the world.'

'You'd soon get tired of it,' he said with the blasé air of the old traveller.

'I'm sure I never should,' she denied. 'It is all so wonderful, I think!'

They passed two steamers tied up to let the mail

75

boat by, and she laughed merrily at the witticisms exchanged between the crews; and even in a dredger, with its Arab sailors, she found something to excite her interest. Everything was all so gloriously novel to Joan, and there were many women on board who looked at her with envy, and sighed for their lost youth; many of whom a prolonged sojourn in India had robbed of two of life's most precious gifts, simplicity and the power of enjoyment.

Presently they heard footsteps, and Miss Gregson joined them, a most bewitching smile on her lips.

'I have never met a brother and sister so devoted to each other,' she said. 'You two positively make me long for a brother.'

Hugh looked at Joan with such a pained expression on his face that it was all she could do to prevent herself from laughing. At the same time she greatly resented the efforts of this woman to capture her brother, and had resolved to checkmate her. Miss Gregson ranged herself on the other side of Shannon.

'I consider you have treated me disgracefully since the night of the dance,' she said. 'You appear to have been avoiding me.'

'I have felt rather embarrassed, Miss Gregson,' replied Hugh, with an effort; 'that is why!'

'Surely not,' she said coyly. 'You and I understand each other too well for that, don't we? And why am I *Miss Gregson* now?'

'Because that is your name,' he said brightly.

'But – but I was *Olive* the other night!'

Joan uttered a sound expressive of disgust.

'I wouldn't think of calling you by your Christian name,' said Shannon.

'But I asked you to!'

'Did you?'

'Oh, Hugh! Don't you remember?' She looked at him reproachfully, and he blanched.

'I – I do remember something to that effect,' he said.

'You are being very, very cruel, Hugh! Your sister will think awful things of poor little me.'

'Why should I?' asked Joan coldly.

'You saw us in a – a rather intimate attitude the other night,' replied Miss Gregson, 'and now Hugh seems to be almost ashamed of telling you—'

'Telling me what?' demanded Joan, while Hugh stared at her in apprehension.

Miss Gregson hid her face with great shyness.

'It is hardly the girl's place to announce an engagement,' she murmured.

'What!' shouted Hugh. Joan clung to the railing in amazement and dismay.

Miss Gregson looked up at the former, and her eyes were filled with tears, while her mouth drooped pathetically at the corners.

'Do you mean to say that you were only playing with me?' she asked, a note of agitation in her voice.

'My dear girl,' said Hugh, gulping hard. 'I have

never given you the slightest reason for thinking that we – we are engaged.'

At that her whole manner changed, her eyes flashed, and her body stiffened. She made no attempt to drop her voice, and Hugh noticed with horror, that several of their fellow passengers were gazing curiously in their direction.

'So that is the kind of man you are,' she said. 'You lead me on and, in my innocence and trust, I grow to – to love you, and then you laugh at me, and throw me aside!'

'How dare you accuse my brother of such a thing!' cried Joan, trembling with indignation.

'And you,' went on Miss Gregson to Joan; 'you have all along been against me!' Her manner once again changed; the tears sprang to her eyes. 'You – you have broken my heart, Hugh!' she sobbed.

'I say I'm awfully sorry if you misunderstood anything I have said or done,' muttered poor Hugh.

'Don't be an idiot!' hissed Joan to him.

'It is no use pretending you're sorry now,' said Miss Gregson in a shrill voice. 'You have made me the laughing stock of the ship, and you'll be sorry in reality for all this before I have done with you!'

And with this threat she turned and stalked off, and down the gangway. A few yards away Hudson was standing smiling sardonically.

Hugh and Joan looked at each other in dismay. 'What an awful woman!' said the latter.

'Good Lord!' muttered Hugh. 'What on earth have I done to make her think that—'

'Say!' said a voice behind them. 'That was the cutest bit of play-acting I've seen for some time.'

They turned and beheld Mr Oscar Julius Miles, an American passenger, who had embarked at Port Said. He was tall and very thin with a gaunt face and deep-set grey eyes, but his mouth was almost eloquent of kindliness and good humour. His hair was a nondescript sort of colour, and he wore tortoise-shell rimmed glasses; his clothes obviously had been made by a first-class tailor, and he wore them with an air of distinction. He looked about thirty-five, but might have been younger. He raised his broad-brimmed grey felt hat and bowed.

'I hope you don't mind my butting in,' he said. 'It kinder got my goat to hear that female letting things rip.'

'I suppose you mean to be polite,' said Hugh stiffly, 'but this is a matter that my sister and I hardly care to discuss with a stranger.'

'I guess not,' replied the American, 'but you see I feel rather an interest in Olive Gregson.'

'You know her then?' asked Joan.

'I reckon I do. She tried the same game with me six months ago travelling from Bombay to Port Said.'

'Good gracious!' exclaimed Joan. 'How awful!'

'Well, I'll say it wasn't nice. All the same I sorter have a sneaking hope that she'll get a husband one of these days – she deserves one.'

'Oh! She makes me hate my sex!' said Joan in disgust, and turned to the contemplation of the Arabian desert.

'Then she makes a habit of this sort of thing?' asked Hugh.

'It kinder looks like it. Say, it wouldn't be a bad notion if I introduced myself. I'm Oscar J. Miles, an American at a loose end.' He held out his hand and smiled, and Hugh grasped it with the feeling that he and this man were destined to become staunch friends.

'My name's Shannon, Hugh Shannon,' he said. 'This is my sister.'

Joan turned round, and held out her hand. She decided that Mr Oscar Miles was a good sort. He took her hand and held it gently for a second.

'I'm glad I made up my mind to return to India, Miss Shannon,' he said. 'I have not made many friends since I left the States.'

'Are you travelling round the world?' she asked.

His eyes twinkled.

'I have travelled some,' he replied. 'I started off two years ago after a breakdown in health, and there isn't much of the little old world I haven't seen since. I spent five months in India and then came to Egypt. During the last six months I guess I've seen all there is to be seen in North Africa.'

'How lovely to travel about like that!' said the girl.

'It kinder gets lonesome after a while,' he smiled, 'and I half made up my mind to go back home, but I decided to have another look at India first.'

'What part are you bound for?' asked Hugh.

'That's just what I can't tell you. I'll lump my bags ashore at Bombay, but there's a whole lot of thinking to be done there, before I move on.'

'We're going to Lahore,' said Joan. 'My brother will be stationed there for three years.'

'Gee! I thought of seeing a little bit of Northern India myself, and Lahore's a great place to be in just now.'

'Why?' asked Hugh.

'There's a whole lot of trouble simmering, I guess, and if a man can butt in without the authorities getting sore, he can have some fun.'

Hugh looked serious.

'Do you mean to say that things are as bad as that there?'

'Well, they might be!'

Hugh looked at his sister seriously.

'I'm beginning to be sorry I brought you now, Joan,' he said.

'Not a bit of it,' said Miles. 'The trouble's in the native quarter, not in the civil station. Miss Shannon won't know there's anything on. Say, what about a drink? Talking is dry work, and I guess there's a smoking room on this vessel with all the usual appurtenances thereto.'

'But ladies are not admitted,' said Hugh.

'Isn't that a mighty shame? Well, we'll find a plate where ladies are admitted!'

Joan smiled.

'I'd rather stay on deck, thank you, Mr Miles. You and Hugh go along to the smoking room.'

'Hugh and I'll sure find our way there,' declared the American, then smiled. 'What do you think of that?' he said. 'That's some familiarity for you!'

Hugh and Joan laughed.

'I don't mind what you call me,' said the former.

'Well, I'm glad of that. My tongue has a bad habit of saying things it shouldn't at times. Are you sure you won't come along, Miss Shannon, and let us find a little corner somewhere?'

'Quite, thanks!'

'Can I send you along a drink?'

She shook her head.

'No, thank you!'

'It surprises me how anyone can get along in this climate without an almighty thirst,' he said. 'Come along, Mr Shannon!'

He swept off his hat and bowed to Joan. Then taking Hugh by the arm, he led him unerringly in the direction of the smoking room. Joan watched them go with a smile, and then returned to her contemplation of the scenery.

The two men settled themselves in a corner of the smoking room under a fan, and ordered drinks. For some minutes the American was busy greeting acquaintances – he appeared to be a well-known figure, and quite a third of the men in the room seemed to have met him at some time or other. Hugh looked at him in surprise.

'You seem to be quite popular,' he remarked. 'Yet you talk of being lonesome!'

'Well, I guess that having a number of "how d'you do" acquaintances isn't calculated to remove one's lonesomeness,' smiled the American. 'You Britishers are too mighty proud to come out of your shells and get down to real friendliness as a rule, especially those of you who live in India. Say, can you tell me why Europeans in India lose all their charm and naturalness and, in the majority of cases, develop into snobs?'

Hugh shook his head.

'I'm afraid I can't,' he replied.

'I guess it's because they've been pampered and spoilt, and taught to regard themselves as little tin gods.'

'But things are different from what they used to be. From my recollection of India there is very little of the tin-god business there now.'

'Granted,' said Miles, 'but the tradition has been handed down, and the present day Britisher hangs on like grim death to every little bit of flattery and adulation he can get from the natives. And they know his weakness and play up to it, too.'

'Aren't you rather too severe, Miles?'

'I guess not. If I were an artist, and wanted to paint a picture of the Britisher in India, I'd depict a man reclining comfortably on a long cane chair, his feet stretched out luxuriously, a table containing whisky and soda by his side, and a bearer standing by ready to refill his glass as soon as it became empty.'

Hugh laughed.

'That sounds rather decadent,' he said.

'It is. And your woman-folk are worse. They have nothing to do, no interests at all but tennis and visiting, and the result is that a whole lot of them spend their time scandalmongering, and lose all their charm, or most of it.' He shook his head solemnly. 'India is sure a bad place for women – it's a mighty good thing that they have a safety valve, even if it is so poor a thing as talking scandal.'

He took a long drink.

'It's a strange thing,' he went on, 'that those women who do retain their natural characters, and mind you, there are some, just stand out and scintillate.'

'Naturally that would be because they are so refreshing after the others,' said Hugh.

'Sure! If you don't mind my saying so, Miss Shannon is the sort of girl who would never lose her charm under any circumstances.'

'I'm sure she wouldn't,' said Hugh warmly.

'I've got to tell you that you possess one of the sweetest sisters who ever went to India, and you'll have a hard job to keep the rotters from her. The men'll be after her like bees round a honeypot.'

'I know that,' said Hugh. 'It was the same thing at home.'

'Gee! You can't compare home with India.' He smiled at Hugh whimsically. 'Say, boy,' he said. 'I'm talking more than I should. You'll be wanting to punch my head, if I don't cut the cackle some.'

'Not a bit,' said Hugh. 'You're rather refreshing.'

'Well, so long as you don't think I'm getting fresh, instead of refreshing, it's all right, I guess.'

'Have another drink?'

'Thanks! As it's getting near luncheon, it's about time I indulged in a sherry and bitters.'

The drinks were ordered, and when they were placed before them, Miles gazed at his seriously for a moment.

'Say,' he said; 'I guess you had a narrow escape with that girl. You have to be mighty circumspect with Eurasians, or they'll raise Cain!'

Hugh looked at him in astonishment.

'Eurasian!' he exclaimed. 'Why she's as pure-blooded as I am.'

'Not on your life! She looks the goods all right, but if you get the chance just take a peek at her finger nails and didn't you notice that peculiar rising inflection in her voice? When you hear that, Shannon, you can bet your bottom dollar the tar brush has been about.'

'Why should she talk about going home on six months' leave then?'

'Say; you're acting innocent, aren't you? Bless you, they love to talk of home and leave! She gave herself away on the other boat – told me her Pa had married in India, and that that was her first trip home. He's made a lot of money in something down South.'

'But the fact that she had never been home before hardly makes her Eurasian, does it?'

85

'Perhaps not! But you see she also said she had persuaded her Ma not to go with her, as she had never seen the sea and was frightened of it! Guess the real reason was that Ma isn't quite the same colour as she is, and she didn't want her to give the show away but you can't get away from the voice and the finger nails.' He shook his head. 'No that sort are good to keep away from; they can be mighty dangerous!'

At that moment Cousins came into the room and seeing Hugh made his way towards him. Miles gave a gasp and rising to his feet held out his hand.

'Say, Jerry,' he exclaimed, 'this is the best bit of luck I've had since leaving the States. Put it there, boy!'

Cousins glanced round hurriedly, and then diffidently took the other's hand.

'Don't be so effusive, you mutt,' he whispered, and then raised his voice, so that all who had noticed the greeting could hear him. 'I am very glad to see you, sir,' he said.

The American gaped at him, and Hugh looked his astonishment.

'Then you have met before?' he asked.

'Yes, sir,' said Cousins. 'I was Mr Miles' valet for close on six years.'

'You what?' gasped Miles, and sat down.

'This is rather a strange coincidence, if I may be allowed to say so, sir,' said Cousins urbanely.

'Almighty strange,' said Miles, looking at him as

though he thought he had gone mad. The little man turned to Hugh, who, having realised the situation, was smiling with a trace of perplexity on his face.

'Will you be good enough to step down to the cabin, sir?' he said. 'There are one or two matters which require your attention!'

'Guess I'll step right along too!' said Miles.

CHAPTER 9

OLD FRIENDS

Once in the cabin Cousins turned to Miles, and held out his hand.

'Now, Oscar, old lad,' he said, 'you can shake it as much as you like.'

The American took him at his word, and for some seconds, used Cousins' arm like a pump-handle.

'I guess I'm falling over myself with astonishment, Jerry,' he said. 'What's the big idea? When did you take to valeting, and what the hell do you mean by saying that you were in my service for six years?'

Cousins shook his head reprovingly.

'Your language hasn't improved apparently,' he said.

'Answer my questions!'

'Well, you big stiff – you notice I am using your own phraseology out of respect for you – I had to say something, when all those fellows in the smoking room heard your absurd greeting. It would look nice for the well-known American traveller to be on terms of friendship with a valet, wouldn't it?'

'Let me get this thing straight!' said Miles. 'Are you really a valet?'

'Of course, I am! I have been with Captain Shannon for years, and I am accompanying him to India, because I could not bear to leave his service.'

'Forget it!' said the American in threatening tones. 'Just blow out the hot air and give me the real facts!'

Cousins' eyes twinkled, and his face creased into smile.

'I am giving you the real facts,' he said. 'I am Captain – now Professor – Shannon's valet, and as Sydney Carton says, "It is a far, far better thing I do than I have ever done".'

Miles seized him by the shoulders, and pushed him on to the settee, then turned to Hugh, who had been watching the two with amusement

'Say,' he said; 'perhaps I can get some enlightenment from you, Shannon. I have known this goop for donkeys' years and we have been firm friends – in fact, he is one of the few friends I have on your side and he occasionally deigns to write to me. Is he really your valet, or is he not?'

'He is!' replied Hugh promptly.

'Well, I'm darned!' exclaimed the other and sat down on Hugh's bunk.

'This is a situation that tickles my artistic soul,' said Cousins. 'Here are two men, each afraid of saying too much in case he gives me away to the other, and each anxious to know how much the other knows. Truly life hath its compensations. One of these days I'll take to play-writing and the present situation will be the basis of my first plot.'

'Look here, Cousins,' commenced Hugh. 'If—'

'Say no more!' said the little man, with a lordly gesture. 'It is a shame to keep you in suspense.' He rose. 'Captain Shannon, may I have the pleasure of presenting Mr Oscar Julius Miles to you as one of America's greatest Secret Service agents. For years, owing to the understanding which exists between our two great countries, he has worked hand and glove with our own service, and our Chief has a particularly high opinion of him.' He turned to the other. 'Mr Miles, you see before you one of the most brilliant of the rising generation of Secret Service men of Great Britain. He goes to India to profess in a college; he has certain other duties to perform with my poor assistance. I trust I have made myself quite clear! Need I say more?'

The two men smiled at each other with relief and a wholehearted pleasure. Instinctively their hands shot out, and they gripped warmly.

'Say,' said Miles; 'this is an occasion. It requires honouring. What's yours?'

'Mine is a Manhattan cocktail,' interposed Cousins.

'You don't count,' said Hugh, with a grin. 'Do you really expect me to drink with my valet?'

'Nevertheless he shall have a treat on this occasion,' said Miles. 'I think three Manhattans will about meet the case. Where's the darned bell push?'

Hugh pushed the button, and at the same moment the luncheon gong went.

'Guess that can wait,' said the American.

Joan had nearly finished luncheon when her brother appeared, looking very much pleased with himself.

'You seem to have found a lot to talk about to Mr Miles,' she said severely. 'Had you forgotten me completely?'

'Never, Joan!' he declared. 'But I found Miles a most interesting fellow.' He dropped his voice and leant towards her. 'He has turned out to be one of us!'

She looked at him inquiringly.

'What do you mean by one of us?'

'He is one of the big men of the American Intelligence Department, and has been working in conjunction with our fellows.'

'How interesting!' she exclaimed. 'But how did you find out? I thought you Secret Service men never gave yourselves away.'

'He and Cousins are old friends. While we were in the smoking room, Cousins walked in to ask me to go to my cabin, and Miles almost gave us away in his enthusiasm at meeting him. We all repaired to the cabin together, and I left them there talking over old times like a couple of boys.'

'I seem to have got mixed up with secret services,' said Joan. 'I think it is time I was counted in also.'

'Why, so you are!' said he.

Presently Miles entered the saloon, and after standing looking round for a moment, approached their table, where two passengers had already finished luncheon and vacated their seats.

'Say, Miss Shannon,' he said. 'Do you mind if I sit here just now? I've been allotted a seat on the other side of the saloon, but I guess I'd rather sit here. I never eat much in the middle of the day, so I won't detain you!'

'Of course I don't mind,' she said. 'It's a pity you can't always sit here.'

'That's real nice of you.' He sent away his soup and ordered an omelette. 'I hope you're not angry with me for keeping your brother away from you?'

She smiled.

'I don't suppose you would mind much if I were,' she replied.

'That is unkind. I wouldn't have you cross with me for anything.'

'Do I look as though I could get very angry?'

'Even angels are reported to get annoyed at times,' he said gallantly.

She laughed.

'Mr Miles,' she said, 'you are nothing but a hollow flatterer!'

'I guess this is where I climb into my shell,' he said sadly. 'I never was much of a hand as a squire of dames.'

'I'm afraid you are a fraud,' said Hugh. 'There's

your omelette. Better get on with it before you give yourself away to my sister further.'

Miles shook his head in pretended despair.

'I reckon I'm a poor mutt with all the world arrayed against me,' he said, and attacked the omelette.

The rest of the voyage proved uneventful, if Miss Gregson's meeting with Miles be excepted. They came upon each other in one of the alleyways outside the cabins and, for once in a way, she was at a loss. Not so the American; he bowed politely and held out his hand, as though nothing could give him greater pleasure than meeting her.

'This is unexpected, Miss Olive,' he said. 'I suppose you got tired of little old England, and decided to go back to the old folks?'

'Not at all,' she returned. 'But I only went for six months. Probably I'll return there for good next year!'

'Is that so? Then you'll be taking your Ma back with you, I guess?'

She changed colour and hesitated.

'It all depends,' she said coldly, then: 'I am surprised to find you here – I thought you had finished with India!'

'Well, I guess your country fascinates me some,' he said slowly, 'so I thought—'

'Are you trying to be insulting?' she asked haughtily. 'India is not my country!'

'Your adopted country then!'

'Nor my adopted country – I think you are horrid!'

'Say, don't be sore! I guess I don't say things as clearly as I might, but it kinder seems to me that if one lives in a country, one adopts it as one's own for the time being.'

She looked at him searchingly.

'I never could make out whether you are as simple as you pretend to be,' she said.

'Believe me, I'm the guy that the poet was thinking about when he created "Simple Simon", only I haven't got the same liking for pies. Well, I guess we'll be seeing a bit of each other for the next week or so.'

'I daresay,' she said, without enthusiasm, and passed on. He watched her out of sight with a quizzical smile on his lips, and then went on to his own cabin, whistling.

Very little was seen of Hudson during the last few days. He took care to avoid both Joan and Hugh and once, when he met the former on a gangway, he drew aside to let her pass without a word and without the slightest sign of embarrassment. He appeared to become very friendly with Miss Gregson, and Joan wondered if she were trying now to capture the Civil Service man. Hugh on the other hand was greatly intrigued by the friendship, and thought it portended danger, or at least unpleasantness for himself. He consulted Cousins about it.

The little man shook his head.

'I can't see what trouble a combination of that sort can hatch,' he said. 'Besides Miss Gregson is bound for Bangalore, and there are not two towns in India much farther apart than Lahore and Bangalore.'

Right on time the great liner drew alongside the Ballard Pier at Bombay. The usual crowd of friends and relations were waiting to greet their pals, sisters, wives and children and once again Joan found a great deal of interest in a novel sight.

As she stood leaning over the rail, Oscar Miles joined her.

'Good morning, Miss Shannon,' he said. She smiled her greeting at him. 'Well, you see yourself at the gate of India. I hope you don't find it disappointing.'

'On the contrary,' she assured him, 'I think it most fascinating. Bombay has a very beautiful harbour.'

'Sure!' he said, 'especially in that direction.' He pointed to Malabar Hill. 'I've a good friend up there. One of my very few English friends, in fact.'

'Oh!' She looked at him questioningly. 'Why do you pretend to have so few English friends, when you seem to have so many?'

He smiled, then looked serious.

'I reckon that the word "friend" includes a whole multitude of things. A real friend is a priceless possession, Miss Shannon.'

'Then a friend to you means more than it does to the average person?'

'I guess so!' he replied after a few seconds' thought.

'I should like you and Hugh to be friends,' she said softly. 'Your kind of friends I mean.'

'I have a feeling that we will be,' he said. He looked troubled for a moment, then added, 'I would like to think that his sister may some day regard me in the same light!'

'I should love to,' she said earnestly.

He looked almost boyish.

'Say, that's the best bit of news I've heard for some time. I only hope it comes off!'

'Why shouldn't it?'

'I feel that I am asking too much.'

'Oh, why? I should so like to have a real man friend. I have always wanted one, but nearly every man I meet seems to think it is his duty to make love to me.'

'Well, you can't blame 'em for that.'

'Now you're being frivolous! Of course Hugh, besides being a brother, is my dearest and best friend – nobody could ever take his place – but all the same I do want a friend who is not a brother, and one who wouldn't consider it his bounden duty to – to propose to me.'

'Well I'm right here if you'll have me.' He smiled, but his face had paled a little as he spoke.

'This is delightful,' she said enthusiastically. 'I'm so glad!'

'And believe me it's real nice of you. Guess I'll have to find a new size in hats now.'

'Oh, you're being flippant!' She looked at him reproachfully.

'Not on your life, Miss Shannon,' he protested. 'I'm trying to show you how I appreciate your kindness to me.'

'Don't put it like that,' she said. 'It will spoil everything.'

'Then I'll just keep mum and think it. Gee!' he exclaimed suddenly.

'What's the matter?'

'Look!'

Visitors were just being permitted to come on board, and amongst others was a large lady, very tall and very fat, notwithstanding the efforts of her dressmaker. She was almost as dark as an Indian, and with her small acquisitive eyes and pendulous cheeks, she was not at all the sort of person one would be enamoured of meeting. She sailed down on Miss Gregson with an air of possession, and as Miles pointed her out to Joan she was engaged in enclosing the fair Olive in a large and ponderous embrace.

'Who can that be?' wondered Joan.

Miles chuckled sardonically.

'Guess it's Ma,' he said. 'Kindly excuse me a moment, Miss Shannon.'

He strolled across the deck to where Miss Gregson was engaged in releasing herself from the maternal hold. The young lady looked anything but pleased, and as Miles came close to them he heard her say:

'Why come all this way, Mother? It was not necessary to meet me at all!'

'Say, Miss Gregson,' put in the American. 'I guess this is your Ma. May I have the pleasure of being presented to her?'

A look of embarrassed fury came over the girl's face, and she performed the introduction almost rudely. Miles stood chatting with them for a moment or two and found the old lady to be coarse in her speech and over-elaborate in her manners; then raising his hat politely he said goodbye and returned to Joan.

'Hugh would have had a handful in Ma if he had been inveigled into a marriage with Olive,' he chuckled.

Joan shuddered.

'Why did you go over to them?' she asked.

'Just vulgar curiosity,' he said. 'I ought to be ashamed of myself, but I'm not. I found out that my suspicions were right – Olive is one part British and ninety-nine Eurasian.'

Hugh joined them soon afterwards, and when he was shown Mrs Gregson, almost collapsed on the deck with shock.

'Let's get ashore,' he said. 'The sooner I am away from Olive Gregson, the better I'll be pleased.'

'Say, Shannon,' said the American, 'you sure are not going off without kissing her goodbye?'

Hugh gave him a look that should have transfixed him, then turning, led Joan down the gangway to the landing-stage, followed by the grinning American.

Cousins insisted on performing his duties as the ideal valet should. He saw the baggage through the Customs and into the train, reserved berths through to Lahore, and generally conducted all necessary details with the gravity and imperturbability of an experienced gentleman's gentleman. Through it all Miles watched him with a smile of admiration.

'Say, Jerry,' he remarked once as the little man was standing near him: 'what an honest to goodness valet you would have made, if your sins hadn't led you into more serious paths!'

Cousins pushed his topee on to the back of his head.

'I always wanted to be a valet when I was a child,' he said. 'When other boys were dreaming about bus conductors and engine-drivers I sighed for the delights of a job like this. I was, as Goldsmith said, "too nice for a statesman, too proud for a wit".'

Even in the midst of his multifarious duties he found time to look round him. He had noticed Hudson leave the ship and meet two men; one was short and inclined to *embonpoint*, the other middle-aged, tall and saturnine, with a moustache that did not hide the cruelty of his mouth. Hudson appeared uneasy in their company, and Cousins spent some seconds speculating on the cause of his anxiety. He contrived to get near without being observed, but their conversation was not at all interesting, and all he learnt was that the three of them were staying in Bombay for a couple of days, and then travelling to Lahore.

Cousins conducted Joan and Hugh to a reserved coupé with the air of a guide expatiating on the delights of some famous work of art.

'Now you have nothing to worry about,' he said. 'Your berth is next door, Miss Shannon, so you will be near your brother all night, as well as with him by day.'

'Where are you travelling?' asked Hugh.

'Oh, I have a second-class compartment a few coaches down, with three cronies I found on board ship.'

'It's a shame that you should travel in the second class,' said Joan.

'Not a bit of it – I like it. My companions are all going to Lahore; one of them is a bandmaster and has a violin with him, another has a flute and as I have a ukulele—'

'You with a ukulele!' laughed the girl.

'Why not? It's not exactly high art, but there is a trace of music in it. So between us, or rather together, we should produce a melody or two to "speed the passing hours". I'm not sure who said that – do you know, Shannon, I – er – mean, sir?'

'No, I don't!' returned Hugh, shortly.

'What a confession for a Professor of English to make!'

'Don't remind me of that for the Lord's sake!'

said Hugh. 'I'm getting thoroughly nervous about it.'

'Never mind!' said Cousins soothingly. 'You've me to fall back upon, and I'll toddle along and help you out with a few quotations. Always at your service, I remain, yours faithfully!'

A bell rang and people began to take their seats.

'Where is Mr Miles?' asked Joan. 'I hope he hasn't gone off without saying goodbye.'

'I lost him ten minutes ago,' said Cousins, 'making his way in the direction of the telegraph office.'

'Then probably he has had his little think,' said Hugh, 'and has decided where to go.'

The second bell rang and the engine gave a piercing whistle in reply. At the same time the object of their remarks could be seen making his way along the platform, with an enormous pile of papers and magazines in his arms. He smiled genially as he came up.

'I was almost late,' he said, and dumped his load into the compartment. 'Something to look at,' he added, by way of explanation.

'How nice of you!' said Joan. 'Thank you so much! Have you decided where you are going yet?'

'Yes! I reckon stay here for a week, and go on a bender.'

'On a bender! And in Bombay!' muttered Cousins.

'Then,' went on Miles, 'I guess I'll come right along to Lahore. I sure am looking forward to seeing a lot more of you folks; and perhaps I can butt in somewhere?' He looked at Hugh questioningly.

The latter nodded, while Joan expressed her pleasure. The American gazed down the platform thoughtfully.

'What are you looking at with such a *wild* expression, Oscar?' asked Cousins.

'Nothing,' replied the other shortly.

'Like Alexander Selkirk,' said the little man; 'you are "monarch of all you survey".'

The train commenced to move and the hand-clasps had to be hasty. Cousins stood talking earnestly to his friend on the platform, and almost missed the train in consequence, but recollecting in time that he was travelling by it, he ran along to his compartment and dragged himself aboard, the American pushing him from behind.

Train travelling is rather a tiring business in India, and even at the best time of the year the atmosphere in a railway compartment is hot and unpleasant. In spite of this Joan found a lot to interest her on the forty hours' journey to Lahore. Everything was so strange and novel, and even Hugh, who had spent some years in the country before, was full of delight as he recognised places he had known. He was never tired of pointing out interesting sights to his sister, and explaining the difference between the various races that they saw during the journey. He had sent a wire to Mahommed Abdullah informing him of their arrival, and asking him to make arrangements for them to be met in Lahore.

He had not exaggerated when he said that he was nervous about taking up the duties of a professor. Although he was a man of splendid qualifications and ability, he had never undertaken such a post before, and he was rather inclined to belittle his chances of success than otherwise. He wondered also how he would fare in his other and more important task. He realised the responsibility that the Chief had put upon his shoulders, and the necessity for using the greatest tact and delicacy in all his operations. He would be compelled, too, to work more or less in the dark, for he could expect no assistance from any Indian public man, and indeed could not ask for it, for fear of causing misunderstanding and, in consequence, suspicion and distrust.

Great Britain's policy of uprooting all causes of trouble in India was an ideal which could easily be open to misconception, and thus the necessity for Hugh to be careful how he set to work. He had one great satisfaction, and that was that he had the assistance of such an astute and capable man as Cousins. The little man was full of resource and seldom made a mistake, and Hugh would have a great asset in the quick wit and deep reasoning power of one of the most successful of Great Britain's secret agents. In fact, Shannon laughed to himself as he reflected that he would probably have to take a back seat

as far as their investigations went, for he acknow-
ledged to himself that he was not the equal of
the little man from Whitehall.

The train raced on by fields, sandy plains,
wooded hills and country districts that at times
almost resembled home. It stopped at all the big
towns such as Indore, Bhopal, Agra, Delhi, and
Ambala, and Cousins spent a good deal of his
time with Joan and Hugh, regaling them with his
witty chat and stories, and once bringing along
his ukulele, when he surprised them by his mastery
of the little instrument; but he never obtruded,
and to the casual observer was in every way the
well-behaved deferential valet.

At last the train drew into the great station of
Lahore, and at once the door of their coupé was
besieged by a crowd of red-coated coolies, clamouring to carry their luggage. Hugh stood on the
step and looked round him. There was a great
crowd on the platform and presently, to his
surprise, he saw Mahommed Abdullah. The latter
saw him at the same time and waved his hand.
Almost immediately there was a rush by a crowd
of cleanly-dressed young men in the red fez, or
turban, long coats and broad white trousers of the
Mussulman. They surrounded the door and
cheered, and Hugh's heart sank with embarrassment as he realised that these were, no doubt, his
future students, who had come to welcome him.
Joan's fate paled nervously, but her eyes sparkled
with pleasure, and she clutched hold of his arm.

Mahommed Abdullah made his way to them, and took Hugh warmly by the hand.

'Welcome to Lahore, Captain Shannon,' he said, and then turning to the students he added loudly, 'Gentlemen, this is your future Professor of English.'

There was another cheer, and immediately several of the young men pushed forward, and Hugh and Joan found their necks encircled by garlands of flowers. Hugh shakily presented his sister to Abdullah, who welcomed her very charmingly. Then there were speeches, and Shannon found himself in the unique position of having to reply from the step of a railway coach. In spite of his nervousness it was quite a good effort, and Joan pleased him afterwards by telling him that it was splendid.

'The students will see to your luggage,' said Abdullah. 'I have obtained rooms for you at the Punjab Hotel for the present; you can make your own arrangements later on. My car is waiting outside and I will drive you there, then perhaps you will lunch with me.'

'It is awfully good of you,' said Hugh, 'but my own man insisted on coming to India with me – I have had him for so long, you see. He will look after the luggage! Here he is!'

Cousins made his way through the throng, his face creased in a hundred wrinkles, denoting his amusement. Abdullah explained who he was to the students, and Cousins received a cheer, and some garlands all for himself.

Then the Principal led Joan and Hugh along the platform to his car, followed by the wildly excited young men, and with Cousins bringing up the rear. Hugh explained to the latter where he was to take the luggage, then entered the car with Joan and Abdullah. There were more cheers and they were off. Cousins stood watching them until they were out of sight.

'Here endeth the first lesson,' he said, and turned to the smiling students. 'Young men,' he added, 'you little know the trials that are before you. However, "where ignorance is bliss, 'tis folly to be wise".'

CHAPTER 10

SHANNON MEETS HIS COLLEAGUES

Joan and Hugh soon settled down in their new quarters at the Punjab Hotel, but as Hugh explained to Abdullah, they would not be able to stay there on account of the expense. No provision was made for European servants, and, therefore, Cousins cost almost as much as each of them did. Abdullah promised to help them to find a bungalow and matters were left at that for the time being.

The day following their arrival in Lahore, Hugh made his first appearance in Sheranwala College. Abdullah called for him and drove him there. He felt extremely nervous, and when he found that he was down on the timetable for four lectures a day, except on Friday, which is a Muslim holiday, he wondered if his throat would stand the strain. Three of these lectures were to the fourth-year students and one to the third.

He commenced his duties at once, and entering the fourth year lecture room, was received in dead silence from about a hundred and twenty Mahommedan young men, whose ages ranged from nineteen to twenty-four. They looked at him curiously and he returned the scrutiny with interest. Most of them looked intelligent – a few had extremely clever faces – but there were also many who, from their expressions, seemed to lack any ability at all. Quietly Hugh summed them up, and his nervousness gradually left him. He made a little speech in which he told them that he was glad to be among them, and hoped that they would find him of great use in their efforts to obtain the degrees of Bachelors of Arts and Science. When he had finished he was enthusiastically clapped and with more confidence than he had expected he started on his work.

To his surprise he found it fairly easy and although the students had a certain amount of difficulty in understanding his pronunciation, he was very patient and was careful to enquire every now and again if he were understood. They appeared, in the majority of cases, to be very keen and listened to him with care and intelligence, but there were one or two who appeared bored, and took no interest in the lecture at all. He felt a delight in asking the latter questions, to none of which they could reply, and they aggravated him by standing up and grinning sheepishly when he spoke to them, and by making no attempt to reply at all. It was the same with all of his classes, and he came to the conclusion that things were not going to be difficult at all. He found the most trouble with the third-year fellows. They were not taking their examination for two years and appeared to consider it unnecessary to work until they were in their fourth year. All of them, both of the third and fourth years, had very little idea of discipline, and on the slightest provocation broke out into loud chatter. Shannon soon made it clear that he would not tolerate such conduct and this appeared to surprise them.

So his first morning passed by, and at half past one, when his last lecture came to an end, his throat was so sore that he could hardly speak above a hoarse whisper. He made his way to the Principal's office in response to a summons, and having been told to take a seat, sat down with a sigh of relief.

'Well, how have you got on?' asked Abdullah.

'Oh, pretty well, thanks,' replied Hugh; 'but it seems to me that I shall have no voice left after a few days.'

The other smiled.

'You will get used to that,' he said.

'Perhaps so; but don't you think that four lectures without a break is excessive. Surely it is overworking your professors to compel them to do so much?'

'It is a lot certainly, but the authorities desire every professor to take twenty-seven periods a week. You have only twenty-two, for I have only given you two on Sunday.'

Hugh looked at him in surprise.

'Am I expected to work on Sunday too?' he asked.

'I am afraid so. You see this is a Mahommedan College and the holiday is on Friday – not, Sunday. Of course if you prefer I could break up your lectures, so that you had two in the morning and two in the afternoon, but I arranged them altogether so that you would have your afternoons free.'

Hugh was thoughtful for a few minutes.

'I think I'd rather risk the strain of the four together,' he said, 'if that ensures my freedom every afternoon.'

Abdullah placed his fingertips together.

'Of course you are expected to take charge of all the sports and I'm afraid that that will take up a great deal of your spare time.'

Hugh laughed.

'Is there anything else?' he asked, with a note of sarcasm in his voice. 'Please tell me now – I think I can bear it!'

Abdullah frowned. After all he was the Principal, and he did not like levity from his subordinates.

'I think that is all – at present!' he said.

'Thank you!' returned Hugh calmly, then he laughed. 'It has its humours!' he said.

'Everything has a humorous side,' said Abdullah, 'and I assure you I agree with you that my professors are overworked. I have already discovered that my post here is by no means a sinecure. I spoke to the governing body about the necessity of engaging at least three other professors, and thus relieving my present staff of some of its work. But they regarded me with horror – their idea is to have as few professors as possible, and to overwork them as much as they can – they do not like paying out money. In confidence, I may as well tell you that they would never have countenanced your engagement – they think it wicked to pay out as much as five hundred rupees a month to one man – if it had not been that the Government refused to give them a grant unless there were at least three men with English degrees on the staff.'

'Then your promise to do your best to get me an adequate salary seems doomed to disappointment,' said Hugh.

'I have already done my best without result,' replied Abdullah. 'I still have hopes, however.'

'Oh, well,' said Hugh calmly. 'I haven't signed their contract yet.'

The Principal looked at him rather anxiously.

'Do you mean to say that you will refuse to sign the contract unless your salary is increased?' he asked.

'I don't know yet – I shall have to think it over.'

'But you accepted their grant for your travelling expenses, and came out with the knowledge of the remuneration they offered. Morally you have already accepted the contract!'

'I also came out on the understanding which your promise gave me,' said Hugh quietly.

'You are placing me in a very invidious position, Captain Shannon.'

'I have no intention of doing that. But you will

admit that you said you thought you could persuade them to make an adequate increase!'

'I know I did. Unfortunately I was foolish enough then to credit them with a greater sense of justice than they appear to possess. I have already wished once or twice that I had not left England.'

'And you have been here—'

'Just two weeks!'

Hugh smiled.

'Oh, well,' he said. 'I'll think things over. I certainly won't let you down, Mr Abdullah, if I can help it.'

'I am sure of that. I hope you are not in a hurry for your tiffin, as I have asked the staff to assemble in their common room to meet you?'

'I would like to be introduced to them, of course,' said Hugh.

'Then will you come along with me?'

Abdullah led him along a corridor, and presently entered a large room, where some twenty-four men were collected. With the exception of two who wore European dress, they were clothed in the usual garb of Mahommedans – white baggy trousers, shirts which fell outside the nether garments and longish jackets. Most of them wore the red fez, but two had on large picturesque turbans.

As Mahommed Abdullah made a short speech of introduction, Hugh studied his future colleagues and came to the conclusion that he had seldom seen a more nondescript lot of individuals. They looked, in the majority of cases, a crude coarse lot, with dirty untrimmed beards, and gross heavy faces. The two in European clothes were of an entirely different stamp, and had an air of refinement about them which none of the others possessed. These two had been to England and were the proud possessors of English university degrees. One of them, a little man about five feet two inches in height caught Shannon's eye, and he reflected that never in his life had he seen anybody quite so ugly. He had small eyes, a broad nose, with somewhat distended nostrils, and an ugly mouth, with thick heavy lips which made him look almost repugnant. It was obvious that his clothes were the factor which gave him the air of refinement, and he certainly knew how to wear them. The other was a nice-looking man of about twenty-five, who looked an athlete, and spoke with an Oxford drawl, though he had been at Cambridge. If his colour had been lighter he would easily have been mistaken for an Englishman.

Abdullah's introduction over, they crowded round Hugh with various expressions of welcome. He liked the athletic man immediately, for he strode forward and shook hands with the firm clasp of the sportsman. Most of the others took Hugh's hand with a jellyfish sort of grip that was unwholesome. One of them, a fat elderly man with a walrus moustache and a series of chins, tried to monopolise him.

'Of course you have not seen much of our

country yet, Captain Shannon,' he said, 'but how do you like what you have seen?'

'I was stationed out here while in the Army,' said Hugh; 'so I know a little about it!'

'Then you speak Urdu perhaps?'

'I am afraid I neglected my opportunities in that direction.' Hugh, in consultation with Cousins, had decided to pretend that he did not know Hindustani. The fat man smiled in his greasy way.

'No doubt you will learn the language?'

'Probably,' said Hugh.

The ugly little man then took possession of him. He spoke English well but with a peculiar emphasis on all prefixes.

'I am Doctor Mumtaz Sadiq,' he said, 'head of the science department here. Perhaps you have heard of me?'

'I am afraid I haven't,' said Hugh.

'Indeed! You surprise me. I became quite well known during my research work in England. Of course I could have taken up an appointment, and in fact settled down there, but family matters demanded that I should return. Among other things I am an expert psychologist, doctor of philosophy, a barrister, and very nearly a qualified medical man. I don't think there is anyone in India so well qualified as I!'

'Are you also a policeman, a bus conductor, and a chauffeur?' asked Hugh, with an appearance of bland interest.

Doctor Mumtaz Sadiq drew himself up to his full height, and looked indignant.

'I was not joking, Captain Shannon,' he declared. 'I have all the qualifications I spoke of. It is difficult for me to decide whether I should continue in this entirely unsatisfactory post here, or take up a position more befitting my attainments.'

'I should wait until the governorship of the Punjab becomes vacant, if I were you,' said Hugh soothingly, and turned to Mahommed Abdullah.

'If you are ready, Mr Abdullah,' he said, 'I think it is time I returned to tiffin.'

'Certainly!' replied the Principal. 'Come along!'

As the car drew out of the College gates, Abdullah turned to Hugh inquiringly.

'What do you think of the staff?' he asked.

Hugh made a grimace. He gave a non-committal reply.

'I think the athletic man is probably a good fellow,' he said.

'You mean Aziz? Yes, he is. He was educated in England, and is almost English. But what about the others?'

'Do you want a candid reply?'

'Certainly!'

'Then I hope for the sake of the College that as professors they belie their looks.'

Abdullah laughed, then became serious.

'I'm very much afraid they do not,' he said. 'They are part of a system of cram. Every one of them has obtained his degree by cramming up textbooks and notes. They have no initiative, no resource, no originality, and they pass on the same ideas to their students and dictate the self-same notes that were given to them. They encourage the wholesale memorising of pages and chapters of textbooks, and are satisfied when, in examinations, their words are repeated with parrot-like exactness.'

'And is that the system of education out here?' asked Hugh.

'Unfortunately it is! I had hoped to be able, in my new capacity, to alter things, but already I begin to despair a little. What can one or two men do, when the same antiquated ideas are prevalent throughout the whole of the University, and no drastic measures are taken to cope with them. The students enter the examination room with their heads full of pages and pages of notes and texts. If they get a question the answer to which they have not learnt by heart, they cannot even attempt to answer it. If they get a question of which they have learnt the answer and a phrase or even a sentence eludes them, they are done. And you and I will not succeed in altering the habits which have been pushed into them from their primary school onwards.'

'Isn't it possible to engage professors with more up-to-date ideas?'

'It is; and of course Government colleges possess some very fine men on their staffs, but the narrow-minded policy of our governing body is to get the cheapest man they can who has a degree. Always

116

our results have been very poor, but what else can you expect from the average type of professor we possess. They do their best, but their best is hopeless. I doubt if more than two or three of them could pass a London Matriculation paper.'

'How awful!' said Hugh.

'It is worse than awful. I came out here with very big ideas, but already I am beginning to find them impracticable. I have three men on my staff with English degrees and ideas above cram; you are one, Aziz is another, Sadiq is the third, but Sadiq will not settle down to his work. He is always thinking that his great attainments, as he loves to call them, would be of more use in another sphere; he does not know his own mind and is a bad case of swollen head. There remain you, Aziz and me; we can accomplish a lot, but we are too handicapped to do much.'

Abdullah spoke with great feeling, and Hugh felt very sorry for him. He could just imagine how the other had accepted the post of Principal with the high hope that he could do much for the advancement of Mahommedan education, and how bitterly disappointed he must have been to find the almost insurmountable obstacles in his path. Hugh decided that his own situation had become very difficult; and with his other job before him, he was going to be placed in a very unenviable position.

The car drew up in front of the Punjab Hotel, and Shannon alighted. He stood watching Abdullah, as he drove away.

'Rotten luck!' he murmured. 'He seems such a good chap, too.'

He had to explain to Joan why he was so late, and she and Cousins listened with interest to his description of the morning's doings. They laughed when he told them about the professors.

'Oh, surely, Hugh,' said the girl, 'they are not as bad as all that?'

'Every bit,' he replied; 'in fact, I have rather flattered them than otherwise.'

'What a dreadful lot they must be!'

'They are!' he said grimly.

After lunch he had a consultation with Cousins.

'I am puzzled how to set about our job,' he said. 'We have come out here with a lot of ideas and suspicions, but without the slightest tangible point to go upon. What do you suggest?'

'Well of course you must become a member of the club as soon as possible. That is essential! In the first place a club in India is the centre of gossip, and it is likely that you may pick up something there. Secondly it is necessary for Miss Shannon, because she will never have any friends unless you are a member – the idea being that those not inside the sacred portals of the club must necessarily be outsiders! For my part I will make acquaintances among the rank and file, and do my best that way. I have already made myself known to a couple of fellows this morning.'

'You haven't lost any time,' grinned Hugh. 'Who are they?'

'Nobody of any account I'm afraid. The manager of Edgar and Watson, chemists, and a sergeant of police named Spink.'

'Did you cable that we had arrived?'

'Yes!'

'Perhaps we will receive some instructions in a day or two. I wonder what happened to Kamper?'

'I wish I knew,' said Cousins. 'That man raises a mildly inquiring curl on my forehead every time I think of him.'

'When Hudson comes you had better watch him as closely as possible. He may lead us somewhere, though I'm afraid if he is in league with the Soviet, he will make it exceedingly warm for us. In fact, Lahore is likely to be rather dangerous.'

Cousins shrugged his shoulders.

'A little danger might make it attractive,' he said.

'Don't you like it?'

'Not a little bit. Lahore is a splendid place to make one reflect what a glorious country England is.'

Hugh laughed.

'You've been very quick in forming an opinion,' he remarked.

'I formed most of it yesterday, and consolidated it this morning. Of course there are some places worse.'

'I like what I have seen of it.'

'Including Sheranwala College?'

Hugh made a grimace.

'No; the College is rather a blot!' he said.

Cousins took out a pipe and filled it.

'I wonder if it would be possible to get a complete list of the members of the club,' he said.

'What do you want it for?'

'We might find out the antecedents of every member and make a list of any doubtful ones.'

'Good Lord, man, that would take ages! Besides I don't see how it would help. The people we are after may not belong to the club.'

'I think they will. They wouldn't lose an opportunity of getting in with the social life, and if they kept outside they would be far more likely to be regarded as questionable characters. I am going to try to get that list anyhow.'

'You have a job before you, and my sympathies! You don't expect the secretary to hand such a thing over to a complete stranger, do you?'

'I have no intention of asking the secretary, my lad.'

'Then how do you propose to set about it?'

'Money talks! Though it doesn't always answer when it's spoken to,' he added.

'I see. You favour bribery and corruption?'

The little man nodded.

'It is a favourite pastime in this country,' he said. 'And when in Rome do as Rome does. At any rate I do not intend to sit down and twiddle my thumbs, do you?'

'Certainly not! But I've got to think a bit before I do anything definite!'

'Well, I don't suppose the Chief expects us to

buzz around without any idea what we are buzzing about. Still I hate doing nothing even in these early days. *Ex nihilo nihil fit!*'

Hugh looked at him suspiciously, and with a smile he got up, and went out of the room.

but a man ade to... in any Idea what we were burning
about. Still I had... been doing nothing about the...
many days...
Clean linked... him sometimes, and with...
...

CHAPTER 11

COUSINS IS ENTERPRISING

Hugh lost no time in making acquaintances, and within a fortnight he had the satisfaction of being nominated as a member of the club. The committee meeting was due in a few days, when his and Joan's names would be put up and the nomination ratified. In the meantime he went daily to his work at Sheranwala College, and began to get on well with the students. He was less successful with the professors. Most of them he found were very harmless, though not at all the type of men with whom he had anything in common, and they seemed to think that flattery would make them popular with him. There was a system of toadyism among some of them with the higher authorities which nauseated him, and in consequence he avoided them as much as possible.

After some consideration he signed the contract which was duly stamped-to his disgust he found that he was expected – to pay for the stamp – and Abdullah reiterated his promise to do all in his power to get the salary increased. Thus he became a fully sworn member of the staff. Among the students he discovered a few with the characteristics of gentlemen, but the majority were quite the opposite. They loved to crowd round him and talk to him, laughing immoderately at the vaguest witticism, run errands for him, and generally do all in their power to curry favour with a view to future profit for themselves. They all looked upon an Englishman in the College as a decided asset, not so much for what they expected to learn from him, as for what he might be able to do for them in the way of obtaining posts in the future. He had not been in the College for more than three days when he was asked for testimonials, and several of them visited the hotel with gifts of fruit, and left cards with their names written upon them so that he might remember them always.

The Indian mind is subtle, but not so subtle that Hugh could not see the purpose that underlay all the extravagant flattery and popularity which suddenly came upon him. He, with Joan and Cousins, laughed many times about it, and the students, and others, would have been surprised had they heard the opinions that were frankly expressed about them.

Cousins, by some means known only to himself, had managed to bribe one of the Indian clerks at the club to make out a full list of regular male members with their professions and addresses, and he spent several days in finding out as much as he could about the doubtful ones. Of course a large proportion were military and police officers and these were passed by. On the Friday he came to Hugh as the latter was preparing to go out, and triumphantly waved a sheet of paper at him.

'Here I have a list of doubtfuls,' he said. 'There are seventeen of them, and the eight with crosses against their names are very doubtfuls.'

'What constitutes a doubtful?' asked Hugh.

'No visible means of support; that is to say they appear to live by their wits. The eight very doubtfuls are either foreigners or of foreign origin.'

'Good Lord! You're a wonder!'

'Dear me! Have you only just discovered that very apparent fact? Why I've known it for a long time!'

Hugh studied the paper carefully.

'Who are the two at the bottom?' he asked.

'Ah! They are the tit-bits, the *chefs d'oeuvres* so to speak!'

'What? Extremely doubtfuls?'

'No; they are not doubtfuls at all. They happen to be men of wide affluence, authority and importance. The first is the head of a large mercantile firm, and the second the principal of one of the colleges.'

'Then why are they on this list?'

'Do their names convey nothing to you?'

Hugh looked at the paper again.

'Novar and Rahtz,' he said 'They're foreign names, of course!'

'My son, they are Russians both of them!'

'How do you know?'

'Because they make no attempt to hide their

nationality, and are registered as such. But that is not the chief point. This is where I come to the climax of my story, as the novelists say. They are the two men whom I saw with Hudson at Bombay!'

'Good Lord!' exclaimed Hugh, and sat down.

'Ah,' said Cousins, with deep satisfaction. 'I have made my point!'

'But how did you find this out?'

'I spent some time waiting outside the house of each, and was rewarded by seeing them, when of course I recognised them.'

'By Jove! This is better! We are beginning to move.'

'There is certainly a suspicion that the cobwebs are being shaken away. What about Hudson? You have spent some time watching his movements. Has anything suspicious transpired?'

Hugh shook his head.

'No; he is leading the life of a respectable member of society, as far as I can make out.'

'You haven't let him see that you are watching him?'

'Of course not!' said Hugh indignantly. 'What do you take me for?'

'A Professor of English literature!'

'Bah!' said Hugh loudly, and with disgust.

Cousins' eyes twinkled, his face creased, and he chuckled.

'"Is life worth living? Yes, so long as there is wrong right. Wail of the weak against the strong,

Or tyranny to fight." Bear up! Remember thy country hath need of thee!'

'For two pins, Cousins,' said Hugh threateningly, 'I'd punch your head.'

'Don't do that! My head is not at its best these days. I think it is suffering from topeeitis. By the way is the bungalow fixed up yet?'

'Yes. At present it is undergoing a much needed coat of whitewash, the furniture goes in tomorrow, and we move in on Sunday.'

'Dear! Dear! On the seventh day thou shalt rest,' murmured Cousins, then added sadly: 'but not in India!'

'Don't remind me of the affliction I have to bear in lecturing on Sunday!'

'I thought you said that Abdullah was arranging to relieve you of duties on that day.'

'So he promised; but he hasn't said anything further!'

'Bless the man! Why you have only been here on one Sunday so far! Well, I suppose I must turn up at the bungalow tomorrow in my character of ideal *valet de chambre* and see the furniture installed!'

'I suppose you must,' said Hugh. 'I'm sorry, but—'

'Don't be sorry! I'm not! I rather fancy myself as a decorator. The position of even a chair in the room makes all the difference to its artistic appeal. Of course you wouldn't understand that. Only Miss Shannon and I could be expected to know whether the leg of a chair should stand in the heart of a rose on the carpet or beyond it.'

'There are no roses on the carpets,' said Hugh triumphantly, 'and they are not carpets, but plain blue durries with red borders.'

Cousins gazed at him sorrowfully.

'You have taken the salt out of my life, Shannon,' he said. 'I had naturally calculated on Persian carpets covered with rugs of priceless worth from Kashmir.'

'Then I'm jolly glad to tell you that you will be disappointed,' jeered Hugh.

'How unkind! How very unkind! "A little word in kindness spoken, A motion, or a tear, Has often healed the heart that's broken, And made a friend sincere."'

'Hugh!' called Joan's clear voice, outside the door. 'How much longer are you going to be?'

'I'm just coming!' he called back, and smiling at Cousins he went off to join his sister.

Through the offices of Mahommed Abdullah, Hugh had succeeded in obtaining a bungalow in Crescent Road, a thoroughfare running parallel to the Mall, and near the gardens. It was quite a small house with six rooms. Four of them with dressing rooms and bathrooms attached were to be bedrooms, for Joan, Hugh, and Cousins, and a spare guest chamber. One of the others was the dining room and the other a sitting room. A shady veranda, a garden large enough for a badminton court, a garage, and extensive servants' quarters

127

completed the premises, and Hugh had obtained the whole for a rental which was almost moderate for Lahore. The garage would not be wasted for, with the knowledge that a car is almost a necessity in Lahore, Hugh had decided to buy one as soon as they were settled in the bungalow.

Joan and Cousins, with the aid of the newly-engaged cook, sweeper and bistee, spent the greater part of Saturday in receiving the furniture and placing it in position. As is often the case with Europeans in India, the furniture had been hired from a dealer in the Anarkali, that crowded commercial thoroughfare in which anything from a pin to a complete suite of furniture can be purchased.

Joan insisted on doing quite a lot herself, which brought forth protests from Cousins, who appeared to be in his element. He bustled his helpers round until they did not seem to have minds of their own, and at his slightest command dashed about with a haste quite un-Indian. Lahore in the cool season is very pleasant, but when Cousins eventually called a halt at six o'clock in the evening, he was drenched with perspiration, and looked gratefully at the whisky and soda which Joan mixed for him.

'You are a brick to have worked so hard,' she said. 'I really don't know why you should.'

'Because it's my job, Miss Shannon. I wish you would get it into your head that I am really a servant.'

'How can I? Anyhow I am grateful for what you have done.'

'Oh, tush!' he said disgustedly. 'You have worked jolly hard yourself. Hugh is the lucky one!'

'That reminds me – I wonder where he is! When he went out after tiffin he said he would be back soon to help us, but it's gone six and there's no sign of him.'

Cousins scratched his head.

'He's somewhere about!' he said with the air of one who has made a very intelligent remark. 'If I didn't know him so well, I should say that he is keeping out of the way on purpose.'

'No,' she said, with decision: 'he is not like that. Perhaps he's at the College coaching them at cricket.'

'If he had been going there he would have said so. Probably he is detained over some private work. Anyhow he'll turn up some time or other.'

Joan looked at him seriously.

'Mr Cousins,' she said, 'is there likely to be any danger to Hugh and you out here?'

'Nothing to speak of,' he replied easily. 'We are here more or less to investigate affairs in this country, so danger is practically – I won't say entirely – a negative quantity.'

'I'm glad to hear that,' she sighed. 'A secret agent's life must be a very dangerous one, as a rule. I shudder to think what risks Hugh may have been running during those two years I was fondly imagining he was merely an ordinary official of the Foreign Office.'

He smiled.

'Oh, well, you didn't know,' he said, 'and were thus saved a lot of anxiety.'

They were silent for a while, then Cousins started to his feet, his face wrinkled with concern.

'What a thoughtless fool I am!' he exclaimed. 'Why, here it is past six, and you haven't had any tea, and I calmly sit down and guzzle a whisky and soda!'

'Really I forgot all about tea until a few minutes ago,' she smiled. 'When you are ready we will take a tonga back to the hotel, and get some.'

'I say; I'm awfully sorry,' he said penitently.

'Don't be, please! I shall enjoy it all the more when we get back!'

She had one more look through the rooms, and then joined him on the veranda.

'It is ever so much nicer to have one's own house, than to live in a hotel!' she said. 'Everything is ready for tomorrow now, and even Mr Miles' room is prepared for him if he turns up. I wonder why he hasn't come!'

'He is probably having a good time with some fellow countrymen of his in Bombay.'

She pouted.

'He might have written, especially as he said he would come to Lahore in a week, and it's a fortnight now since we left.'

A tonga came rattling through the gates, and Hugh jumped out.

'Oh, I say, I'm so sorry!' he said. 'Are you people just going?'

'We are!' said Cousins sternly. 'You have managed to work things rather well, my son!'

'What do you mean?'

'Well, you waited until we had done all the work before you turned up!'

'Oh, you rotter!' said Hugh. 'I have been chasing round Lahore all the afternoon trying to find someone.'

'Whom?'

'Of course, I may have been mistaken, but as I came out of the College about three, a taxi passed by, there were two men in it, and I could have sworn that one was Kamper. I noted the number of the car and have been trying to find it since in the hope that the chauffeur would tell me where he took them.'

Cousins whistled.

'So the fellow has got here after all!' he murmured, almost to himself.

'Mind you, I couldn't be certain. I may have made a mistake.'

'Not you,' said Cousins. 'If you are pretty sure you saw Kamper, then Kamper is here. As a matter of fact I was expecting him. He has only arrived rather sooner than I anticipated.'

'Who is Kamper?' asked Joan.

'A rather elusive friend of ours,' replied the little man. 'Come along! You must have that tea!'

* * *

131

When they had installed themselves in the bungalow, there was nothing much to be done except unpack the boxes, and Hugh was in his room busily engaged with his, when Cousins joined him. The latter sat on the bed and watched for a few minutes.

'I suppose I ought to be doing that,' he remarked, at length.

'Nonsense!' said Hugh. 'We haven't got to carry on the pretence so much here, and what's more, I'm going to get a bearer. You can chivvy him round if you like, but he'll do the work.'

Cousins smiled.

'You're a marvel!' he murmured. 'You have a bungalow, hire furniture, keep your sister and an English valet as well as a cook, and other servants, and you receive a salary of five hundred rupees a month!'

'Well, I've made no secret of the fact that I have private means.'

'Your new friends must think you a bit eccentric to take up a post like this, when you have private means, don't they?'

'Not a bit of it! They know I have come out partially through a desire to return to India and partially because I am interested in Muslim education.'

Cousins chuckled. Hugh stopped in the act of putting a coat on to a coat hanger.

'If you've finished unpacking your stuff,' he said, 'why don't you go out and see if you are any more successful in tracing that car than I was? I told you the number!'

'My son, it has been done!'

'Good Lord! When?'

'When you and Miss Shannon piously went to church this morning, I looked up my police sergeant friend and asked him where I was likely to find taxi number seven-nine-seven-six. I might say that I invented a totally fictitious story to account for my inquiry. He told me of several taxi stands, and after visiting two, I ran the car to earth on a rank near Queen Victoria's statue.'

'Well?' asked Hugh eagerly.

'The driver proved to be a Sikh of much hair and more stupidity. At first I could get nothing out of him – my Hindustani and his English being more or less negligible. However, to cut a long story short—'

'Yes do!' said Hugh sarcastically.

'I discovered that he had driven the two men to Martin's in the Mall.'

'You mean the restaurant?'

'Yes. I went there, but there was nothing doing. None of the waiters or the manager remembered to have seen the man I described. When I asked the hall-porter, he looked at me blankly, until he caught the word "man" issuing from my lips, whereupon he broke into a torrent of Punjabi, which I translated as meaning that mangoes were not in season!'

'Damn!' said Hugh with emphasis.

'Why? Are you fond of mangoes?'

'Don't be an ass! That fellow Kamper is like will-o'-the-wisp. What are we to do now?'

Cousins shrugged his shoulders.

'What's the hurry?' he asked. 'We have three years.'

'Yes, but two of them are not necessarily to be spent twiddling our thumbs, and from signs around us I should imagine that there is something happening.'

'You mean the arrival of Kamper?'

'Yes; and Hudson being met by those two fellows in Bombay!'

The ideal valet nodded his head slowly.

'I have an idea,' he said, 'that Kamper has known of your voyage and its purpose all along, and that is why he is in India now. Furthermore that is probably the reason why those two fellows met Hudson at Bombay.'

'How could they know anything about it?'

'Shannon, Shannon,' said Cousins reprovingly, 'where are those supposedly quick wits of yours? Either Hudson or Kamper could have cabled to them from Port Said, or Hudson might have wirelessed.'

'Of course!' said Hugh. 'But why should they meet him at Bombay?'

'Why shouldn't they? Hudson does not know that we suspect his association with these people and—'

'By Jove!' said Shannon suddenly. 'They all stayed in Bombay, probably to meet Kamper!'

'I think you have hit the nail on the head,' said Cousins. 'I thought of that when I heard that the three of them were staying behind, and I asked Miles to keep his eye on them. That's why I am so bothered about not hearing from him.'

'Do you think that anything could have happened to him?'

For once in a way Cousins' mild expression left his face, and a look of inflexible resolve and grim purpose took its place. Hugh had never seen such a transformation in the little man before, and a new feeling of respect and confidence took possession of him.

'If anything has happened to Miles,' said Cousins, through set teeth, 'then God help those who have touched him.'

For a moment there was silence, then he looked at Hugh and smiled.

'There aren't many men with the cleverness of Oscar Miles,' he said, 'and I have never met a man better able to look after himself!'

There came a loud knocking at the front door. Cousins stood up and settled his jacket to his figure.

'This is where my duties commence,' he said, '"*iacta alea est*". Are you at home, may I ask, sir?'

There was another and even louder knock, then the sound of the wire doors opening.

'Say,' called a well-remembered voice; 'is every darn soul out?'

'Miles!' exclaimed Cousins and Hugh together, and dashed out of the room.

Joan was before them, and the three surrounded the American, who was grinning with delight. After vigorously shaking hands with them all, he was escorted into the sitting room. Then placing a hand on the shoulder of each of the men, he looked at them grimly.

'Say, boys,' he said. 'I guess I've tumbled on one of the finest plots that ever was. If you two don't get busy right now, there's going to be a sensation that will set the world aflame.'

CHAPTER 12

WHICH TELLS OF AN
AMAZING PLOT

There was a silence for several seconds as the three looked at Miles. He was not the type of man to raise needless scares, or, in fact, say anything without being perfectly sure of his ground. Shannon and Cousins felt that he had news of the gravest import to tell them, but Joan was the first to speak.

'Where is your luggage, Mr Miles?' she asked.

'It's at the hotel,' he said. 'When I arrived in Lahore I went straight to the Punjab Hotel and they told me where to find you, so I dumped my baggage there and came right along.'

'Well, you had better send for it. We have a room here ready for you!'

'That's real nice of you, but I couldn't think of putting myself on you like that.'

'There's no question of putting yourself on us,' said Hugh. 'We shall be disappointed if you don't make this your home, while you are in Lahore.'

'But I guess I shall be here for a long time.'

'That doesn't matter!'

He looked from one to the other, and smiled.

'Well, it would be churlish of me to refuse such a kind invitation. I've kept the taxi waiting outside, and I'll tell him to go back for my bags. Can you provide me with paper so that I can send a note to the manager?'

The paper was speedily forthcoming, and the taxi sent to the hotel.

'Now as tiffin is nearly ready,' said Joan, 'perhaps you will postpone your talk, which I suppose is going to be a long and serious one, till afterwards?'

'Yes,' said Cousins 'I consider that a very good idea. One can always talk better after victuals – I can.'

'Guess nobody wants you to talk, Jerry,' remarked Miles, 'at least, not until after I have said my little bit.'

'I suppose I shall have to keep out of the way?' said Joan a trifle wistfully.

The three men looked at each other.

'She's my sister, and I'll go bond for her, if—' began Hugh.

'A woman's mind often goes right bang to the point,' said the American, 'and I would take my solemn oath that anything Miss Joan hears in this room will never go further.'

Cousins looked from Joan to the men and back again.

'Miss Shannon,' he said, with a bow, 'obviously everyone is in favour of admitting you to our secret council – I can only express my delight.' He bowed deeply.

Joan looked at them with glowing eyes.

'How perfectly sweet of you all,' she cried. 'I am so pleased.'

'The pleasure is entirely ours, Miss Shannon,' said Miles. 'This is going to be some combination!'

After tiffin they adjourned to the sitting room, and when everyone was comfortably settled, the American began his tale.

'When I say I have tumbled on a plot against Great Britain,' he said, 'perhaps I am going a little too far. As a matter of fact I found out that there is a plot and what it is about, but the details are missing – those we shall have to discover, and mighty quickly, too.

'Jerry here asked me to keep an eye on Hudson and the two fellows with him and find out if a little Russian Jew called Kamper arrived in Bombay. Well, his description of Kamper was so good that I couldn't have missed him in a fog, but Hudson knows me; so I went back to the wharf after you had left and rang up the American Consulate. There's a little fellow there who's as cute as pork and beans, and he's nothing much to look at; the sort of mean little guy that nobody would gaze at twice, kinder like Jerry in fact.'

Cousins grunted and Hugh grinned.

'Well, I'd better get right along and miss the frills, I guess,' went on Miles. 'I told Parkinson to meet me on the wharf at once – Hudson and company were still hanging round, apparently waiting for some one, and they were still waiting

139

when the little fellow arrived. I took him behind some cases and told him to watch them and report to me. I also described Kamper, so that there couldn't be any mistake. Then I beat it for the Consulate and sat down and waited.

'At three-thirty Parkinson rang up to tell me that the three had met another man, who had arrived on a boat from Basra, and that they had all gone along to the Taj Mahal Hotel. It wasn't Kamper, for this guy was fat and tallish. So I went right along and booked a room too. That evening I came upon them all in the lounge comfortably settled round a group of cocktails. I greeted Hudson like an old friend, and would have passed on only, to my surprise, he seemed tickled to death at seeing me and introduced me to his three friends, whose names were Novar, Rahtz, and Oppenheimer. They were all so mighty glad to meet me that I got a hunch that there was a catch somewhere, but I had no objection to drinking their cocktails and accepted their invitation to join them. Conversation was very ordinary and general for a time, and then came the catch, as I expected. Hudson turned to me in a casual manner and said, "You were rather friendly with Shannon, and his sister, Miles; what did you think of them?"—Say, Shannon, I don't want you to get annoyed at what I replied,' he broke off.

'I suppose you gave me a bad character,' grinned Hugh.

'No; I didn't go as far as that, but I said that I

140

thought you were a bit slow on the uptake and a few things like that. Then, still in the same casual way, Hudson said, "He always gave me the idea that he had some other reason for coming to India than to take up the post of professor in a college. Did he ever hint to you what it was?" The other three guys all appeared most uninterested, but I could see that they were waiting keenly for my answer. I laughed and said that it was obvious Shannon had only come to India for one purpose, and that was to profess, because he was always so full of how he was going to raise Muslim education, and so on. That didn't appease Hudson, and he kept on at me to cast my mind back in the effort to remember if you had ever let anything drop which would suggest another motive, but of course I remembered nothing; and then I suddenly asked him why he was so almighty anxious to know. That caused some confusion, but Hudson gave a lame reason, and nothing more was said. Later on that night after dinner I watched the four of them go off to an entertainment, so I looked through the visitors book and found out the numbers of their rooms. They were all on the same corridor, and when there was nobody about I nipped into Novar's room – I have a bunch of little instruments in my pocket that will open most doors.'

He smiled and paused to light his cigar which had gone out. His three auditors waited with impatience until it was going again.

'Well, what did you find?' queried Hugh.

'Just nothing! That is, nothing of the least interest to you or me. I was disappointed some, for Jerry had made me get down to things with my old instincts. However, I reflected that if there was anything crooked about Novar and Rahtz they were too fly to leave anything about, and that I was far more likely to find something in Hudson's room. So I went in there. I searched thoroughly, and it seemed that I was due for another disappointment, when just as I was leaving I noticed a lounge jacket hanging on the end of the bed. I searched the pockets and I found something which was mighty puzzling, and might prove useful, so I kept it for further reference.'

'What was it?' demanded Shannon.

'I'll show it you when I'm through. There wasn't time to search any more rooms that night, so I beat it before they came back and caught me. All next day I had Parkinson tracking them, but with no result, and I had a casual drink or two with them. I told Hudson that I was coming to Lahore some time or other and accepted his invitation to look him up. Novar and Rahtz also held out the welcoming hand and I promised to give them both a call.'

'Who is Oppenheimer?' asked Cousins suddenly.

'He a fat German guy! What he had to do with the others I couldn't quite figure out but he told me he was in India for some time on business for an educational firm. But I guess this is becoming a mighty long yarn; I had better cut it short.

That night they again went out and I got into Rahtz's room. I had almost finished my search with the same negative result, when I guess I got a jar – I heard somebody at the door.'

Joan sat up with excitement and Cousins and Hugh leant forward more intently. For a moment there was silence, then the American went on:

'Luckily I had locked myself in,' he said, 'so I had a moment in which to look round, while the key was being fitted into the lock and turned. There was nowhere to hide except the bathroom, a large wardrobe, or under the bed. I chose the wardrobe, and only just got inside when the door was opened. I felt real queer when I heard the voices of Oppenheimer and Rahtz. They were presently joined by the other two, and I was in a fine trap.

'"Shut the door!" said Rahtz and I heard the door closed and locked.

'"Now, gentlemen," he went on in German, "I think that our preparations are almost complete. We have only to wait for the signal from Moscow which will convulse the world. But we must not remain idle – all those in India who have been persuaded into our service will have to be kept up to scratch; the invasion cannot take place until September next – nearly ten months – and the waiting is likely to break the spirit of our allies in this country unless something is done to keep them enthusiastic."

'"Why delay till next September?" asked the voice of Hudson.

'"Because my friend," replied Rahtz, "the entire force in Russia will not be complete till July, and as the monsoon will then be on, we must wait till September. Once the invasion commences there must be no hitch, no mishap; the startling suddenness of it all will ensure its complete success. Our friend, Herr Oppenheimer, has brought us the news that Germany will be ready to act immediately – the Russian fleets have swooped on India, and doubtless our other allies will fall into line without fail. Everything must work with clockwork smoothness."

'Oppenheimer grunted agreement and Novar laughed.

'"What a surprise for England," he said. "Lulled into security by the apparently chaotic state of our country and the quiescence of Germany, and acting as policemen in China over a nation which for their benefit is pretending to be at sixes and sevens, they are benevolently backing the League of Nations and pushing disarmament. And not only that but their labour party sympathises with poor downtrodden Russia, and is doing its best to help her. Was there ever a more amusing situation?"

'There was a general laugh at this, and Oppenheimer used some particularly choice expressions to denote his contempt of England.

'"Still we must take no risks," went on Rahtz. "England is always lucky and on many occasions has been saved by sheer good fortune. The Spanish

144

Armada was scattered by the elements; we must ensure that our armada does not suffer a similar fate. At last," he added enthusiastically, "Russia is within grasp of the ambition which has been hers for decades."

'"Have you thought of America?" asked Hudson. "She will, of course, side with England."

'"By the time America knows anything about events it will be too late, and then she'll find it to her advantage to keep quiet, otherwise our German friends will settle her."

'The German agent grunted his agreement – That man seemed to be full of grunts.

'"And France?" asked Hudson.

'There was a chorus of contempt from the other three.

'"France and Italy will go into the melting-pot of Germany," replied Novar.

'"And now," said Rahtz. "We must watch that fellow Shannon. You are sure he is a secret agent, Hudson?"

'"Absolutely certain," was the reply; "and Kamper will confirm it. He had a very narrow escape when he was in London recently from being captured by Shannon."

'"Kamper takes too many risks," said Novar; "he should not have returned to England."

'"It is lucky he did," replied Hudson significantly. "I might have had the wool pulled over my eyes by Shannon, but for Kamper's discoveries."

'"That's true," replied Rahtz, "but what a devil

Wallace is! He obviously sent Shannon out here on suspicion that something was wrong. He is the most dangerous man we have to face."

"'It's time he was put out of the way," said Novar.

"'He bears a charmed life," remarked the other. "It would be impossible to count the number of times he has escaped death by a miracle. But now he has sent Shannon out, we'll have to watch that young man with the greatest care, and if he becomes a nuisance – well, he must be killed. Kamper will look after him, and I have already warned two other fellows who have been entered as students in his college to shadow him, so we have nothing to fear from him, or from his pretended valet."

"'Then you think Cousins is also a secret agent?" asked Hudson.

"'Of course he is!" said Rahtz. "And now, gentlemen, remember that there is a very important meeting in Lahore on December the twenty-first. The time and place will be notified to you later on, and very important representatives of our other allies will be present. Shall we now go below and refresh ourselves? Perhaps that foolish American with the glasses will join us! I confess he amuses me."

'To my relief they then departed, and when I was sure that it was quite safe, I came out of the cupboard. I was cramped some, and I had to give myself a mighty rubbing before I could move much. Then I cautiously left the room, and as

Rahtz showed such an inclination for my company, I obliged him by going downstairs and joining them.'

His three hearers were sitting in a state of absolute amazement. Joan's face was white with excitement and fear; Hugh was biting the end of his pipe with such force that it presently snapped, and Cousins looked straight in front of him, his face creased in a conflict of emotions. Nobody spoke, and after a moment Miles went on:

'The next day Parkinson again followed them, and sure enough Kamper arrived. He had apparently disembarked at Goa, in Portuguese territory, and travelled to Bombay by train. They met him at the station. They avoided me more or less that day, but in the evening invited me to dinner, as Rahtz, Novar and Hudson were leaving for Lahore the following morning. We had a real merry time, believe me! Kamper, of course, was not present. When the three had left the next day, I stopped behind and kept Parkinson shadowing Kamper, until he also left for Lahore. In the meantime I sent along a cable in code to my headquarters telling them that I was stopping in India for some time on urgent business and promising a long report. I stayed in Bombay until Oppenheimer left for Calcutta – he told me he would be in Lahore himself later on – It strikes me all roads lead to Lahore!

'And now, Miss Shannon and gentlemen, that's my story, and I'm here to help see this thing through. The United States is in this little affair up to the neck.'

He stopped talking and with a sigh took another cigar from his case. Hugh got up and walked thoughtfully up and down the room.

'It seems to me, Oscar,' remarked Cousins, 'that the British Secret Service has a lot to thank you for!'

'I guess not,' replied Miles. 'You put me on to those guys. I reckon you saw through them and the credit's yours.'

Hugh stopped walking, and looked keenly at the other two.

'Just imagine!' he said. 'Here have we been thinking that Russia was only harmful in an insidious way that she could merely stab us and other nations in the back, by means of Bolshevik propaganda, and all the time she is preparing to invade India, and is in alliance with Germany, whom we thought crushed. Good Heavens! It's absolutely astounding. But how on earth is this invasion to take place!'

'You've got me there!' said Miles. 'At her most powerful period Russia couldn't manage an invasion, and I'm darned if I know how her fleet can swoop on India. Even if she has built a hoard of ships, they've sure got to come a mighty long distance from either direction to get here.'

'Great Scott!' ejaculated Cousins.

The others looked at him in surprise.

'What's getting you, Jerry?' inquired the American.

'I think I've got it,' said the little man. 'The fleets they mean are not battleships and cruisers, but *airships*!'

Hugh whistled.

'I believe you've hit it!' said Miles.

'That's it,' said Hugh, with decision. 'While we've been watching their Communistic antics with contemptuous indifference, they've been secretly building airships, perhaps for years, and for Germany as well as for themselves.'

'And China, too,' nodded Cousins. 'I suppose behind all the disorder in that country, which we sent our troops to check, the Russians and Germans are drilling and equipping an orderly army and building airships somewhere in the interior. Certainly, Oscar my lad, you have tumbled on the biggest plot that has ever threatened the peace of the world.'

'And we know so much, and yet so little,' said Hugh. 'When did you say that meeting was to be held, Miles?'

'On December the twenty-first! I don't know where, or at what time, of course.'

'That's got to be found out, even if I have to wring someone's neck for the information. Today is the eighteenth of November, so we've got a month. I shall be present at that meeting!'

'Sure!'

Joan went white.

'Oh, Hugh!' she said. 'Will that be necessary?'

'Absolutely!' he replied.

'Perhaps Miles or I will go instead, Miss Shannon,' said Cousins.

She looked at him gratefully.

'No!' said Hugh with determination. 'That is my job and I'm going to do it. Joan knows that it is my duty, and naturally she will agree that I must not back out!'

She nodded her head slowly, and her face was whiter than before.

'Of course not,' she murmured; 'but now I know more than I ever did the terrible dangers you Secret Service people must face.'

Miles leant forward and patted her hand.

'I guess you're built of pluck, Miss Joan,' he said. 'Don't worry! Jerry and I'll see Hugh through. In fact,' he added whimsically, 'we'll see each other through, I reckon.'

'Now,' said Cousins to Hugh, 'what are you going to do about Rahtz and the rest?'

'Let 'em carry on, of course,' said Hugh, with decision. 'The time hasn't come to pull them up yet!'

Miles nodded approvingly.

'If you had them arrested now,' he said, 'it might precipitate the whole show, and God knows what would happen then, for neither my country nor yours would be ready.'

'I shall send a coded report of what Miles has discovered to the Chief,' went on Hugh.

'And I'll send one through to my headquarters,' said the American, 'then my Foreign Office can communicate with yours, and once they get going – my! I guess there's a surprise coming all right, but not the surprise Russia and Germany anticipate.'

'Don't forget that there are two spies in your college watching you Shannon!' warned Cousins.

Hugh grinned.

'Most interesting!' he said nonchalantly. 'I shall have to discover who they are. Kamper's more likely to be dangerous; anyhow I can always have him arrested without raising any suspicion – he's wanted so badly already.'

'The only thing is that you've got to catch him first,' said Cousins dryly.

'By the way, what did you find in Hudson's pocket, Miles?' asked Shannon.

'I'd almost forgotten about that,' replied the other. 'Here it is!'

He took a large wallet from an inside pocket, and searching inside it, drew out a small folded sheet of paper. He handed it to Hugh without a word.

The latter took it, and examined it critically. On it was a roughly drawn map of India, with a dragon neatly sketched on the eastern side, an eagle to the north, and another on the north-west, and an eagle and dragon side by side in the centre.

'I wonder what that means!' he said.

'I took it to mean that the Chinese attack comes from the east, and the Russian from the other points, and that they will meet in the centre,' said Miles.

'H'm!' grunted Hugh. 'There doesn't seem to be much significance in that – rather absurd in fact. I think there must be a deeper meaning behind it. You'd better keep it! We may find out what it really is for!'

He handed it back, and Miles gave it to Cousins who glanced casually at it and then gave it up with a shrug. They were about to resume their discussion when there came a knock at the front door.

'Visitors!' said Hugh. 'Damn!'

'Hugh!' said Joan reprovingly.

'Well, I don't want visitors just now.'

'I guess I'd better scatter,' said the American. 'I'll do some unpacking.' And he went off to his own room.

Cousins rose to his feet with a sigh.

'Oh, woe is me!' he said. 'This answering of knocks does not fit in with my idea of a valet's life. *Mauvais honte* fills my breast!'

He left the room with the expression of a man going to the scaffold. Two minutes later he was back, a curious look on his face.

'Mr and Mrs Rahtz!' he announced.

Joan went white, and Hugh started with surprise, but recovered himself immediately.

'Be careful, Joan!' he hissed.

Cousins bowed the visitors in and withdrew.

CHAPTER 13

A VISIT FROM RAHTZ

Mr Rahtz was tall, dark-visaged, and possessed a large greying moustache, which apparently he had cultivated to hide the cruelty of his mouth. Mrs Rahtz was florid, fat and overdressed, in a style suitable to a girl twenty years her junior. She wore shingled hair which had been dyed a reddish brown and clashed badly with her dress of emerald green, and a small brown hat with a large brown feather. Joan almost blinked as she looked at her. Rahtz was probably three or four years his wife's senior, but Mrs Rahtz was obviously on the wrong side of forty-five.

She greeted Joan with a simper, while Rahtz shook hands with Hugh in a bluff hearty manner that somewhat belied his appearance.

'We heard you were settled in your bungalow, my dear,' said Mrs Rahtz, 'and thought we would be among the first to call on you. I hope we have not called too soon?'

'Not at all,' replied Joan, 'but as a matter of fact, we only came in this morning.'

'Really! I thought you had been here for three

or four days. You seem to have settled down very quickly.'

'We have a very efficient man,' said Joan, 'and it was mainly through his efforts that the house was ready before we took possession.'

'You are lucky to have been able to bring an English manservant with you, Shannon,' said Rahtz. 'Most of us have to put up with natives, and they are very slow and not altogether trustworthy.'

'As a matter of fact,' replied Hugh, 'I was going to leave him behind, but he wanted to come so much that I hadn't the heart to refuse him. You see he has been with us so long. Luckily I have an income of my own, so there was no real reason why he should stay at home.'

'No, of course not!'

'Mr Abdullah told us all about you,' simpered Mrs Rahtz, 'and naturally we were eager to meet you. Such a charming man, don't you think?' she added to Joan.

'Mr Abdullah?'

'Yes!'

'Yes, he is. I like him very much, and so does Hugh.'

'Of course, when we heard of your arrival, my husband was a wee bit jealous of Mr Abdullah's luck in getting you. He badly wants a first-class man at the head of his own English department.'

Rahtz nodded.

'Yes,' he said; 'I am not too well served in that

154

direction in my college. I have three or four Indian professors, who have specialised in the English language, but that is not the same thing as an Englishman, and like all Indians who teach English, they are inflated with their own importance and imagine they know a lot more than they do. I contend,' he went on, 'that in order to teach a language properly, the professor should be a native of the country whose language he teaches. Even I, though I was educated and partially brought up in England, do not feel myself a master of English.'

'Are you not an Englishman?' asked Hugh innocently.

'No, I am a Russian!' He looked at Hugh keenly as he spoke.

'Are you really?' asked the latter, with an appearance of quiet interest.

'I would never have taken you for anything but an absolute Englishman,' said Joan.

Rahtz smiled.

'Of course I spent many years in England,' he said; 'and I have been in the education department of the Punjab for ten years.'

'Mr Miles described you as a regular Englishman,' said Joan naïvely. 'You met him in Bombay, didn't you?'

For a moment a startled expression appeared on Rahtz's face, and he glanced hurriedly at his wife.

'Miles?' he said, as though trying to remember the name. 'Oh, yes! He's the toll American, isn't he? A most charming fellow. I happened to be in

155

Bombay with a friend of mine for a conference a couple of weeks ago, and we met Hudson, who introduced us to him. They were fellow passengers of yours, were they not?'

Hugh nodded.

'I remember now he spoke about you. For a moment his name eluded me. That is the young man I told you about, my dear,' he added turning to his wife.

'Oh, yes, I remember,' she said. 'You asked him to call, did you not?'

'Yes.' He turned to Hugh. 'He must have arrived in Lahore already then?'

'He called on us today,' replied Shannon, 'and we invited him to stay here. I believe he is unpacking his bags at the moment. He'll be delighted to see you again – he spoke so highly of you. I'll go and get him!'

A puzzled expression crossed Rahtz's face, as Hugh left the room. He looked like a man who was not quite sure of his ground. Mrs Rahtz and Joan chatted amiably.

'Of course you will become members of the club?' said the former. 'You will meet most charming people there. Life is very slow out here, unless one belongs to a club.'

'We have already been nominated,' replied Joan. 'I expect we shall be elected in a day or two.'

'Really! That is unusually quick work. Generally it takes such a long time to become a member. They are so particular, you know.'

'Surely you are not a Russian, Mrs Rahtz?' asked Joan suddenly.

The other woman looked questioningly at her, then smiled. 'No, dear,' she said. 'I was born in Australia, but have lived most of my life in India.'

Miles came in, followed by Hugh. He shook hands cordially with Rahtz.

'This is a great pleasure, Mr Rahtz!' he said. 'I'm very glad to meet you again.'

He was introduced to Mrs Rahtz, and bowed low over her hand.

'I was looking forward to calling on you, Mrs Rahtz,' he said gallantly. 'Your husband gave me an invitation, of which I intended to avail myself in a day or two.'

'We shall be delighted to welcome you at our home, Mr Miles,' she replied with another of her girlish simpers.

'I was surprised to find that you had already arrived, Miles,' said Rahtz.

'I came up sooner than I first intended. And I surely did not expect such a welcome as I got. Miss Shannon and her brother have insisted on my staying here.'

'So she told us. She has anticipated an invitation which it would have been our pleasure to have given you.'

'It's very good of you, Mr Rahtz. I kinder feel that I have almost come home, with all this kindness flowing about.'

Rahtz looked at him sharply, as though he half

suspected that the American was laughing at him, but all he saw in the latter's face was a look of bland innocence. Tea was served shortly, and Cousins brought in the things and waited on them with a gravity and thoroughness that made Joan want to laugh. He wore a dark suit with a black bow and looked every inch the well-trained manservant.

Shortly after tea Mr and Mrs Rahtz rose to take their leave, and invited the Shannons and Miles to dine with them one day during the week, an invitation that was accepted apparently with pleasure by all. When they had gone, Miles threw himself into an armchair, and chuckled.

'Old Rahtz made an early call,' he said. 'I suppose he wanted to see you for himself, Shannon, and perhaps find out a thing or two. I bet that man's mind was mighty busy all the time he was here.'

'He had a surprise when he heard that you were staying with us,' said Hugh.

'Did I do right in mentioning that Mr Miles had spoken of Mr Rahtz?' asked Joan.

Hugh grinned.

'There was no harm in it,' he said. 'He'd be bound to know sooner or later that Miles was here, and it made everything look above board. As a matter of fact, Joan, it was clever of you to mention our friend here in the way you did. I told Miles when I called him, and he roared with laughter.'

'Sure!' said the American. 'I was tickled to death.'

Cousins came in, and stood respectfully by the door.

'May I sit down, miss?' he asked humbly.

Hugh pushed him into a chair.

'You old humbug,' he said, 'I know I shall laugh one of these days when you're acting the well-disciplined servant.'

'Why? Don't I do it all right?'

'You do it as though you were born to it, Jerry,' said the American.

'I was in your service for six years remember!'

'I just forgot that – so you were!'

Hugh looked at Miles seriously.

'Are you really coming into this business with us?' he asked.

'I sure am! It's to the interest of the USA that I should ally myself with you.'

'Good! I'm rather handicapped by being at the College most of the day, and besides I appear to be a carefully watched man, so a lot will depend upon Cousins.'

'I guess he's going to be mighty closely watched too,' said Miles. 'It'll take him all his time to shake off his watchers. That leaves me – I'll have to get busy.'

'If I can't shake off any little fellow who's got his eye on my movements,' said Cousins with contempt, 'this hand has lost its cunning and this brain its power. No, Oscar, my lad, you needn't think that you're going to do all the dirty work, while I'm about.'

159

'Well, I'll call on our friend Hudson tomorrow – there may be some information to be gained from him somehow. Say, I don't think a whole lot of that fellow; he's an all-fired traitor, and there's a whole lot of trouble coming to him later on.'

'There is,' said Hugh, through set teeth, 'and I hope it will be my job to bring it to him. Well, we all know pretty well what we are going to do – I must get that report of mine off tonight.'

'Say,' said Miles suddenly, 'I must get a bearer. I knew there was something I had to do.'

'I have half a dozen coming tomorrow for selection,' said Hugh. 'Perhaps you'll find one to suit you among them.'

'Sure thing! But what do you want a bearer for? Isn't Jerry the goods?'

'Look here, Miles—' began that worthy.

'Now then, little man, don't get sore!' chuckled Miles. 'I was thinking that you were the best manservant that ever was. You ought to take that as a compliment!'

Cousins threw a cushion at him, and then apologised to Joan for throwing her furniture about. There came another knock at the door.

'If that is another caller,' said the little man, 'I'll jam him in the door, and dance with glee at his agony.'

He went out and came back with a telegram in his hand.

'Telegram!' he said laconically.

Tearing open the envelope, Shannon glanced hurriedly through the wire.

'Cable from the Chief,' he said. 'Get the code book, Cousins, like a good chap!'

The small book was brought quickly from the despatch case, in which it was always kept locked and, while the others talked in subdued voices, Hugh carefully decoded the cablegram. When he had finished he threw down his pencil and whistled. Three pairs of eyes looked at him eagerly.

'Just listen to this!' he said.

'Wait a minute, Shannon,' said Miles, and rising from his chair, he walked quickly to the windows, and out on to the veranda. Presently he returned and, shutting the windows carefully, resumed his seat.

'I thought I saw a shadow pass by. It might have been the sweeper or somebody harmless, but it's just as well not to take any risks, especially as we know this house is watched.'

Hugh nodded, and Joan looked round apprehensively.

'It is sent direct from the Chief,' said Shannon, 'and reads:

Believe Kamper has got through – watch carefully – understand events may be developing – arrange meet two men – Novar – Rahtz – both prominent Lahore of Russian nationality – deeply suspect them – report – Chief.

161

'I take off my hat to your Chief,' said Miles. 'How in the name of all that's holy did he cotton on to Novar and Rahtz?'

'The British Secret Service is a live organisation,' said Cousins. 'We do not spin, neither do we sew, but we get there all the same!'

'Well, anyway,' said Hugh, 'we have already got on to Rahtz and Novar and know Kamper is in Lahore, so we're well prepared.'

'You also know that events are developing,' said Joan.

'We sure do!' murmured Miles.

CHAPTER 14

COUSINS HAS A BUSY EVENING

For several days nothing of importance took place.

Joan and Hugh duly received a letter from the secretary of the Club informing them that they were elected as members and asking politely for their entrance fee. Hugh and Miles each engaged a bearer, and Cousins' domestic duties were considerably lessened in consequence, and in fact became practically nil. Miles called on Hudson, as he had determined, only to find him out, so he left his card and received an invitation to dine with the civil servant a week later. Joan had several callers, and was invited with Hugh to numberless teas and dinner parties. She was a very fine tennis player, and in consequence found it very easy to get a game whenever she wanted one. Of course, as Miles had prophesied, the men began to crowd round her, and Hugh found himself remarkably popular all of a sudden, a popularity which he reflected cynically was due to the possession of a beautiful sister.

It was not long before the young secret agent began to feel almost an admiration for his enemies.

He knew he was watched, and yet, try as he would, he could never discover anybody following him, or taking the least interest in his movements. Even in the College where he had information that two men had been placed as students to shadow him, he was quite unable to find out who the two were. Kamper appeared to have entirely disappeared, and neither Hugh, Miles nor Cousins were able to come across the slightest clue as to his whereabouts, yet they knew that he must be very close at hand.

Hugh had sent a long cabled report to the Chief in code telling him of Miles' discoveries, and in return, received the following:

> Your information of immense value – acting on it immediately – am informing authorities Lahore in secret of your position – they will communicate with you later – hope you will succeed in attending meeting – very important.

'All very well,' murmured Hugh to himself, as he read the cable over again before destroying it; 'but how am I to be present at the meeting! I've got to find out where it will take place first.'

The dinner party at Rahtz's house was attended by several other people besides themselves, and Hugh and Joan were introduced to Novar, who in his smug way laid himself out to be pleasant to them. Miles, on this occasion, rather gave emphasis

164

to the fact that he was a wealthy, amusing American with a love for travel and a very ordinary amount of intelligence. Hugh smiled to himself as he noticed the impression the American was deliberately creating, and wondered what Rahtz and Novar would think if they found out who he really was.

A week went by. On the night that Miles was dining with Hudson, Joan also was fulfilling a dinner engagement with some friends, to which Hugh had been invited, but was unable to accept owing to having previously promised to take the chair at a lecture in the College. Cousins went out at half past nine and strolled in the direction of Novar's house, a beautiful, large bungalow lying well back in extensive grounds, and situated on the Mall. Knowing that he was probably followed, the little man walked slowly in order to give an impression that he was merely out for a stroll. He entered the Lawrence Gardens – Lahore's beauty spot – and passing the zoo, turned sharply up a path that was so overhung with trees that it was in pitch darkness. Then suddenly stepping behind a fine old banyan he crouched low and waited. At once he became aware of the soft, almost imperceptible tread of someone approaching. The individual crept by, and the footsteps receded – it was so dark that Cousins was only aware of the vaguest outline. He immediately went back the way he had come, and hurried along the Mall to Novar's bungalow.

He waited in the shadow of the gate for nearly half an hour before venturing to move, watching the road anxiously the while to find out if he had been followed again. Satisfied at last he took a pair of socks from his pocket, and pulling them over his shoes to deaden the sound of his movements he drew quietly towards the house. There appeared to be nobody about, so after waiting again for some time, he commenced to encircle the building, looking for some means of entry.

All the windows were covered by the wire mosquito netting, which is to be seen in almost every house in India, and the doors also were protected by the same fine mesh. Cousins had almost encircled the building when he found a small service door which by some accident had been left open. Merging himself into the shadows round it, the secret agent worked his way along, then with a sudden glide was inside with such rapidity that it would have taken a quick-eyed man to have noticed him.

'Well, I'm in!' he muttered with satisfaction. '"*Audaces fortuna juvat*!" Now for the most ticklish part of the job!'

The lights were on all over the bungalow, which made his task all the greater, because he could be seen so easily from outside as well as by anyone within. But such considerations did not worry Cousins much. He found his way past the service rooms to the main corridor. On his right was apparently the dining room, and next to that the drawing room, both of which he decided were not at all likely to contain anything of interest to him. They were both empty, and taking a deep breath he stepped out into the corridor, and hurried along to the first room beyond the drawing room. This was obviously a lady's bedroom, and giving a rapid look round he stood behind the heavy curtains which hung by the door for a minute and listened intently for any sound indicative of an alarm being raised. As the silence remained undisturbed, he emerged once more into the corridor, and went along to another room. Just as he was about to enter it he heard the sound of subdued voices, and carefully looked in. It was another bedroom, and two Indian servants were apparently engaged in folding clothes in the little dressing room adjoining it.

'That looks as though it might be Novar's bedroom,' muttered Cousins. 'Dash those bearers!'

He moved on, and came to another bedroom, which was obviously a guest chamber. He spent very little time there, and continued his way along the corridor. Presently he came to a narrow passage, which led to a room in darkness. He entered this, and feeling for the door closed it upon himself, and stood for a moment breathing deeply like a man who has been through a nerve racking experience. Then taking an electric torch from his pocket he held it downwards and flashed it on for a moment. The illumination thus afforded enabled him to see a large window, by the side of which hung long thick curtains. He went forward and drew them together so that not a vestige of light could penetrate to the outside world, and returning to the door repeated the performance with the curtains which hung there. That done he uttered a sigh of relief, and switching on his torch looked round him with curiosity.

He found himself in the study of an obviously busy and prosperous man. A thick carpet lay on the floor with a couple of valuable-looking rugs spread thereon. In the middle of the room, facing the window, was a large oak desk, with a swivel chair before it. On his right was a row of book-shelves containing a great number of books of all descriptions, and on his left a fine open fireplace, with a large safe let into the wall on one side and a long, comfortable leather couch on the other. A couple of armchairs, also of leather, completed the furniture. There were a few tasteful pictures hanging on the walls, and the mantelshelf was crowded with photographs in silver and black-wood frames. A telephone, books of reference, and various papers were on the desk, as well as a reading lamp with a heavy brown silk shade.

Cousins found the switch of the electric lights and turned them on, then crossing to the door he locked it.

'Now may the gods grant that I am uninterrupted for an hour or so,' he murmured. 'Novar can't return from his appointment till twelve at the earliest, and it's only a quarter past ten now.'

He took off the overcoat he was wearing and placed it over the back of a chair. Then he sniffed.

'H'm!' he said. 'There's a smell of stale cigar smoke about, so there can't be any harm in my adding to it.'

He took out a cigar and lit it.

'Now for work!' he said.

He drew a pair of thin rubber gloves from his pocket and put them on – Cousins was always thorough – and sitting down before the desk, proceeded to go carefully through the papers scattered before him. He read every one, and replaced them in exactly the same position in which they had been before he touched them. Every now and again he carefully shook his cigar ash into a pocket of his coat. None of the papers proved of any value to him, and he picked up three letters, which were lying unopened upon the desk, and examined them critically. Two of them were obviously business communications, and these he replaced; the third aroused his curiosity, and after a little thought he took a thin, razor-like instrument from his breast pocket, and carefully inserting it under the flap of the envelope, slid it along until the flap came open. He then withdrew the sheet of paper from the envelope and read it, Immediately a look of keen interest showed on his face.

'Ah!' he said. 'This is more like it!'

He took a notebook from his pocket and copied every word of the letter, after which he put it back carefully into its envelope. Producing a tube of thin fish glue, he carefully spread some on the flap, and closed it again. When he had finished, the envelope had no appearance of having been touched. He placed it on the desk.

'Now for the safe!' he muttered.

After gazing at the solid-looking affair for a few minutes, he knelt down and commenced to turn the combination handle, listening with delicately attuned hearing to the sound of the tumbril. In a short while a smile creased its way across his face.

'It's easier than I expected,' he murmured.

Ten minutes later he sat back on his heels with a sigh of satisfaction, and pulled open the door of the safe. Inside were bundles of papers, letters and documents of all sorts, as well as negotiable securities and banknotes for large sums of money, which showed that Novar was ready to fly at a moment's notice, if necessary.

Cousins went through every document with meticulous care, and every now and again copied rapidly into his notebook something of interest to him. When he had examined the safe thoroughly, he selected two papers from the collection, and putting them in his pocket, replaced the rest as he had found them then carefully closing the door, he reset the combination, and rose to his feet. His cigar had long since gone out, and he had put it among the ashes in his coat pocket. Now he took out another, and lit it. He looked at his wristwatch.

'Dash it!' he said. 'I have already been an hour and five minutes.'

Crossing quickly to the bookcase, he selected a book here and there, and examined them, then he tapped the woodwork gently in an effort to discover secret hiding places. He was unsuccessful, however, and at last after a careful look round to make sure that everything was as it had been left, he switched off the lights, and going to the window drew aside the curtains. He then felt his way to the desk, and picking up his overcoat, put it on. He drew off the rubber gloves, put them in his pocket and, damping his fingers, extinguished his cigar.

'A pleasant evening's amusement,' he murmured, as he made his way to the door and, drawing back the curtains, gently unlocked and opened it.

For a few minutes he stood listening intently, but no sound disturbed the stillness, and he crept quietly along the passage towards the brilliantly lighted corridor.

Then suddenly there was the sound of a car drawing up outside, and he heard the voices of a man and woman and the creak of the wire doors, as they entered the house.

'Dear! dear!' muttered Cousins. 'He has returned half an hour before he should have done. How awkward!'

He retreated to the study, and stood behind the curtains, listening. A small revolver had appeared in his hand. Apparently the man and woman had gone into the dining room or drawing room, for there was silence for some minutes, and Cousins was about to venture out of his hiding place when he heard a voice say distinctly, 'I'll go and get it,' and the sound of rapidly approaching footsteps came from the corridor. Presently Novar appeared, and walked straight into the study, his body actually rubbing against the curtain behind which the secret agent crouched. The Russian, who was humming to himself, switched on the desk lamp, and crossing to the bookshelf selected a large volume, and carried it to the desk. It was apparently a work of reference, for he turned page after page before, finding what he wanted, he uttered an exclamation of satisfaction and replaced the book on the shelf.

Then returning to the desk, he was about to turn off the light, when he noticed the three letters lying there. He took up the one that Cousins had examined, and tore it open. As he read he ceased humming, and for some minutes afterwards stood tapping his foot on the floor like a man in deep thought.

During all this time Cousins remained where he was hidden by the curtain, hardly daring to breathe. He knew that if Novar turned in his direction the latter could not fail to notice him, and he held the revolver ready, while his teeth were tightly clenched and his eyes screwed up with the grimness of a man who recognises death to be hovering uncomfortably near.

At last, carefully putting the letter in the inside pocket of his dress-coat, Novar turned off the light and made his way past Cousins down the passage and disappeared. The little man chuckled to himself.

'So near and yet so far,' he murmured. 'And now the sooner I am out of this place the better I shall be pleased.'

Without a sound he crept quietly into the corridor and, with his heart thumping against his ribs, moved slowly down towards the service passage, expecting every moment that Novar would emerge from the room again, and confront him. His luck, however, stood him in good stead, and he reached his destination and glided into comparative safety. The passage was now in darkness, but he felt that that was all to the good.

Before going farther he decided to try and catch a glimpse of the lady with Novar – no doubt his wife – so that he would know her at any future time. They were apparently in the drawing room, so cautiously Cousins stretched his head round the corner until he could see into the room. To his surprise there were two women with Novar. One, a prim middle-aged lady, wearing pince-nez, was apparently looking at a fashion book; the other, a fair-haired girl, had her back turned to him, and was examining something with Novar leaning over her shoulder. The latter made a remark, which made her look up at him with a laugh – Cousins caught a glimpse of her face and drew back into the passage with a gasp.

'Would you believe it!' he muttered. 'The plot indeed thickens!'

He delayed no longer, but found his way towards the door. This time it was closed, but not bolted, and he pushed it gently open, and, going out, as gently closed it, and slid away into the darkness. Avoiding all light he made his way very cautiously towards the gates. On the way he very nearly walked into the chowkidar, who was sitting crouched up by a tree, with a lathi held in his hand. The man apparently heard him, for he stood up, and peered round him as though trying to discover what the darkness held. But with a stealth that would have done credit to a Red Indian, Cousins crept away and reached the gates. Here he took off the socks, and waiting until he was absolutely sure there was nobody watching outside the house, he turned into the Mall, and strode away towards Crescent Road.

There was still an adventure before him, however, for he had hardly entered the drive leading to Shannon's bungalow, when he became aware of two shadows that dived into the undergrowth at his approach.

'Watchers of the night!' he murmured, and continued on his way, with his eyes cast warily in the direction in which the shadows had disappeared.

Suddenly two forms silently sprang upon him. He heard the hiss of a knife and felt the ripping of cloth accompanied by a burning sensation in his left arm. He had been ready, however, and at the identical moment that his assailants attacked him, he skipped aside and fired. There was a yell

174

of agony, one of the shadows staggered, but appeared to recover, and the two darted away into the darkness and disappeared. Almost immediately the sound of running footsteps could be heard coming from the direction of the bungalow. Cousins stood where he was, and his face started to crease into a broad grin.

'A most interesting evening on the whole,' he chuckled aloud.

He was presently joined by the two runners, who – as he had guessed – were Shannon and Miles.

'What has happened?' asked the former, when he discovered Cousins standing in the path.

'I think our friends have decided that I am becoming a nuisance,' replied the little man. 'I was attacked by two – er – shadows.'

'Are you hurt?' inquired Miles anxiously.

'No, I don't think so, at least not much. I am afraid though, that Messrs. Rahtz, Novar and Company owe me a new coat.'

CHAPTER 15

CONTAINS NEWS OF OLIVE GREGSON

There was no chance of their finding the assailants, so presently the three men entered the house. Joan had gone to bed, and apparently had not been disturbed by the revolver shot, as she did not come from her room to ask what had happened. Once in the sitting room the three noticed that the left sleeve of Cousins' coat had been slit from shoulder to elbow. There was a trickle of blood running down the arm, and Miles quickly helped the little man off with his coat and jacket and found a nasty cut about two inches long.

'Say, boy,' he said, 'you've had a darn narrow escape. Get some warmish water, Hugh – I've some lint and bandages in my room – and we'll dress this.'

Both Miles and Shannon were quite expert at first-aid work, and they made a very good job of the bandaging, much to Cousins' disgust.

'Why make such a fuss over a little scratch like that?' he asked. 'What bothers me is the damage to my coat!'

'Blow your coat!' said Hugh. 'Thank God you weren't badly hurt! What I can't understand is why you were attacked. It seems a bit weak to show their hand like this, and right inside these premises too.'

'Was it you who fired the revolver, Jerry?' asked Miles.

Cousins nodded.

'Yes,' he said; 'and I think I gave one of them more than I received. Anyhow he let out a yell and staggered, but was able to run away.'

'Well, I guess that don't help any. They didn't expect you to shoot, and got an unpleasant surprise when you did.'

'We might as well sit down,' said Cousins. 'I have a lot to tell you and I prefer to tell it from a chair.'

He sank into a comfortable armchair and the others followed suit, Hugh first taking care to see that the windows and door were closed, and the curtains drawn.

'First of all, Oscar,' said the little man; 'did you have any luck with Hudson?'

'Not a bit! There were two other men dining. He showed a great deal of interest in Shannon, however, and wanted to know a lot of things I didn't tell him. He is sure puzzled about my staying here; I told him that I had been invited to stay till after Christmas. Darn cheek, I know, but I had to say something!'

'Nonsense!' said Hugh. 'You'll be staying longer than that.'

'I guess not! Novar and Rahtz and their little crowd will get mighty suspicious if I do. But, Jerry, I'm doing all the talking – this is your innings.'

Cousins at once described his adventures of the evening, right from the time when he gave his shadower the slip in the Lawrence Gardens, until he was attacked. Neither of his hearers uttered a word until he had finished; Hugh sat puffing at a pipe, while Miles chewed a cigar. The latter had laid aside his horn-rimmed glasses, and it was surprising the difference the lack of them made to his face. The indolent look of good humour had gone and the strength of the face now seemed to have come out almost aggressively. From time to time Hugh glanced at him in wonder; he had never seen Miles without his glasses before. At last Cousins finished, and a slow smile appeared on the American's face.

'Not a bad evening's work,' he said.

'What was in the letter, Cousins?' asked Hugh eagerly. 'You can read it for yourself – it's in German and from Oppenheimer.'

He took his pocket book from his pocket and, opening it at the page whereon he had copied the letter, handed it to Hugh. Miles drew his chair close to the latter's, and they read together. It was dated from Calcutta, and after a long vague preamble about Oppenheimer's work among participants in the activity in Calcutta, none of which were mentioned by name, it went on – 'I am distressed that the conference is to be held in

Lahore, instead of Karachi where you informed me it might take place. If it had been Karachi, I would have been on the spot to leave for Germany; as it is I will have to travel many additional hundred miles by train, and train travelling in this country is an abomination. However, that is a detail, and I suppose the Mozang College is, as you say, an ideal place for a meeting of such educational importance. Is the new English professor of Sheranwala College proving himself to be the man his authorities desired? I am glad to hear that Mr Rahtz is taking such an interest in him, and watching his progress so carefully.'

The letter ended in the writer begging Novar to convey his felicitations to all his friends, and assuring the Russian of his eagerness to be at a meeting of such worldwide educational interest.

As he came to the end Miles lay back in his chair, and roared with laughter.

'I guess that's the cutest letter that ever was,' he said.

'It is clever,' admitted Hugh; 'damnably clever! Nobody reading that would ever think that Oppenheimer was anything but a man interested in the progress of education, and that the meeting was anything but an educational one. I begin to grow interested in our German friend.'

'He's a fat old boy,' said Miles, 'who talks English with an accent as tough as Indian steak. But what a piece of luck to find out about the meeting. I was beginning to wonder how it was to be done!'

Hugh's face was all smiles as he handed back the pocket book to Cousins.

'You've jolly well earned your supper tonight, old chap,' he said. 'Rahtz has invited me to call at Mozang College one day, and he'll show me over it. You and I had better go together, Miles, and then we can compare notes about the lay of the land.'

'Sure thing! The only thing we don't know now is the time.'

'Well,' said Cousins, 'that doesn't matter much we know the place and date.'

'I suppose,' said Hugh suddenly, 'this can't refer to another conference?'

'Not on your life,' said Miles. 'Anyhow we'll keep Oppenheimer well under observation from the time he arrives till he leaves for Karachi. We'll get a railroad official to watch for his arrival. Now then, Jerry, what are the other tit-bits you've collected?'

Cousins turned to another page of his notebook.

'I will now, gentlemen,' he said, with the air of a lecturer, 'proceed to read you a few extracts, which I think it will be as well to send to head-quarters at an early date.'

The first was a suggested plan of the disposition of the Russian forces in India, and another of the Chinese. After that followed a note of great interest. 'Among our active allies,' it ran, 'Turkey will keep the English engaged in Egypt and Mesopotamia,

Afghanistan will open all the passes to our military trains, and invade the north-west frontier; and China, besides participating in the invasion of India, will attack Hong Kong and keep the English forces in the East occupied. Persia will close her ports to British ships and be prepared with all the ships she can gather together to transport the second Russian army down the Persian Gulf to India, as soon as the first has carried out the invasion.'

Hugh whistled long and softly, when he had heard that, and Miles sat back in his chair and looked across at Cousins.

'Say, Jerry,' he said, 'when you burgled old Novar's house, had you any idea that you were going to find this stuff?'

'No; only hopes! But I've thought for a long time that Novar was really the moving spirit out here. And when I found out that he was attending the ball at Christopher's tonight, I thought I'd have a shot at burglary.'

'It's been a jolly fine shot too,' said Hugh admiringly.

'I take back what I said about your being a born valet,' remarked the American. 'You're a born burglar instead.'

'"Thank you, sir," he murmured with real gratitude,' said Cousins.

'I reckon my thinking apparatus is getting out of tune – I could have sworn that old Rahtz was the big noise!'

'Well, anyhow I didn't,' returned the little man; 'he might be as brainy as Novar, but he has less caution and self-control. He's full of a treacherous, vindictive cunning and cruelty, but when it comes to finesse, give me Novar every time. And now in support of my theory, I produce my last two efforts.' He took two documents from his pocket. 'Letters actually written and signed by the Soviet Minister of Foreign Affairs to Novar – one giving him instructions to do all in his power with the aid of Rahtz to undermine British power and harm British prestige in India, and the other informing him that Germany had actually and irrevocably cast in her lot with Russia, and had sent German experts to aid in the building of airships at Bokhara and Samarkand.'

He handed the letter to Shannon.

'Good Lord!' ejaculated the latter. 'Then we have proof that it *is* to be an invasion by air. But, dash it all how can you read this stuff? It's in Russian!'

'So were practically all the documents in the safe.'

'Then that language is one of the six?'

Cousins nodded almost apologetically. Hugh looked at him with pretended resentment.

'Is there anything you don't know?' he asked.

'Algebra!' replied the little man sadly.

'Say,' put in Miles, 'I guess when your Chief receives all these little bits, he will dance with excitement.'

'May the gods grant that I will be present when

182

Sir Leonard Wallace shows excitement,' said Cousins earnestly.

'Is that all?' asked Hugh presently.

'Isn't it enough?'

'Good Heavens, yes! Cousins, your King and Country are indebted to you; you've done a hefty night's work, my lad!'

'Sure!' said Miles heartily. 'And I reckon the USA will feel grateful too. She isn't directly interested, but she is indirectly. You and I had better take a back seat after this, Shannon, and give the little man the glad hand while he gets busy.'

'For two pins, not to mention needles, Oscar Julius Miles,' said Cousins with a frown, 'I'd pulverise you!'

The American grinned.

'Start right now!' he invited.

Cousins looked him up and down.

'Ugh, you big bully!' he said.

'Well,' said Hugh thoughtfully, 'it almost looks as though Great Britain will have to turn once again from peace and gaiety to war!'

'"From jigging veins of rhyming mother wits, And such conceits as clownage keeps in pay, We'll lead you to the stately tent of war",' quoted Cousins.

'That is Shakespeare, or I'm a Dutchman!' said Hugh.

'You're a Dutchman,' said Cousins solemnly. 'It's a bit of Christopher Marlowe!'

'But what about that girl who gave you such a

surprise in Novar's house, Jerry!' said Miles. 'Who was she?'

'Ah! That is the *piéce de resistance*!' returned the little man. 'I bet neither of you fellows can guess.'

'I'm not going to try,' said Shannon, who was rather irritated that he had mistaken Marlowe's words for Shakespeare's.

'And I'm darned if I know enough people to make a guess!' said Miles.

Cousins leant forward impressively.

'It was Miss Gregson!' he said.

'Holy smoke!' exclaimed the American. 'Not Olive?'

'In very truth the same!'

Shannon sat bolt upright in his chair.

'What in the name of all that's mysterious can she have to do with Novar?' he cried.

Cousins shrugged his shoulders.

'"A woman scorned—" You know the rest!' he said.

'Oh, but that's absurd and I didn't scorn her. I suppose a man's not bound to marry a woman if he doesn't want to?'

'No; but the fair Olive has made up her mind to marry someone, and she obviously took a fancy to you. No doubt she thinks she has been treated churlishly.'

'Hugh,' said Miles, 'I begin to see daylight. Do you remember that she suddenly became very friendly with Hudson after you gave her the go-by on the boat?'

Hugh nodded.

'Well, I reckon that Hudson saw the way the wind was blowing, and got her to pour out her young heart to him. Then he spoke about it to Novar and Rahtz and the three of them decided to get her to come to Lahore in order that she could start some scandal against you which would mean your having to leave the place.'

'But what scandal could she possibly cause?'

Miles shook his head.

'That remains to be seen,' he said; 'but you may bet your bottom dollar that Hudson will stop at nothing to do you harm. And a man who is a traitor to his country is the worst kind of scoundrel.'

'Oscar is right,' agreed Cousins; 'Hudson won't forget what happened on board ship in a hurry, and he'll take any chance he can to ruin you. Besides, if he thinks you are becoming dangerous, he'll do his utmost to get you out of the way.'

'You're a couple of dismal jimmies,' growled Hugh.

'Well, if he starts something in conjunction with Olive, or without her,' said Miles, 'we'll start something that will give him a shock.'

'But we can't do anything without giving the whole show away,' objected Shannon.

'There are ways and means,' returned the other. 'I guess you'll just have to leave it to me if Olive starts scandalising! Well! It's getting late – I'm going to bed!'

He rose, and the others presently did the same.

'I'll have to send a long report and those two letters to the Chief by this mail,' said Hugh. 'Would you like to send copies to your headquarters, Miles?'

'No; I guess not. Your Foreign Office will no doubt communicate with mine. I'll just cable them to the effect that important information and documents have been sent by you to the British Foreign Office relative to the Russian activity.'

'If you're wise,' said Cousins, 'you'll send them by hand and not through the post.'

'I was thinking of something like that myself,' said Hugh, 'but whom can I send? I can't go myself and I certainly can't spare you.'

'I'll take them to Bombay, and put them in charge of the captain of the mail boat,' suggested the little man. 'They'll be perfectly safe then, and you can cable to say they are coming and how.'

'That's a good notion,' put in Miles. 'Novar and Co. will be on the lookout for all letters, and they're bound to have people in the post office in their pay.'

'Well, that's decided,' said Hugh, with a sigh of relief. 'I'll leave you to discover the best way to shake off anybody who starts to follow you, Cousins.'

'Trust me to do that,' said the little man confidently.

While this consultation was going on in Shannon's bungalow, Novar was talking angrily to two Indians in the dining room of his.

One of them, a young man in the semi-European dress affected by so many Indians, was sitting in a chair, his drawn countenance denoting that he was in pain; the other standing by his side was watching Novar with a look of fear. And at the moment the latter was not a pleasant sight. His flabby, usually good-humoured face was as dark as thunder, and his eyes flashed with the vehemence of his words, while every now and again his lips were drawn back in a snarl that made him look like a wild beast.

'Fools! Imbeciles! Idiots!' he stormed. 'You may have done irreparable mischief by this altogether uncalled-for assault. In the devil's name—why did you do it?'

'I have told you, sahib,' said the man who was standing. 'Sayed here as usual followed the little man when he left the house. He was close behind him all the way into the Lawrence Gardens, and then he lost him—'

'Dolt!' snapped Novar. 'Well, go on!'

'He made many efforts to find him, but it was of no use, so he returned to me. You had given us instructions that if ever we suspected either Shannon sahib or the small man of doing something by means of which they may have gained information, we were to knock them down and search them. We consulted for a long time before deciding. We saw the tall Englishman and his sister and the American sahib return one after the other, but the servant did not come till late. In that time he could have done much harm, so when he entered the gate, I sprang on him with a knife, but he eluded me, and fired. A bullet hit Sayed, as you see, and he is badly hurt.'

Apparently not knowing enough expletives in Hindustani, the Russian broke out into a string of his own. For several minutes he walked up and down the room swearing to himself, and then turned once more and confronted the two Indians.

'You've made absolute fools of yourselves,' he said. 'The man was probably out for mere harmless amusement, and you've raised suspicions that we wanted to avoid. Obviously in the first place he found out that he was being tracked and I told you to be careful not to let either of them suspect they were being watched. Then to take the risk of attacking him without any adequate reason, and to make such a mess of it, and above all to assault him inside his own grounds—' He raised his hands above his head as though he were about to dash them into the faces of the two men who cringed before him. At that moment the fellow in the chair gave a low moan and crumpled up in a dead faint.

'Where was he hit?' demanded Novar.

'In the right side I think, sahib.'

Novar, assisted by the other, examined the wounded man, and found that a bullet had entered apparently just below the ribs, and was probably imbedded there.

'This is a nice thing,' growled the Russian. 'He'll have to be seen by a doctor and what explanation are you going to make? The devil! Were there ever such fools? Help me to lift him on to that couch!'

They placed the sufferer on the couch, and Novar sent the other Indian to get water and try to bring him round. He himself went to the telephone and rang up Rahtz.

'Have you gone to bed yet?' he inquired, when he was through.

'Just going,' was the reply,

'Then don't! A *contretemps* has occurred and I'd like you to jump into your car, and come here!'

'What has happened?'

'Tell you when you arrive! Be as quick as you can!' He rang off.

In ten minutes there was the sound of a car drawing up outside, and as Rahtz left the driving seat, Novar came out of the house to meet him. He took him straight into his study, and explained what had happened. Rahtz listened, and then he, too, swore, but he did not appear to be so affected as Novar had been.

'After all, the only harm that can possibly come of the business,' he said, 'is that Shannon will arrive at the conclusion that the people he has come to watch have discovered it and are watching him. If he is out here on behalf of the British Secret Service, he is a very poor member of it.'

'You should never underrate your opponents,' said Novar.

'Bah!' returned the other. 'He is not worth considering.'

'I'm not so sure. At any rate this affair tonight will make him suspect that there is somebody about who regards him as dangerous, and what is more, he will immediately recognise that Cousins also must be known to us as a secret agent.'

'Of course it is very annoying and idiotic,' said Rahtz, 'that this should have happened, but they will never suspect you or me.'

'Why not? They know our nationality!'

'Quite so! We have never made the slightest effort to hide it; in fact have many times talked about it, and in that lies our greatest security. These obtuse Britishers will search for Russians who are hiding their race under the guise of Britons.'

'I hope you are right,' said Novar doubtfully.

'I'm sure I am! Was Cousins wounded?'

'No; I don't think so. From what Mushtaq told me I should think that he must have been expecting an attack since he got out of the way and fired so rapidly.'

Rahtz looked thoughtful.

'I don't like the look of that, or of the fact that he knew he was followed and gave Sayed the slip. We shall have to watch these gentry more carefully than ever after this. Perhaps it would be better to leave it to Kamper.'

Novar shook his head.

'Kamper cannot watch them both and all the time. Besides if he is recognised it'll mean very short shrift for him.'

Rahtz nodded.

'Still he's quite the best man we have out here, and if there is anything to be discovered about Shannon and his pretended manservant, he'll discover it. I suppose there is no news from the postal department?'

'No; so far only three letters of Shannon's have been intercepted and they were perfectly harmless. Now what is to be done about Sayed? He is badly wounded and must have a doctor, and if he does all sorts of inquiries will be made. The police out here are very interested in cases of shooting and stabbing, you know.'

'They shouldn't have come here – the fools!' growled Rahtz. 'If they had gone to their own homes and reported it as an attack by Hindus, it would have been put down as due to the communal feeling.'

'I'm glad you take the matter so coolly,' said Novar, rather impatiently.

'There is no reason for taking it in any other way. It is very unnecessary and irritating, but that's all.'

'Come along and see Mushtaq!'

When they entered the dining room, they found that Sayed had recovered consciousness, and his companion had done his best to make him a little comfortable.

'Well, you're a nice pair of bunglers,' said Rahtz gruffly. 'You've behaved like a couple of madmen!'

Mushtaq started to explain all over again.

'I don't want to hear your excuses,' interrupted

191

the other. 'Since you did attack Cousins, why the devil didn't you make a better job of it. As it is,' he added callously to the wounded man, 'it's rather a pity he didn't finish you off! It would have saved a heap of trouble.'

'Talking like that won't get us anywhere,' put in Novar. 'What is to be done with him?'

Rahtz thought deeply for a moment with a scowl on his face, then:

'I've got it!' he said. 'There's a small hospital of sorts near my place, and I know the doctor in charge. I'll take Sayed there, and say that I found him lying wounded in the Lawrence Gardens, and that as it is obviously a case of Hindu–Muslim trouble he had better keep it quiet. Now, you two,' he added to the Indians; 'all you know is that you were fired at by a Hindu in the Gardens – you wouldn't recognise him again as it was too dark! Do you understand?'

They both nodded. Novar took Rahtz aside.

'Supposing that Shannon and Cousins report the matter; what then?' he asked.

'It's the very thing they will not do, as you know. Besides, I'll see that not a whisper gets outside that hospital!'

A few minutes later the wounded man was helped into the car, and Rahtz drove away.

CHAPTER 16

SNOBS

Cousins took extraordinary precautions in order not to be followed to Bombay, when he left with Hugh's bulky despatch for the Chief. Shannon was now the proud possessor of a small, speedy car, and on the evening of mail day, he took Cousins for a run in the direction of the Cantonments and then doubled round on to the Grand Trunk road and headed for Amritsar. They soon left all motor traffic behind and, with the exception of occasional bullock carts and tongas, had the road to themselves on the thirty-three mile run to the Sikh city.

Cousins had been busy in the tonneau with a box of grease paints, a looking-glass and a few other odds and ends, and when Hugh stopped the car on the outskirts of Amritsar a fresh complexioned little man, with a dark pointed beard turning grey, stepped from the car and hailed a tonga.

'Splendid!' said Hugh admiringly. 'If there is a spy on the train he'll never recognise you in that make-up!'

The tonga drove up, and Cousins transferred a small suitcase and his roll of bedding – which had been hidden under a rug on the floor of the car – to the vehicle.

'Our faithful watchers will be much intrigued when you arrive back without me,' he said. 'Goodbye!'

'Goodbye!' said Hugh. 'Be very careful!'

He turned the car and drove away. Cousins was conveyed to the station where he had a wait of three hours before the mail train for Bombay was due. However, he left his luggage in charge of a ticket collector, and had a leisurely dinner in the first-class refreshment room. He then booked a berth in the name of 'Mr Sutton' – Sutton being his home – and sat down in the waiting room to wait with exemplary patience for the train.

It ran slowly into the station at last, and he found his compartment – a coupé – which he was to share with a frank-faced, boyish-looking Englishman, who turned out to be a subaltern of a famous line regiment on his way home for a spell of leave. The young man was delighted to be going to England, and his jolly chat and high spirits kept Cousins very entertained on the tedious journey to Bombay. He saw nobody he could regard with suspicion, and the great seaport was reached without incident.

Leaving his belongings in the cloakroom at the station, Cousins went straight to the ship and asked to see the Captain. He found it rather a difficult matter, but when he sent a message on board to the effect that he was on private Government business, he was shown to the

Captain's cabin, where that important personage was awaiting him.

'I'm afraid I cannot give you more than five minutes, Mr—?' He looked inquiringly at Cousins.

'It doesn't matter about my name, sir,' said the latter briskly. 'I am a member of the British Intelligence Department, and I am here to ask you to convey, under your personal care, a despatch to Sir Leonard Wallace.'

The Captain, who was a genial man of about fifty, looked surprised, then smiled.

'In other words you want to make a secret agent of me, eh?' he said.

'Put it that way if you like, sir; but the information contained in the despatch is extremely important, and we dare not risk sending it through the ordinary channels.'

'Where is the despatch?'

Cousins took it from the breast pocket of his jacket, and held it out to the other, who read the superscription, and examined the seals.

'H'm!' he grunted. 'I suppose you can show me some proof of your authority. You see, one has to be very careful in a mar like this.'

In reply Cousins undid his waistcoat, and opening his shirt, disclosed a belt made of soft leather in which were two or three pockets with buttoned flaps. Opening one of these he drew out a folded parchment, which he handed to the Captain. The latter unfolded and read it, then returned it with a look of interest at his visitor.

'Thank you!' he said. 'I shall be only too delighted to carry your package home for you. To whom am I to deliver it?'

'You will be met at Marseilles, probably by one of the King's Messengers. At all events whoever asks you for the despatch will produce ample authority.'

The Captain rose and, taking the large official envelope across to a safe hidden behind a curtain, he locked it away, and returned to his desk.

'You would like a receipt, of course?' he asked.

'Please!'

When Cousins had put the receipt in his pocket, the Captain held out his hand.

'I am glad to be of service to you,' he said.

'And I thank you for your courtesy, sir,' replied the little man. 'You understand, of course, that nobody knows that you have that packet!'

'Nobody will know,' replied the bronzed sailor. 'Goodbye!'

Cousins left the ship, and waited about on the wharf until she sailed.

When two days later he arrived back in Lahore and drove to the bungalow in a tonga, having once more resumed his normal appearance, it was immediately reported to Novar and Rahtz, who had been much intrigued by his disappearance, that he had returned with a suitcase and a roll of bedding. This caused a good deal of conjecture to the Russians, who felt uneasy over the business.

'My friend,' said Novar to the other, 'if this man

can disappear so simply and leave no trace, depend upon it we have a much more dangerous proposition in him and his master than we thought. They obviously know that they are watched.'

'Oh, nonsense!' replied Rahtz. 'It was the foolishness of the driver of your car, which enabled Shannon to slip away on the Cantonment road.'

'Our shadowers have twice been slipped now,' Novar reminded him.

On the night of Cousins' return there was a big dance at the Club, to which Joan and Hugh went. By this time they had made many friends, some of them being very nice people, and as soon as Hugh walked into the gentlemen's cloakroom he was greeted on all sides. One man, a small, straight fellow, with a dark, rugged face, and a large military moustache, welcomed him with particular warmth.

'Come and have a drink!' he invited, in a hoarse voice. 'I haven't seen you lately.'

'Presently!' said Hugh. 'I must see my sister settled first!'

The other laughed.

'There will be plenty of men to see to Miss Shannon's comfort,' he said.

'I prefer to see to it myself,' said Hugh, and leaving the room, he met Joan who had just emerged from the ladies' retiring room. He found a couple of cane chairs and a table in a corner and escorted her to them. Immediately they were joined by a tall, willowy girl with a bored expression on her face, and a most affected air.

'You two are always together,' she said languidly, dropping into the chair Hugh pushed forward for her. 'Do you always intend keeping the men from your sister, Mr Shannon?'

Although she knew Hugh was a captain, she never, under any circumstances, gave him his proper title, probably because her fiancé, the man who had spoken to Shannon in the cloakroom, had risen to the *temporary* rank of captain during the war and was never now known by any other title than plain mister. She was the type of girl who considered that she first, and her fiancé second, should be the centre of interest always; she expected every other man to take a back seat when he was present, and she loved to bask in his imagined importance. He was entirely the right man for her, for he also looked upon himself as a born leader, and was surprised when people did not hang on his words with the respect and deference which he considered was his right.

'I've no desire to keep anyone from my sister, Miss Palmer,' said Hugh.

'Well, you are always hovering over her like a sentry,' replied Miss Palmer disdainfully. 'That sort of thing might be all right for England, but things are different in India.'

'I like Hugh to hover over me, as you call it,' said Joan.

'But, my dear, it's not done. Anybody would think he was a lover, instead of a brother.'

'I prefer to have a brother, thank you!'

Miss Palmer laughed in a tired way.

'Are you afraid of the men out here?' she asked. 'Of course not!'

'You can always choose your own friends, you know. I do, and I'm naturally most particular. One can't know everyone!' She laid emphasis on the 'know'.

At that moment a nice-looking boy came up, and asked Joan for a dance. The latter smiled, and a moment later was fox-trotting happily with her young partner. Miss Palmer sniffed.

'A nice boy,' she remarked, 'but he's so young, and in such a subordinate position. It does not do to encourage people like that too much.'

'Most people have to start in a subordinate position, Miss Palmer,' said Hugh. 'And I'd rather that boy danced with my sister than a good many of the senior men – that fellow, for instance!'

He indicated Hudson, who was passing on the other side of the room.

'Mr Hudson!' she exclaimed, almost in horror. 'Why, he's a most charming man! Do you know that he draws over two thousand rupees a month?'

'I wouldn't mind if he drew twenty thousand, my opinion would remain the same.'

'How perfectly ridiculous you are!' she said. 'I don't suppose that Mr Hudson would bother about your opinion. You see he occupies rather an important position, and after all, you are only an assistant in an obscure college, aren't you?'

She expected to irritate him, but when he laughed

with whole-hearted enjoyment she bit her lip with annoyance.

'Shall we dance?' he suggested.

'No; I don't want to dance just yet, thanks!'

'Snubbed!' thought Hugh to himself and smiled again.

At that moment the Deputy Commissioner came up. Miss Palmer put on her best smile; surely he must be coming to ask her to dance, it was rather more than she had expected, but after all only her due. Apparently he thought differently, for he merely bowed slightly to her, and held out his hand to Hugh.

'How are you, Shannon?' he said. 'Can you spare me five minutes some time this evening?'

'Of course!' replied Hugh.

'Good! I'd like to have a chat with you. By the way, remind Miss Shannon that she promised me a dance tonight, will you? I'll come and find her myself later on,' he added, and with a nod, and another formal bow to Miss Palmer, he passed on.

'Will you excuse me?' said Hugh, turning to Miss Palmer. 'I promised Groves to go and have a drink with him.'

'Tell him I am waiting here, will you?' she said, an angry spot on either cheek.

'With pleasure!' he murmured, and wandered away.

He found Groves in the bar in the centre of a crowd of cronies.

'You've been a long time,' the dark man said. 'What is yours? A peg?'

'Thanks. A small one! I've been talking to Miss Palmer. She told me to tell you that she is waiting for you.'

'Isn't she dancing?'

'No. I asked her, but she said she didn't want to dance just yet.'

'She wants her Basil,' said one of the other men, and Groves joined in the laugh which followed.

Hugh gritted his teeth. He wondered what he would have done, if he had been engaged, and any man had spoken of *his* fiancée in a tone like that.

'I won't be very long,' said Groves.

For ten minutes Hugh listened to the conversation, which was mainly about girls. Opinions were expressed to which he was unused, and his companions began to sicken him. They discussed people with a familiarity that was almost indecent, and spoke of marriage as a necessity that must be regarded from the point of view of one's future welfare. Girls who were daughters of men with not very important positions were talked of as 'nice little things' to have a bit of fun with, but there the line must be drawn.

At last with a feeling of nausea Hugh made an excuse and wandered away. Groves followed him.

'Must do a little dancing,' he said. 'Women expect it, although it doesn't appeal to me much.'

Hugh was puzzled regarding Groves. He spoke without any trace of the Eurasian about him, but he was so dark, admitted being born in India and spoke Hindustani so perfectly, that it certainly seemed that there was a trace of the mixture somewhere. Yet, whenever he spoke of the half-breeds, he expressed the most utter contempt, and derided them at every possible opportunity. But Miles had said that Eurasians always made a point of running their own people down, unless they were so dark that they knew they gave themselves away. And Groves was not too dark – many Englishmen who had spent their lives in India were as brown as he. Hugh, with a growing contempt in his heart, decided in his own mind that the man was – more than doubtful.

He drifted away from him and paid his respects to various people. He had been looking for some of the friends whom he really appreciated, but tonight he seemed to be unlucky. Time and again he was compelled to speak to women whose whole object in life appeared to be a desire to pull their neighbours to pieces. They criticised other women's gowns, spoke openly of their family affairs, discussed how much each man they noticed earned, and how much he allowed his wife. These women comprised the usual social stratum of Lahore, and were typical of most towns in India; and their men-folk, in their own way, were as mean, intolerant and despicable in the expression of their opinions as were their wives. Hugh began to look with horror and loathing upon an existence which appeared to sap all that was best and sweetest out of life, and transformed it into a hideous, grasping, money-making, place-seeking travesty. Above these people, however, there was a society which had the freshness, and the charity, the purity and the toleration of the best circles at home, and that, Hugh knew, circled round the Governor. He had never met the gentleman who controlled the affairs of the Punjab, but he had met many of the people who were in the confidence of His Excellency, and he knew them to have all the attributes of the true, straight Englishman. Sir Reginald Scott, then so ably administering affairs as Governor, would have none but the very ablest, the very finest and the most honourable men round him. And those men had wives who were imbued with their own spirit, and would glorify the name of Great Britain anywhere.

After dancing twice with people he would rather never have met, Hugh found his way to the corner table he had reserved for Joan and himself. It was vacant and he sank into a chair with a feeling of intense boredom. Presently Joan arrived on the arm of one of the men who had formed a circle around Groves at the bar. It almost hurt him to see his sister in such company, but there was nothing he could do but bow to the inevitable of Indian social life. He forced a smile as Durrell, a fair-haired, conceited fop, led Joan to her chair.

'I have been trying to persuade your sister to take part in a charity concert I am getting up,' said the elegant, 'but she will not give a definite answer. You'll add your persuasive powers to mine, won't you?'

'My sister is her own mistress!' said Hugh. 'I'm afraid I cannot influence her.'

'I'll think it over, and let you know in a day or two, Mr Durrell,' said Joan, smiling at him in a manner that had captivated many impressionable young men.

He bowed and withdrew, his eyes eloquent of unspoken thoughts.

'Oh, Joan!' groaned Hugh. 'Isn't this atmosphere awful? I am longing for some wholesome, outdoor air to chase away the thoughts of these people, and their narrow, mean outlook on life.'

She touched his arm.

'I know, dear,' she said. 'I feel just like you. I often wish that I had never left England. But we'll stick it, Hugh, until your work is finished.'

'I hate to think of your being thrown among these creatures, Joan.'

'I know you do, dear old boy, but I've got you to look after me and there are Mr Miles and Mr Cousins and a few others who are – gentlemen!'

'Say,' said a voice behind them, 'I've been looking for you folks all the evening.'

Miles looked at them with the pleased smile of one who had found friends.

'Pull a chair up, and have a drink, Oscar!' said Hugh, using the other's Christian name for the first time. 'You're the man we've been waiting for!'

'How did you know I was coming here? I remember saying, when I went out to dinner, that I didn't think I would.'

204

'I know. Perhaps I should have said, you're the *type* of man we've been waiting for.'

Miles looked at him curiously.

'Guess something's got your goat, Hugh,' he said.

'Yes; these awful people have!' muttered Shannon.

The other grinned.

'Don't let them worry you any!' he remarked. 'They can't help themselves – I think the climate may have something to do with it and certainly the life that some white people live out here is real bad for them in many ways. They regard themselves as the Lord's chosen, and everybody else as dirt beneath their feet. It can't hurt you or me, or Miss Joan, so I guess it's best to let them tread their rotten little path, and not bother about them.'

'But one has to meet them, to listen to them, to dance with them and if one disagrees with their snobbishly expressed opinions they look as though they have met some strange insect which should be put out of the way. Only a few minutes ago I ventured to disagree with a certain lady's unkind comments upon a young man, whom she considered was not the type who should be admitted to the Club. He had received a first-class education, but had not been to a public school, and above all was in a most subordinate position.'

Miles chuckled.

'I can just imagine the dear old thing speaking,' he said; 'nose in air, a dainty sniff at intervals, and a pained droop of the eyelids. You'll be getting yourself unpopular if you disagree with these dames. What did she say when you dared to contradict her?'

'She looked me up and down, gave a wintry smile and turning to another woman the same type as herself said, quite distinctly enough for me to hear, "Professor Shannon is quite nice, but has the most extraordinary ideas!" And the other remarked that most professors were eccentric.'

Joan and Miles laughed, and presently his sense of humour getting the better of him, Hugh joined in.

'It has its funny side,' said Joan, 'though it is rather pathetic to reflect that those people are our countrymen and women.'

'And what makes it worse,' went on Hugh, 'is that nearly every man here tonight swears he is from an English public school. They go about in the daytime sporting old boys' ties; and I bet not half of them have the right to wear them.'

'How do they get them then?' inquired Miles.

'Why there are shops in London where one can buy ties of any old boys' association. Man alive, the spirit of a public school dies hard in one, and a real public school man would never stoop to the petty meanness that these fellows show. I bet I could pick out the real old boys amongst them.'

'This public school spirit is a bit of a shibboleth with you folks, isn't it? We've got nothing like it in the States.'

'It is at home, but out here it is ruined and made a laughing stock of by the conduct of the men who are supposed to be the results of a public school education. I sometimes think that you, Oscar, and people of your nationality must quietly laugh at us and feel rather a contempt for our cheap egoism.'

'You're being a little drastic, Hugh,' returned Miles. 'I have some sense; quite enough to know that it is only in India that your compatriots lose their best characteristics; and that is because they are members of the ruling race.'

'Ruling race, pshaw!' said Hugh in deep disgust. He swept his arm round in a comprehensive gesture. 'Behold the rulers!' he said bitterly.

'I get you,' nodded the American. 'About one half look as though they couldn't rule a dustbin!'

'They've no broad-mindedness, no understanding, they are puffed up with their own imagined import- ance. If a little bit of scandal touches one of them, the rest edge away, raise their noses in the air, and look at each other askance, while all the time their own inner lives wouldn't bear looking into. Thank God, there are some people here in India who retain all that is best in them, and, by Jove! It is jolly good to get among them, and away from the snobs and their erotic sycophants!'

'Forget it, Hugh!' said Miles, patting him on the shoulder. 'Miss Joan, I came from that dinner on purpose to ask you for a dance.'

A minute later he and Joan whirled away to the strains of a waltz.

CHAPTER 17

MISS GREGSON CAUSES A SENSATION

By the time the supper interval arrived, Hugh's good humour was completely restored. He had found some of the people he appreciated, and had danced twice with Miss Rainer, the Deputy Commissioner's daughter, a pretty dark-haired girl, who possessed an abundance of common sense as well as good looks.

He took her in to supper, and they sat with Joan and Miles at a table in a secluded part of the room. Close by were Groves and Miss Palmer seated with a plump little lady, Mrs Renfrew – who knew all about everybody in Lahore and added a great deal more – and her attendant cavalier, a tall, thin, vacuous-looking man, who possessed a wife, but was never seen with her.

Shannon introduced Miles to Groves and his party, and Miss Palmer immediately started talking to the American about her *Besil*, as she pronounced his name in her affected way. Miles listened politely, occasionally getting a word in himself, and at last he leant back towards Groves, who was behind him, and said, in a tone of admiration.

'Say, *Besil*, I guess you're some fellow. I'm real glad to make your acquaintance!'

Proceedings threatened to become dislocated for a moment. Joan stuffed her handkerchief into her mouth to prevent herself from laughing. Helen Rainer actually did laugh, while Hugh grinned. Groves smiled as though he was not quite sure what to make of the American, but an angry frown appeared on Miss Palmer's brow. The other two merely looked surprised. Miles glanced round with an expression of such bland innocence that presently normality was restored. But Miss Palmer felt impelled to say something to protect her fiancé's dignity.

'Mr Groves is not usually called by his Christian name,' she stated.

'Is that so?' asked Miles in a puzzled tone. 'What's it for then?'

'I mean to say that only his great friends, and of course myself, call him by it.'

'That's a pity! *Besil* is a nice name.'

Groves gave one of his hoarse laughs.

'Miss Palmer is rather foolish at times!' he said.

She gave him a look that should have quietened him, but Groves prided himself on his reputation for hearty good fellowship.

'We'll have something worth drinking,' he said loudly. 'Boy!'

A bearer was immediately forthcoming, and was given an order for champagne. As soon as it was brought, Groves insisted upon the occupants of both tables being served, and would take no refusals. Then raising his glass:

'Here's prosperity!' he said, in a voice which carried halfway across the room.

Thereafter Miss Palmer was unable to control the conversation, and she became petulantly quiet in consequence.

An extraordinary thing about dance suppers in Lahore is that the *piéce de resistance*, as Hugh described it, is invariably sausages and mashed potatoes. Miles regarded his plate with amusement.

'I guess the little fellows have lost their way,' he said.

Mrs Christopher, who did the catering at most functions, and on special occasions appeared herself, happened to be passing at the time. She was a large ample lady of stately aspect who moved with all the dignity of one of Nelson's three-deckers.

'Is there anything else you would prefer?' she asked in a deep voice.

Miles looked up at her pleasantly.

'Not on your life, Ma,' he replied. 'I'm tickled to death, and give the little fellows a hearty greeting.'

With slow and solemn steps she passed on.

'Gee!' said the irrepressible American. 'I've met my affinity, Hugh. When Oscar J. settles down, if ever, it would gladden his heart to see Ma seated at the other end of his connubial table.'

Mr Rainer came up towards the end of supper, and asked Joan for the dance she had promised him. She smilingly went off with him followed by Miles with Miss Rainer, whom he kept in a state of amusement the whole time they were dancing. Hugh once more offered himself to Miss Palmer. This time, a little to his surprise, he was accepted, for he thought that he had offended her and she was not the sort to forgive easily. However, he soon knew the reason for her acceptance; she kept up a running commentary on the American all through the dance, some of her remarks being more than a little barbed. He decided not to argue with her, as the best means of quieting her, and she became more and more annoyed when she saw the little effect her words had upon him, while his unruffled smile made her want to box his ears. At last the dance was over, and she refused an encore.

'Take me to *Besil*, please!' she said peremptorily.

When the Deputy Commissioner brought Joan back, he bowed her into her chair, then turned to Hugh:

'Perhaps you can spare a few minutes now, for our little chat, Shannon,' he said.

They found their way out of the ballroom into the bar, and presently settled themselves in a quiet corner. Mr Rainer ordered drinks and not a word was spoken until the bearer had placed them on a small table before them, then:

'Of course I cannot say much here,' began the Deputy Commissioner in a low voice, 'but I wanted to tell you that Sir Reginald Scott has received a private despatch from the India Office informing him of certain things, and enclosing a letter from Sir Leonard Wallace—'

Hugh nodded.

'In that letter,' went on Rainer, 'Sir Leonard informs His Excellency of your secret activities out here. I was immediately sent for and, under the pledge of secrecy, told of the fact. The Governor of course is highly intrigued, and desires me to take you to him tomorrow evening at six o'clock. You will make that time convenient?'

'I am at His Excellency's service at any time,' replied Hugh.

'Good! I must say,' he smiled, 'that I am surprised myself. I had no idea that you were anything but the professor you appear to be. I know Sir Leonard Wallace well, and we in India are under a great debt of obligation to him. But I thought that he had entirely cleansed this country of spies a year or two ago, and yet from what the Governor let drop, I should imagine that your activities are connected with the same thing?'

Hugh smiled.

'When I tell you what we have discovered,' he said, 'I rather fancy you will be amazed.'

'You raise my curiosity, Shannon! But you said "we". Have you an assistant with you?'

'Cousins, my valet, is in reality a member of my department.'

The Deputy Commissioner whistled.

'Indeed!' he murmured. 'I have heard about him.

In fact,' he smiled, 'one or two people have made rather caustic remarks, in my hearing, about what they described as the absurdity of a man in your position having an English manservant with you.'

'I expected that,' laughed Hugh. 'I have also another assistant,' he went on, 'one who attached himself to Cousins and me quite voluntarily. We met him on the boat and it turned out that he and Cousins are warm friends.'

'Does he know much about – things?' asked Rainer.

'He knows all. In fact, he was instrumental in finding out a great deal.'

The other frowned slightly.

'Is it not rather injudicious to take into your confidence a man not in your service?' he asked thoughtfully.

'Not in the least,' smiled Hugh, then added in a whisper. 'It is Miles!'

'Miles!' exclaimed the man known to everybody as the D.C. 'Not the American?'

'Yes! He is a member of the United States' Secret Service, and is in this business with us on behalf of his own country!'

'Great Scot! You amaze me! Why nobody on earth would imagine Miles to be anything but a harmless and wealthy wanderer.'

'All the better,' said Shannon. 'As a matter of fact he is remarkably astute. I owe all I know to him and Cousins. The job would have been too big for me alone!'

'Then the position is serious?' Rainer asked eagerly.

'It is very serious. I will tell you this much now: there is the greatest plot brewing against Great Britain that probably the world has ever seen.'

'Good heavens!'

'By the way, sir, we must not go to Government House together tomorrow!'

'Why not?'

'Because I am watched!'

Rainer started.

'Who is watching you?' he asked.

'Spies of the other party! I can hardly make a move without its being known. Tomorrow you must go alone. I will shake off my shadowers somehow and come along in my little car.'

'Then your real position is known?'

'To these people, unfortunately, yes. I daresay that I am even being watched tonight.'

The Deputy Commissioner sighed.

'You live a very dangerous life,' he said.

'It has its compensations,' said Hugh; 'and I would not change it for any other. I was at the Foreign Office for some time, but I found things too dull for me there. It was chiefly through the help of Major Brien that I was transferred to the Intelligence Department.'

Rainer smiled.

'Major Brien is another man for whom I have a great admiration,' he said. 'He was out here with Sir Leonard. By the way,' he asked, 'does

Miss Shannon know of your connection with the Secret Service, and the real reason for your presence in India?'

'She knows everything,' replied Hugh.

'Ah!' said the Deputy Commissioner. 'I can see that she is as reliable as she is beautiful!'

'She is the best sister in the world,' said Hugh, with a totally uncalled-for emphasis.

Rainer nodded understandingly.

At that moment Novar and Rahtz entered the room. They came across to Rainer and Shannon and greeted them rather loudly. Hugh caught a swift glance of suspicion exchanged between them.

'The Professor and the Deputy Commissioner,' laughed Novar. 'A strange combination surely!'

'Not so strange as it may look,' smiled Rainer. 'Captain Shannon and I come from the same little bit of England, and I knew his parents very well indeed.'

Hugh chuckled inwardly at his companion's quick wit.

'Ah!' said Rahtz. 'The combination is explained. We must drink to further combinations.'

Shannon wondered what he meant, but accepted the drink he ordered.

When the four had the glasses of whisky and soda in their hands, Rahtz held his high.

'I'll give you a toast suggested by this happy meeting of our respected D.C. and Shannon. The world is small; may it grow smaller!'

The toast was drunk laughingly, but there was

a warning gleam in Novar's eyes as he looked at his companion.

For some minutes the four stood talking, then Hugh excused himself, and went off to find his sister. A dance was in progress when he entered the ballroom, and for a few minutes he stood watching the efforts of the various couples to do the Charleston. Presently he espied Joan and Miles near the centre of the room, and stood lost in admiration. The Charleston is not a pretty dance, but when done by experts it can be made quite artistic. Joan was a glorious dancer, and every movement she executed was full of grace, but what surprised Hugh was the discovery that Miles was such a graceful performer. He watched them enraptured. They made the dance almost a poem. And others were watching them too, for gradually the other dancers stopped to look on until at last Joan and Miles were alone. Then there broke out a great spontaneous burst of hand-clapping from all parts of the vast room.

Joan looked round, realised the situation, and suddenly stopped dancing; and, with her face as red as fire, ran to her chair, followed by the American. From everywhere came demands for an encore, and prolonged clapping, but to all requests Joan turned a deaf ear, until Hugh made his way to her side, and added his entreaties to those of the rest. Then, now pale when before she had been crimson, she walked out with Miles to the centre of the floor; the band struck up, and she and the American gave an exhibition of the

Charleston that Lahore had never seen before, nor dreamt of seeing. As they went on she forgot the crowd watching and danced exquisitely. Joan and her partner became famous, and their dance was talked of for long afterwards. At last it was finished and amidst thunderous applause she walked back to her seat a little unsteadily, followed by her grinning companion who took it all apparently in the most composed fashion.

'Oh, Hugh,' said Joan with embarrassment, 'it was awful!'

'I guess we'll have to go on the halls after this, Miss Joan,' said Miles.

'I don't believe you minded a bit.' She looked reproachfully at him.

'I didn't,' he confessed. 'I enjoyed every minute of it.'

'If only Cousins were here,' sighed Hugh, 'what a chance he would have had for one of his quotations!'

'Poor old Jerry!' said Miles. 'He gets all the work, and none of the fun.'

'I'm not so sure about that,' put in Joan. 'I think he has quite a good time with his friends at the Railway Institute. Only the other day he told me that he danced quite a lot there!'

'I guess Jerry didn't put it like that,' said the American.

She laughed.

'No. As a matter of fact he said that he occasionally twiggled a terpsichorean toe!'

217

There was a lull in the proceedings while the band took a much needed rest. Close to their corner Miss Palmer, Groves and their friends were seated, and near by some of the old dowagers, who spent their time in scandal-mongering.

Miss Palmer leant across to Joan.

'You danced beautifully,' she said. 'I did admire it so. I suppose you have done it professionally, haven't you?'

'Of course not!' replied Joan indignantly.

Then Miles clutched Hugh's arm.

'It's come!' he said tensely. 'Get a tight hold on yourself, boy!'

Hugh looked up in astonishment, and his heart missed a beat; he felt a premonition of coming evil. Right across the middle of the floor, in all the glory of a mauve evening-gown, the cynosure of all eyes, and looking insolently from side to side, came Olive Gregson, and she was making straight for their table. Joan went as pale as death, while Miles swore under his breath.

The newcomer stopped, and there was a smile of contemptuous amusement on her face. Hugh rose clumsily to his feet.

'Good evening!' he said, and swallowed hard.

'Good evening!' replied Miss Gregson mockingly, and her voice was raised, so that all in the neighbourhood could hear. 'I am glad to see you are enjoying yourself so much, Hugh Shannon!'

'Thanks!' he stammered awkwardly.

'Please don't thank me! It is hard to think that

you who stand there are the man who has wrecked my life!'

'Wrecked your life! What do you mean?'

'Oh, don't pretend because all these people are around you!'

'If you have anything to say let us go somewhere else,' he said desperately.

'No!' She raised her head high. 'I prefer to say what I have to say – here!'

He shrugged his shoulders, and sat down. Miles stepped forward and took her by the arm. She pulled herself away.

'Miss Olive,' said the American coaxingly, 'whatever you are sore about can be put right elsewhere. Have a little consideration.'

She looked coldly at him.

'You, I know, are in league with that cad there, or else you would not interfere!'

'But—'

'Be quiet!' she almost shouted, then went on hurriedly to Hugh. 'You made love to me on board ship, you made me love you and promised to marry me. Then when you had tired of me you threw me over like any old rag. I went back to Bangalore heartbroken, but—'

'Stop!' cried Joan in a voice of agony.

'I will not stop! Your brother has ruined me, and I have come to him for reparation. I loved him – I trusted him, and—and he took advantage of me. I went back to Bangalore and tried to forget him. But when I found what had happened I came here

219

as fast as I could. He must – must marry me to save me from disgrace!'

She covered her face with her hands and sobbed. Miss Palmer rose from her seat, and with a look of the deepest contempt walked away followed by her companions, the two men grinning cynically. Then by ones and twos the rest of their neighbours rose and departed, first casting looks of scorn at Hugh. Joan had sunk over the table, and with her head pillowed in her arms was crying as though her heart would break. Miles caught Miss Gregson by the shoulders.

'You she-cat,' he ground out, and nobody would have recognised the calm, easy-going American now. 'You all-fired liar! You'll take back every word that you have spoken before I have done with you!'

She dragged herself away from him.

'Don't dare to speak to me like that!' she cried. 'I am going back to the Royal Hotel, and tomorrow I expect Hugh Shannon to make all arrangements for the wedding.'

And turning she walked out of the room, and disappeared. Miles laid his arm on Hugh's shoulder.

'Say, Hugh,' he said, 'I'm sorry! I expected something; but hell – nothing like this!'

'Let us go home!' said Hugh miserably.

At that moment the band struck up, prompted by some kindly spirit, and under cover of the dancing Hugh and Miles escorted Joan, who was still crying bitterly, to the ladies' retiring room. Then the two men with grim, set faces sought their own coats and hats. There were one or two acquaintances of Hugh's in the cloakroom, and they drew aside with shrugs which were more eloquent than words. Miles was about to remonstrate with them, but Hugh caught his arm.

'It's no use, old chap!' he said. 'Come along!'

They drove home in grim silence.

In the early hours of the same morning, Miss Gregson was seated in the comfortable drawing room of Novar's bungalow, puffing a cigarette. Rahtz and Hudson were lolling in large armchairs with whiskies and sodas by their sides and cigars in their mouths, while Novar was leaning against the mantelpiece similarly equipped. He was speaking.

'The moment was admirably chosen,' he said, with deep satisfaction, 'and everything went off much better than I anticipated. I congratulate you on your admirable stage-management, Hudson, and you, Miss Gregson, on your perfect acting of a most difficult part.'

'It was pretty nerve-racking I assure you,' said the girl. 'I felt rather awful standing there with all those people around, and saying what I did.'

'Well, it's done now, and you have had the satisfaction of ruining Shannon,' put in Rahtz, lazily flicking his cigar ash on to the carpet. 'I shall see that the whole facts are placed before the Principal of his College today, and he will be compelled to resign. Such a thing as this would never be tolerated by the Muslim community. After that he will find Lahore an impossible place for him. Yes; you have done well – very well indeed!'

'I can't help feeling rather guilty,' said Olive. 'It was awfully mean, wasn't it?'

'Not a bit,' said Hudson. 'Remember the indignity he put upon you on board ship!'

A hard smile came into her face.

'Well, I have repaid him with interest,' she remarked.

'Compound interest, I should say,' smiled Rahtz. 'That reminds me,' he added to Novar, 'I think that Miss Gregson might now receive the remuneration we promised her for her services.'

'Quite so!' said Novar.

He took a roll of banknotes out of his pocket.

'Let me see!' he went on. 'You have received money for all your expenses have you not, Miss Gregson?'

She nodded.

'Then I have much pleasure in handing you the thousand rupees promised for tonight's entertainment!'

He counted out ten hundred rupee notes, and handed them to her with a little bow. She took them and smiled up at him.

'Thank you!' she said. 'May I know now why you three men are so anxious to ruin Captain Shannon?'

They looked at each other.

'Let me remark, Miss Gregson,' said Novar, 'that that is a matter which only concerns us. You have had your revenge! Surely that is all that matters to you!'

'Or why not put it in this way,' remarked Rahtz. 'We deeply sympathised with you, and wanted to help you!'

'And so you not only did that!' she said cynically, 'but paid me a thousand rupees and my expenses as well.' She shrugged her shoulders. 'Oh, well, as Mr Novar says, it is only a matter that concerns you!'

'Just so!' said Novar. 'And we have your word that you will never let any mention of this – er – little transaction pass your lips.'

'You may be sure I shall not speak,' she replied. 'I am hardly likely to, am I?'

'You must leave for Bangalore without fail today!' said Hudson suddenly. 'That is imperative!'

'Can't I wait until tomorrow?'

'No; it would be most foolish. Shannon will not lie down under the insult you have put upon him.'

'But I told him I was staying at the Royal Hotel, not the Northern India!'

'That does not matter! Lahore is not a very large place, and it would be dangerous for you to stop a minute longer than necessary.'

'I agree with Hudson,' said Novar. 'We are sorry to hurry you off, Miss Gregson, but we have no choice.'

'Oh, all right!' she said. 'But it isn't Shannon I'm afraid of. He's a broken man! It's that American – Miles!'

Rahtz laughed.

'You needn't fear him,' he remarked. 'He's a harmless fool! As a matter of fact I expected him to shun Shannon like the rest of the dear, eminently proper and shocked assembly. He rather touched me by his true-friend-in-a-calamity behaviour.'

'If you had only seen his face and heard his voice when he caught hold of me,' she said, 'you'd understand why I fear him.'

'Well, you'll soon be away from both of them,' said Novar; 'and now I think perhaps a little rest will do you good before your journey!'

'I'll drive you to the hotel,' said Hudson.

'Thank you!' she replied insolently. 'I hardly intended to walk!'

CHAPTER 18

SHANNON IS ASKED TO RESIGN

It was a very miserable party which entered Shannon's bungalow on their return from the Club. Cousins was sitting in an armchair before a large fire in the sitting room reading the newspaper. He rose and looked curiously at the unhappy trio.

'What on earth has happened?' he began. 'You all look as though—'

'For the love of Mike, fetch some whisky and sodas like a good chap,' said Miles 'and some port for Miss Shannon.'

'I don't want anything, thank you,' murmured Joan.

'I want you to be guided by me in this, Miss Joan. A glass of port will do you a world of good.'

'All right!' she said in the same low, colourless voice.

Without another word Cousins went off to do the American's bidding, and nothing more was said until everybody was supplied with a drink. Hugh sat in a chair, his legs stretched out, his chin resting on his breast, gazing at the fire; Miles chewed savagely at a half-smoked cigar; Joan sat bolt upright, her head drooping pathetically. As for Cousins, he glanced from one to the other with a puzzled frown on his face. Presently Joan broke the silence.

'What a little idiot I was to – to cry!' she said bitterly. 'I wish now that I had faced the whole roomful of people, and defended Hugh!'

'It wouldn't have been of much use,' remarked Miles.

Cousins sighed gently.

'Am I not to be informed of the trouble?' he asked plaintively.

In a few short, pithy sentences the American told him what had happened. The little man's teeth snapped together as he listened, and his eyes flashed with a look that was seldom seen in them.

'Great Heavens!' he exclaimed. 'I knew there was some mischief brewing, but this—' A sound very much like a curse came from him.

Hugh sat up.

'It was devilishly engineered,' he said. 'The band had stopped, the floor was clear, and Joan and Miles had just previously brought attention on our corner by doing a special dance. A better opportunity couldn't have been found. All those round us were the greatest scandal-mongers in Lahore, people without understanding, without mercy. There is not a soul in the whole of the civil station who won't know all about it today, with a few picturesque details added. I'm ruined – absolutely and irrevocably.'

'I guess not,' growled Miles. 'I'm going to make that dame eat her words!'

'You can't!' said Hugh. 'If you did you would have to tackle Hudson and Novar and Rahtz and it would mean disclosing our knowledge to them, giving away your own position, and spoiling everything!'

'I reckon there's a way somehow, and I'm going to find it!'

'I'm hanged if I can think of anything,' said Cousins mournfully. 'If only we could have foreseen this!'

'Well, we didn't, and that's that!' replied the American with an irritation which was foreign to him. 'I'll see that girl anyhow, and if I can't think of anything else in the meantime, I'll put the fear of the Lord into her.'

'You'll have to be quick,' said Cousins. 'She'll be away for Bangalore by the first train she can catch tomorrow, or rather today?'

Joan looked up hopefully.

'Won't that make people realise that she was not telling the truth?' she asked.

'Not on your life, Miss Joan,' replied Miles. 'Their evil minds will at once come to the conclusion that your brother has bought her off. Where did she say she was staying, Hugh?'

'At the Royal!'

'Then it is certain,' put in Cousins quietly, 'that she will be elsewhere.'

'Yes,' said Hugh; 'she'll probably be at Novar's

where Cousins saw her first, and where you can't possibly get at her.'

'No,' said the American; 'your brains are dusty, and I don't wonder. Novar's bungalow, or Rahtz's, or Hudson's are just the very places she won't be. None of those guys are going to bring the least suspicion on themselves by a fool idea like that.'

'Who's to know?'

'Such a thing is always likely to be found out. No; she's staying in some hotel in Lahore, but not the Royal as Jerry says, and I'm sure going to find out right now.'

'How?' asked Joan.

He smiled for the first time since they had left the Club.

'There's a dandy little instrument hanging in the corridor, Miss Joan, called a telephone, and with it is a directory. With the aid of those two, one can find out a mighty lot!'

Hugh rose from his chair, with a cry of impatience.

'What's the use?' he said. 'The mischief is done I'll be asked to resign from the Club, the Governor will hear of it – everybody. My name will be anathema in Lahore. No doubt I shall be politely requested to hand in my resignation at the College. Even the Chief will probably hear, and I shall be ruined in every respect. It's – it's damnable!'

'Say, don't be a greater fool than you can help, Shannon. The Chief isn't going to take any notice of idiot reports like this, and once you have explained everything to the Governor – you say you have an appointment with him this evening – he's going to understand. I have met Sir Reginald Scott twice and he struck me as being a man of sense.'

Hugh smiled wanly at him.

'You people are jolly decent,' he said, then gritted his teeth while an expression of despair came into his face. 'But how do *you* know this thing is false?' he went on. 'Perhaps, unknown to you, I was philandering with that girl on the ship! You have only my word against hers!'

'Oh, Hugh!' cried Joan. 'Don't be such an utter baby! It is cruel of you to say a thing like that!'

The American rose from his chair.

'Shucks!' he said in a tone of disgust, and went off to the telephone.

'Some are born idiots; some achieve idiocy; others have idiocy thrust upon them!' muttered Cousins.

Then suddenly Hugh smiled; it was rather a pale smile, but it had a sparkle of the old Hugh about it. He looked tenderly at Joan.

'I'm sorry, old girl,' he said; 'I hardly knew what I was saying. This thing has rather bowled me over, especially as it happened before the very people, who, I know, are only too eager to snatch at a crumb of scandal to ruin a fellow. They got a whole loaf,' he added bitterly. 'But I'm going to fight!'

'Of course you are,' said Cousins approvingly. 'None of us thought otherwise!'

Joan caught her brother's hand and pressed it.

'You'll win through,' she said. 'I know you will.'

In the meantime Miles was busy ringing up every hotel in Lahore. He could get no answer at all from two, while the others informed him that there was nobody of the name of Gregson on their books. He returned to the sitting room and sank into his chair.

'I wasn't too lucky!' he said. 'I couldn't get an answer from the Gordon, nor the Northern India, and all the rest informed me that they had nobody of the name of Gregson staying there. None of them appeared to be falling over themselves with delight at being rung up at this hour; in fact the fellow in the Punjab Hotel was even kind enough to tell me that it was nearly half past two!'

'Well, that narrows the search down,' said Cousins.

'Perhaps she is not using her proper name,' said Hugh. 'Anyhow I don't see what you can do, even if you do find out where she is.'

'I've no very clear notion myself at present,' replied Miles, 'but I've given you my word that I'll see that that woman makes restitution, and I've never broken my word yet. You've got to leave it to me, Hugh!'

'Very well!' replied Shannon. 'Since you wish it!'

'I do! And now you and Miss Joan go along and hit the hay! Jerry and I are going to sit right here and have a few thinks.'

'Oh, but I say—' began Hugh.

'Do what you're told, Shannon!' said Cousins. 'You're not on in this act! Oscar and I are used to each other's brainstorms.'

'And something always happens, when we get busy in the upper storey,' added Miles.

Hugh shrugged his shoulders.

'Come on, Joan!' he said. 'These fellows make me feel like a naughty child, who has overstayed his bed hour.'

'So you have,' replied Cousins.

After Joan and her brother had departed, the other two made themselves perfectly comfortable, replenished their glasses and lit their pipes. Joan, whose room was next to the sitting room, heard the sound of subdued voices, occasionally punctuated by long periods of silence, for some time before she fell into a troubled sleep. It seemed to her semiconscious mind that just before she lapsed into slumber someone laughed.

Hugh and his sister met at breakfast and both showed signs of the trouble they had gone through. Miles did not put in an appearance – Cousins, of course, had his meals in his own room – and Hugh concluded that the American was still in bed. He made a poor attempt at eating and then went along to see him as soon as he had finished, but the bedroom was unoccupied. Feeling somewhat puzzled he entered Cousins' apartment, but here again the room was empty. He returned to Joan and told her of the absence of both. She smiled.

'Depend upon it, Hugh,' she said, 'they have

thought of some way out of this awful business, and perhaps they are even now making that terrible Gregson woman confess that all she said was untrue.'

He smiled.

'You are an optimist, Joan,' he said.

Miles' bearer passed through the room. He was a young smart-looking man with a cheerful smile. He had once been a soldier, and he brought his hand up to his turban in a military salute, as he said, 'Salaam!' Even before the servants Hugh kept up the pretence of knowing no Hindustani.

'Where is sahib?' he asked.

'Going out too much early, sahib,' replied the bearer, who prided himself upon the knowledge of a little English.

'What time?'

The other thought deeply for a moment, and crossing to the mantelshelf consulted the clock thereon, then he turned triumphantly to Hugh.

'Seven o'clock going!' he said.

'And Cousins? Where is he?'

'Him going out with sahib!'

Shannon looked at Joan.

'I wonder what they are up to!' he said.

He was later preparing to go down to the College to commence his daily work, and walked round to the garage to get his car out, when he discovered, somewhat to his indignation, that it was not there. He went back to the bungalow.

'It's all very well,' he complained to Joan. 'I don't

232

mind their taking the car when I don't want it, but I've left myself barely a quarter of an hour to get to the College, and now there's no car to go in. A tonga will take more than twice as long!'

'Never mind, Hugh,' said the girl; 'and don't be ungrateful! They have gone out for your sake!'

He smiled and sent his bearer for a tonga. The small vehicle had arrived, and he was about to get in when the car, driven by Miles, tore in through the gateway and came to a stop with a jarring of brakes.

'I'm sorry to keep you waiting,' said the American, as he descended from his seat. 'And I hope you don't mind my commandeering the bus. But I didn't want to wake you and ask permission, when I knew it would be granted.'

'That's all right,' replied Hugh. 'I was going in a tonga.'

He took out a few annas, and was about to give them to the tonga-wallah, when Miles interposed.

'Don't send him away!' he said. 'I'm going out again after I've had some eats!'

'You can have the car if you like!'

'Not on you life! An ekka, or tonga, or whatever they call 'em, is quite good enough for me.'

'Just as you like,' said Hugh, and getting into the car he drove away.

'Do tell me what you've been doing,' pleaded Joan eagerly, as she accompanied Miles into the dining room.

He smiled.

'Well, I found out where the Gregson woman is staying!'

'Where?'

'At the Northern India Hotel! I first went with Jerry to the Gordon and asked for her, but there was nothing doing, so we found our way to the other – a sure enough hotel, but a place where I wouldn't advise my worst enemy to stay. She was there right enough.'

'Well?'

'We couldn't pull even Olive out of bed at that hour besides there were one or two other things to be done first. I told the fellow in the office that I'd be right back. Then Cousins and I went to see a particular friend of his, and we had an almighty earnest talk with him while he was shaving. So earnest, in fact, that he cut himself. When we asked him to do a certain thing, at first he refused point blank, but old Jerry has a mighty persuasive manner, and he agreed in the end.'

'What was it?'

'I'm sorry, but I can't tell you just yet, Miss Joan!'

She pouted.

'You've made me horribly curious!' she said.

'You shall know everything before long. I left Cousins with his friend, so as to keep him up to scratch.'

'Is there any chance of this horrible business being put right?' she asked earnestly.

'Miss Joan,' he replied in as earnest a tone as

hers, 'if Hugh's name isn't absolutely cleared in the course of the next few hours, I shall be the most amazed man in the whole of this world!'

'Oh, Oscar,' she said impulsively, 'you're a dear!'

Then as realisation of what she had said came to her, she blushed a vivid scarlet. He half rose in his chair, and a look of delight shone on his face.

'I'm – I'm so sorry!' she stammered.

'Don't spoil it!' he said. 'What is there to be sorry about? I never thought much of my name, but when you say it, it has possibilities I never noticed before. I hope you're always going to remember that Oscar sounds a deal better than Miles!'

She looked at him and smiled a trifle shyly.

'Would you like me to?' she asked.

'Surest thing you know!'

'Then perhaps I may – sometimes!'

He looked at her very seriously for a moment, like a man who has something to say, but does not know quite how to say it. Then, rather nervously – a most unusual state for Oscar Julius Miles – he leant towards her.

'Say, Miss Joan,' he said. 'I'd like to tell you a little story some day, may I?'

'Will it be a nice story?' she asked.

He hesitated, then:

'Well, you might not like it, but it appeals to me,' he replied.

She walked to the door.

'Then I think,' she said, and there seemed to be

235

a strange new tone in her voice, which he had not heard before, 'that if it appeals to you, it very likely will appeal to me also – Oscar!'

He crossed the room hurriedly, and held the door open for her to pass through.

'I've a mind to tell that story right now,' he said.

She shook her head.

'There's no time now,' she remarked. 'Remember you have an appointment!'

He looked a little crestfallen.

'That's true, Miss Joan!' he nodded.

She smiled up into his face.

'I think I shall love to hear it later on,' she said softly. 'In the meantime "Joan" without the "Miss" has possibilities, which I may not have noticed before.'

She was gone. For two or three moments Miles stood where he was, still holding the handle of the door, a broad smile on his face. Then he hurried back to the breakfast table, drained a cup of coffee and picked up his topee.

'Gee!' he exclaimed. 'Some angel!'

He dashed out of the house, and slapped the tonga driver on the back.

'Drive to the Northern India Hotel, son,' he said, 'and I'll give you a tip that'll buy you a new pony!'

Hugh arrived at the College, feeling quite disinclined to lecture to a crowd of uninteresting students. However, he forced himself to go through with his first period, though he dismissed the class a little earlier than the scheduled time. He was walking slowly toward the staffroom, when a chaprasi handed him a note from the Principal, asking him to go to the office. He found Mahommed Abdullah sitting at his desk looking extremely serious. Hugh guessed what was coming, and decided to open the proceedings himself.

'I should imagine,' he said, 'from your expression, that you have heard the news?'

'It depends what you mean by the news,' replied Abdullah cautiously. 'I have certainly heard something, which has upset me, and I have therefore asked you to see me with a view to a possible explanation.'

'I think it would be better, Mr Abdullah,' said Hugh, 'if you spoke out!' His voice was calm, level, emotionless, but there was a glitter in his eyes which was not lost upon the Principal.

'Very well, as you wish it!' said the latter. 'I received a telephone message a few minutes ago, informing me of a certain unfortunate incident that took place during a ball you attended last night. I need not say that it came as a very great shock to me. Perhaps you will tell me if this – er – incident actually took place?'

Hugh nodded.

'You admit it?' demanded Abdullah.

'I admit the incident,' replied Hugh.

'That a certain lady made an accusation against you in front of a crowd of people – a most terrible accusation – and demanded redress?'

'Yes.' Hugh looked down at Abdullah. 'And now,' he went on, 'perhaps you, in turn, will be good enough to tell me to whom I am indebted for the fact that this was reported to you!'

'Does that matter?'

'It certainly does. But if you are not inclined to tell me, I shall find out elsewhere.'

'Sit down, Shannon!' said Abdullah. 'Let us discuss this matter calmly!'

Hugh sank into a chair.

'I have no objection to giving you the name of my informant,' went on the Principal, 'but first of all I want to ask a question for my own satisfaction.'

'Naturally,' said Hugh. 'You are going to ask me if I am actually guilty of the conduct I have been accused of!'

'Exactly! I'd like you to know, however, that I personally feel certain that you are not, and I also made a point of telling my informant so.'

'That is good of you,' said Hugh, with real gratitude.

'Not at all! I think I know you well enough – I only want your word for it!'

'Then you have my word that the thing is absolutely false!'

'Thank you!' Abdullah held out his hand, which Shannon clasped warmly. 'I was told,' continued the former, 'by the Principal of Mozang College, who was present at the dance and heard everything.'

Hugh nodded, and his teeth came together with a click.

'I guessed it was Rahtz,' he said, more to himself than to the other.

Abdullah looked at him in surprise.

'Why?' he asked.

'Oh, just a thought,' said Hugh.

For a moment there was silence, then:

'Who is this person?' asked the Principal.

'A girl I met on board a ship!' He proceeded to tell the other all about her.

When he had finished Abdullah smiled rather grimly.

'She appears to be a most unpleasant lady,' he remarked. 'Of course,' he went on, 'this will reflect very much on the College, and I am afraid that if it gets to the ears of the governing body, they will be up in arms. They are frightened of scandal of any sort. Is it likely to be disproved?'

'I sincerely hope so,' replied Hugh. 'In fact friends of mine are engaged at this moment in doing all they can to help me.'

'I'm very glad to hear it!'

At that moment the Chairman of the College Board was announced. He was a man whom Hugh had only met once, and to whom he had taken an instinctive dislike. He had small ferrety eyes, a broad nose, and an untidy straggling beard, which he had a habit of caressing lovingly, whenever he was thinking deeply. He wore the ordinary garb – never over clean – of a true Mussulman.

239

'Perhaps you will see me later on, Shannon!' said Abdullah.

Hugh rose to go.

'There is no need for Professor Shannon to go,' said the Chairman, in his careful English, 'I am here on a matter concerning him.'

A quick look passed between the Principal and Hugh, and the former frowned.

'Some very unpleasant information has come to us,' went on the Chairman. 'It is to the effect—'

'There is no need to repeat it,' interrupted Abdullah. 'Professor Shannon and I have been discussing it.'

The bearded man shrugged his shoulders.

'It is very painful,' he said. 'You will understand, Professor Shannon, that such a thing cannot be tolerated here. The scandal would have a most bad effect on students and College.'

Hugh clenched his fists.

'Do you mean to say,' he demanded, 'that you accept this thing?'

Again the shrug.

'We have no choice. A woman would not make such a statement – so unpleasant to herself – before others, if it were not true!'

'I am, therefore, condemned without a hearing?'

'What can you say?'

'I have Captain Shannon's word for it,' interposed Abdullah, 'that there is no truth in the accusation, and I never believed in it for one moment.'

A sarcastic smile crossed the Chairman's face.

240

'You are a trifle – what is the word – quixotic, Mr Abdullah,' he said, 'And, of course, are interested in Shannon—'

'*Professor* or *Captain* Shannon, if you please,' growled Hugh.

'Professor Shannon, then. But I am afraid very much, and regret very deeply—'

'Spare me the regrets!' interrupted Hugh.

The other cast a malignant glance at him.

'It would be perhaps as well,' he said in a harsher voice, 'if you resigned as soon as possible!'

Abdullah rose from his seat.

'This is absurd!' he said.

'Not at all! There will be a meeting of the Board this afternoon, and it would be better – much better – if I were to convey to them that Captain Shannon had resigned, than that they should demand his resignation!'

Abdullah was pained and he looked it.

'But why should such a drastic course be necessary?' he asked. 'The matter will be put right in a day or two.'

'Things like this must not be allowed to besmirch the good name of the Muslim Community,' said the Chairman unctuously.

'I am a Mahommedan,' said Abdullah, and his face showed the intensity of his feelings, 'and, I hope, a good one. Such a course as you suggest is against all ideas of Muslim justice.'

The Chairman frowned.

'I am surprised to hear such an expression of

241

opinion from you, Mr Abdullah,' he said. 'I repeat that Professor Shannon will save much unpleasantness both to himself and to others, if he resigns quietly, and at once!'

'I refuse to acknowledge your right to interfere in any way with me,' snapped Hugh. 'I am responsible only to the Principal of this College, and then only in matters in the College, or affecting the College. You can say what you like, or do what you like, but I will *not* resign!'

Once more the bearded man shrugged his shoulders.

'You will be sorry!' he sneered.

Hugh turned to Abdullah.

'Do you wish me to resign?' he asked.

'Certainly not!'

For a moment the Chairman looked furious, then he smiled.

'That is unfortunate!' he said.

'Bear this in mind!' said Hugh to him. 'I'll make you apologise to me for the insult you have put upon me today! If you don't mind, Mr Abdullah,' he went on, 'I'll miss the rest of my lectures this morning.'

'Do,' said the Principal. 'I can quite understand your feelings.'

'I am sorry Professor Shannon has taken the matter like this,' commenced the Chairman. 'I think that—'

Hugh turned his back on him, nodded to Abdullah and walked out of the room.

Dr Mumtaz Sadiq was hovering about outside. He tried to take Hugh's arm in what he considered a friendly manner, but it was shaken off.

'This is a bad business,' he said.

Hugh glared at him.

'What do you know about it?' he demanded.

'Only what the Chairman told me. It's not nice for you – I'm really sorry!'

'Good of you!' said the other shortly. 'I wasn't aware that I had asked for your sympathy.'

'Of course it was mad of you to get entangled with a woman of that type,' said Dr Sadiq, shaking his head reprovingly. 'It's all a question of psychology, you know,' he went on. 'Of course I understand the mentality of these people, and with my vast knowledge I can help you, if you'll let me take her in hand.'

'Go to the devil!' snapped Hugh.

CHAPTER 19

MILES GETS BUSY

Miles arrived at the Northern India Hotel, and told the tonga wallah to wait. He marched straight into the dilapidated little office, where he found Cousins and a friend of the latter's – a police sergeant named Spink – awaiting him.

'I'm glad you've arrived,' he said.

'We've been here for some time, sir,' replied Cousins, playing up to his character of valet before the policeman.

'Then I'm sorry to have kept you waiting,' said Miles cheerfully.

The assistant manager, a small, lean Goanese, who had been watching them curiously, here interposed a remark.

'I should theenk, sare,' he said, 'that Mees Gregson is in breakfast room at thees time. Shall I go and tell her you waiting?'

'No thanks!' replied the American. 'I'll find her myself. Where is the breakfast room?'

It was pointed out to him, and he was about to cross the compound, when Spink followed him outside, and touched him on the arm.

'Don't bring me into this business if you can possibly help it, Mr Miles!' he said.

'Don't you worry!' was the reply. 'I don't think there will be any need for such a drastic step, and I guess, even if there is, we won't get so far as the police court.'

He smiled, and continued on his way. He did not want Miss Gregson to see him and take alarm, and for that reason had not permitted the under-manager to announce him. He approached the door of the breakfast room cautiously and looked in. There was a sprinkling of guests seated therein, but no sign of Miss Gregson. He called the head waiter, and inquired if she had had breakfast. It took the man some time to understand, but at last his face brightened and, by means of signs rather than words, he indicated that the lady was taking breakfast in her room that morning. Miles wandered back to the office.

'What is the number of Miss Gregson's room?' he asked.

'Seventeen, sare!' replied the clerk.

'You boys had better come right along!' said the American. 'We'll wait on the veranda outside room seventeen until she is ready to see us. Gee!' he went on, as the three of them walked round the compound towards Miss Gregson's apartment. 'I guess she'll be some surprised to see us!'

There were several cane chairs on the veranda outside the block of rooms of which seventeen was the centre, and drawing one close to the door,

Miles calmly sat down and lit a cigarette. Presently a bearer crossed to the room from the kitchens with a dish of something in his hands. The American intercepted him.

'Say, bearer,' he asked, 'is Miss sahib in bed?'

The waiter indicated that she was, and disappeared within.

'I guess we've got a long wait,' said Miles.

'That bearer will probably tell her we are waiting,' said Cousins, 'and describe you, sir.'

'Yes; darn it! Therefore it'll be best if I send in my card right now. Is there another way out, do you think?' he asked Spink.

'Bound to be, sir, through the bathroom, but that wouldn't help her much. I know this place. There is a high brick wall behind the block, and only a narrow passage. If she makes her way along that, in either direction, she's bound to emerge into our view.'

'Good!'

At that moment the waiter returned and Miles gave him a card, which he told him – through the medium of Spink, who acted as interpreter – to give to Miss Gregson, and inform her that he would wait until she was ready to receive him.

Olive had been sitting up in bed quietly enjoying her breakfast. Her trip to Lahore had cost her nothing, she had had a very ample revenge for the way Hugh Shannon had turned her down on board ship, and, in addition, she had received a thousand rupees. The world appeared a very bright place to her that morning, and now all she had to do was to get up casually, bath and dress, and catch the train for beautiful Bangalore. A nuisance that journey, of course, but it was quite worth it considering everything. She stretched herself luxuriously as the waiter entered with the second course. Then came rather a jarring note to her enjoyment.

'There is a sahib waiting to see you, Miss sahib,' announced the bearer, as he laid down the dish on the bedside table.

She stopped stretching, and stared at him.

'A sahib!' she exclaimed. 'Who?'

'He did not tell me. He asked if you were in bed. There are two other sahibs with him I think.'

For a moment a dreadful fear entered Olive's mind. Three men! Perhaps Shannon, Miles and the valet! Then she assured herself that it could not be – they would think she was at the Royal, not here. It must be Novar, Rahtz and Hudson, although none of them had come to the hotel before – Hudson in fact had dropped her outside the gates when he had brought her from Novar's bungalow, as though he had no intention of being seen on the hotel premises with her.

'What is the sahib, who spoke to you, like?' she asked in rather a shaky voice.

'He is tall, I think, although of that I could not be certain, as he was sitting and he wears glasses!'

She went pale. The description certainly fitted Miles.

'I cannot see anyone,' she said nervously. 'I – I'm not dressed.'

The bearer inclined his head, and went out. Presently he was back, and handed her a card.

'The sahib says he will wait until you are ready to see him,' he told her.

She took the piece of pasteboard in trembling fingers. One glance was sufficient. She dropped it on the bed, a half-stifled groan issuing from her lips.

'Tell the sahib,' she said, 'that I will see him in an hour.'

By that time, she thought, she would be able to get away from the hotel. He would be sure not to wait. She had lost all interest in her breakfast now, her appetite had completely deserted her, and as soon as the waiter had left the room, she jumped out of bed and ran into the bathroom bent on making a hasty toilet, and getting away as soon as possible. How on earth, she wondered, had they found out where she was!

Miles received the message with a smile, and getting up he winked at the others, and led the way through the hotel gates and across the road to where a group of shady trees enabled them to conceal themselves and watch the door of Miss Gregson's room.

'I guess we shan't have to wait half an hour after all,' said the American. 'She'll be out of that room, and make for the station in a remarkably short space of time.'

Cousins laughed, and Spink grinned.

'This business is quite interesting,' said the latter. 'I only hope that it won't go wrong, and put me in the soup.'

'There's no danger of that,' said Cousins. 'Once Mr Miles talks to her, she'll come to earth – *voila tout!*'

'I reckon that as soon as she's dressed,' said the American, 'she'll hop over to the office and pay her bill to save time, come back, grab her bag and beat it.'

He proved to be a true prophet. In less than a quarter of an hour Miss Gregson came from her rooms cautiously, glanced anxiously about, then made for the office.

'Now, boys,' said Miles. 'This is where I get busy. I'm going to wait in her room. If you'll just saunter up after she has returned, Spink, so that I can show her your uniform if necessary, everything will be bully.'

Without waiting for a reply he walked rapidly back into the hotel compound, and coolly entered number seventeen. Almost every bedroom in the Northern India Hotel has a tiny anteroom leading into it. These apartments can hardly be described as sitting rooms as they are too small, and only contain a couple of chairs and a table. Miles found himself in Miss Gregson's, and selecting a chair, sat down and placed his topee on the floor beside him.

In the meanwhile Olive had entered the office

and demanded her bill, explaining that she was in a hurry to get away. The under-manager, who also acted as cashier, leisurely turned over the books, and carefully selecting a pen, started to make out the account as though he knew not the meaning of the word 'hurry'. Miss Gregson watched him, her irritability mounting every minute.

'Oh, for goodness' sake,' she exclaimed impatiently, and vulgarly, 'buck up!'

He looked at her in surprise, then smiled in a manner that irritated her the more.

'Did you see your friends, Mees?' he asked. 'They was so anxious to see you that they came here first at soon after half past seven!'

She bit her lip.

'Yes, I – I saw them,' she said untruthfully.

'I know the poleece sergeant werry well!' he said, and bent once more to his task.

She gasped. Police sergeant! What had he come for! Olive Gregson began to wish that she had never left Bangalore. Presently the little Goanese rose, and handed her the bill with a bow. She paid it mechanically, took the receipt and change, and hurried back to her rooms. She pulled aside the curtain and entered. The next moment she reeled against the door post.

A familiar figure rose from a chair and bowed to her courteously.

'Good morning, Miss Olive,' said Miles.

For a moment she could not speak, then:

'Didn't you get my message?' she demanded.

'I sure did, but it occurred to me that the bearer had made a mistake, and I guess I was right!'

'How dare you enter a lady's rooms without permission?'

He looked round with a puzzled air.

'Gee!' he said apologetically. 'I thought these rooms were yours.'

She went crimson.

'Have you come here to insult me?' she asked angrily.

'Not on your life! I came to have a little talk.' He pushed a chair forward. 'Sit down, and let us be comfortable about it.'

'No!'

He shrugged his shoulders.

'Just as you like, of course, Miss Olive.'

'What do you want with me?'

'Well, that's a mighty strange question. Last night you demanded, before a whole host of folks, that Captain Shannon should make arrangements to marry you. I reckon that as I am his friend, and the obvious best man, it is naturally my duty to make those arrangements.'

She stared at him in amazement.

'What do you mean?' she asked.

'I just can't see why you ask a question like that!'

'Do you mean to say that he is prepared to marry me?'

'Well, wasn't that your ultimatum?' He smiled.

She did not like that smile; it sent a cold shiver down her back. For a moment she hesitated, then:

'I've changed my mind,' she said.

He looked at her reproachfully.

'A woman can't make the statements you did before a crowd, demand restitution from a man who has wronged her, and then change her mind.'

'Well, I have!' she said defiantly.

'Why?'

'That's my business!'

'I guess I've made it mine!' He still spoke in the same careless voice, but there was a subtle difference in the tone. He leant towards her. 'Perhaps it's because you told a whole heap of lies last night?' he suggested.

She stamped her foot.

'I suppose you think you're funny,' she said. 'Well, I don't, and the sooner you clear out the better I'll be pleased.'

'I'll clear out, Miss Olive, when you have decided to take back publicly all you said last night.'

She laughed in a shrill voice.

'You'll wait here a long time!' she said.

'No; I don't think so.'

He moved a little closer to her, and she shrank back.

'Don't you dare touch me!' she cried.

'I've no intention of touching you,' he said. 'I came here hoping to fix this little matter without any trouble, but I guess I've got to talk almighty plainly. You did an unforgivable thing last night. You tried to ruin the character of a man who has never done you any harm; you hurt his sister grievously, and she's a girl whose shoes you aren't fit to black. I told you what you were last night and I repeat it again. Now you'll just come right along with me to the Club and tell the Secretary the whole darn truth.'

She shook with rage.

'How dare you speak to me like this,' she almost shouted. 'You're nothing but a brute and a bully, and I'm not afraid of you!'

A gleam came into his eyes, which in spite of her anger frightened her.

'Your opinion of me doesn't hurt me any. I've said what you're going to do, and you're going to do it, or else—'

'Or else what?'

'I have means which will persuade you!'

There was a tense silence for a minute or two. Then she shrugged her shoulders; and walked towards the bedroom. He barred the way.

'No, you don't!' he said.

'Will you let me pass!' she demanded furiously. 'I have a train to catch, and I want to get my things.'

'It's almighty strange that you have a train to catch, when you were supposed to be waiting for Shannon to make arrangements to marry you!'

'I told you that I have changed my mind!'

'You mean to say that you came here fully intending to make him marry you?'

'Yes!'

'That's why you told him you were staying at a

hotel which you have never visited, I suppose?' he said sarcastically.

'I – I intended to change to the Royal today!'

'Golly!' he ejaculated. 'You're a mighty fine liar!'

She glared at him fiercely.

'Let me pass!' she said.

He made no movement.

'I suppose you'll say next that you are in reality in the condition you said you were before those people,' he went on inexorably, 'and that Shannon has really ruined you?'

'You utter brute!' she stormed.

'Not a bit!' he replied calmly. 'I only want to be sure. Are you?'

For answer she slapped his face.

'Now perhaps you'll let me go!' she shouted.

'Not a chance in Hades,' he said. 'But I guess it's time this little affair was brought to a close. God knows why you did this thing. Of course there was somebody behind you who paid you well, but that doesn't interest me.'

She looked startled and drew back.

'What – what do you mean?' she stammered. 'Hugh Shannon treated me badly, and I meant to have my own back – that's all!'

'You know darn well that is not all,' he said, 'and you also know that Hugh Shannon did not treat you badly. But I'm getting mighty sick of all this tongue music. I ask you once again – Are you coming with me to the Secretary of the Club to tell him the truth?'

'I am not!' she replied defiantly.

'Then I've got to be a little unpleasant!'

He strode to the door, and lifted the curtain. She watched, a look of fear in her eyes. Just outside a European policeman was standing. He stepped forward.

'Do you want me, sir?' he asked.

'Not for a moment or two, I guess,' he answered, then dropped the curtain and looked at her.

She had gone as pale as death, and stood where she was, trembling. Then her nerve broke down, she ran to him and clutched his arm.

'What is he there for?' she cried. 'What does he want?'

'He wants you!'

'But they can't arrest me for – for what I said!'

'Of course that depends upon Shannon. He certainly can bring an action for slander. But this policeman is here for a much more serious reason!'

'But I've done nothing – nothing!'

He pushed her into a chair, and stood looking down sternly at her.

'You trumped up a beastly, underhanded, false charge against Shannon, and I guess I can fight you with the same weapons you used against him.'

She was nervously biting her handkerchief, and tearing it to pieces in her agitation.

'It's almighty easy to frame a charge, if one wants to. I'll tell you what is in store for you, Miss Gregson, if you don't do what I wish. You will be arrested for passing dud notes!'

'What?' she gasped.

'There have been a whole crowd of spurious notes put into circulation during the last four days, which coincides with the time you have been in Lahore. That policeman outside is waiting to search you and your belongings and arrest you!'

She was terror-stricken.

'But I haven't passed the notes! You know I haven't!' she almost sobbed.

'That remains to be seen. You have a considerable amount of money in your possession, which you will have to account for, and when you are searched there will be found several bad notes.'

She started from her chair, and in her frenzy she clutched the lapels of his jacket and strove to shake him.

'You're doing this to ruin me – you know I have not brought bad notes into Lahore. You're—Oh, you're a devil!' she ended and sank back into the chair sobbing.

'Say, Miss Gregson!' said the American gently. 'I don't want to hurt you any, but I want justice done to Shannon. If you will come with me to the Club and confess everything, why, I'll send that policeman about his business, and tell him you're not the person he wants.'

She cried bitterly, and Miles watched her with a pained expression on his face. At length she looked up.

'I'll – I'll do anything you wish!' she sobbed.

'I only want you to tell the truth!' he said, an immense relief in his voice.

He dabbed his forehead with his handkerchief.

'Gee!' he murmured to himself. 'Some job!'

He went to the door, hesitated, then came back to her.

'If I send the cop away,' he said, 'can I rely upon you to go through with what I've asked you to do? If I can't I'll take him with us.'

She turned to him a face full of misery, her cheeks wet with crying, and her eyes in a hopeless mess with the mixture of tears and black cosmétique.

'Please, please send him away!' she implored.

He nodded and going outside spoke to the two men.

'I guess everything's all right,' he said. 'There's no necessity for you to stay, Spink.'

The policeman sighed with relief.

'I'm glad to hear that, sir,' he said. 'I didn't like the job, though I wanted to help in clearing up the matter.' He shook his head with disgust. 'It was a scandalous business,' he went on. 'What a woman!'

He shook hands with Cousins, saluted Miles and turned away.

'Jerry,' said the American, 'call a taxi, will you? There's a rank somewhere handy.'

With a nod Cousins went off to do his bidding, and Miles returned to Miss Gregson. He found her still sitting in the chair, the picture of dejection.

'Say, Miss Olive,' he said kindly, 'I'm sorry to have been so darned hard, but I guess it couldn't be helped. Just run along and wash away the sorrow from your face. I've got a taxi coming right along!'

Without a word she went.

CHAPTER 20

IN WHICH HUDSON HAS A SHOCK

Miles threw himself into a chair and, taking out a cigar, he carefully lit it.

A car drew up outside and there was a knock on the door.

'Come right along in!' invited the American.

Cousins looked in.

'The taxi's here, sir!' he announced.

The other grinned broadly.

'I shall be glad when we get somewhere where I can punch your darned head, Jerry,' he whispered cheerfully.

'Why should you want to interfere with my devoted cranium?' asked the pseudo valet.

'Well, just because I'm sick of all the respect and deference you've been unloading on to me this morning. You're too almighty like the real thing when you get busy.'

'Pshaw!' muttered the other in disgust. 'You're jealous!'

He disappeared, and a few minutes later Miss Gregson returned with all the effects of the tears cleared away.

'I'm ready!' she said in a subdued voice.

He bowed and lifted the curtain aside for her to go out. Cousins opened the door of the car, standing respectfully with his topee in his right hand.

'I beg your pardon, sir,' he said, before closing the door again, 'but I understand that the lady will be leaving for Bangalore today. As the train goes out at twelve forty-five, sir, there is only an hour and ten minutes left. Might I suggest that we take the luggage with us, and then the lady could be driven straight to the station after – er—' He paused and coughed discreetly.

'A very good notion, Cousins, my man!' replied the American, putting emphasis on the 'my man'. 'Don't you think so, Miss Olive?' he asked.

She nodded.

'There are two suitcases,' she murmured, almost inaudibly.

The luggage was stowed in the car, and three or four servants appeared with many salaams on the lookout for tips. Miss Gregson started to open her handbag, but Miles stopped her.

'Cousins, tip those fellows!' he ordered in lordly fashion.

The little man's eyes gleamed as he obeyed.

There was hardly a word spoken as the car ran rapidly to the Club. Miles once asked his companion if she would tell him who was behind her in the plot to ruin Shannon, but she refused to say.

'Well,' he said. 'It doesn't matter, though I think I know!'

She looked questioningly at him, but he said

no more. Arrived at the Club, he immediately entered the secretary's office. A clerk gazed at him inquiringly.

'Where's the secretary?' asked the American bluntly. 'I've a whole heap to say to him.'

'I regret he is engaged, sare,' replied the clerk smoothly. 'Is there some message, please?'

'I can't help whether he's engaged, or not. I've got to see him right now.'

'But, sare, there is an emergency meeting being held!'

'Where?'

'In the committee room!'

'I'll go right along!' said Miles.

He knew where the room in question was, and he went straight to it followed by the protesting clerk. The door was shut, and a murmur of voices reached him from within. He knocked loudly, and after a second or so the door was opened. The secretary himself looked out and, seeing Miles, frowned.

'I cannot see you now,' he said, 'there is a meeting—'

'Say, just answer one question! Has this meeting got anything to do with Captain Shannon, and the affair last night?'

'Really, Mr Miles, I do not see—' began the other indignantly.

'I'm sorry to butt in, but it's on account of that business that I'm here, so now please answer my question.'

'Well, yes it is!'

'Excuse me!' said Miles, and pushed past him into the room.

There were five important members of the Committee seated round the table, and they looked up with annoyed surprise at his intrusion.

'I've got to apologise, gentlemen,' said the American, bowing, 'but I understand you are discussing what happened last night, probably with a view to blackballing Captain Shannon.'

A stern, military-looking man, obviously the chairman, rose angrily to his feet.

'This is most unwarrantable, sir,' he said. 'How dare you—'

Miles held up his hand.

'I have the lady in question with me. She wishes to make a statement!'

His announcement caused a stir.

'I do not see in what way a statement from her can interest us,' said the chairman pompously.

'You will find that it does!' was the reply. 'May I bring her along?'

The military man sat down, and there was a hurried interchange of views, then he looked up.

'This is most unusual,' he said, 'but we will give her five minutes.'

Miles went back to the car, and asked Miss Gregson to accompany him. He ushered her into the presence of the Committee, who looked at her curiously. She was given a seat.

'I understand, Madam,' said the chairman, 'that you wish to make a certain statement.'

'I do!' she said in a low voice, and hesitated.

'We are prepared to hear it!'

Then, with several pauses, she told her story. To Miles' surprise she did not spare herself, and went through the ordeal as though determined to make amends. She even told how she had done all in her power to get Shannon to propose marriage to her on board ship, and when she failed had attempted to coerce him. It was a very sordid tale and most of the men there looked at her with disgust long before she had finished. She made no mention of anybody else being concerned with her in the plot to ruin Hugh.

'That is all!' she ended. 'Mr Miles has shown me the awful thing I was doing. I am very sorry now.'

A few questions were asked, then she was bowed coldly out of the room. The chairman detained Miles as he was about to follow her, and held out his hand.

'Mr Miles,' he said, 'I thank you on behalf of the Committee and myself for bringing that woman here. We might have done an irreparable wrong to Captain Shannon. Will you convey to him our deep sympathy for what happened last night and assure him that everything will be done to clear the scandal from his name?'

'Sure!' said the American, and shook hands warmly with every member of the Committee.

On the way to the station he turned to Miss Gregson.

'It was fine of you to go through with it like you did, Miss Olive,' he said.

'I only did what was right,' she murmured. 'You have shown me what a horrible creature I am.'

'Were!' he remarked. 'That's all over now, and you've proved yourself a darn fine girl, believe me!'

He saw her into her compartment in the train and bought her some magazines. Hardly a word was spoken until the time of departure drew near, then:

'Mr Miles,' she said confusedly, 'there were other people behind me in – in this—'

'I know that,' he said.

She did not heed the interruption.

'I cannot tell you who they were, but – but they paid me some money to do it. Will you take the money and give it to any charity you like!'

She fumbled in her bag. He caught her hand.

'That's fine of you,' he said, 'but you keep it. It'll make up for what you've had to suffer today.'

'I'm glad I've had to suffer,' she said. 'It has taught me a lesson I'll never forget. Would you mind asking Captain Shannon and his sister if they will try to forgive me?'

'Rather!' he said enthusiastically. 'And I guess they will.' He shook hands with the girl.

The train began to move, and at that moment Hudson came hurriedly along, searching in the carriages as he came. He did not notice them until he was almost upon them when he looked dumbfounded and stopped in his tracks, his face going

264

a sickly white. Miss Gregson gasped, but said nothing. Miles had watched Hudson's advent with a grim smile.

'I won't forget your messages, Miss Olive,' he murmured. 'Goodbye!'

Then turning to Hudson, he took him by the arm.

'Say, this is a surprise,' he said. 'Have you come to see anybody off?'

Hudson murmured something inarticulate, and the American's smile became grimmer than ever. He glanced round in the direction of the receding train once more, and waved his topee to Miss Gregson, who was leaning out of her window, then, looking the civil servant straight in the face:

'Gee!' he remarked. 'You look mighty queer, Hudson. Come right along and split a bottle of beer with me!'

Hudson had received a very bad shock, and he permitted Miles to lead him towards the refreshment rooms, almost as though he were bereft of the power either to resist or acquiesce. Once seated at a table, however, he made a big effort to pull himself together; he even succeeded in producing an imitation of a smile.

'I hardly realised where you were bringing me!' he said. 'I suddenly became faint! Very stupid of me, of course, but I'm not usually afflicted in that way.'

'You looked pretty seedy,' said Miles. 'Will you have a beer, or do you prefer something less plebian?'

'Beer will suit me admirably, thanks!'

The American turned and gave an order to a waiter. While he was thus engaged, the other studied him surreptitiously, wondering, with a great unease, how he had been present to see Olive Gregson off, and if he had learnt anything from her of harm to himself and his fellow conspirators. Miles turned suddenly and noticed the anxious look in Hudson's eyes. He guessed what was passing in his mind, and looked forward to an amusing ten minutes.

'Say,' he said, 'you look better already!'

'Oh, I'm all right now!' replied Hudson shortly.

'Of course, I'm a bit of a fool sometimes,' remarked Miles apologetically, 'but when you turned up and suddenly looked so bad, I thought for a moment that you were upset at seeing me, or Miss Gregson!'

Hudson laughed unsteadily.

'How absurd!' he said. 'Why should I be?'

'Darned if I know,' smiled the American, 'but I often get fool notions in my head. I daresay it's because I'm not over supplied with grey matter.'

'As a matter of fact I came to see a friend off, and was looking for him, when that fainting attack came over me!'

The beer arrived and both took a long drink before saying any more. Hudson seemed to regain his faculties entirely; the colour returned to his face, and he smiled across the table at his companion.

'I say,' he said, 'that was a pretty beastly affair last night at the Club, wasn't it?'

'Damnable!' agreed Miles.

'I was astounded! I can't say I ever liked Shannon, but I certainly didn't think he was that sort.'

'I guess not!' murmured Miles. This was sheer enjoyment to him, and he took another drink in appreciation of what was to come.

'What puzzles me,' went on Hudson, 'is to find you, his friend, here at the station seeing Miss Gregson off, and apparently on the best of terms with her.'

'Well, there's nothing extraordinary in that. Miss Olive and I have a great understanding of each other.'

'But why is she leaving Lahore? I thought she had come to demand reparation from Shannon for the wrong he had done her?'

'And you think it looks mighty queer her beating it so suddenly?'

'Well, it is, isn't it? And especially with you to see her go!' He leant forward. 'Has Shannon bought her off?' he asked.

A gleam of anger came into Miles' eyes, but was gone immediately.

'Shannon does not do things like that,' he said quietly. 'Besides there was no need!'

'What do you mean?'

'She and I had a heart-to-heart talk this morning at her hotel and—'

'Her hotel!' exclaimed Hudson in sudden

consternation. 'How did you know where to find her?'

Miles looked at him with an expression of amiable surprise.

'Why,' he answered gently, 'she told us last night that she was going to the Royal Hotel.'

'But she wasn't there!' said the surprised Hudson.

'How do you know?' snapped the American, and the other realised what a bad mistake he had made.

'I – I—' he stammered in confusion. 'I can't for the moment recall how I heard, but—'

He stopped, utterly at a loss what to say. Apparently Miles was not interested for he went on:

'Shannon and I had a talk last night, and I told him to leave everything to me. She wasn't staying at the Royal as you say, but I found her at the Northern India getting ready to beat it. When I had talked to her for half an hour like a granddad, she saw the error of her ways. We went right along to the Club; there was an emergency meeting on, and I'm darned if she didn't butt in, and tell them the truth. My! They were astonished!'

Hudson jumped to his feet, and his face was as pale as death.

'What!' he almost shouted.

'Don't get excited! It's nice of you to be pleased like this – I was mighty glad myself.'

The civil servant sank back into his chair.

'What did she say?' he gasped.

'She told the whole darn story!'

His companion looked a pitiable sight, but Miles did not appear to notice his condition.

'Do you mean to say,' gasped Hudson, 'that she did that of her own accord?'

'Sure! She turned out to be quite a fine little girl in the end. I brought her to the station, and, as you know, saw her off. Say, you won't guess what she wanted to do!'

'What?' asked the abject-looking specimen of humanity before him, licking his dry lips.

'There was someone behind her in this plot – Why, man, I guess you look almighty queer again! Have some brandy!'

'No, no! Go on!'

'Well, as I was saying, there was someone behind her who had given her a whole heap of money, and she wanted me to take it and give it away to charity! Now wasn't that mighty fine of her?'

'Who – who was behind her?'

Miles purposely took a long drink, watching the other over the rim of his glass. Then he leant back in his chair with a sigh of regret.

'I couldn't get her to tell me that!' he said.

An expression of the utmost relief replaced the terror-stricken look on Hudson's face. He sank back.

'I think I will have that brandy,' he murmured. 'I do feel pretty bad!'

The brandy was forthcoming, and he gulped down the neat spirit without a pause. Then he tried to smile.

'Do you feel better?' inquired Miles, who looked the picture of anxiety.

'Much, thanks! I – I must be off, if you'll excuse me!' He rose unsteadily to his feet.

'I had better come with you in case you're taken bad again,' said the American.

'Not at all! I'm quite all right now. Can't understand what has happened to me this morning!'

Miles thought he could, but did not say so.

'I'll tell Shannon how pleased you are that the scandal has been cleared from his name,' he said pleasantly.

'No; please don't! I'd much rather you didn't,' said Hudson earnestly. 'Shannon hasn't much regard for me. He – he might resent it. Goodbye!'

He made his way out of the refreshment rooms, and as soon as he had gone Miles lay back in his chair and laughed so loudly that the waiters in the vicinity thought he had gone mad. Presently he called for his bill and, having paid it, wandered off to the entrance of the great bare station, where Cousins was still waiting for him with the car. The little man wore a look of pain on his usually cheerful face.

'What on earth have you been doing all this time?' he asked resentfully.

'Jerry, I've been having a dandy time,' chuckled Miles.

'Stop grinning like a Cheshire cat, and tell me the joke!'

'No time now, my son; I'm beginning to feel sadly in want of some eats!'

270

'Look here—' began Cousins.

The other slapped him on the back.

'Home, James!' he said.

The ideal valet climbed into the seat beside the driver with a frown on his face, which promised a searching inquiry later.

'*Quantum mutatus ab illo*!' he muttered.

'Oh, say!' said Miles suddenly. 'I left a tonga at the Northern India – I forgot all about it. Better drive there first. I owe the driver a pony!'

CHAPTER 21

HIS EXCELLENCY THE GOVERNOR

When eventually Miles and Cousins reached the bungalow, they found Joan eagerly awaiting them on the veranda.

'Well?' she asked, and at the sight of Miles' beaming face the look of trouble began to leave her own.

'Has Hugh come back yet?' he inquired.

'Yes; he came home ages ago. They know everything at the College and he was asked to resign, but he refused. He is in an awful state about it!'

'Well, Miss Joan, just you go right along to him and tell him that Olive Gregson has been before an emergency committee at the Club, and confessed everything; that I have seen her leave for Bangalore, and that she has asked me to request you and your brother to forgive her.'

'Oh, Oscar!' she cried, her eyes shining with such happiness that Cousins felt an uncomfortable lump in his throat. 'Is this really true?'

'Sure! And not only that, but the chairman of the Club has asked me to convey his sympathies, and those of the other committeemen to Hugh, and to assure him that everything will be done to clear the scandal from his name.'

'Oscar, you dear!' she cried, and ran off to tell Hugh the good news.

Cousins looked at Miles in perplexity.

'Good heavens!' he exclaimed. 'Can it be possible that a lean, ugly, grinning specimen of what a man might come to, like you, has found his way into that dear girl's heart!'

'Gee! If only I could think so!' sighed the American.

'Do you mean to say—?'

'I just mean to say that I would sell my soul for Joan!'

Cousins held out his hand.

'I wish you luck, old chap. You make sentiment rise in my breast, and I can almost feel the weight of years rolling away from my shoulders. I also love Miss Shannon!'

'You what?' demanded Miles.

'As a father, of course,' said the little man hastily; 'though I must confess that even I, in spite of all the cold, calculating reason that inhabits my cranium, am capable of feeling *la grande passion*. "A warmth within the breast would melt The freezing reason's colder part, And, like a man in wrath the heart, Stood up and answered 'I have felt'."'

Hugh was sitting moodily on the bed, when Joan burst into his room, her face all aglow with delight. She repeated what Miles had told her without stopping for breath. He started up and caught her by the shoulders.

'What is this?' he demanded.

She told him all over again, and then threw her arms round him and kissed him.

'Oh, Hugh!' she said. 'I am so happy!'

He was a different man as he returned her caress.

'By Jove!' he said. 'How splendid!'

'And it's all due to Oscar – every bit of it!' she cried.

He looked at her and smiled.

'Oscar!' he remarked. 'Since when—?'

She blushed and hurried from the room.

For a few minutes he stood looking after her, and then he followed. He found Miles explaining to Cousins and Joan how careful one should be in mixing a cocktail and, without regard for cocktails or the interested listeners, he clasped the American's hand and interrupted him.

'Miles!' he said, with deep gratitude in his voice, 'I'm a rotten hand at expressing my feelings, but—'

'Shucks!' interrupted the other. 'Don't say anything more about it! Besides, Jerry here had as much to do with it as I!'

Cousins got behind a table.

'If you do the gratitude stunt to me,' he threatened, 'I'll burst into tears! Go away! Anyhow the man's a confirmed liar – I had nothing to do with it, except act the ideal valet as usual. And a pretty time I've had,' he complained.

Tiffin was late that day. The bearers and cook became plaintive over the fact that the viands were getting cold. But no one heeded them. Miles told the whole story of the morning's doings right up

274

to the appearance and subsequent torture of Hudson. The laughter was unrestrained as the American described how he had baited the civil servant, and Cousins magnanimously forgave the narrator for the long wait he had had while the process was going on.

A happy party sat down to luncheon, the only jarring note being the necessary absence of Cousins from the table. The cold food tasted delicious to them all, and they declared that they had seldom enjoyed a meal more. They discussed the change in Olive Gregson at great length, and Joan decided that, if she could only discover her address, she would write and tell her that everything was forgiven and forgotten, and thank her for what she had done.

'Say,' put in the American, 'I can make a good effort at remembering the address. She told me when I first met her on the way from Bombay to Port Said!'

'Splendid!' cried Joan and Hugh together.

A few minutes before six that evening Shannon drove away from the house and made a leisurely tour of the Lawrence Gardens, all the time watching through the mirror attached to the windscreen to see if he were followed. He soon decided that there was no doubt about it as, a hundred yards or so behind, a large touring car glided along in his wake, slowing down and accelerating when he did. He smiled to himself.

'Clumsy!' he murmured.

Entering on to a circular road, running round the cricket ground, he suddenly increased his speed, but as soon as he got among a grove of trees which hid him from sight, he pulled up dead, and waited at the side of the road with his engine running. Almost immediately the big car tore round the corner; there was a jarring of brakes, and it stopped almost alongside. Hugh grinned at the success of his manoeuvre, and looked curiously at the two occupants of the other car, both of them very uninteresting-looking Indians wearing bright coloured turbans. They were obviously surprised, and consulted hastily together then one got out and lifting up the bonnet proceeded to make a great show of examining the engine. Hugh puffed placidly at his pipe, and watched the performance.

'Something gone wrong?' he inquired presently.

The driver looked at him uneasily, but the other man glanced round.

'It missing one cylinder, sahib!' he said.

Hugh got out of his car and joined him.

'Which one?' he asked.

'I think this one!' replied the other.

'Better take out the sparking plug and have a look at it,' said Hugh casually.

The man shook his head.

'It not matter, sahib,' he remarked uneasily.

'Well, of course, that's up to you, but I should. By the way,' he added, 'you're right in the way here. If another car comes round the corner there'll be an accident!'

He helped the other man to push the vehicle in front of his own.

'Now, let us have a look at that plug!' he said in an authoritative voice.

Apparently the fact that their car was directly in front of his made the two Indians feel that he could not very well get away from them, for they produced a spanner and went through the performance of taking off the sparking plug and examining it. Hugh took it into his own hand and looked at it critically.

'There doesn't seem to be much wrong with it,' he said. 'Try the next!'

That also was unscrewed, and Hugh held them both.

'This one is perfectly all right!' he said. 'We had better look at the lot. Well, it's no use letting my engine go on wasting petrol. I'll shut it off, and assist you to put this matter right!'

He took off his coat as he spoke to lend colour to the remark that he would help, then strolling back to his car, the two plugs still in his hand, he threw the coat in, and suddenly jumped in himself. He put the car into gear, and swerved by the other. There was a shout of fury from the two men, and Hugh smiled.

'Catch!' he cried, and threw the sparking plugs towards them.

In a moment he had swung round the bend and out of sight, and a few minutes later entered the main gates of Government House.

'What absolute fools!' he laughed, as he drove up the beautiful avenue that led to the Governor's residence.

He found the Deputy Commissioner awaiting him on the terrace in front of the house. Hugh rather expected a cold welcome, considering that Rainer had been present at the incident of the night before. Instead he received a very warm greeting from the alert, sharp-featured man upon whose tact and ability the peace of Lahore and district depended to such a great extent.

'Sorry I'm late, sir,' said Hugh, 'but as I expected, I was followed, and it took me some time to trick my shadowers.'

Rainer looked interested.

'Of course I'm eager to hear all about it,' said he, 'but His Excellency will be waiting.'

They sent their names in by a secretary, who returned almost immediately and ushered them into a large, softly carpeted and quietly furnished room where Sir Reginald Scott sat before a desk writing. He threw down his pen and rose as they entered.

The Governor was over six feet in height, and powerfully built. His features were cast in a large mould, his complexion was as fresh as that of a man on the very threshold of life. His mouth was humorous, but at the same time incisive, and he possessed a pair of kindly grey eyes, which nevertheless suggested great strength of character. He shook hands with Rainer, then turned to Hugh.

'I don't think you have ever met Captain Shannon, sir,' said the former.

'No!' replied His Excellency. He held out his hand. 'I am glad to make your acquaintance, Captain Shannon,' he said.

He invited them to be seated and, pulling round the chair at his desk, sat down facing them.

'If you would care to smoke, gentlemen,' he said, 'you will find cigars and cigarettes on that table. I prefer a pipe.'

Hugh asked and obtained permission to smoke his own pipe, whilst Rainer helped himself to a cigar.

'Before we discuss the matter which brought you here, Captain Shannon,' went on Sir Reginald, 'there is a certain question I wish to ask you. I heard, in quite a roundabout way, that an unsavoury incident occurred at the Club last night which reflects on your honour. Would you mind telling me the facts of that incident?'

'Certainly not, sir,' replied Hugh promptly. 'In fact, I had intended to tell you the whole truth of the matter.'

Rainer looked at him appraisingly.

'If I may be allowed to say a word relative to that affair, sir,' he said to the Governor, 'I happened to be present and saw what took place. I came to the conclusion that there was more behind it than appeared on the surface, and felt perfectly certain that Shannon was the victim of a vile plot.'

His Excellency nodded.

Hugh at once plunged into an account of

Miss Gregson's accusations, and then went on to tell how Miles had made her confess that the whole thing was a fabrication. Both the Governor and the Commissioner laughed heartily over the account of the American's busy morning.

'I am very glad,' said Sir Reginald, 'very glad indeed that the matter has been put right so promptly. And who do you think these people are who were so obviously behind the woman?'

'They are the men whom we are watching, sir,' replied Hugh.

'Indeed! Then you have actually discovered something with reference to the real object of your visit to India?'

'We have discovered a most amazing plot, sir,' replied Hugh quietly.

'Before you go into that, Shannon, I must tell you that I received a communication from the India Office in which I was informed that certain things had been discovered which pointed to the fact that there was a Russian plot against India, and that Lahore was apparently the centre of activity. I also had a letter from Sir Leonard Wallace telling me of the real reason for your presence in Lahore. I was greatly surprised, and am naturally eager to know what you have found out.'

'It is a long story, sir,' said Shannon, 'and first it is necessary to let you know that I have with me, presumably as a valet, one of the astutest men in the Intelligence Department. He has already done a considerable amount of first-class work, and I have him to thank, and Miles, for what I know.'

'Miles!' exclaimed His Excellency. 'Do you mean to say that he is also a member of your Department?'

'No, sir! He belongs to the American Secret Service.' He went on to explain how Miles had become associated with Cousins and himself. 'He is absolutely invaluable,' he concluded, 'because he is unsuspected, while Cousins and I are watched from morning to night!'

'I must say you have astonished me,' said the Governor. 'I have seen the gentleman once or twice and it occurred to me that he was merely an American on the lookout for amusement.'

'Most people think that,' smiled Hugh, 'even the very energetic representatives of the Russian Government!'

'Who are they?' demanded Sir Reginald, and Rainer leant forward.

'One is a man named Kamper, who was deported from England, and who, I think, followed me out here. His position is rather mysterious. The others you know by name. They are Novar, of the firm of Novar and Company; Rahtz, the Principal of Mozang College, and—'

His Excellency sat back and looked dumbfounded; Rainer started to his feet.

'Are you absolutely certain of this?' demanded the former.

'Absolutely, sir!'

Sir Reginald's face became stern.

'Who else?' he asked.

'Hudson of the Secretariat!'

'What!' gasped the Governor. 'Why, he is a man in whom I have always put the greatest reliance! You must be mistaken!'

Hugh shook his head.

'There is no mistake, sir,' he said emphatically.

The Deputy Commissioner clutched the back of his chair like a man who was not sure whether he was dreaming or not.

'But,' he stammered, 'Hudson is an Englishman!'

'He appears to be,' said Hugh sternly; 'I sincerely hope that he turns out to be something else.'

His Excellency rose from his chair, and for a few minutes paced up and down the room. Then he sat down again.

'I think you had better tell us everything, Captain Shannon,' he said.

Hugh told him all that he and his companions had discovered. His auditors listened with growing amazement and, when eventually he had finished, there was a tense silence for several minutes. At last the Governor knocked out the ashes of his pipe.

'The whole thing sounds like part of a particularly imaginative novel,' he remarked. 'And you have actually sent those two letters home?'

'Yes, sir!'

'Well, it looks, Shannon, as though you and your companions have saved Great Britain from disaster. God only knows what would have happened if we had never known these things. Of course the home Government will deal with the matter as soon as it is in a position to act. What a blow for the League of Nations and our hopes of disarmament!'

'That meeting on December the twenty-first will be interesting,' remarked the Deputy Commissioner.

'I shall be there!' said Hugh quietly.

'How are you going to manage it?' queried His Excellency.

'I don't know yet,' was the reply; 'but it is absolutely essential that I should be present. In fact what action Great Britain takes will depend upon a complete report of the meeting being placed before the Government.'

Sir Reginald smiled.

'Now that I know these things,' he said, 'it is going to be a difficult matter to remain inactive. I shall feel like an idler, who watches while great stakes are being played for. A tremendous responsibility rests on your shoulders, Shannon!'

'I realise that, sir, but with Cousins and Miles to share the work with me, I have no fear of the result. Of course, you and Mr Rainer will be careful to let no suspicion reach either Rahtz, Novar, or Hudson that you are aware of anything?'

'Certainly not,' said His Excellency.

Rainer sighed.

'I wish I could arrest the three of them now,' he said.

'Such a thing would be ridiculous at the present juncture,' said Hugh. 'They have no idea yet that

I suspect them, and when they find out, if they do—' He paused and smiled grimly.

'Did you say they are watching you?' said the Governor.

'Every movement, sir!' returned the secret agent. 'But they are watching me because they know why I am in India. At present they haven't the vaguest idea that I have discovered anything.'

'You will keep me well posted about events?' asked the Governor.

'By all means, sir!'

'And, of course, Rainer will always be ready to supply you with any help.'

The Deputy Commissioner nodded quickly.

'I'm only sorry,' he said, 'that I cannot take a hand now.'

Hugh smiled.

'You'll probably have all the excitement you want before we are finished.'

His Excellency put a few more shrewd questions, during which he and Rainer learnt, much to their amusement, of the way Hugh had tricked his two shadowers in the car. Then the latter took his leave, accompanied by the Commissioner. They stood talking on the terrace for a few minutes before parting.

'I am looking forward to meeting Cousins,' said Rainer. 'It appears to me from what you have told us about him that he is the sort of man one reads about but seldom meets.'

'He is!' smiled Hugh. 'Cousins is in a class by

himself, and is one of the most brilliant men we have.'

Soon after that they shook hands and Rainer drove away. Hugh gave him a few minutes and then followed. It was quite dark by this time, and it was necessary to have the powerful headlights on. He did not hurry, being too engrossed in his thoughts to desire speed. He turned into Crescent Road, and had reached the gates of his bungalow, when gently he pulled up and at the same time switched off the lights. He had caught the sudden flash of an electric torch at the side of the house, and it gave him cause for reflection. In the first place, the servants were quite likely to use such torches, but their quarters and the kitchen were on the opposite side of the house; secondly, he knew that Miles had a bridge appointment at the Club and that Cousins had expressed his intention of having a glance, as he called it, round Rahtz's house. Therefore only Joan was in. Hugh came to the conclusion that the owner of the torch was someone who had no business there. He got out and, releasing the brakes, quietly pushed the car half way down the drive, and left it there. Then gradually he crept nearer and nearer to the bungalow.

Again came the flash, and he saw that it was focused on the bathroom door of his own rooms. He noticed that the door was being pushed open, then the light disappeared. Hugh entered the bungalow as quietly as he could, crept by the sitting room where Joan was curled up in an

285

armchair reading a book, and reached his own bedroom. The door was open, but the room was hidden by a curtain. He listened intently, but not a sound reached his ears. Taking a small revolver from his pocket he carefully drew aside the curtain, and quietly entered. The room was in pitch blackness and he stood for several minutes wondering where the intruder was. At last, came a slight sound from the direction of the dressing room, and he caught the reflection of a light, which immediately disappeared again. He moved to the electric switch and placed his left hand on it.

A minute went by, then he heard the swish of the curtain which hung between the bedroom and the dressing room, and knew that the man was actually in the room with him. A few seconds later and the electric torch was switched on and the light focused on the floor. It gradually moved higher and round the room. When it had almost reached him, Hugh turned on the lights.

'This is an unexpected visit, Kamper!' he said grimly, as he recognised the other.

A vicious oath came from the startled visitant.

'Put your hands up, and keep 'em up!' commanded Hugh. 'I've been wanting to have a little talk with you for a long time!'

CHAPTER 22

KAMPER APPEARS AND DISAPPEARS

Rather to Shannon's surprise the small, sallow-faced man with the shifty eyes made no effort at resistance. He calmly sat on the bed, and put his torch in his pocket.

'I did not invite you to sit down,' said Hugh.

The other shrugged his shoulders.

'Vell, it can't hurt you if I do, I suppose,' he said, speaking in a heavy nasal voice, which suggested that he was suffering from adenoids.

'I have no objection to your sitting, as a matter of fact, but there are several chairs in the room!'

The Jew rose, sauntered to an easy chair, and threw himself into it with an appearance of utter nonchalance, which annoyed his captor.

'You take things very coolly, my friend!' he said.

'Zere is not a great deal of good doing othervise,' was the reply.

'I'm glad you are so sensible!'

A sneering smile appeared on the Jew's face.

'I vould be very annoyed at this accident, only I happen to know that you vill have to let me go.'

'Indeed! Perhaps you will tell me why?'

'Simply because you vould have to give away the

real reason vhy you are in Lahore, if you handed me over to the police!'

'Oh!' Hugh began to feel vastly amused at the calm insolence of the other. 'You think so, do you? I'm afraid that you are in for an unpleasant shock.'

The Jew smiled unbelievingly.

'Bluff!' he said quietly and calmly.

'No, Mr Kamper, it is not bluff! Quite apart from whether I give myself away or not, and I assure you there is nothing to give away, you seem to forget that I can have you arrested for the very serious crime of housebreaking!'

That appeared to give the man something to think furiously on. He bit his lips, and his shifty little eyes, for the first time, looked at Hugh. What he saw in the latter's face did not seem to reassure him.

'You dare not!' he growled, but in rather a doubtful tone.

'There is no question of daring,' said Hugh firmly, 'and such is my intention! At the same time it may please you to know that what I was and what I am are two entirely different things, and though I am now merely a professor in a college, I have not so far forgotten my old profession as to also forget the connection you had with it. In fact I can and *will*, tell a most interesting story to the authorities here. No; keep your hands up!'

'How can I keep my hands up?' grunted Kamper.

'Getting tired?' inquired Shannon. 'Very well,

stand up, and when I have relieved you of any lethal weapons you have upon you, you may put your hands down.'

The Jew refused to move, and Hugh approached to within a foot of him.

'Stand up!' he snapped. 'I won't have any nonsense and as sure as my name is Shannon, I'll shoot you if you don't do as you're told.'

It takes a man of great courage to refuse to obey an order in the face of a revolver pointed firmly at him, and Kamper was not a man of great courage – in fact like most of his breed he was a coward at heart. Also he knew that Shannon would do as he threatened, a glance into those steel grey eyes assured him of that. He rose to his feet, his hands still held high above his head.

Hugh had no intention of merely feeling for weapons, and so with the revolver pressed against a spot over Kamper's heart, he went thoroughly through the latter's pockets. He found a long stiletto-like knife in a curiously fashioned sheath, the electric torch, a revolver, a few letters written in Russian, some banknotes, and a watch; that was all. But when he removed the watch the Jew made an effort to prevent him, immediately stopped by the pressure on his breast.

'You can put down your hands now!' said Hugh. He sat down on the bed, the watch in his left hand. 'Apparently this is the object you least desired me to have,' he went on; 'therefore worth examining,'

'It is vorth a lot to me,' said Kamper, sullenly, 'It vas a present, and I don't vant to lose it.'

'You're not going to lose it, my friend!'

Hugh opened the back of the watch, and at the same time the Jew made a convulsive leap forward, only to be brought up by the cold touch of the revolver against his head.

'Sit down!' said Shannon sternly. 'If you make a move like that again I'll shoot. You had a very narrow escape then!'

Slowly the fellow slunk back and sank into the chair. Hugh found a folded piece of paper in the back of the watch. With the other's eyes following his movements with a look of hatred, he straightened out the paper, and glanced at it. What he saw there almost made him start with surprise. It was a replica of the drawing on the sheet of paper that Miles had found in Hudson's coat pocket in Bombay, with the addition of three figures written in the centre of the map – just under the eagle and dragon – '8. 21.'

Hugh leant forward.

'What is this?' he asked.

'Can't you see vot it is?' replied Kamper sulkily.

'I wouldn't ask if I could. I recognise a map of India, but what do the eagles and dragons imply?'

'Eagles and dragons, I suppose!'

'It might be to your advantage to answer my question properly,' said Hugh quietly.

'I have answered it. I suppose I can draw eagles and dragons, and lions and tigers, if I vant to!'

'And then put the drawing carefully away in the back of your watch,' remarked Hugh sarcastically. 'I did not know that you were an artist, Kamper!'

'Vell, you know now!'

'I remain unconvinced. This was not drawn by you, my man.'

The Jew glanced quickly at him, then shrugged his shoulders.

'Oh, well, if you won't tell me,' went on Hugh, 'I daresay I can puzzle it out; also the meaning of the figures!'

'Vot figures?' cried Kamper, and started to his feet.

'Ah! So you had forgotten them!' grinned Shannon. 'They must be important, too, I should think from your look of alarm. Oh, well, we're getting on! Are you quite determined not to explain the meaning of this?'

He waved the paper. Kamper looked as though he would have liked to have made a grab at it, but refrained.

'Zere is nothing to explain,' he growled. 'You can tear it up if you like.'

'Of course I can,' laughed Hugh, 'but I won't!' He put it in his pocket. 'Now,' he said; 'I want to know first what you are doing in Lahore; secondly, why you are in my room?'

The Jew maintained a sullen silence in spite of repeated efforts by Hugh to get him to talk. At last the Englishman gave it up.

'As you won't confess,' he said, 'nothing remains

to be done, but to hand you over to the authorities. I might as well tell you that I have known of
your presence in Lahore for a considerable time
– I was waiting for you to come out into the open
and proclaim yourself!'

Kamper shot him a look in which fear and
surprise were equally blended.

'How did you know?' he gasped.

'You were seen some weeks ago in a motor car.
I think it must have been the day you arrived.
Now then, come along into the corridor: I am
going to ring up the police and tell them to come
and collect you.'

The Jew rose quietly enough, Hugh watching
him carefully the while, prepared for an attempt
at escape. But he was not quite prepared for
what actually did happen. He was standing
slightly sideways and close to the other man as
the latter rose. Suddenly Kamper kicked hard
and viciously at a spot behind Hugh's right knee,
and the latter staggered and almost fell. Before
he could recover, the Jew dashed into the bathroom and away.

Shannon was after him in a flash, but the kick
had numbed his leg and when he followed the Jew
outside the latter was nowhere to be seen. He
hobbled down the path, searching in the bushes
on either side as he went, but Kamper had
completely disappeared.

Hugh presently reached the car which was
standing, of course, where he had left it, and

leaning on the radiator bitterly reproached himself for not being more careful. He stood there for some time listening and endeavouring to search the darkness for a sign of the fugitive, but nothing suspicious occurred and, at last, he got into the car and drove it to the garage where he locked it up for the night.

When he entered the house Joan was still in the sitting room reading. Apparently nothing had disturbed her.

'Hullo, Hugh!' she said. 'You've been longer than I expected.'

He smiled grimly.

'I've been in for some time,' he replied. 'While you were sitting here, I was entertaining Kamper in my bedroom.'

She looked at him in wide-eyed surprise. He told her of the Jew's visit, and how he had let him escape.

'Good gracious!' she exclaimed. 'I heard nothing! Are you hurt?'

'No,' he replied shortly; 'my leg was a bit numb for a few minutes. It's all right now! But what an utter fool I was to let him get away!'

'You couldn't help it; but why didn't you call me? I could have telephoned to the police for you.'

'I wish I had,' he groaned. 'That fellow is as cute as a cartload of monkeys.'

When later Miles and Cousins returned – the latter reporting that he could not get into Rahtz's bungalow as there was a party on, though as far as he could make out Rahtz himself seemed to be absent – Hugh repeated to them the story of his encounter with Kamper.

'Rotten luck!' sympathised Cousins over the escape. Miles nodded.

'Perhaps it's as well though,' he said thoughtfully. 'Handing Kamper over to the authorities would have meant their asking an endless stream of questions.'

'I would have referred them to Rainer,' said Hugh. 'Besides the Jew will tell the others that I have that paper with the map on it, and I have an idea that it is rather important.'

'M'm, yes; that's true!'

'Let us see it!' said Cousins.

Hugh took it from his pocket, and handed it round. Joan examined it as eagerly as the two men.

'It's just the same as the other,' remarked Miles, 'except for the figures. I wonder what they mean!'

'I wonder what the whole thing means,' said Hugh almost in exasperation.

Various explanations were mooted and put aside as being absurd, then Joan gave a little cry. The others looked at her inquiringly.

'I think I've got it!' she exclaimed. 'Didn't you say that the meeting was to be held on the twenty-first?'

Hugh nodded eagerly.

'Well,' she went on, 'this twenty-one stands for that date, and the eight means the time that the meeting is to be held!'

'Golly!' said Miles. 'You've hit it, Miss Joan!' She looked at him half shyly, half reproachfully. 'I mean – Joan!' he added with a broad smile, and she looked wholly shy.

'Trust a woman's wit!' remarked Cousins. 'Now let me see, there should be a quotation from—'

'Never mind your quotations,' interrupted Hugh. 'We now know practically all there is to know about that meeting. Probably the drawing is a kind of passport those fellows carry about with them, so that they can prove their bonafides to each other.'

'Far more likely,' said Joan, 'it is a passport to the meeting!'

Cousins whistled; Hugh stared; Miles slapped his leg.

'I'll bet my bottom dollar she is right,' said the American. 'Joan has more brains than the rest of us put together.'

'Well, I'll carry one with me on the twenty-first,' said Hugh, 'and, if it becomes necessary, try it on.'

'And I've got a hunch I'll carry the other,' said Miles.

'Where do I come in?' asked Cousins indignantly.

'You, Jerry, will stay at home like a good dutiful valet.'

'To borrow a little of your own picturesque phraseology,' replied Cousins; 'you have another think coming!'

'What about the letters, Hugh?' asked Joan.

'Yes,' said the American, 'perhaps they contain some information.'

Hugh went to his room and brought back the letters and other things he had taken from Kamper.

'Quite a collection!' murmured Cousins. 'A nasty-looking knife, that! I don't suppose he exactly carried it to trim his fingernails, so it's as well you relieved him of it.'

'He professed to have a great sentimental desire for the watch,' remarked Hugh, 'but that was before I found that sheet of paper in it! What are these about, Cousins?'

He handed the letters to the other, who read them through and then handed them back with an air of disappointment.

'They're only ordinary,' he said. 'One is from a brother telling him about his troubles on a farm near Ivanovo, another is addressed from the post office at Nijni Novgorod telling him that his mother is dangerously ill, and the other is from his mother herself saying that she is better, but doesn't expect to live long, and would like him to come to her.'

Hugh grunted, while Miles grinned.

'Somehow,' he said, 'one doesn't associate Kamper with a mother, but I suppose he's only human after all!'

After dinner Miles was left alone with Joan in the sitting room – Hugh and Cousins were apparently busy elsewhere – and he made a great pretence of reading the newspaper, but his eyes kept straying to the glorious picture of young womanhood, who sat curled up in her favourite attitude in a chair before the fire. Joan was dressed in a simple little evening frock of cloudy blue georgette, which suited her colouring wonderfully. Miles thought he had never seen anything more beautiful, and likened her to an angelic figure poised on the clouds.

Joan was reading a book, at least it would be more correct to say that she was trying to read a book, but her thoughts must have been far away, for nearly half an hour went by and she had only turned over one page though, as a rule, she read quickly. At last she even gave up trying and, putting the novel down with a sigh, sat gazing into the depths of the fire, which seemed to her to be winking at her in the most outrageous manner.

Miles had discarded the newspaper long since, his cigar had gone out, and though he was sitting in a very comfortable chair, he had the appearance of a man who was anything but satisfied with himself. Once or twice he leant forward as though to address the silent figure near the fire, thought better of it, and sank back with a frown on his face. He took off his glasses, and polished them abstractedly . . . After a little while Joan turned to him, and started with surprise.

'Good gracious!' she exclaimed. 'How different you look!'

He smiled at her.

'You mean without glasses?' he inquired.

'Yes!'

'I guess it does make a difference.' He was about to replace them when she stopped him.

'Need you put them back just yet?' she asked.

'Not if you don't want me to.'

'I think I like you better without them – do you mind very much?'

'I guess not,' he answered. 'I don't wear them because I have to. They're only plain glass!'

'Why on earth wear them at all then?' she asked in surprise.

'Well, you see, Miss – er – I mean Joan, they give me the appearance of an amiable, harmless sort of guy, and I like to encourage that impression.'

She laughed.

'I don't wonder,' she said. 'You don't look harmless with them off – I mean to say,' she added hastily, 'you look like a man who was used to the big things of life; one who would never deviate from the path of honour and duty, who would fight to the very last to obtain what you wanted. I—oh! What nonsense I'm talking!'

'Don't say that! It's mighty good to hear you talk in that way – Do you really feel like that about me?'

She nodded – rather shyly. He rose and walked to the fireplace and stood looking down at her.

'It might be true to a certain extent,' he said earnestly. 'But the thing I want most in life I can't fight for at all. When I try to make an attempt, all the courage seems to ooze right out of my body and I feel like a darned jellyfish.'

She smiled at him, but there was a misty

something in her eyes which he found infinitely attractive.

'I don't believe you,' she said. 'I could never imagine you lacking courage, no matter what you had to face.'

'Not even at the crisis of my life?'

'No; less than ever then!'

'I guess you're wrong, Joan, for the crisis is here right now; but I haven't any courage!'

She looked at the carpet, her face beginning to burn. She knew that she, too, was facing the crisis of her life, and though she felt unutterably confused, her heart was singing within her and a great thrill of wonder and joy was permeating her whole being. And thus, for some minutes, these two remained without speaking; the one longing, but dreading to declare his love, the other aching to hear him speak, and wanting to help him, but not knowing what to do, or what to say. At last he spoke, and his voice was hoarse with emotion and doubt.

'Joan,' he said, 'do you remember I promised to tell you a little story this morning? Gee, it seems longer ago than that!'

She nodded, but did not raise her head.

'Say,' he went on desperately, 'I'm a presumptuous fool ever to think that – that I could reach up to the heights and ask an angel to come down to me; to share my life; to give me a happiness I have never known. Joan, dear, that little tale was the story of my love – *I love you!* Only God knows how much!'

Then she looked up. Her face had become more scarlet than ever, but in her eyes was the glory of a love which even he could not mistake. With a great, passionate cry of joy he was on his knees in front of her chair, and had gathered her into his arms.

'Joan, my little Joan!' he murmured.

'I told you you would never lack courage, dear,' she said softly.

A little later Hugh, wearing a pair of carpet slippers, came quietly along the corridor and into the sitting room, stopped dead, backed out and retraced his steps. He met Cousins, and took him by the arm.

'The sitting room is no place for you and me, old chap,' he said. 'Come along to my bedroom!'

A smile appeared on the little man's face, and went on spreading until nothing could be seen but a mass of wrinkles, each one of which seemed to contain a smile of its own.

'I am undone,' he said sadly, though his looks belied his words. 'I, too, loved that lady fair. I hope she won't rob me of the little love she had for me. "Then mourn not, hapless prince, thy kingdom's lost; A crown, though late, thy sacred brows may boast; Heaven seems, through us, thy empire to decree, Those who win hearts have given their hearts to thee".'

Hugh stopped and looked at the other.

'I had no idea,' he said, 'that I was going to lose

a sister, and gain a brother-in-law. They seemed to have entirely forgotten that such mundane creatures as you and I existed!'

Cousins nodded solemnly.

'"How hard it is his passion to confine, I'm sure 'tis so if I may judge by mine!"' he said.

'For the Lord's sake come along, and have a drink,' said Hugh, 'and let us toast them. A whisky and soda may wash down your poetry, though I doubt it.'

'It's atmosphere!' said Cousins apologetically. 'Just atmosphere.'

CHAPTER 23

WHICH CONTAINS ANOTHER PLOT

Once again Novar, Rahtz, and Hudson were gathered together in the former's bungalow, and, judging from the expression on their faces, their thoughts were far from pleasant ones.

After his encounter with Miles, Hudson had left the railway station a very worried man. He had driven straight to Novar's office, where he had poured into the latter's ear the story of all that had taken place. The Russian used very expressive language in describing his feelings, and immediately got on the telephone to Rahtz, who promised to call at the former's bungalow in the evening, despite the fact that he had a large party to dinner at his own house. Then again Hudson told his story, and the Principal of Mozang College was even more forcible than Novar had been.

'That comes of trusting a woman,' he said, when he had used all the oaths he could muster. 'To think that all our plans to rid ourselves of Shannon should be brought to naught by a female fool with a conscience!'

'We've had a narrow escape,' remarked Novar

uneasily. 'Supposing she had divulged our connection with the business!'

'You're sure she didn't?' inquired Rahtz sharply of Hudson.

'Perfectly certain!' replied the latter. 'Miles is too ingenuous not to have given away the fact, if he had known.'

'Do you think that the American is such a fool as he looks?' asked Novar doubtfully. 'I don't like his putting up with the Shannons all this time.'

Rahtz smiled sarcastically.

'Oh, Miles is a fool right enough! I suppose it is the girl who is the attraction!'

Hudson started to his feet and swore.

'If that is the case,' he said, 'he has me to deal with. I want Joan Shannon and I'm going to get her!'

'Don't be an idiot, Hudson!' said Novar. 'We have more important things to think of than fooling about with women.'

'Nevertheless, I mean to have Joan!' muttered the other.

'So you shall when Shannon is out of the way,' laughed Rahtz. 'In the meantime I am of the opinion that we must put our heads together and devise some means of removing him. I don't think he is dangerous, but he is a nuisance and nuisances should be obliterated.'

'I agree with you,' nodded Novar. 'I have a feeling that sooner or later he will stumble on to our track. He may even suspect us now! I did not like his being in such close conversation with Rainer at the Club last night.'

'Oh, that was natural enough,' replied Rahtz. 'The D.C. is just the man in whom he would confide, and no stretch of imagination would make Rainer suspect us. I am quite certain that Shannon is feeling bewildered and probably hopeless at his non-success.'

'But now he knows that someone was behind the Gregson woman in that little affair,' said Hudson, 'he has something to go on.'

'What? He will probably guess that the people he is looking for know him and are watching him, that's all!'

'But don't you see? If this hadn't occurred he would have sent a statement to his chief eventually telling him that there was nothing suspicious going on, and now he will know there is.'

'There's certainly something in that,' agreed Novar.

'Yes,' grunted Rahtz; 'and then he would have been recalled and we might have had Sir Leonard Wallace out here again.'

'God forbid!' murmured Novar fervently, and Hudson went pale.

'I wonder if there is a likelihood of his coming out in any case!' said the latter.

'Not unless there was something very drastic taking place,' replied Rahtz, and added viciously, 'Even if he did come we should know, and Wallace would be a dead man within half an hour of his arrival in India.'

They were busy with their own thoughts for some time after that, then Novar helped himself to a cigar and lit it.

'We've had a nasty set-back,' he said, 'and I confess that I don't like it. I don't like the part Miles has played in it either. They were very quick in finding out where Olive Gregson was really staying, and must have suspected that she gave the wrong address.'

'Undoubtedly they acted at once,' said Rahtz.

'And that is the very reason why I think that Shannon is perhaps more dangerous than we are aware.'

'Oh, rubbish!' grunted the other. 'It wouldn't take much perspicuity to discover where the girl was living, once they found she was not at the Royal. At the same time I am tired of being bothered by Shannon's presence in Lahore. We had better remove him without further ado.'

'You don't mean to kill him?' asked Hudson.

'Yes; why not?'

'Such a course would cause a tremendous sensation, and be too dangerous to risk!'

'Not a bit,' scoffed Rahtz. 'There are many ways of dying in this country. You did not think that I was contemplating an ordinary murder, did you?'

Hudson nodded slowly.

'My dear fellow,' went on Rahtz, 'please give me credit for a little more sense. Shannon's death would be the most ordinary event in the world, so ordinary that not even the greatest stretch of imagination would make anyone suspect anything but natural causes. And you and Novar and myself would show our great respect for the deceased by following the funeral and sending a wreath – I think forget-me-nots and violets would be most appropriate!'

Novar laughed.

'You are delightfully callous, my dear Rahtz,' he said.

'Not callous!' protested the other. 'Say rather, helpful. You know what Shakespeare made Cassius say? Every man fears death and in cutting off Shannon now, at the age of thirty or so, we might be doing him the service of saving him thirty or forty years of worry about dying!'

Hudson shuddered, and Rahtz laughed.

'Squeamish, my friend?' he asked. 'Well, I won't ask you to participate in the ceremony; I won't even invite Novar – I'll do it all myself. I assure you that the result will be eminently artistic and satisfactory to all parties.'

'At the same time,' interposed Novar, 'I should like to know how you propose to set about it?'

The door was flung violently open, and Kamper appeared on the threshold. The other three gazed at him in alarm. Then he closed the door behind him and advanced into the room.

'Give me a drink!' he demanded in Russian.

Novar hastened to supply him.

'What has happened?' asked Rahtz.

The Jew took a long drink, then commenced

to gabble out his story, but Novar held up his hand.

'You had better speak in English,' he said, 'as our friend Hudson does not understand Russian.'

Kamper reverted to the other language and proceeded to tell them of his encounter with Shannon.

'You were a fool!' said Rahtz harshly, when he had finished. 'What did you enter the house for?'

'To search his rooms, of course,' replied Kamper. 'You may not think he is very dangerous to our plans, but I have a different opinion. That's vhy I vanted to see if I could find anything to prove that I vas right.'

'You were lucky to escape!'

'I vas – I admit it.'

'What makes you think he is dangerous?' asked Hudson anxiously.

'Because I knew him in England, and saw his vork; that's vhy!'

Novar walked up and down the room in agitation.

'Was there ever such misfortune!' he groaned. 'Two events have happened in one day to prove to him that there is something taking place.' He turned on the Jew viciously. 'Damn you, Kamper!' he said. 'He knows you are in Lahore now, and I was most anxious to avoid that.'

The other smiled sardonically.

'He has known it ever since I first arrived,' he said.

'How do you know?' shot out Rahtz.

'He told me so! He said he vas just vaiting for me to proclaim myself!'

Hudson jumped to his feet in alarm.

'Look here, Rahtz,' he said, 'something will have to be done. This fellow Shannon is not the fool we have thought.'

'That is unfortunately now evident,' put in Novar.

Rahtz held up his hand.

'Of course you told him nothing, Kamper?' he asked.

'Vot you take me for!' said the Jew indignantly. 'I'm not a mad man. He, however, did search me, and in the back of my vatch he found the paper vich admits to the meeting.'

'Good God!' said Novar. He sat down shakily.

'What did he do with it?' demanded Rahtz, who was by far the coolest of the three.

'He asked me many questions vich I vould not answer, then he put it into his pocket, and said he vould puzzle it out for himself.'

'Well, he can never do that!' said Rahtz. He turned sharply on Hudson who was looking thoroughly alarmed. 'Pull yourself together, you coward!' he said. 'Shannon doesn't know anything more than he did before, and that is nothing!'

'What if he discovers the meaning of the drawing?'

'Bah! He can't do that!'

'Nevertheless,' said Novar, 'I wish I could arrange to have the design altered, but unfortunately there is no time.'

'I tell you,' said Rahtz impatiently, 'that it is impossible for him to find out the meaning of that diagram. Why, he would have to know about the meeting itself to guess what it is for. All the same I must admit that he begins to get on one's nerves – the sooner he dies the better. Did he find anything else incriminating on you, Kamper?'

'No. A few letters of no use to him or anybody else vere in my pockets, and a revolver and knife, besides my vatch. All of them I have lost.'

'Serves you right for being a fool!' A dangerous gleam came into the Jew's little eyes.

'Take care!' he snarled. 'I don't vant nothing like that from you, Rahtz!'

The other smiled sneeringly at him.

'Rubbed you up the wrong way, have I?' he asked. 'Why, you little rat, I'll break you in two if you cheek me!'

'That's enough, Rahtz!' interposed Novar with a frown. 'We've other things to think about besides quarrelling, and naturally Kamper's experience has upset him.'

'Vell, I'm going,' said the Jew, 'and if Shannon crosses my path ven there is nobody about, he'll get six inches of cold steel in him. I've got more than vone knife.'

'Don't be such a fool!' said Novar. 'You'll bring a catastrophe upon us if you do anything like that. Rahtz and I will deal with Shannon and in a way that will be safer and more subtle than, yours.'

Kamper shrugged his shoulders.

'Have your own vay,' he said. 'I von't argue the point.'

With that he nodded to the three curtly and walked out of the house. He had hardly gone when there came a timid knock at the door and a bearer entered to announce that a Hindu, Malawa Chand, was waiting to speak to Novar.

'Tell him to come in here!' ordered the latter. 'It is one of the fellows I set to follow Shannon whenever he went out in his car,' he added to his companions.

The man entered with many salaams and an anxious expression on his face.

'Well, what is it?' demanded Novar in Hindustani.

The other broke into a voluble description of how he and his mate had been tricked by Shannon, when they had followed him in the car, and that, in consequence, they had lost him and could not report where he had gone. This fresh incident roused a regular devil in Rahtz and catching the fellow by the scruff of the neck he kicked him out of the house. Hudson tried to stop him, but was pushed aside without ceremony.

'Look here, Rahtz,' he said, when the Russian returned to the room wiping his hands on a handkerchief, 'if you treat these fellows like this, you'll have them turning on us and giving us away!'

'Not a bit of it,' replied the other. 'They're all too frightened of the police to do that.'

Novar nodded.

'We took care to choose men we knew were

criminals,' he said. 'I possess ample proof of crime against each. Most of them are murderers!'

'A nice thing for us,' muttered Hudson, 'to be surrounded by murderers and criminals!'

Rahtz laughed harshly.

'What about yourself?' he asked. 'A theft of two lacs of rupees is not criminal when *you* do the thieving, I suppose?'

Hudson shrank back into his seat. The other two looked at him ironically.

'Well well,' Novar said, 'we won't talk of that little affair. It put you into our hands, and you have done some good work for us in consequence. And now you are so deeply involved that I have come to regard you almost as a Russian.'

'My mother was Russian!' said Hudson hoarsely.

'Quite so!' replied Novar urbanely. 'But I'm afraid that won't save you from being treated as a traitor if you are found out.'

'Is there any chance of the – the plot being discovered, do you think?' stammered Hudson.

'Not the slightest,' replied Rahtz. 'But you may rest assured of this, my friend, that if by some chance it were, Novar and I would make quite sure that your part in it became known. So don't think that there is any possibility of your escaping!'

'Why are you threatening me?'

'I'm not! I am merely mentioning a fact.'

'Come, come! This is unfriendly talk,' said Novar. Then his brow clouded. 'We have had enough proofs today that Shannon is cleverer than we thought him,' he went on, 'to make it imperative that measures should be taken to render him harmless. It was very cute of him to remove those sparking plugs from the car!'

'Devilish!' snapped Rahtz. 'He and that fellow Cousins seem to be able to avoid detection whenever they wish. To my mind it is obvious that he was out on some errand tonight and did not desire to be followed.'

Novar nodded.

'I wonder where he went,' he murmured. 'However, we do not know, and that is all the more reason why he should die. Such a drastic course is to be deplored, and he is quite a nice fellow, too. If it were not that he is in the way, I might even be inclined to regret his demise.'

'I'm afraid he will get no regrets from me,' grunted Rahtz. 'I did my best to make it impossible for him to remain in Sheranwala College and now I suppose I shall have to withdraw my words and apologise. Such a thing as an apology is distasteful to me. I think he had better die before it becomes necessary.'

'We must not be hasty, my dear Rahtz,' said Novar smoothly, 'otherwise we may spoil the full artistic finish that you – er – promised us.'

'There is no fear of its being spoilt,' replied the other, with an ugly laugh. 'I will use the utmost care!'

'I should like to know how you propose to relieve Shannon of the necessity of living?'

Rahtz stood smiling for a few moments as though the contemplation of his plan was affording him some amusement, then:

'You know, of course, that there is a very well-equipped laboratory in my College?'

The other two nodded.

'In that laboratory,' he went on, 'there is a sealed tube containing enough cholera bacilli to kill twenty people. I intend removing a certain quantity from the tube, resealing it, and putting it back in its place. Shannon and Miles are visiting me to look over the College very soon. What more natural than that they should have a drink with me afterwards? *And Shannon's glass will contain his death*!'

Hudson shivered as though with the ague, but Novar laughed as if he had just heard a very good joke.

'A splendid notion, my dear fellow,' he said, 'and one that appeals to me immensely. Two or three days later our friend will be no more! Splendid! There is only one point that occurs to me which may possibly spoil it. That is, that perhaps Shannon may refuse a drink!'

'I'll see that he doesn't!' said the other with conviction.

Novar rubbed his hands together and looked pleased.

'You must take care in removing the bacilli,' he remarked.

'I'm not a fool!' retorted Rahtz.

The other turned to Hudson.

'What do you think of the idea?' he asked. 'Our friend is certainly artistic, is he not?'

'He's a devil!' said Hudson hoarsely.

CHAPTER 24

RAHTZ MIXES A COCKTAIL

The next few days contained almost a series of triumphs for Hugh. The Committee of the Club made special efforts to clear his name, the secretary making an official announcement whilst a crowded dance was in progress and a statement even being put into the local paper. Everywhere he went he was greeted by people anxious to show their friendship, and those who had been the first to turn their backs on him were now among the first to fawn upon him. They declared that they had never believed a word of the accusation and made Hugh thoroughly sick with their smug assurances of unshattered faith in his honour. Invitations poured in for various functions, and altogether he was made as much of as though he had performed something notable. Rahtz, who had tried so hard to damn him with the College authorities, now telephoned to explain matters and apologise, and Hugh felt a real sense of triumph when the Chairman of the College Board, by force of necessity, came to beg his pardon.

Among the many visitors were Groves and

Miss Palmer. The latter walked into the bungalow as though she owned it, whilst Groves blustered his way in, the hearty good fellow as ever.

'Of course, you knew that we never believed such a scandalous thing,' said the former to Joan. 'It sounded false, and I could see in the woman's face that she was lying. It was so obvious and I really felt very sorry for your brother.'

'I noticed that as you walked away,' put in Miles, who happened to be present.

'I walked away to show my disbelief, and because I thought it would be embarrassing to you if I stayed. *Besil* agreed with me!'

'Sure!' said the irrepressible American, '*Besil* would!'

'It was a bad business,' said Groves in his strange voice. 'But you can never trust a half and halfer and she was one, absolutely – I saw that at once. Keep away from 'em, is my advice, now and always. I loathe the breed. They'll turn a harmless flirtation into God only knows what, and—'

'I didn't even have a harmless flirtation,' interrupted Hugh.

'Of course not; still there you are! A drink? Yes, I don't mind, thanks! It's just about peg time!'

Two days after his encounter with Kamper, Hugh received a letter from Rahtz, saying that he would be delighted to show him and Miles over Mozang College on the following Sunday morning, if they would call about eleven. In reply Hugh rang him up and told him that they would be glad to come along and would be there at the time appointed.

Sunday arrived, and they were about to set out when Joan came to them.

'Be careful, both of you,' she said. 'I suppose I am very silly, but I have a premonition that you are going into danger.'

Hugh laughed.

'There won't be any danger today,' he assured her.

'Don't you worry any, Joan!' said Miles. 'I'll look after Hugh!'

'You be careful too, Oscar!' she said with an adorable smile.

'I'll take care of him,' said Hugh, 'and return the compliment; so we'll both be well looked after.'

On the morning after his confession of love to Joan, Miles had come to Hugh and told him the news. Hugh had listened solemnly and when the American asked formally for his sister's hand, pretended to hum and haw as though very doubtful. Miles immediately said that he knew that he was asking for an awful lot, but would make Joan very happy and would give her everything she wanted as he was a fairly wealthy man. Thereupon Shannon had laughed and confessed that he had almost walked in upon them the night before. He also said that he could not wish for a better brother-in-law and many other things to the same effect. That was a day of rejoicing in the bungalow, and the congratulations, intermingled with quotations, were kept up by Cousins until late at night. Miles borrowed the car during the afternoon and went out and purchased the most expensive engagement ring he could find – an exquisite affair of sapphires and diamonds.

Arrived at Mozang College they found Rahtz waiting for them at the gate, and he conducted them to his office, where he offered them cigarettes before starting out on their tour of inspection.

'The first thing I must do, Captain Shannon,' said the Russian, 'is to apologise most humbly for believing the accusations that were made against you at the Club, and for reporting the matter to your authorities. I'm afraid I felt very strongly about it at the time, and allowed my indignation to outweigh my better judgment – I am sorry!'

'Please say no more about it!' said Hugh. 'You made ample amends by telephoning to explain matters, when the truth was discovered.'

'It is kind of you to remember my reparation and not my faults!'

'At least you admit that you believed in my guilt,' said Hugh, 'while the others who turned their backs on me that night, now come forward and protest that they knew the girl was lying all the time!'

'Indeed!' murmured Rahtz. 'But that is typical of the people here, I'm afraid.'

'I guess you're right there,' remarked Miles. 'I doubt if I have ever struck a bunch of folk I despised more.'

Rahtz smiled.

'You seem to be bitter,' he said.

'I am, when they show themselves to be so darned narrow-minded!'

'I can't understand what object the woman could have had,' said the Russian.

'Haven't you heard that she had someone behind her?' asked Hugh.

'Really! And who was this person?'

'I guess it was more than one person,' put in Miles.

Rahtz darted a look at him.

'How do you know that?' he asked.

'Guessed it for one thing, and she admitted it for another,' was the reply. 'Unfortunately she wouldn't say who they were.'

'Ah! Then you have no means of discovering the identity of these people?'

'Well, I'm in the dark, but I've got a hunch that Shannon will do the trick. He's got a nice little bunch of brains in that head of his.'

Rahtz looked at the man of brains, and there was a gleam in his eye which did not escape the notice of the American.

'You, no doubt, suspect somebody, Shannon?' asked Rahtz.

'Can't say that,' replied Hugh; 'but when I find them, if I do, there'll be trouble.'

A faint smile passed across the Russian's face.

'But why should anybody plan such a plot against you?' he said in a puzzled tone. 'You surely haven't made any enemies out here?'

'I made one, besides Miss Gregson, on board,' said Hugh, looking straight at him. 'He treated my sister abominably, and we had a bit of a row. He's the type of fellow to do anything mean and underhanded.'

'Who is that?' asked Rahtz, almost sharply.

'I'd rather not discuss the matter any more, if you don't mind,' said Hugh.

'Just as you like, of course,' said the other courteously. 'Let me show you round now!'

Mozang College was a much better building, and far better equipped than Sheranwala College, and apart from the real object of their visit, which was to take a mental note of the place Hugh and Miles found a great deal to interest them. Rahtz proved an able cicerone, and he dilated at great length upon the various places and objects which claimed their attention. They wandered over the whole of the premises, including the playing fields, gymnasium and library, and spent some time in a students' hostel near by, inspecting the cubicles, arrangements for meals, and the reading and rest rooms.

'Unlike your College, Shannon,' said Rahtz, as they walked away from the hostel, 'we have students of all creeds, but they live separately. This place, for instance, is exclusively devoted to Hindus, and there is one for Mohammedans, with a small mosque attached, and another for Sikhs, but they are both some distance away.'

'Do you ever have trouble between the Hindus and Muslims?' asked Hugh.

'Not the slightest!'

'What do you do when communal riots take place?'

'Nothing! Of course we keep a close watch on the students, but there has never been any cause for misgiving. During every riot that has taken place while I have been here, the fellows have behaved in an exemplary manner.'

He took them into the laboratory, which they found most interesting. He himself was a doctor of science, and he seemed to be in his element as he spoke, at great length, of the research work his science professors were carrying on, and became quite enthusiastic as he showed them the apparatus, which was certainly very up-to-date. At last they returned to his office, where Hugh and Miles expressed their thanks for his courtesy in showing them round.

'It has been a great pleasure,' he declared. 'And now you must come across to my bungalow and have a drink!'

Both Shannon and the American protested that they felt no inclination to drink just then, but Rahtz was so insistent that they gave in in the end for fear of appearing rude, and accompanied him across the road to his bungalow, a very fine place lying back amidst a perfect riot of colour from the beautiful flowers, which were growing all round it.

Rahtz apologised for the absence of his wife, who, he explained, was lunching out. He showed them into an exquisitely furnished drawing room done completely in the Indian style, with rich hangings from Kashmir, rugs from Afghanistan, brasses from Benares, marble work from Agra and Lucknow, and curios which seemed to have been collected from all parts of the country.

'What will you drink?' asked their host, as soon as they were seated.

'Let it be something light,' replied Hugh; 'I couldn't face beer or whisky.'

'I guess I feel the same,' said Miles.

'What about cocktails?'

'That sounds good to me,' nodded the American.

'The only thing I can think of with equanimity,' agreed Hugh.

'Well, if you'll excuse me for a few minutes,' smiled Rahtz, 'I'll go and mix them. I never allow such a sacred rite to be performed by a servant.'

He hurried from the room. As soon as he was out of earshot Miles leant across to Hugh.

'Say,' he whispered, 'I'd like to know why he was so almighty anxious for us to have a drink.'

'Wanted to impress us with his friendship, I suppose.'

'I wonder!' murmured the American, and sat back.

In five minutes Rahtz was back followed by a bearer carrying a tray on which were three glasses full to the brim with a sparkling amber liquid. He handed one each to his guests, and took the other himself.

'You must tell me how you like this, gentlemen!' he said. 'It is a concoction of my own. Here's to your very good health!' There was a slight emphasis on the last word.

He raised the glass to his lips, and the others followed suit.

'Gee!' exclaimed the American suddenly, and Hugh stopped in the act of drinking to stare at him. 'Have you a telephone, Mr Rahtz?'

'Yes; why?'

'Can I borrow it? I forgot to cancel a luncheon appointment, and it's nearly one now!'

'Of course! Come this way!'

He put down his glass and led the way from the room, followed by Miles, who, before going, whispered tersely in Hugh's ear:

'Change your glass for his!'

When they had disappeared into the corridor, Hugh smelt his cocktail, and examined it curiously, then with a smile and a shrug of his shoulders he pulled Rahtz's glass a little towards him, and put his in its place. He knew that Miles had no luncheon appointment, and he walked across the room to look at a picture wondering what had made the American suspect that there was any danger to be apprehended from an apparently innocent-looking cocktail. He was inclined to ridicule the whole thing. It was absurd to think that Rahtz would dare to make an attempt on his life in circumstances when his guilt would be so evident. But Miles was no fool and Hugh had placed the glasses close together in order that the drama could have a fitting climax if the American was disposed to give it one.

In the meantime Miles telephoned to a friend of his. He was immediately answered by the man himself, who listened in a state of bewilderment while the former apologised profoundly for not ringing up sooner to say that he was unable to come to luncheon. The poor man tried to explain that the American had not been invited, as far as he knew, whereupon Miles threw him into an even greater sense of stupor.

'Thanks very much,' he said. 'I guess you're a darn good sort to take it so well. Another day? . . . Sure, I'll be delighted!' And he placed the receiver back on its hook.

He turned and smiled at Rahtz.

'I guess I'm a forgetful sort of guy,' he said. 'I'll be getting myself a bad name if I break appointments like that.'

He linked his arm in the other's in the most friendly fashion, and they returned to the drawing room.

Hugh was still gazing at the picture, but he turned as they entered, and seeing Miles looking at him questioningly nodded significantly towards the glasses. Rahtz picked up the one he thought was his.

'Why, you haven't touched your cocktail yet, Shannon,' he said.

'I naturally waited,' was the reply.

He raised the glass, the three men pledged each other, and sipped the liquor.

'It's jolly nice,' said Hugh.

'Bully,' agreed Miles.

'I'm glad you think so,' said Rahtz, sitting back in his chair and apparently well pleased with the praise. 'I always mix this cocktail for special guests, and I've had no end of fellows bothering me to give them the recipe, but I always keep it to myself.'

'I guess you do,' said Miles. 'Say, Rahtz,' he went on, 'let me see your glass, may I?'

The Russian handed it to him, and watched with a frown on his face while Miles examined it with a look of curiosity.

'I like this ornamental ring round it,' he said. 'It's sure artistic!'

'Ornamental ring!' gasped Rahtz, and his face went a sickly white.

Miles nodded.

'I thought I noticed it on Shannon's glass, when you first handed them round,' he said carelessly.

'Perhaps it was,' said Hugh. 'I suppose Rahtz picked up mine instead of his own – they were close together!'

'Give it to me!' almost screamed the Russian.

He took one glance at it, and put it down on the table with a groan of agony.

'My God!' he gasped. 'Oh, my God!'

He looked wildly from one to the other, then starting to his feet he staggered from the room. Hugh had gone white at this manifestation of

Miles' suspicions, but the latter only smiled calmly as he looked across at his colleague.

'I guess there's some subtle poison in that glass that isn't going to work for a while,' he said. 'Our friend has gone to try an antidote!'

He took a self-filling fountain pen from his pocket and crossing to a large aspidistra that stood near the window, he emptied out the ink, cleansed it from a sarai of water that stood outside on the veranda and, returning to the table, refilled the pen from the cocktail which had caused Rahtz to behave in such an extraordinary manner.

'I'll take this right along and have it analysed,' he said.

For five minutes they waited for the Russian's return, then a bearer entered.

'*Sahib salaam do!*' he said. 'Too seeck, not coming, very sorry!'

'By which I guess you mean that he sends his salaams and asks us to excuse him because he's sick?' said Miles.

The man nodded.

'Very well,' went on the American. 'Tell him we are very sorry he is ill, and hope he'll soon be better!'

The bearer bowed and departed, and Miles picked up his topee.

'Come along, Hugh!' he said.

They crossed over to the college courtyard, where they had left the car. As they were about to get in, Hugh held out his hand.

'I owe my life to you,' he remarked.

'Shucks!' said the American. 'Get in, and don't be such a darn fool!'

'What made you suspect that Rahtz would put poison in my glass?' Shannon asked on the way back.

'I didn't like his anxiety to get us to have a drink,' was the reply. 'But I only told you to change the glasses as a precautionary measure. Naturally the telephone message was a fake.' He laughed. 'I guess Holden, whom I rang up, was a mighty surprised man!'

'But what about your cocktail? Perhaps that was poisoned also!'

Miles shook his head.

'No,' he said. 'He wouldn't want to get innocent me out of the way. Still I didn't drink it, to make sure.'

'He must have been jolly desperate to do such a risky thing,' said Hugh reflectively.

'I reckon the poison, whatever it is, wouldn't have worked for hours, so that he couldn't be suspected. I'm mighty curious to find out exactly what he did put in that cocktail. He got the fright of his life, when he discovered that he had drunk some of it. I wish I had let him drink the lot, but I wanted to see if there was anything in my suspicion.' He chuckled, and added, 'There sure was!'

'Of course he'll know now that we are aware of his connection with Kamper and company,' said Hugh. 'He's hardly likely to be such a fool as to think that the changing of the drinks was a sheer accident.'

'I guess not,' said Miles. 'And he'll know I'm interested in the game, too; still it can't be helped.'

'Perhaps he'll die!'

Miles shook his head.

'He'll get mighty busy with antidotes right away, and prevent that,' he said. 'All the same I hope he has a bad time before he recovers – the devil!'

'Well what impression did you from of the College?' asked Hugh, after a pause. 'Where do you think the meeting will be held?'

'In the room on the first floor just over the laboratory,' replied Miles promptly, 'where Rahtz told us board meetings are held.'

'I agree with you. It's an ideal place for the purpose. There's only a narrow corridor leading to it, which can be guarded easily, and it is absolutely isolated. I thought as soon as I saw it, that they couldn't have found a better place in Lahore. And did you notice that under the roof of the passage there is a row of beams quite close together?'

'Sure!'

'Well if we could only manage to get on them somehow, we could look right into the room and hear what is said, for there is a fanlight over the door.'

'That's a great idea,' nodded Miles. 'Let us hope that they will meet there!'

A few minutes later they reached the bungalow, and found Joan awaiting them on the veranda.

They had decided to say nothing to her of Hugh's narrow escape, therefore they greeted her with cheerful smiles as she ran down the drive to meet them.

'I'm so glad you've come,' she said. 'I've been feeling so anxious – I don't know why. Silly of me, wasn't it?'

'We've been having a dandy time,' said Miles. 'What you might call a cocktail time!'

CHAPTER 25

SHANNON MAKES A CALL

A few mornings after Hugh's narrow escape, he came in to breakfast looking particularly thoughtful. Miles was already half way through his meal and he also looked grave, but it was from a different cause.

'Look here!' began the former. 'I've been thinking that it wouldn't be a bad idea to call on Hudson, and accuse him of being behind Miss Gregson in that affair. What do you think?'

'No harm in it as far as I can see,' replied Miles. 'You had a row with him on boardship and afterwards saw him with Olive, which is quite good enough reason for you to suspect him. But what's the big idea?'

'Well, I thought that perhaps I might frighten him into making some disclosure!'

'What disclosure can he make?'

'I'd like to find out what connection he has with Novar and Rahtz.'

'I don't think you'll get anything out of him about that. Why, man, it would be tantamount to imprisoning himself for life, and I don't think anything you can say to him will so frighten him as to make him give himself away to that extent.'

'Still I think I'll have a talk with him!'

'Sure! Have you heard the latest?'

'What?'

'Rahtz is seriously ill, but is expected to recover. A rather complicated attack of enteric is suspected, but he seems to have got over the worst!'

He handed Hugh a newspaper.

'Yesterday's,' he said 'but it is a small paragraph tucked away in a corner and none of us noticed it.'

Hugh read the few lines and handed the paper back.

'Enteric!' he exclaimed. 'How on earth—'

Miles smiled a trifle grimly.

'I guess he dosed himself so much that when the doctors examined him they mistook his condition for enteric,' he said. 'As a matter of fact it is, or rather was, cholera!'

'Good Lord! How do you know?'

'Read that! I received it by this morning's post!'

Hugh took the letter the American held out to him. It was from a well-known medical man in Lahore.

'"Dear Miles"' – he read,

In accordance with your request I have analysed the contents of your fountain pen, and find strong evidence of cholera bacilli. Perhaps when you come to get the pen, which I have cleansed and sterilised by the way, you will tell me how such dangerous germs got there.

Hugh handed the letter back, and his face had paled.

'The fiend!' he said. 'The utter fiend!'

'Well, he's been hoist with his own petard,' said Miles. 'I'm beginning to think that it's time we came out into the open a bit,' he went on. 'He is bound to suspect now that you know more about him than he thought, and I've no doubt he has even formed certain suspicions of me. Therefore, if you were considered dangerous enough to be exterminated before, you – and I, too, in all probability – will be in continual danger henceforth. Anyhow, there can't be any harm in our calling on him, and asking what he meant by attempting to give you cholera.'

'Right!' agreed Hugh. 'As soon as he is well enough to see us, we'll go and interview him. In the meantime I'll have the chat I promised myself with Hudson.'

'And I guess Jerry had better confine his attentions to Novar; what do you say?'

Hugh nodded, and just then Joan made her appearance.

House examinations commenced in the College that day, and Hugh found his morning engaged in superintending the students, while they tussled with questions which most of them could not answer.

Those who could, wrote page after page on each question, and when he came to examine his papers later on, he almost went crazy with the awful repetition with which he had to contend. It was a very boring business watching them write, relieved occasionally by his catching some of them attempting to use unfair means. These he sent marching, followed by reports to the Principal anent their misdeeds. At last one o'clock came and he watched the papers being collected with a sigh of relief. Before he could leave the College, however, he was met by three of the wrongdoers who, with hands joined in supplication, entreated him to spare them the shame of being reported for cheating, and promising to pray for his long life and happiness if he were merciful to them.

'My report has already gone to the Principal,' he said curtly. 'You had better go and say your prayers to him.'

Other students of his own class surrounded him, and asked him quite openly to be kind to them, when he examined their papers. They mentioned their roll numbers in the fond belief that he would remember them, and give them extra marks. A few, indeed, even wrote their numbers down on scraps of paper, and tried to get him to accept them, while one actually announced how many marks he desired. Altogether Hugh was nauseated by their unprincipled behaviour, and his reply, in every case, was short, sharp, and very much to the point, while he threatened to give no marks at all to those who had badgered him.

He left the College that morning with a new insight into the character of the Indian student, and he was doomed to get an even greater understanding of it. During the days on which he was engaged in examining the papers, his bungalow was besieged by students requesting to see him on some plea or other, and they brought baskets of fruit and various other gifts with them. Always before they left, they asked for a concession in his marking of their particular papers. Some fellows brought relations to plead for them, and, in one or two cases, even attempted to bribe him in some subtle manner. To all his reply was more forcible than polite and entirely decisive, and during that examination time he lost a great deal of the popularity which had enshrouded him before. He became so thoroughly disgusted, that he longed to be relieved of his duties at the College, and confided to Joan and his companions that he could not understand how English professors lasted for so long in a country of such corrupt ideas, and, in fact, appeared to be quite happy in their work. Joan and Miles merely laughed at his disgust. Cousins found appropriate quotations with which to soothe him, but they quite failed to have any effect.

It was in no very good humour, therefore, that he sat down to tiffin, on the first day of the examination, and as he had decided to call on Hudson that very afternoon, Miles remarked that the signs boded ill for the civil servant. However, Shannon was a very good-tempered fellow really, and after he had eaten heartily and been in the company of Joan and Miles for some time, he began to recover his spirits and with them, see the humorous side of Indian College life.

He had decided to call on Hudson at his office. At half past two, therefore, he drove his speedy little car down to the Secretariat and made his way to a door over which a printed inscription informed him that the great man sat within. He knocked and a voice bade him enter.

Inside sat Hudson, a cigar in his mouth, looking anything but busy. As soon as he recognised his visitor, however, he started with surprise, and his face changed colour.

'Good afternoon!' said Hugh calmly, and without waiting to be invited, seated himself in a chair on the side of the large flat desk directly opposite to the other.

'To – to what am I indebted for – for this visit? stammered Hudson.

'A burning desire to have a few words with you,' replied Hugh.

The shining light of the Indian Civil Service pulled himself together and looked haughtily at his visitor.

'I can only see people here,' he said, 'who have business with my department, and I presume yours is not!'

'Not exactly!' admitted Hugh.

'Then perhaps you will be good enough to call

at my bungalow, if you desire to talk to me on a personal matter. I am a busy man!'

'You look it!'

'Whether I look it or not has nothing to do with the matter. Will you be good enough to go?'

'No,' said Hugh; 'I have come to talk to you here, and I am going to talk here.'

Hudson rose indignantly.

'Look here, Professor Shannon—' he began.

'Sit down, Hudson, and be sensible!' interrupted Hugh. 'It's not the slightest bit of use your taking that tone. How's your friend Rahtz, by the way? I was sorry to hear that he is so ill – Enteric, isn't it?'

Hudson sank into a chair, his face pale, his eyes searching his visitor's face affrightedly.

'What – what do you mean?' he asked.

Hugh looked at him in pretended surprise.

'That's rather an extraordinary question, isn't it?' he inquired. 'What explanation can a simple question like that require? I saw in the paper that Rahtz was ill – in fact, Miles and I were with him when he was first taken ill – and knowing you to be a friend of his, I naturally inquired after his health.'

'I'm no more a friend of Rahtz's than you are – in fact, I don't like the man very much!'

'Don't you?' said Hugh pleasantly. 'I thought you and he were great pals.'

'Not a bit,' said Hudson eagerly. 'I suppose Miles put that into your head, because he saw us together in Bombay. But I met Rahtz and – and—'

'Novar!' supplied Hugh.

336

'Novar – quite by accident, and naturally, they being from the same district as myself, you understand, we spent some time together.'

'I see! But why this long explanation? It is immaterial to me whether you are friendly with Rahtz or not. I merely asked you how he is?'

'Quite! Quite! But I'm afraid I can't tell you. I only knew he was ill through seeing it in the paper, just as you did.'

'H'm!' grunted Hugh. 'Beastly thing enteric, as bad as smallpox and – cholera!'

'Cholera!' gasped Hudson, and his face became positively ghastly. 'What do you know about cholera?'

'Nothing much,' said Shannon calmly, 'except that it is a pretty rotten disease. The very mention of it seems to upset you!'

'I – I've had it once, that's why!'

'Oh!'

Hudson slowly recovered himself, and the colour began to come back to his face.

'Do you mean to say,' he asked querulously, 'that you actually called here to ask me about Rahtz's condition?'

'No.' Hugh leant forward. 'I came to ask you why you persuaded Miss Gregson to do the dastardly thing she did?'

'I?' almost screamed Hudson. 'How dare you suggest such a thing?'

'Now don't get excited!' said Hugh. 'I am not suggesting it. I am quite well aware that you arranged it. I want to know why!'

337

'I did not arrange it – I knew nothing about it!'

Hugh shook his head reproachfully.

'You're lying, Hudson!' he said. 'I know it, and you know it.'

The other began to bluster.

'You're insulting, damnably insulting, sir. You'll hear more of this,' he croaked.

'That's why I've called,' said Hugh patiently. 'I'm waiting to hear more!'

'Leave my office at once!'

'If I leave your office without your admission, I'll tell the Committee of the Club the whole truth of the matter, and let you taste a little of the medicine you administered to me. Further, I will also inform the Governor, who, it appears, heard of the incident at the Club.'

'Don't be such a fool, Shannon!' said Hudson, and he no longer blustered. 'It's untrue, I tell you absolutely untrue! Who has been maligning me to you?'

'Nobody! I have the facts in my possession.'

'You think that because of what occurred on board ship, I was trying to have my revenge. But you're mistaken, hopelessly mistaken. I would not think of doing such a thing!'

'Oh, look here!' said Hugh in disgust. 'Why the devil don't you act the man for once in your rotten life, and tell the truth!'

'I am telling the truth! I assure you I am!'

Shannon rose to his feet.

'Very well!' he said. 'I'll carry out my threat. You

worm,' he went on, 'you haven't one spark of manliness in you, and I'll regret to my dying day that I didn't throw you overboard when you so grossly insulted my sister. You're riding for a fall, my man, and it is going to be a pretty desperate one when it comes. And to think that a fellow like you is supposed to uphold Great Britain's prestige out here! Why you're not fit to associate with the lowest coolie!'

He walked to the door and was about to step outside, when:

'Stop!' cried Hudson in accents of utter misery. And truly he looked a wretched object.

'Well?' said Hugh coldly.

'Please sit down!'

Shannon returned to his seat.

'I'm going to make a confession to you, Shannon,' went on the broken man before him.

Hugh's heart missed a beat. Was he going to find out what tie bound Hudson to Novar and Rahtz!

'Go on!' he said.

'I suppose it is no use denying any longer that I did help to persuade Olive Gregson to – to do what she did. I suppose she told you that?'

'No; she did not!'

'Well, she told Miles then?'

'Nor Miles!'

'Then how did you know?'

'That is my business, and I am not prepared to discuss it with you. Is that the extent of your confession?'

'Will you promise not to report me to – to the Governor, nor to any one else?'

'I'll promise not to speak of your connection with the happening in the Club, if that's what you mean?'

Hudson nodded slowly.

'I arranged with Miss Gregson to come to Lahore,' he said, 'and thereby try to ruin you, but there were others besides myself!'

'Ah!' ejaculated Hugh. 'Who were they?'

'I cannot tell you,' said Hudson in a tone of abject misery. 'If I did, my life would not be worth a moment's purchase. And if they didn't kill me, they would ruin me.'

Hugh stared at him.

'You're being rather theatrical, Hudson,' he said sternly. 'This is the twentieth century, and you're apparently trying to transport me back a hundred years or so.'

'I'm telling you the absolute truth now,' groaned Hudson, and the wretchedness depicted on his face carried conviction.

'Do you mean to say that you are being black-mailed by somebody?'

'In a sense; yes!'

'Well, be a man and report it to the police!'

'I can't – I only wish I could. If the police knew they would—' He stopped suddenly and bit his lip as though realising that he had said too much.

'I see,' said Hugh quietly. 'Sometime in your past life you did something, shall we say, illegal? These people, whoever they are, found out all about it, and thus got you into their power. Now they compel you to do all they decree with the threat of exposure hanging over your head. Is that it?'

'Yes!'

'And you won't tell me who these people are?'

'No; I can't – I can't!'

'Very well! I won't press you! And they persuaded you to get Miss Gregson to come to Lahore to slander me?'

'Yes!'

'Think again, Hudson!' said Hugh sternly. 'How did they know of the existence of Miss Gregson?'

Hudson's wretched-looking eyes gazed at him in quick alarm.

'I told them about her – and you,' he said slowly.

'Quite so! And suggested the plot?'

Hudson nodded.

'You – you made me hate you!' he said, almost in a whisper.

'Because I protected my sister from a skunk,' remarked Hugh bitterly.

He rose from his seat once more.

'Well, I've made a certain promise, Hudson,' he said, 'and I'll keep it. But, if a word of warning from me is any good, I advise you to get away from your fellow conspirators as soon as you possibly can, or you'll find yourself in the queerest street you've ever imagined.'

He strode to the door, and turned. Hudson's eyes followed him.

341

'I've spared you today,' went on Hugh, 'but, if you cross my path again, God help you!'

He went out, and stopped dead. A car had just drawn up, and Novar was getting out. As the latter saw Hugh, his face blanched, and he looked at him like a man who had received a shock.

'Hullo, Shannon!' he said, with an attempt at unconcern. 'Have you been in to see Mr Hudson?'

'Yes,' said Hugh. 'And I presume you are here for the same object?'

'Well, yes I am!' said Novar looking at him searchingly.

'I'm afraid you'll find him a bit limp,' said Shannon. 'He doesn't seem to be very well today!'

Novar frowned.

'What is the matter with him?' he inquired.

'I really couldn't say! By the way, that reminds me, how is your friend Rahtz?'

For a moment the two men looked straight into each other's eyes.

'He is improving, I am delighted to say,' said Novar at last.

'I'm glad to hear that. I must call and see him, as soon as he is able to receive visitors.'

'I daresay that will be in a day or two,' replied Novar.

'Of course, you've been already,' said Hugh; 'but you and Mr Rahtz are such old friends, are you not?'

Again the Russian looked at him, as though

striving to penetrate right into the inner recesses of his mind.

'We are rather – er – friendly,' he admitted.

Hugh smiled.

'Have you ever played poker, Mr Novar?' he asked, *à propos* of nothing.

'Poker! Good gracious, no! Why do you ask?' inquired the other in surprise.

'I thought not,' said Hugh calmly. 'People who play it, and play it well, get what is known as the poker face. Cheerio!'

And with this remarkable observation, Hugh climbed into his car and drove away.

Novar watched him until he was out of sight, a worried frown upon his brow. Then he knocked hastily upon the door of Hudson's office. There was no reply, so without further ado he entered.

A quarter of an hour later, he emerged, and entering his car was driven rapidly to Rahtz's bungalow. In spite of the serious condition of the latter, Novar remained with him for some time, and when he eventually came forth, there was a look on his face that promised ill for some one. He drove away as though in a great hurry. As he disappeared, a small man emerged from among some bushes, and cautiously made his way into the road where a bicycle was leaning against a tree.

'Well, the afternoon has not been wasted altogether,' said Cousins to himself. 'First Kamper and then Novar, and from the look of the latter I should think that war has been declared! *Bella! Horrida bella!*'

CHAPTER 26

A DEPUTATION TO NOVAR

Hugh and Miles made two attempts on successive days to see Rahtz, only to be told on both occasions that he was too ill to receive visitors. They had a long chat with Mrs Rahtz on the second day, and came away wondering what she knew. She had been very nice to them, and spoke as though she was quite convinced that her husband had had a sharp attack of enteric, and they were both persuaded that she had little, if any, idea of his antagonism to Shannon and the cause of it.

They were soon aware that war had been declared in very earnest against them. On the day after Hugh's visit to Hudson he had a narrow escape from colliding with a brick wall, owing to the steering-gear of his car becoming loose. On examination he found that it had been tampered with, and resolved to lock the garage up at night. The next evening he was out with Joan and Miles when a large touring car swung round a corner in front of them, and missed them by inches, chiefly owing to Hugh's presence of mind and his skilful manipulation of the wheel. Miles, too, had conclusive proof that he was also a marked man, for he was attacked by three men with lathis when walking home from the Club after a bridge party one night, and it was only the unexpected approach of a car with powerful headlights that saved him. Things were becoming exciting indeed, and when Cousins was also attacked, but got away through deeming discretion the better part of valour, as he put it, Hugh and Miles tried to persuade Joan to leave Lahore and visit some friends in Delhi until all danger was passed. She, however, refused to go, and no amount of persuasion could influence her.

Every precaution the three men could think of was taken; none of them ever went unarmed, and Cousins added to his domestic duties by hovering round the kitchen while meals were being served, in order to guard against any attempts from outside to poison the food. They considered Joan to be in almost as much danger as themselves and she was never permitted to go anywhere without one or the other of them being with her. Naturally this duty almost entirely devolved upon Miles, to the satisfaction of the two of them.

At last things came to a head. A few evenings before the meeting Hugh walked to the gate of the bungalow just before dinner to watch for the American and Joan, who had gone out in the car and were rather late. He was standing leaning against the gate post, when something whizzed by him, and stuck quivering in the woodwork. It was

345

a long, ugly knife! He swung round, drew his revolver, and tried to pierce the darkness with his eyes. But there was not a sound for some minutes. To his hypersensitive mind every second seemed to be laden with peril, even the woodland creatures appeared to have become silent in expectation of tragedy. All his world was in fact at a standstill as though watching with bated breath for the attack which it knew was imminent. Hugh Shannon was a brave man, but there is something fantastic and unnerving in waiting in the dark, knowing one is surrounded by enemies, being unable to see them, and yet every moment expecting a knife to fly through the gloom and pierce one. As he stood there, every nerve, every faculty strained to its utmost, he felt a creepy sensation in his spine.

Presently he moved gently towards the place from which the knife must have been thrown, then, suddenly, there came a rush of feet. A shadow loomed in front of him, and without hesitation, he fired, but at the same moment his arm was struck up, and he was grappled, apparently by two men from behind, presently aided by two others who attacked him in front. The revolver was wrested from his grasp and flung away, but Hugh, exerting all his magnificent strength, fought like a veritable Titan. Back and forth the combatants swayed and not a word was uttered by any of them, the only sounds that disturbed the stillness being the crunch of feet and the laboured breathing of the five men. Hugh twisted and tore, doubled up and butted at his opponents, but they clung like leeches, and do what he would he could not shake them off, until at last, with a superhuman effort he freed his right arm, and laid about him with a will. Two men went down and were immediately up again, but he had been given the opportunity of freeing himself from the other two, and with a mighty heave he threw one right over his shoulders, and shook the other off.

They were in front of him now and he retreated until he was standing with his back to the gate post. Then again two flew at him with knives raised to strike; the first he hit with all his force on the point of the jaw, and with a queer groan the fellow dropped and lay motionless; the other Hugh caught by the wrist, which he bent until there was a snap and a howl of agony. In a flash the remaining two were upon him again.

'Cousins!' he shouted.

'I'm here!' replied a voice close by. And the ideal valet, who had heard the sound of a scuffle while standing by the kitchen, and had come to investigate, joined in the fray with a vigour that showed the state of his feelings.

Hugh's assailants were thrown into confusion by this unexpected attack, and drew back for a fraction of a second, and in that infinitesimal space of time Hugh collected all his strength into one huge blow, which landed between the eyes of the man nearest him, and the latter crumpled up and fell without a groan. The other fellow, whom Cousins was pummelling with a will, then tore himself away and fled. And at that moment the whole place was lit up with a brilliant radiance, the car turned into the drive and, with a jarring of brakes, came to a standstill.

'Holy Mike!' exclaimed the voice of Miles. 'Have you fellows been practising for the world's heavyweight championship?'

And indeed, the headlights of the car revealed a strange sight. The two men whom Hugh had hit lay on the ground, one completely unconscious with a lump the size of a duck's egg between his eyes; the other groaning in a state of semi-sensibility with a fractured jaw. Another man was sitting at the side of the road nursing a broken right arm, and intermingling his groans with curses. Hugh's clothes were torn, his hair tousled, and an ugly bruise disfigured his left cheek, while he stood looking down at his victims, with his fists clenched and breathing deeply. Cousins completed the picture. He was standing with his hands in his pockets and not a hair out of place, surveying the stricken field with an air of curiosity tinged with disappointment.

Joan jumped from the car and ran to her brother's side.

'Are you hurt, dear?' she asked anxiously.

'No; a bit blown that's all,' he smiled, and stooped to pick up his revolver which he saw lying by the side of the road.

'Gee!' exclaimed Miles, joining them. 'You and Jerry seem to have had quite a pleasant evening.'

Cousins uttered a sound expressive of disgust.

'I only arrived on the scene when he was polishing them off,' he said. 'There were four; the other fellow got away!'

The American looked at Shannon, and his eyes expressed his admiration.

'Great snakes!' he ejaculated. 'I'd have given a whole lot to see you in action, Hugh.'

'Better get inside,' said the latter curtly. 'Obviously the enemy are desperate. Cousins, go and get the servants and tell them to carry these two into the house! The other fellow can walk!'

Miles looked at the figure of woe sitting by the roadside.

'What's getting him?' he asked.

'I'm afraid he has a broken arm,' said Hugh. 'Come along!' he added to the man in his own language.

The fellow got up without a word, and followed his captor to the bungalow, all his spirit gone. Joan watched them go with glowing eyes.

'Your brother's a real he-man, Joan,' said Miles quietly, with a note of intense respect in his voice.

'Hugh always was like that,' she said. 'But, Oscar, how long is this terrible business going on? I am so frightened for you all, dear. It would kill me if – if I lost Hugh, or you!'

He took her hand and patted it gently.

'Don't you worry any, little girl!' he said. 'You're not going to lose Hugh, or me either!'

Presently Cousins returned with the two bearers, and the cook. Loud were the exclamations of the three servants as they saw the prone men, but Cousins gave them no time for wonder. He made the two bearers take one fellow, while he and the cook lifted the other between them and carried him to the bungalow, followed by Miles and Joan in the car.

While Hugh was changing his clothes and having a much-needed and refreshing wash, Cousins got some lint and bandages and proceeded to do all he could for the injured prisoners, assisted by Joan and the American. He made a rough splint and, starting on the man with the broken arm, set the injured bone and bound it up, then tied up the fractured jaw of the second, and bathed and bandaged the head of the third.

'This fellow will be a good many hours, perhaps days, before he resumes acquaintance with the world,' he said. 'Shannon has a punch like the kick of a mule, and I believe he has fractured this sinner's skull. My word! 'Twas a goodly blow!' he added with satisfaction.

Joan shuddered. Presently Hugh reappeared looking practically himself again except for the red weal on his cheek. The injured captives were put into Miles' dressing room, and locked up for the time being. Cousins remained in the dining room, while dinner was being served, in order to take part in the discussion about the disposal of the three.

'Of course, the ordinary thing to do is to hand them over to the police,' said Hugh, 'but that would mean having to answer an uncomfortable lot of questions, and I don't want to have to do that yet. Besides, they are only instruments. We can't keep them here though; that is out of the question, especially as they may need a doctor.'

'May!' exclaimed Cousins. 'Why, my dear chap, they'll keep a doctor busy for many weeks!'

'I'm sorry I had to be so drastic,' said Hugh regretfully, 'but it couldn't be helped, and if I hadn't disabled them, they would have got me.'

'Why the dickens didn't you shout for me sooner?' asked the little man in tones of reproach.

Shannon smiled.

'It didn't occur to me at first,' he said. 'By the way, did any of you pull that knife out of the gate post?'

'What knife?' asked Miles.

'I was waiting for you and Joan there, when they opened the proceedings by throwing a knife at me; it stuck in the post!'

'Oh, Hugh,' said Joan tearfully, 'do be careful! Why did you go out when you knew it was so dangerous?'

'I didn't expect them to attack so close to the bungalow,' said Hugh. 'I'll be more careful in future.'

'They attacked Mr Cousins!'

'Yes but I am convinced that they were acting contrary to orders then.'

'Well I guess they weren't tonight,' said Miles. 'I bet they were waiting on the off-chance of getting you, or one of us, and you obliged them by walking right along. But, golly,' he added with a chuckle, 'they got an honest to goodness surprise.'

'I can't understand how I avoided their knives when they were all on top of me,' said Hugh. 'I was jolly lucky!'

'Don't let us talk about it any more,' said Joan with a shudder.

Hugh smiled at her and tackled a cutlet.

'We haven't decided yet what to do with the prisoners,' he said between mouthfuls.

'Look here!' said Miles, waving his glasses to emphasise his point – he never wore them in the house now. 'This is obviously the work of Novar; Rahtz is too sick, and Hudson, from what you told us, Hugh, is merely a tool. I suppose Novar still thinks he is unsuspected. I guess it's high time we gave him a hint that he's not so darn secure as he thinks he is!'

'I'm beginning to feel the same,' said Cousins. 'It certainly can't put us in any more danger anyhow.'

'That's true enough,' remarked Hugh; 'but how does it dispose of our present problem?'

'I suggest that we take his men right along, and give them back to him with our compliments! That'll give him the necessary hint, and relieve our minds of injured prisoners, doctors and all the worry!'

Hugh and Cousins laughed outright. The suggestion appealed to them immensely. But Joan did not see it from their point of view.

'You will be running into danger again,' she said.

'Not on your life, dear,' replied Miles earnestly. 'We'll all three go, and I guess Novar doesn't keep an armed guard at his house. Even if he does he's not such a fool as to declare himself so openly.'

'Why not, when he finds out that you know what he is? And he will have you all together – just what he wants!'

'My dear girl,' said Hugh reprovingly, 'we are out here to do a certain job, you know, and we've got to do it. It's not like you to raise objections.'

'I know you've got your duty to do, but this is not duty. It seems to me that it is running an unnecessary risk.'

'Joan, darling,' said Miles soothingly, 'there is no risk at all. You see, we have the advantage of giving him a surprise. If he were expecting us, I guess it would be a different matter. Besides,' he added, 'you know that I'm the last man in this world to take risks.'

She laughed at that.

'Oscar,' she said, 'you're a humbug! Very well, if you must, you must, I suppose, and I've no right to interfere. But I make one stipulation!'

'What is that?' asked Hugh.

'That you take me with you!'

The three men looked inquiringly at each other, then Hugh shook his head.

'I don't think that would be wise,' he said.

'Ah! Then there is danger?'

'Not at all, but I don't want you to be mixed up in an unsavoury business like this.'

'And you'd all go out and leave me in the house alone? I should hate to be left all by myself now that these things are happening.'

'There's a whole lot in that, Hugh,' said Miles seriously. 'And Joan can keep well in the background.'

Hugh laughed heartily.

'Oscar,' he said, 'you've got to learn a lot about my sister. I can see that she is going to spend the rest of her life twisting you round her little finger.'

'That's what her little finger's for, bless it!' said the American.

They rose from the table.

'Very well, Joan,' said Hugh, 'you've won!'

She danced with delight.

'You're a dear!' she said to her brother, and kissed him. 'And you're a darling!' she added to Miles and repeated the performance.

He took her in his arms and returned the caress with compound interest.

'And what am I?' asked the plaintive voice of Cousins.

'You're one of the nicest men I have ever met!' she said with conviction.

'Thank you!' he replied, bowing. 'But – er – don't I get the doings?'

She looked at him half shyly, half smilingly.

'Well, perhaps just a teeny one!' she said, and

glancing round to see that no servants were about, she kissed him gently on the forehead and ran from the room.

'The touch of an angel's wing,' he murmured. 'But you notice,' he went on, 'that granddad only gets a kiss on the forehead! Ah! To be young again!'

'Go and have your dinner, Jerry!' laughed Hugh. 'Then as soon as you're ready we'll beard the lion in his den.'

'A bear, not a lion, I reckon,' said Miles; 'and by the time we have finished with him, he'll have the sorest head that any bear ever had!'

Cousins did not take very long to eat his dinner and, when he had finished, the injured men were taken out to the car, and put in the tonneau with him to look after them. Hugh, Joan, and Miles squeezed into the front seat. It was rather a tight fit, but Joan and Miles seemed to like it, and apparently, in their desire to allow Hugh room to drive, they crushed together into a remarkably small space, and he actually found more room than he needed. However, he made no comment, which shows that Hugh was a tactful person.

As they passed the gate post they saw that the knife was still sticking where it had been flung. Shannon pulled up, and Cousins got out of the car, and obtained the dangerous-looking weapon. He threw it on to the seat, and they drove on.

It did not take very long to reach Novar's bungalow, and they arrived to find a car standing in the porch. Hugh pulled up just behind the other machine.

'It looks as though he has visitors,' he said.

'No,' said Cousins; 'that's his own car. I know the number remarkably well.'

Shannon, Miles, and Cousins got out and lifted the recumbent form of the fellow with the fractured skull on to the ground. He still showed no signs of returning consciousness, but the man with the broken jaw had regained his senses on the way. He was helped out also, while the other man was able to step out without any assistance. The three were taken to the veranda. Then Cousins came back.

'Sit tight, Miss Shannon!' he said. 'And if anyone comes near you, call out!'

'Very well,' she promised, and he returned to the others. Hugh knocked loudly on the door, and after a moment's delay, a servant came.

'*Sahib salaam do!*' said the former.

'*Jih, sahib!*' said the man, and held open the door for them to enter.

Hugh indicated that they would stay where they were, and the bearer went off to inform his master. After some minutes the heavy tread of Novar was heard from the corridor. Shannon turned and smiled at the others. Miles winked.

'Jerry,' he said, 'there's a switch there! Let us have all the light we can on this historical scene!'

Cousins switched on a powerful light, which illuminated the whole veranda, and at that moment the door opened, and Novar appeared before them.

'Good evening,' he said. 'What can—'

Then he recognised his visitors, and a spasm passed across his face, but he recovered himself instantly.

'This is a pleasure,' he said, but the tone of his voice denied the assertion. 'Come in!'

'No, we won't come in, thanks very much!' said Hugh. 'We just called to return some belongings of yours.'

'Some belongings of mine?' questioned Novar in a surprised tone.

'Yes; they gave me a little trouble, but they're nearly intact!'

'I don't understand you,' said the astounded man. 'When did I leave any possessions of mine with you?'

'You didn't leave them,' replied Hugh. 'You merely sent them along! I'm afraid they are not in such good condition as they were!'

'What on earth do you mean?' Novar's face expressed a most remarkable mixture of emotions: surprise, doubt, distrust, fear, all were there.

'You are a forgetful fellow!' said Hugh chidingly. He was enjoying himself. 'Perhaps you'll remember when you see them.'

He stepped aside. Cousins and Miles did the same, and Novar's horrified eyes beheld three Indians, whom he knew very well indeed. One had his arm in a sling, another had a bandage round his face – these two were sitting miserably on the floor. The other, with his head wrapped in bandages, was lying prone, and appeared to be asleep.

Novar leant, against the door post; his face had gone the colour of chalk and seemed to be more flabby than ever. His teeth clenched together and a hissing sound came from between them. For a moment there was a silence which was so pregnant with feeling that it seemed almost noisy. At last Hugh spoke again:

'Well, aren't you grateful?' he asked.

Novar's hand stole to his jacket pocket, but Miles made a slight movement, and a revolver gleamed in his hand.

'Don't be a fool, Novar!' he said, and his voice sounded like steel. 'There are three of us and when it comes to drawing a gun, I guess any one of us could pull three before you got your finger on the trigger of yours. You kinder look foolish sliding your hand about in that baby fashion.'

'What are you all talking about?' the other asked, almost pathetically. 'Is this some elaborate practical joke?'

'Don't try to bluff, Novar!' said Hugh sternly. 'I told you you ought to learn to play poker, didn't I? Here are your possessions! They all want medical attention. You had better have them seen to as soon as possible.'

'But I've never seen these men in my life before!' protested the Russian.

'Gee! That's mighty strange!' said Miles sarcastically. 'Did you give them their orders with your back turned towards them, or were you blindfolded?'

'Gentlemen,' said Novar, spreading his hands

out in a gesture of hopelessness. 'I give you my word that you have made some extraordinary mistake. Come inside, and let us talk this matter over!'

'No, thanks!' said Hugh. 'I prefer to be on the outside of this house. We have done what we came to do – there are your goods; take them! And next time you send your emissaries to commit murder, be more subtle about it. We know you, Novar, and we're not to be deluded. You had better go and talk this over with your friend Rahtz – that is if he has recovered from cholera yet!'

With that the three turned and walked down the steps and re-entered the car. Hugh backed slowly up the drive, Cousins and Miles keeping their hands on their revolvers the while. Novar stood like a statue where they had left him, and gradually there came over his face a look of diabolical fury. With a glance of malignant scorn at the three miserable wretches in front of him, he turned suddenly and entered the bungalow, slamming the door behind him. He went straight to the telephone, and rang up Hudson.

As soon as they were outside the gates of Novar's grounds, Miles and Joan sat in the tonneau, and Cousins joined Hugh in front: thus they proceeded home. They were well satisfied with their visit to Novar, but resolved to redouble their precautions against attack of any kind for the future. Joan went to bed fairly early, but the three men stayed up talking for a considerable time. Before they retired they made certain that every door in the house was securely locked and bolted, and with a final whisky and soda wandered off to their various rooms.

Hugh found it difficult to sleep that night and when he did eventually fall into a troubled slumber, it seemed to him that it was only a few minutes before he was awake again with a feeling that there was something wrong. He listened intently, but nothing was to be heard save the ticking of his clock on the mantelpiece, the luminous dial of which showed him that it was twenty minutes past two. He smiled to himself, and came to the conclusion that the events of the evening had reacted on his mind. Making himself as comfortable as he could, with his arm under the pillow in a favourite attitude, he tried to get to sleep again. Then suddenly he was sitting up, every nerve on the alert. He had distinctly caught the sound of soft footsteps.

Getting quietly out of bed, he put on his dressing gown and slippers and moved to the door. He had almost reached it, when there was a piercing scream, and the front door slammed. With a horrible dread in his heart he dashed into the corridor, at the same moment as Miles switched on the lights, and Cousins made his appearance.

'My God! What was that?' cried the latter.

'It's Joan! See to Joan!' shouted Miles in agony.

Hugh was in his sister's bedroom, and had switched on the lights in a second. One glance revealed to him an empty bed and the bedclothes thrown back. He called to the others and they entered. The door communicating with the bathroom was locked on the bedroom side, and there was no sign of the poor girl anywhere.

'They've got her!' groaned Hugh. 'The fiends! They've got her!'

'After them!' cried Cousins. 'Go and get the car out, Hugh! And you, Oscar, put on a dressing gown and shoes – hurry!'

The little man rushed away to garb himself, while Hugh dashed frantically to the garage. Miles hastily put on some shoes, and an overcoat. His face was white, his teeth clenched, and there was a look almost of madness in his eyes.

'If one little hair of her darling head is hurt,' he muttered, 'I'll tear the devils to pieces with my own hands.'

CHAPTER 27

THE KIDNAPPING OF JOAN

Novar rang up Hudson with his mind in a perfect tumult of emotions. Recent events had convinced him, as well as Rahtz, that Shannon had, by some means or other, discovered that the Principal of Mozang College was in Lahore for other reasons besides the education of the young Indian. But Novar fancied himself secure, had not imagined for one moment that he also was suspected. The arrival of Shannon, Cousins and Miles with their injured prisoners – the men he had sent either to kill or seriously disable Shannon – had, therefore, come as a terrible shock to him. His mind was in a state of chaos, he was almost bereft of the power of thought; he was only aware of a blind fury, intermingled with a dreadful fear, as he waited for Hudson to come to the telephone in reply to his urgent call.

At last he heard the voice of the other.

'Is that Novar?' it asked.

'Yes! Get into your car quickly, and drive to Rahtz's bungalow! I'll meet you there.'

'What has happened?'

'You'll know all presently! Hurry!'

He rang off, and calling for his chauffeur had himself driven to Rahtz's bungalow, without bestowing another glance at the three men on the veranda. He met Mrs Rahtz at the door of her house talking to a woman visitor, who was just going. It needed a gigantic effort to hide the agitation which was consuming him, but he succeeded tolerably well, and raised his hat with a pretence of his usual suave politeness.

'I am afraid my husband is asleep, Mr Novar,' said Mrs Rahtz.

'I wouldn't think of disturbing him at such an hour,' said he, 'but as I was passing I called in to ask how he is.'

As he spoke he looked meaningly at her.

'Come in for a few minutes!' she said. And saying 'goodbye' to her visitor, she ushered him into the drawing room.

As soon as they were inside he threw off the cloak of urbanity.

'I must see Rahtz immediately,' he said. 'It is a matter of the gravest importance. Hudson will be here in a moment also.'

'What has happened?' she asked, her face paling.

'Never mind that now!' he replied. almost curtly. 'Go and wake Rahtz, if he is really asleep!'

She went without another word, and Novar spent the time until her return in walking about the room, with hands behind his back and muttering to himself. Hudson arrived just as Mrs Rahtz was on her way back to the drawing room, and entered the house without ceremony.

'Is Novar here?' he asked eagerly.

'Yes!' she replied. 'Mr Hudson, *what* is the matter?'

'I haven't the vaguest notion,' he said. 'Where is he?'

She led the way into the room.

'My husband is waiting for you,' she said to Novar.

He nodded curtly to Hudson.

'Come with me!' he said, and without taking any further notice of Mrs Rahtz walked off to the bedroom followed by the civil service man.

Rahtz was sitting in bed propped up by pillows. He looked years older, and his face was white and haggard; even his moustache seemed to be drooping and lifeless, but there was a gleam in his eyes which showed that his mind was still in its most active state.

'Find chairs and sit down, both of you!' he said in a thin voice, and when they were seated: 'What's the matter, Novar?' he asked.

'We've absolutely underrated Shannon and Cousins,' burst out the other. 'And Miles, too, is hand in glove with them. Something must be done immediately, or we are ruined!'

Hudson clutched the arms of his chair, and looked at the speaker with eyes of frightened inquiry. Rahtz frowned but made no comment.

'Tonight,' went on Novar, 'I've had a visit from

all three of them, and they brought back three of the four men I sent to Crescent Road in the hope of killing Shannon!'

A particularly ugly oath burst from between Rahtz's bloodless lips.

'Then they know—' began Hudson hoarsely.

'They know that I am a Russian emissary as well as Rahtz,' interrupted Novar. 'I am wondering what else they know!'

'Do you think they also know of my connection with you?' asked the terror-stricken Hudson.

'Of course they do!' said Rahtz brutally. 'What fools we've been. I see it all now: they must have suspected us right from the beginning. Perhaps Miles stayed in Bombay to watch us, when we met you and Oppenheimer there, and they've watched us ever since. The devil take them – and us, for imagining that they were fools!'

'If they know about me, what am I to do?' moaned Hudson, and he was shaking in every limb.

'Pull yourself together and don't be such a coward!' said Novar.

He himself was not in much better condition, Rahtz as usual being the most composed. The latter looked bitterly at the civil servant.

'It's worms like you that ruin everything!' he said. 'I wish we'd never met you.'

'How have I ruined everything?' asked the other, with a glimpse of spirit.

'Oh, don't let us quarrel again,' said Novar. 'The

position is desperate, and we've got to face it. Attempts have been made to do away with Shannon, and Cousins, and even Miles – they have all failed! Now what is to be done?'

'I wonder who Miles really is?' said Rahtz. 'It's through him, I feel sure, that we were first suspected. Oh, idiots that we were to think him a harmless fool!'

He ground his teeth with rage.

'I can't understand why they have not put the police on our track!' said Novar.

'Because they want to find out what we're doing,' replied the sick man.

'But that doesn't explain why they have shown their hand now,' muttered Hudson.

'I think I can see why they have done that,' said Rahtz. 'The attempts that have been made on them lately, though unsuccessful, have worried them, and so they have come out into the open as a sort of warning to us to stop. But, by Heaven!' he cried, 'it won't stop us! Now is the time to make some drastic move that will keep them quiet, or destroy the three of them entirely! What did they say to you tonight, Novar?'

The latter repeated the conversation, and Rahtz's face was an unpleasant sight.

'So he told you to talk it over with me, did he?' he snapped. 'And how the devil did he know I had cholera?'

Novar shrugged his shoulders hopelessly.

'How does he know anything?' he said.

The three men sat thinking for several minutes. Each showed his temperament by the expression on his face. Rahtz's was brutal in the intensity of his hatred; Novar's was twitching, half with fear, half with cruelty and cunning; Hudson's was wholly terror-stricken, the face of an arrant poltroon. Yet he was the first to speak, and he even spoke with a semblance of spirit.

'It seems to me,' he said, 'that we can't carry on any longer as we have been doing. You two don't stand to lose much. I, on the other hand, lose my post – everything. I daren't return to the office again, and neither of you can risk going on with your work openly. For all we know the police may have been informed already!'

Novar nodded.

'There's a lot in what you say,' he said. 'It certainly would be safer to go into hiding until after the meeting is over, and then we can disappear and lay low in Peshawar or 'Pindi.'

'Bah!' said Rahtz. 'That is all very well. But do you suggest doing this without striking another blow at Shannon?'

'No, I don't!' cried Hudson, and his face was distorted with hatred. 'I, for one, want to see him suffer hell, and that brute Miles, too!'

'Why Miles?' inquired Novar.

'Don't you know?' went on the civil servant, still in the shrill voice of the coward forced to action. 'He is engaged to Joan, and *I* want her. I'll have her if I wreck the schemes of the whole world!'

He rose to his feet and there was madness in his eyes.

'You'll sit down and talk sense!' commanded Rahtz, and he looked meaningly at Novar, who stood up and, taking Hudson by the arm, helped him back into his chair almost gently.

'No use getting excited, Hudson,' he said. 'We've got to discuss this matter calmly. I think we had better go into hiding, and at once,' he went on. 'Only four days remain until the meeting and it would be worse than rash to risk our liberty, when it is so essential that we should be free to receive our friends. Possibly the slightest hint of anything going wrong may seriously injure our cause, and we must not allow them to become alarmed!'

'You are right!' nodded Rahtz. 'I propose, there-fore, that the three of us disappear tonight. All our preparations are made, luckily. And' – a hateful smile came into his face – 'I have thought of the very means to make Shannon and Miles suffer to the utmost, and at the same time protect ourselves and give Hudson his heart's desire.'

'What is that?' asked Novar quickly, and Hudson leant forward eagerly.

'Kidnap the girl! We can then send a note to Shannon telling him that she will be perfectly safe while he and his friends remain inactive, but if he attempts to find us or her' – he spread his hands out significantly. 'That I think, will make both him and Miles suffer very acute agony and, at the same time, Hudson can have the girl and do what he likes with her!'

'A splendid plan, my dear Rahtz,' said Novar, rubbing his hands together softly, while Hudson sat back in his chair, a gloating, horrible look in his eyes.

'How do you propose to do it?' he asked.

'I don't propose to do it at all,' replied Rahtz sharply. 'As soon as you two have gone I shall get up and go to our little retreat, and I advise you two to follow my excellent example. Bring all papers of any importance with you and be careful to leave nothing incriminating behind. All of us, I believe,' he looked from one to the other with a smile, 'have put our money in safe places, so we will lose nothing but our furniture and unnecessary clothing.'

'Are you well enough to travel, Rahtz?' asked Novar.

'Yes; I have been in the garden for a little time today. Besides,' he smiled again, 'it is not far to our haven of safety!'

'But what about the girl?' demanded Hudson querulously. 'It is all very well to leave it to us, but—'

'You will find Kamper in The Retreat. I should advise you to get there as soon as possible and put it in his hands. I know of no one more likely to tackle a matter of that sort successfully. Of course as soon as she has disappeared Shannon and his friends will come clamouring to our houses, but they will find empty shells!'

'And your wife?' asked Novar.

'She will stay here for a day or so; nobody can harm her, as she knows very little, and that she won't divulge. She will put it about that I have gone away for a change and make it right with the doctors. You, my dear Novar, are lucky that your wife. has already gone away for Christmas and it is known that you were to join her. Your servants must be told to say that you have gone a little earlier than you at first intended. I did not expect that we should have to use The Retreat quite so soon; however, I have no regrets!'

'And what about me?' cried Hudson. 'I can't put a report about that I have gone away for a change or a holiday!'

Rahtz looked at him with a sneer.

'Your disappearance will merely be a nine days' wonder,' he said. 'And, after all, you will have the girl.'

'Yes,' said Hudson in a voice that would have repelled any decent man. 'I shall have the girl!'

'And now, gentlemen,' went on Rahtz, 'you had better go and make your preparations at once. I am rather weary and I must rest before I move, besides which I have a lot to say to my wife.'

The other two rose.

'Au revoir for the present!' said Novar, in a much more complaisant tone than he had used when he first entered the room. 'We will meet later!'

He left, followed by Hudson. They each went straight to their respective homes. Hudson collected together everything he considered of importance and bundled them into a large suit-case, which he carried out to his car and, without a word to the servants, drove away. Novar was more meticulous and made a careful examination of every room in the bungalow. Once or twice he sighed when he looked at favourite articles of furniture and reflected that he would have to leave them behind. He spent more than half an hour in his study going through the drawers in his desk. He destroyed a pile of papers in the fire which was burning in the grate, and placed others in a bag which he had procured from his dressing room. He then opened the safe and, taking out everything inside it, put the contents into the bag with the other papers. That done, he sat down and wrote a letter.

When he had finished writing he called for a servant.

'You will take the boxes, which are packed, and this letter for memsahib by the first train for Delhi tomorrow. I am leaving now in the car and am staying with friends on the way, so I will not arrive at Delhi for some days. You understand?'

'Yes, sahib!'

'If, before you leave, some men call to ask for me, you must know nothing, and if possible, get away tomorrow without anyone knowing where you have gone, as I do not want memsahib troubled by inquiries for me.'

'Very well, sahib!'

'Here is money for all your expenses and pay the other servants before you go!'

'What about the three sick men, sahib? What is to be done with them?'

'Damn them!' muttered Novar in Russian. 'I had forgotten them.' He thought for a few minutes. 'Get a tonga and send them to the hospital!' he said at last. 'Pay the tonga driver well and tell him to say that you found them after a fight. They won't give themselves away; that's certain!'

A smile showed on the face of the servant. He knew a good deal and, if the truth were known, was almost as great a scoundrel as his master.

'I will see to it, sahib,' he said.

'Good!' said Novar. 'Now be discreet! Lock up the house before you go away, and keep the keys till I arrive. Send the chauffeur to me!'

When the man had left the room, Novar walked to the bookcase and selected half a dozen volumes, which he put with his papers in the bag. Then securely locking the latter he carried it into his bedroom and changed his clothes. While he was thus engaged, the chauffeur knocked at the door.

'Come in, Jai Singh!' called Novar, and as the man entered: 'we go to The Retreat,' he said.

'So soon, sahib?' queried the tall, bearded Sikh.

'Unfortunately, yes! Carry out those two suit-cases and put them in the car!' He pointed to two large leather cases, which he had kept packed in case of necessity.

'And this bag, sahib?'

'I will bring it myself!'

The Sikh left the room and a few minutes later Novar followed him. He used a few expletives expressive of his hatred of Shannon and regret at leaving his home as he entered the car, and presently was on his way to the house he called The Retreat.

On the other side of the city, on the road to Shadrah, stood a large oriental building of two stories in its own picturesque grounds surrounded by high walls. It was a flamboyant place of blue and yellow painted stone with verandas running completely round each storey. It belonged to a wealthy Parsee gentleman, who was reputed to live in Bombay, and who was seen very seldom, therefore, in Lahore. But he was understood to have a liking for the Punjab, and had purchased the house for this reason. A staff of servants was regularly kept employed, despite the master's absence, and the house and rounds were well kept. The Parsee gentleman was Novar, and the servants were, almost without exception, men whom the superintendent of police would have been well-content to have had within his clutches, if he had only known who they were.

After a run of a quarter of an hour, the car drew up outside the iron gates of this imposing mansion, which Europeans regarded as an eyesore even in a city of clashing colour schemes like Lahore. The driver rang a bell which communicated with a small lodge just within. As he did so a man got down from his perilous perch on the luggage-rack at the back of the car, and drew back into the darkness. He was a slightly built Indian of middle height, dressed with care in the usual garb of the Mahommedan, and wearing a red Turkish fez upon his head. He watched the gates being opened, and then locked again after the car had entered. For half an hour he waited, then strolled away.

In the meantime the car had continued on its way up the drive until it stopped by the front door. Novar immediately entered the house carrying his precious bag, followed by the chauffeur with the two suitcases. He went straight to a suite of rooms, which he had reserved for himself.

Half an hour later a stoutish, dark-visaged Parsee gentleman, wearing a long, dark-blue coat buttoned up to the neck, and the peculiar shaped headgear of the sect, emerged from the rooms and, walking along a passage, knocked at a door. He was bidden to enter, and found within two other gentlemen of the same race, who greeted him soberly.

'My dear friends!' he said in English, 'the transformation is wonderful. If I did not know, I should never have recognised you.'

'And you, Novar,' said one, who was lying on a couch, and spoke in the voice of Rahtz, 'look the ideal Parsee gentleman – I congratulate you!'

Rahtz had cut the ends of his moustache as well as darkened his face, and no disguise could be more perfect than his. Hudson, too – who was the third, of course – looked very unlike the civil servant. These men were thorough in most things they did, and in disguising themselves as Parsees they were strictly correct in every detail.

'Now you have come,' continued Rahtz, 'I am going to bed. Kamper has already gone off on his kidnapping expedition, with three assistants, and Hudson is in a state of impatience and doubt. Take him away, my dear fellow, and give him a drink!'

'Which car did Kamper take?' questioned Novar.

'Mine!' was the reply.

'I hope the number plates were not forgotten, in case of accident!'

'Are they ever forgotten?' said Rahtz impatiently. 'We have such a supply of different numbers,' he laughed, 'that it would be a pity not to use them!'

Novar also laughed and, taking Hudson by the arm, the two bade Rahtz 'goodnight' and left the room.

In the meanwhile Kamper and his assistants had driven to Crescent Road. As Rahtz had said, Kamper was an expert in this type of villainy and, having left the car hidden among some trees with one of the men to look after it, he and the other two – burly Sikhs both of them – crept cautiously towards Shannon's bungalow. When within a few yards of the house he bade his two companions wait among a group of bushes while he went forward. He noiselessly tiptoed on to the veranda and heard voices coming from the drawing room, but try as he would he could distinguish nothing, then moving round to the other side he tried the windows of the dining room. They were closed, but not fastened, and gradually he pushed them open, stepped within, and as gradually closed them again. The room was in darkness and, feeling his way with the utmost caution, he presently reached the dining-table, which was covered by a large cloth. For some minutes he stood listening, trying again to catch what was being said in the sitting room, then crept quietly under the table.

It was not long before he heard the sound of movement, and Miles entered the room and, switching on a light, walked to the windows and securely fastened them, after which he turned out the light again and disappeared. Kamper heard other doors and windows being bolted and the cheery 'goodnights' of the three men. Then there was silence.

The Jew composed himself for a long wait and, being unable to smoke, took a plug of tobacco from a pocket, bit off a piece and started to chew. He made himself comfortable and seemed quite content to remain under the table, for an hour went by before he moved. Then rising gently he made his way into the corridor, listening outside every room to find out if the occupants were asleep. Satisfied, he returned to the front door and, with the greatest care and patience, began to withdraw the bolts, an operation which took him some time, but which he at length accomplished without making a sound.

It was a calm night and there was no danger of

the doors banging, so, leaving them ajar, he went outside and softly signalled to his companions, who joined him almost instantly. Whispering his instructions to them in a sort of mixed Hindustani and English, and making sure that they understood him he led them into the house. He already knew which room was Joan's and without a sound the three reached it and paused outside.

The door was half open, but a heavy curtain veiled the entrance. This was drawn softly aside and held up by one of the Sikhs. The other entered the room behind Kamper, who switched on an electric torch, and shielding it with his hand looked round to take his bearings. Joan was lying on her side fast asleep, and the Jew looked at her for a few minutes with an appraising smirk on his mean little face, before picking up an evening cloak which lay over the back of a chair. He then nodded to his companion who, with one movement, picked up the girl from the bed in such a way as to enable him to put a hand over her mouth at the same time.

In a moment she was wide awake, and great terror-stricken eyes looked at them. Then, as she was carried out into the corridor, she kicked and struggled, but could not utter a sound for the cruel clasp of the hand on her mouth. Kamper and the other man led the way to the front door and, just as they reached it, she succeeded in freeing her mouth and emitting the scream which brought her brother and friends out of their rooms. But in a moment the three kidnappers were out of the house and running up the drive. As they drew near the gate Kamper whistled and the car came gliding quietly up. Joan was placed in the middle of the back seat with the Jew on one side of her and one of the Sikhs on the other. The former threw the cloak round her shoulders.

'Keep quiet, Miss!' he hissed, 'and ve von't hurt you. Make a sound and ve'll be rough!'

The other Sikh got in beside the driver, and they were off, just as Hugh drove his car out of the garage.

The poor girl knew it was useless to cry out with a man sitting on either side of her ready to use drastic measures to quieten her, so she sat still, praying with white lips for her brother and the others to come to her rescue. The car skirted Lahore, making many sudden turnings to put their pursuers off the scent and, at last, reached The Retreat. The gates were opened in response to Kamper's ring and, in a couple of minutes, the car glided up to the front door of the house and stopped. Two Parsees appeared as Joan was carried in, and one of them made a movement towards her, but the other held him back.

'Not tonight, my friend!' said Novar. 'She will hardly be in a condition to receive you. Tomorrow you can have your own way with her. Be content that we have her. And now come and let us get Kamper to tell us how he accomplished the deed!'

Hudson looked at first as though he intended

dragging himself from the Russian's grasp and following Joan, but after some hesitation he agreed to wait.

In the meantime the girl was carried to a room in the middle of the house, from which no sound could reach the outside world. The Sikh threw her on to a bed, and Kamper stood by the door until he had gone, then:

'If you make any sound,' he said, 'no vone will hear you, so take my advice and go to sleep!'

'Why have you committed this outrage?' she demanded, her eyes flashing from her white face with indignation.

He grinned.

'You'll know soon enough,' he said. 'Don't worry, ve'll give you a good time!'

'My brother will never rest until he finds me,' she said fiercely, 'and then – God help you!'

A savage look came into the Jew's ugly face. Then it changed into a leer. He kissed his hand to her.

'Goodnight, sweetie!' he said and going out closed and locked the door.

It was not until she heard the sound of the key turning that the full horror of her position dawned upon Joan, and almost in a frenzy she hurled herself against the door and beat frantically upon it with her little fists. She shouted for help until she was hoarse, then realising the futility of her efforts, threw herself upon the bed and cried until she could cry no longer, and an uneasy sleep came to give her anguished mind a little relief.

CHAPTER 28

THE COMING OF ABDUL RAHIM

Cousins and Miles came running out as Hugh drove the car to the front door, and in a second they were tearing up the drive, having shouted to the servants to lock up the house and stay up until they returned. They swung into Crescent Road just as the other car disappeared in the distance. Hugh pressed his foot hard on to the accelerator, and sat leaning forward over the wheel, the muscles of his face working with emotion, and a terrible look in his eyes. The other two were no less affected, and their set, stern faces boded ill for anyone who had dared to assist in the kidnapping of Joan.

They turned on to the Mall and were forced to pull up. There was not a sign of their quarry anywhere. At last, after a short, sharp discussion, Hugh decided to drive straight on towards the law courts, but there was no traffic about at all. He asked two policemen if they had seen a car pass that seemed in a hurry, but both replied that they had not seen any motor cars of any description for nearly an hour.

When they reached the post office Hugh stopped.

'It's no use,' he groaned; 'we've lost them. The only thing to do is to drive to Novar's bungalow and force the truth out of him.'

'I guess you're right, Hugh,' muttered Miles.

The car was turned and they went back the way they had come, and in five minutes pulled up in the porch of the Russian's house. The car had hardly stopped when Cousins and Miles were hammering on the front door to be immediately joined by Hugh. For five minutes they startled the neighbourhood with their knocking, but there was no response.

'I'll get in if I have to smash all the windows,' ground out Hugh.

He was about to carry out his threat, when Cousins, who a minute or two before had gone round the side of the house, reappeared dragging a native servant with him. Hugh strode to them and catching hold of the man by the shoulder:

'I want your master,' he said. 'Get him!'

'He has gone away, sahib,' replied the man in a terror-stricken voice.

'You lie!'

'No, sahib, I do not. He went away in a great hurry tonight at half past eleven.'

Hugh frowned at him a moment.

'Is memsahib in?' he asked.

'No, sahib; she went away three days ago.'

'Bring me the keys of the house! Hurry!'

'But, sahib—'

'Hurry!' stormed Hugh, and the man ran off to do what he was told.

Hugh told his companions what the bearer had said.

'I was afraid of that,' said Miles. 'It stands to reason that he would go away in the circumstances.'

'And Rahtz and Hudson will be gone too,' put in Cousins.

'Rahtz won't,' snapped Hugh. 'He is too ill to go anywhere, and I'll throttle him, sick as he is, if he won't give us any information.'

The bearer came back with the keys of the house and they searched every room and anywhere where a man could hide, but of course were unsuccessful. Hugh turned to the servant again and a terrible anger showed in his face.

'Where has your master gone?' he demanded.

'I do not know, sahib.'

'Don't lie to me! I'll shake the truth out of you, you little rat, if you don't answer truthfully.'

'I would say if I knew, sahib – I swear it.'

In his rage Hugh caught the fellow by the throat and shook him like a terrier shaking a rat.

'Where – is – your – master?' he shouted.

It looked as though he would strangle the man in his anger, and Miles caught him by the arm.

'I guess it's no use killing him, Hugh,' he said. 'It's Novar we want.'

Shannon looked at him, still holding the bearer by the throat.

'You're right,' he said. 'Come along! We'll go and talk to Rahtz.'

He released his hold and the man, who was almost

half-dead already, fell to the floor. Then hurrying from the house, Hugh and his companions jumped into the car and tore once more along the Mall in the direction of Mozang College. They passed the same two policemen, who stared in astonishment at the three wild, dishevelled men in a car that must have been travelling at nearly fifty miles an hour, and who took out their note-books – too late – to record the number, with a view to a summons for exceeding the speed limit so grossly.

The car turned into Rahtz's gate almost on two wheels, and Hugh pulled up with a jerk that nearly unseated the occupants. Once again the three men banged on a door without ceremony, and after a continuous rat-tat for five minutes had the satisfaction of seeing the lights switched on in the passage. Presently a frightened voice, which they had some difficulty in recognising as that of Mrs Rahtz, asked who they were and what they wanted, from the other side of the door.

'It is I – Shannon!' said Hugh. 'Open the door, please!'

After what seemed to them an unnecessary delay the bolts were withdrawn and the door opened, and they were confronted by Mrs Rahtz, whose ample figure was clothed in a startlingly purple dressing gown and whose usually florid face was pale in patches. She wore a beflowered boudoir cap, which in her agitation had become awry, and presented a most comical figure. But neither of the three was in a mood to be amused.

'I do not understand the meaning—' she began, but Hugh and his companions pushed past her into the house.

'We want Rahtz!' said the former.

This demand, spoken in such a tone, roused her resentment.

'This is not the time to come asking for my husband,' she said. 'How dare you enter my house in such a manner?'

Then she saw how they were dressed – Hugh and Cousins in dressing gowns, but showing their pyjamas beneath, and Miles in a coat, which displayed even more of his. She was astounded and for a moment could not speak. Then drawing her flabby form up as stiffly as she could:

'Are you all drunk?' she demanded. 'And what do you mean by bringing this man, a servant' – she pointed at Cousins – 'into the house?'

'Mr Cousins is not a servant, Mrs Rahtz,' replied Hugh. 'He is an official of the British Government.'

He entered the drawing room and, finding the switch, turned on the lights.

'We have come to see your husband,' he said, 'and we mean to see him before we leave this house!'

Her woman's curiosity got the better of her indignation.

'What do you want with him?' she demanded.

'We will discuss that with him and not with you,' replied Hugh curtly.

'Then you can't,' she said in triumph; 'he has gone away!'

There was silence for a few seconds at that, then: 'Where has he gone?' asked Hugh quietly.

'What has that to do with you?' she blazed forth.

'Everything,' was the quiet reply. 'I don't want to have to disbelieve your word, Mrs, Rahtz, but if you still insist that he is not in this house, I will go and search every room to make certain.'

'You dare! You dare!' she cried in a shrill voice.

'Keep your eyes on her!' said Hugh to his companions, and made for the door.

She strove to stop him, but he shook off her arm and left the room. Miles and Cousins took an arm each and led her to a chair as gently as they could considering that she struggled violently. They pushed her into the chair and she glared for some moments speechlessly from one to the other.

'It's not pleasant to treat a lady in this fashion,' said Miles soothingly, 'but, believe me, madam, we have no choice.'

'You brutes,' she shrieked, getting her voice back at last; 'you'll pay for this insult. If only my husband were here, he'd – he'd—'

'If he's not,' said Cousins, 'it is to our regret more than yours, Mrs Rahtz.'

'Don't dare to speak to me, you – you valet!'

After some minutes Hugh returned.

'I have searched everywhere,' he said, 'but he's not here!'

'Perhaps you are satisfied now!' snapped Mrs Rahtz.

'I am certainly satisfied that he is not in the

house,' replied Hugh, 'but I want to know where he is.'

'Then go and find out!'

'I would prefer you to tell me.'

'I would not tell you if I knew, you coward,' she cried. 'And I am firmly convinced that you came here to molest a poor defenceless woman, because you knew he was absent.'

'Mrs Rahtz,' said Hugh sternly, 'it is no good your taking that tone, and I advise you to tell us where your husband is. Otherwise I am afraid you will find yourself being asked that question in a court of law.'

She was frightened now, and her face lost all its floridness and became sickly white.

'What do you mean?' she gasped.

'Exactly what I say. We have no wish to war against a woman, but if you will not answer my question, we shall have no option.'

'Who are you?' she asked in a terrified voice.

'Never mind who I am,' he answered. 'Tell me where Rahtz is!'

'I don't know – really I don't! He told me tonight that he was going away, but he would not tell me where. He was not well enough to go and I tried to dissuade him. It was after – after—' She stopped and bit her lip.

'After what?' he demanded.

She hesitated, then:

'After he had had visitors,' she murmured.

'Who were they?'

'I can't tell you.'

'They were Novar and Hudson, were they not?' he demanded.

She shot a half-surprised, half-frightened look at him.

'There is no need to answer,' he went on sternly. 'I can see from your face that they were. Do you know the connection those two men have with your husband?'

'I know they were engaged with him on some scheme, which had to be kept a profound secret,' she replied, almost in a whisper.

'I'll tell you this,' he said, and his voice was almost deadly in its calmness, 'those men were engaged on a most unlawful enterprise and tonight because they feared what I might disclose they have kidnapped my sister!'

'It's not true! It's not true!' she cried in horror.

'It is true!' He paused a moment, and then went on. 'I am going to believe that you do not know where Rahtz is, but you are not to leave this house until you are given permission to go by the Deputy Commissioner; do you understand?'

'Who are you to dictate to me?' she demanded, with a touch of her old spirit. 'I intend to leave Lahore for a holiday tomorrow and you can't prevent me going.'

'If you leave this house you will be arrested,' he replied ominously.

She began to cry.

'What have I done?' she sobbed.

'As far as I know you have done nothing, but I am taking no risks: You have heard what I have said, and I am not speaking idly. This house will be under continual surveillance. Take my advice and stop inside and save yourself unpleasantness. In the meantime I am going to find your husband and his friends if I have to pull down every brick in Lahore.'

'Don't – don't hurt him!' she whimpered.

'Mrs Rahtz,' he said, and his voice cut like a knife, 'your husband and I have a reckoning to settle, and I am not disposed to be merciful to him. It may be news to you that he tried to give me cholera in a cocktail he offered me in this house. Luckily the glasses were changed and he drank some of the infected liquid himself – that is why he was ill!' She was gazing at him in absolute horror. 'I am disposed to forget that incident as it affected only myself, for your sake. But, I tell you candidly that if he or his companions harm my sister in the slightest degree, I'll kill him with my own hands!'

She fell back in her chair with a moan, and covered her face with her fat, podgy hands. Hugh signed to Cousins and Miles and the three left the house.

'Of course Hudson will have gone too,' said Shannon, 'but we'll try his house.'

He drove the car to the civil servant's bungalow, but, as they expected, there was no one there but the servants, who were obviously surprised at their master's absence and could not tell where he had gone. They searched the house as they had done the other two, but found nothing to give them a clue as to his whereabouts. At last, when dawn was breaking in the eastern sky, they returned home worn-out in body and mind, and full of the most dire forebodings.

None of them went to bed, and soon after seven o'clock Hugh, dressed and shaved, drove to the Deputy Commissioner's bungalow, and asked to see him. Mr Rainer was already up and in a very short time he was with Shannon, listening to his tale.

'Good God!' he exclaimed, when the latter had finished, and his face had become as white and drawn as the younger man's. 'What on earth is to be done?'

'It is time you took a hand in the game, Mr Rainer,' said Hugh. 'Will you send out search parties all over Lahore to look for Joan? It is going to be a difficult matter I know and doubly difficult as neither Rahtz nor Novar must be arrested if they are discovered.'

'Why not?'

'Because the meeting must not be interfered with in any way and it takes place the day after tomorrow. As soon as it is over we'll trail either, or both of them. The Chief must have received my despatch long before this and I'm hoping that I'll get a cable before Tuesday telling us to arrest every one who attends the conference. Then I'll leave all arrangements about surrounding the place to you. But I cannot act without official instructions.'

'Then all I can do is to search for clues of Miss Shannon's whereabouts,' said Rainer.

'That's all, I'm afraid. If recovering her means preventing Rahtz and Novar from attending the meeting, then she must be left in their hands until afterwards. It's a case of duty, you see.'

Rainer put his hand on Hugh's shoulder.

'Poor old chap,' he said 'I know how you feel, and I can't express my sympathy – it would sound too banal anyway. I'll get hold of the superintendent of police and explain matters to him at once.'

'I'm afraid I've given you a very delicate job,' said Hugh, and smiled wanly, 'but you, of course, understand how things are. I think a clue might be found if a careful watch is kept on Rahtz's house.'

'Mrs, Rahtz is still there you say?'

'Yes; and I gave her to understand that if she left the premises you would arrest her. I'll leave that to you though.'

Rainer nodded.

'You don't think she knows the whereabouts of her husband?' he asked.

'I feel sure she doesn't, and certainly she knew nothing about the kidnapping of Joan.'

'All the same I think I'll go and have a talk with her myself some time this morning. Have you any objection?'

'Not the slightest.'

A few minutes later Hugh took his departure, having refused breakfast and even a cup of coffee. Rainer at once drove to the bungalow of the superintendent of police. He was closeted with that official for half an hour, and when he departed he left an exceedingly astonished man behind him.

The Deputy Commissioner breakfasted with his wife and daughter and smoked a pipe in his study before starting off to interview Mrs Rahtz. As he puffed at his favourite Dunhill his thoughts were long and profound, and it was with a feeling of annoyance that he heard his bearer announce that a man was waiting to see him.

'Who is he?' asked Rainer irritably.

'A Mahommedan, sahib. His name is Abdul Rahim.'

'What is his business?'

'He did not say.'

'Tell him I cannot see him today, and that if his business is pressing he must go to Brooks sahib.'

'I do not want to see Brooks sahib,' said a voice in perfect English and, swinging round, Rainer beheld a slightly-built Indian standing at the door in a careless attitude, his left hand thrust into the pocket of his coat.

The newcomer was dressed with great care in the broad, spotlessly white trousers affected by the Muslim community, a long black coat buttoned up to the neck and a red cap with a silver tassel. He possessed a most attractive face, the humorous

391

curves of which were seldom seen on the face of an Indian.

The Deputy Commissioner gazed at him wrathfully.

'How dare you enter my house without permission? Go at once!'

'Don't be hasty, Mr Rainer,' said the other calmly. 'It grieves me that you do not recognise an old friend.'

'Your face is certainly familiar,' said Rainer, 'but old friend or not, you have no right to intrude in this manner. If you have business with my department, go and see Mr Brooks, my assistant.'

'I am very sorry I intruded,' said Abdul Rahim, 'and I ask your pardon. I am afraid I took advantage of our past friendship.'

'You talk about friendship, but I have no recollection of any friendship between you and me, and certainly there is no Abdul Rahim on my visiting list. So go!'

He turned his back on his visitor. Apparently that did not daunt the latter, who will be recognised as the man who watched Novar, enter The Retreat the night before after having had a ride on the luggage carrier of the Russian's car. He smiled for a moment at the Deputy Commissioner's back, then:

'Perhaps you will be more prepared to listen to me,' he said, 'if I am permitted to whisper two words in your ear.'

'Haven't you gone yet?' thundered Rainer, and

there was an ominous frown on his brow, as he once more glanced round.

'Not yet!' And with a laugh he strode forward and, bending down, said something very softly.

A remarkable change came over the other's face.

'Good Lord above!' he ejaculated.

Lahore's esteemed Deputy Commissioner proceeded to give a splendid imitation of a country bumpkin for fully fifteen seconds, his mouth being open to its widest extent, and his eyes apparently doing their best to burst from their sockets. Then he bounded from his chair, and grasped the Indian's hand.

'This is one of the biggest surprises in my life!' he exclaimed. 'How did—'

'S'sh!' warned Rahim. 'Walls have ears you know, at least you English very often say so.'

Rainer laughed, and turning to his servant, who had regarded his master's transformation with rank amazement, ordered him from the room. After that he locked the door and for over an hour was engaged in close conversation with his visitor.

Hugh was in a terrible state of mind when he arrived at the College that morning. The examinations were still on, which was a lucky thing for him, for it is certain that he could never have lectured. On the following day the College closed for the Christmas holidays, otherwise he would have taken the morning off. He tried every means he could think of to take his mind away from his trouble but failed entirely, and several of the young Muslims seated before him looked up from their papers and wondered why the Englishman's face was so pale and so set in its expression.

The morning dragged on its weary way and to Hugh every minute seemed an hour, every hour a day, and when he glanced at his watch and saw that it was only twelve, with another hour still to be borne, he cursed savagely under his breath, a thing that was, as a rule, foreign to the nature of Hugh Shannon.

Five minutes later an interruption came. The Principal himself appeared at the door of the room and beckoned to him. With a sense of relief Hugh left his seat on the rostrum.

'Come with me!' said Abdullah. 'Aziz will take your place.'

The athletic young professor came along the corridor at that moment and, smiling at the other two, entered the room. Abdullah took Hugh by the arm, in his habitual manner, and led him to his office. Once inside:

'I have received a telephone message from Government House,' he said, looking at his companion rather curiously. 'His Excellency desires your presence there at once!'

'Oh!' said Hugh without enthusiasm.

Apparently the Principal expected his announcement to cause Shannon some excitement, for he looked disappointed.

'You do not seem very interested,' he said. 'Were you expecting the summons?'

'Not exactly,' replied Hugh. 'I had better go now,' he added.

'Yes; the message was most urgent.'

Hugh left the office, and a highly intrigued Principal. Abdullah was a very nice fellow, but he was not without curiosity and it was unusual for the Governor to ring up a college and summon a professor to Government House on an urgent matter of business.

On this occasion Shannon did not trouble to ascertain whether he was followed or not. He drove there rapidly and on the way, strangely enough, his mind was temporarily relieved of its burden of sorrow. He was thinking of the College and Abdullah, the man who stood at the helm in the face of overwhelming obstacles and who was fighting bravely to raise his institution to the level of other colleges belonging to the group under the University of Northern India.

Hugh disliked Sheranwala College, disliked the governing body with its petty meannesses, its hypocrisy, and its narrow outlook; he could not get on with the staff – except Aziz the sportsman – because of its jealousies, its intrigues for favour, its deceit, and above all its insincerity. But he liked Abdullah. He had an admiration for the genuineness of the man and the latter's belief in his power to raise the Muslim standard of education; and he felt sorry for him in the knowledge that his task was a hopeless one in face of the smugly sanctimonious and utterly incompetent people with whom he had to deal on the board of governors.

'He is true blue,' murmured Hugh to himself, as he swung round a tonga that seemed bent on collision. 'He is a sahib in the true sense of the word. This city seems to consist of a few sahibs, such as the Governor, Rainer and a dozen others, and hosts of snobs! I don't know how to describe Novar, Rahtz and their kind, unless it is as sinners.' The alliteration rather pleased him. 'Sahibs, snobs and sinners!' he muttered.

The thought of Novar and Rahtz took his mind back to Joan's peril, and the hard, fierce, wretched expression returned to his face.

'Oh, Joan, Joan,' he groaned, 'to think that I have brought you out to India to this. May God forgive me!'

CHAPTER 29

A LETTER FROM THE CHIEF

Sir Reginald Scott paced his study, his hands behind his back, his face reflecting the sternness of his thoughts. Hugh sat in a chair watching him. Presently the Governor ceased his walking and stood looking down at him.

'What you tell me is awful – horrible!' he said. 'And you have no clue to your sister's whereabouts?'

'None whatever, sir! Of course I shall be able to track Novar and Rahtz on Tuesday night after the conference, but in the meantime—' He stopped and the pain in his eyes was reflected in the other's.

'Yes,' said the Governor almost mechanically; 'what is going to happen in the meantime.' His teeth clenched. 'Is there nothing we can do at all? Has Rainer no suggestions to offer?'

Hugh shook his head.

'I feel myself to blame for openly defying Novar last night,' he groaned. 'My disclosure that I knew him must have made the man desperate, and this is the result.'

'But how does he think that kidnapping your sister will help him?'

'I daresay I shall receive a letter warning me that

if I take any action against him or his companions harm will come to her.'

'Then if you appear to do nothing perhaps Miss Shannon will be safe.'

'She'll never be safe while that brute Hudson is near her, sir. I told you what happened on the ship coming out.'

His Excellency nodded moodily.

'What step is Rainer taking?' he asked.

'He is having the whole district searched, and both Miles and Cousins are out making enquiries, but I have very little hope that anything will come of their efforts. Novar and Rahtz are far too clever to leave any trace.'

'Then you think they are still in the environs of Lahore?'

'I'm sure of it, sir. They would not go far away with this meeting so imminent; besides Rahtz must be too ill to travel far. Personally I have a feeling that they are quite close to Mozang College, and Cousins is devoting himself to that neighbourhood.'

'It is a terrible thing,' said Sir Reginald, 'and I only wish I could do something to help your sister and relieve you of the agony you must be suffering.'

'You are very kind,' murmured Hugh.

The Governor turned on him almost irritably.

'The matter is too serious for banalities, Shannon,' he snapped, then smiled. 'I am afraid my inability to think of any way to confound these scoundrels has made me irritable,' he went on. 'But I must explain why I sent for you.' He sat down at his desk and unlocking a drawer took out a large official envelope. 'This arrived yesterday morning from England by air. The pilot made a record trip and left within five days of the receipt of your despatch to Sir Leonard Wallace. It will please you to know that the British Government acted immediately; the American and French Ambassadors were shown the two letters from the Soviet Foreign Minister to Novar, and the whole plot was reported at once to Washington and Paris, with the result that the United States and France are taking action with us. I have the whole report here in this letter which is from Sir Leonard through the India office. He asks me to arrange for your release from the contract with Sheranwala College. Therefore, instead of three years as a professor your term will be reduced to three months.'

Hugh started to his feet, a smile of pleasure on his face. 'Then he considers that there is no longer any necessity for me to remain in India, sir?' he asked.

'I cannot say anything about that, but there certainly is no reason for you to remain a professor. You have accomplished in three months what he expected would take a considerable time; besides your real profession may come to light in the course of the next week or so. During that time, Shannon, very stirring events are going to take place. I think you may consider yourself the saviour of your country.'

'I am afraid I have done very little, sir,' said Hugh modestly. 'The credit belongs to Miles and

Cousins. But I am delighted that I need no longer work as a professor of English literature. It isn't that I dislike the work, but I loathe the College and those in authority who call themselves the governing board.'

His Excellency laughed.

'I know quite a lot about them myself,' he said. 'Their methods are certainly not to be commended, but all the same from what I have heard of you, you will be badly missed. I must have a talk this afternoon with Mahommed Abdullah about your leaving. By the way, to revert to our former discussion, there will be no need for you to track Novar and Rahtz on Tuesday night. Your instructions are to surround the building and permit nobody to escape – but read Sir Leonard's enclosure to you!'

He took a letter from the envelope and handed it to Hugh. It was in the Chief's own writing, and was dated from his private address.

Dear Shannon (it ran),
Your communication with enclosures arrived in good time, and I am glad you took such precautions to get it here safely. I need not say that your information is of the most tremendous importance, and was immediately placed before the Government with the result that action is imminent.

Your association with Mr Miles of the United States Intelligence Department is a happy accident, and I congratulate both you and him, and of course Cousins, on the wonderful results which have accrued from your efforts. The country owes a great debt of gratitude to you, and I am more than delighted that you have proved so worthy of my confidence in your ability. In sending you out to India I was aware that an event of some magnitude was pending, but had no idea that it would prove to be a colossal plot against Great Britain, almost ready to burst into a conflagration that would have had results too awful to contemplate: I fully expected that you would have been occupied in your inquiries for very nearly, if not quite, three years. As it is there is no necessity for you to stay in Sheranwala College, and I have asked Sir Reginald Scott to obtain your release on plea of some Government employment.

I desire you to be present at the conference which is due to take place on the 21st December. Make arrangements for the building to be surrounded and everybody present arrested. There are likely to be some very important men there and I want you to take them all. My old friend Rainer, the Deputy Commissioner, will help in arranging details and you could not have a better man. But wait till the meeting is finished before disclosing your presence. I want everything that is said to be reported by cable the same night. As soon as the report is received, Great Britain, the United States and France will move.

I will cable further instructions to you through
His Excellency after Tuesday.
  The Prime Minister has asked me to convey
his appreciation to you and your companions.
  Please give my regards and thanks to Messrs.
Miles and Cousins.
  Sincerely yours,
  Leonard Wallace

A glow of genuine pleasure filled Shannon when he had read the letter. It was most unusual for the Chief to write to any of his agents in such a congratulatory vein, and Hugh knew that he would rather receive such a communication than any number of decorations and honours. Sir Leonard Wallace had the power of making his assistants adore him. There was not a member of the Secret Service who would not gladly give his, or her, life for the rather mild-looking man who controlled the department which was Great Britain's eyes and ears. Hugh realised with a thrill that the receipt of such a document would make him the envied of his colleagues.

The Governor smiled, as he noticed the delight depicted on his companion's face.

'I can see that Sir Leonard has expressed his appreciation,' he said. 'And I can guarantee that it was deserved. If you are an example of the men of the Intelligence Department, Shannon, there is no doubt that it must be a remarkably efficient service.'

'I don't think I honestly deserve all this praise, sir,' replied Hugh. 'Cousins and Miles accomplished the really vital work. If I didn't admit that, I should feel that I was sailing under false colours. And,' his voice became bitter and his face clouded, 'I did not prevent my sister being kidnapped.'

'Neither did your companions! Have you any idea how it was done?'

'We can only conjecture, sir. Every door and window was locked before we went to bed last night and on examination none of them were found to be tampered with in the slightest degree. It is fairly evident, therefore, that they, or one of them – for there must have been more than one – entered the house before we went to bed and hid somewhere.'

'Whoever it was did not lack daring,' commented His Excellency.

'Daring of a sort,' groaned Hugh, 'with a poor girl, who has never harmed a soul, as a victim of their courage!'

Sir Reginald crossed to him and placed a hand on his shoulder.

'Bear up, Shannon!' he said. 'Do not give away to despair. Remember you have much to do yet, and you must be in a condition to do it.'

'You are right, sir,' said Hugh, rising. 'It is foolish to let my feelings get the better of me but she is just everything in the world to me.'

'I quite understand,' said the Governor gently. 'And now tell me; what are your plans?'

'I shall go straight home,' replied Shannon, 'and see if Miles or Cousins have any news. Then the three of us will call on Mr Rainer and make arrangements for our *coup* on Tuesday night.'

'I should very much like to be present at your discussion so perhaps you will hold it here?'

'Certainly, sir!'

'I will send a message to Rainer. Will seven o'clock suit you?'

'Admirably, sir.'

'Good! I hope you and your companions, as well as Rainer, will give me the pleasure of dining with me afterwards?'

For a moment Hugh hesitated. He had no desire to dine out anywhere while the burden of his sister's disappearance oppressed his mind. But he could not very well refuse an invitation of this sort, so accepting on behalf of his companions and himself, he presently took his leave.

As he left the house a car drove up and from it descended the Deputy Commissioner and Abdul Rahim. Hugh hardly glanced at the latter, his eyes being entirely occupied in watching the Commissioner's face; and truly it was a sight for a sick heart. Rainer appeared so thoroughly pleased with himself and the world in general, that he wore a broad smile, which threatened to be the prelude to a roar of laughter.

'Hullo, Shannon!' he called cheerily.

'You seem jolly pleased about something,' said Hugh eagerly. 'Have you any news?'

'Lots,' said Rainer vaguely. 'I've met an old friend, and failed to recognise him, and—'

'Oh, hang your old friend!' exclaimed Hugh rudely. 'Have you any news of Joan I mean?'

'Well, my friend has,' replied the other, without showing any resentment. 'Let me introduce you to Mr Abdul Rahim.' He indicated the Indian. 'Captain Shannon!' he added to Rahim.

Hugh bowed mechanically and turned back at once to Rainer.

'Where is your friend, and what does he say?' demanded Hugh.

'You've just bowed to him rather coldly,' chuckled Rainer. 'Perhaps he will tell you his news himself!'

Shannon looked at the Mahommedan in astonishment.

'I am sorry if I appeared rude,' he said, 'but I am worried. Apparently from what Mr Rainer says you know of the disappearance of my sister.'

The smart-looking Indian bent his head in acknowledgement. He was standing in what appeared to be a favourite attitude of his – his left hand stuck into a coat pocket.

'I heard it from his lips this morning,' was the reply spoken in perfect but rather sibilant English. 'And it was a very strange coincidence, because last night I happened to see the man you are after enter a house on the outskirts of Lahore, and as he did not emerge again, I presume that he lives there. Since Mr Rainer told me of your sister's disappearance, we have both agreed that it is very likely she was also taken there.'

'Where is this house?' demanded Hugh excitedly.

'Look here, Shannon,' put in Rainer, 'you leave this to us. You said yourself that Novar and Rahtz must not be interfered with before the meeting, so—'

'Shut up, you fool!' hissed Hugh.

For answer, and still smiling, the Commissioner took him by the arm and led him a little away from the Mahommedan.

'You need not worry about Rahim,' he said, 'he is the soul of discretion.'

'I don't care what he is,' said Shannon bluntly. 'You had no right to say anything to him.'

'I have hardly said a word. Do I look the sort of fool to go blabbing, especially when I know what great issues are at stake?'

'No, you don't,' admitted Hugh.

'Well, listen! As luck would have it he knows where Novar is. He spent some time near the house this morning, and heard that the owner, a Bombay Parsee merchant, arrived yesterday. He is quite convinced that the Parsee is Novar and I am inclined to agree with him. Now where Novar is we can be pretty certain Rahtz and Hudson also are and where they are Miss Shannon is sure to be.'

'Yes, yes,' said Hugh. 'Go on!'

'He proposes to get into the house and rescue your sister tonight, and he can go where we could not without bringing all the occupants on us,

406

and in consequence being compelled to arrest them.'

'How is he going to do it?'

'He won't tell me that. Take my advice, old chap, and leave it to him. He'll get her away somehow I am certain and without interfering with the liberty of Novar and the others. Of course, they'll disappear again, but that doesn't matter – your sister will be restored to you – and they will be free to turn up at Mozang College on Tuesday night.'

'Can you rely upon him?'

'Absolutely!'

'Then I suppose I must leave it to him,' said Hugh reluctantly; 'but I'd like to be at hand in case of mistakes.'

'You can take my word for it,' said Rainer earnestly, 'there won't be any mistakes.'

Hugh smiled with real gratitude, he felt as if an enormous load had been lifted from his heart.

'You are a brick, Rainer,' he said. 'But for God's sake,' he added, 'don't say too much about our plans to him!'

'I won't,' the Commissioner assured him.

'Who the devil is he?'

'One of the greatest detectives in the world,' said Rainer, and they returned to Abdul Rahim.

'I don't know how to thank you for what you are about to do for my sister and me,' said Hugh. 'God grant you will be successful!'

The Mahommedan bowed with true Oriental politeness.

'Allah always looks after his chosen,' he said. 'I shall succeed!'

Hugh held out his hand impulsively, the other clasped it, and they looked into each other's eyes for a second, then turning to the Deputy Commissioner:

'The Governor has a lot to tell you,' said Hugh. 'You have come at a most opportune time.'

'Good!' exclaimed Rainer. 'I have few things to tell him also.'

He nodded cheerfully and went up the steps with Abdul Rahim.

Hugh watched them disappear, then with a song of gladness in his heart, jumped into his car and drove home. He found Miles and Cousins awaiting him with such unhappy faces that he knew at once that they had failed in their quest. Miles handed him a letter which had been delivered by hand. Hugh tore open the envelope and discovered a single sheet of paper on which half a dozen lines had been typewritten:

Miss Shannon is perfectly safe and will come to no harm, unless any further efforts are made to interfere with us, or she is searched for, when she will disappear for good.

That was all – there was not even a signature. Hugh read the warning aloud, but neither of his companions made any comment.

The three sat down to lunch – there was no longer

any reason why Cousins should play the servant, at any rate in the house – and, without preamble, Hugh plunged into an account of his interview with the Governor, and handed round the Chief's letter. For a moment Cousins and Miles forgot the shadow of sorrow that was resting on their spirits and delighted grins and mutual congratulations passed between them. Miles even insisted on their drinking a toast – 'Great Britain and the United States!' – and they stood up and drank it with the emotion of true patriots. But afterwards the gloom returned with redoubled force, whereupon Hugh told them of his meeting with Rainer and Abdul Rahim. Then gradually the sorrow left their countenances, and when Shannon had finished speaking, Miles leant across the table, the light of a great hope in his eyes, his voice trembling with eagerness.

'Hugh,' he said, 'do you really think this guy will do it?'

Hugh nodded.

'I don't know why,' he said, 'but when I was speaking to him, something told me he would never fail in anything he undertook. He did not say much, but there was a sort of inflexible purpose underlying his words and I have only once or twice met men who gave me such utter confidence. I never thought I should meet an Indian with a personality like that. Rainer has no doubt whatever!'

Miles rose from the table.

'I can't eat any more,' he said apologetically. 'I feel kinder choky.'

At five minutes to seven that evening the three men, who in such a short time had done so much and had become such inseparable friends, entered the main gates of Government House, not bothering in the least whether a whole army of spies was tracking them or whether they entered unnoticed. Cousins was the only one who felt in any way disgruntled with his lot, and his dress suit was the cause. He had brought only one to India with him and, in his role of valet, had regarded even that as impedimenta; thus he had left it in his trunk without ever bothering to take it out and give it an airing. The result was that when he drew it forth that afternoon it was so creased that Hugh, who watched the ceremony, declared rudely that it resembled its owner's face. With the assistance of all the servants, including even the cook, the erstwhile valet did his best to press it, and when it was hung out in the sun it looked more like what a dress suit should be. But, alas, when he came to adorn himself in it, it was apparently so annoyed at its long disuse that it bunched itself up in unfamiliar places, and flopped plaintively in others; also, sad to relate, the moth had been having a bean feast in one or two hallowed spots. However, when arrayed, Cousins was assured by his companions that it looked splendid; nevertheless, on the way to Government House he felt awkward, which to say the least of it was most unusual with him and, in consequence, bothered him considerably.

They were shown straight into the Governor's study, which by now had become quite familiar to Hugh. There whisky and sodas, cigars and cigarettes were placed before them, and they were informed that His Excellency would join them in five minutes. In that time exactly he appeared, followed almost immediately by the Deputy Commissioner. He was introduced to Cousins and shook hands with Miles.

'It is a great pleasure to meet men like you, gentlemen,' he said gracefully, 'who devote their lives to their countries, and risk everything in serving them. You, Mr Miles,' he smiled, 'have been a great surprise to me. I never thought, on the few occasions we met, that you were anything but an American traveller getting the best out of the world. You are one of those who hide your light—'

'Under a pair of spectacles, sir,' interposed Cousins. ''Miles' benevolent look is entirely due to wearing those tortoiseshell abominations of his. If he would take them off you would see the cunning, hard man underneath.'

There was a general laugh, after which the Governor turned to Hugh.

'I have spoken to Mr Abdullah,' he said, 'and although he is very upset at losing you, he understands that it is a matter against which neither he nor his board of governors can protest. He will make arrangements for you to be relieved of your duties in Sheranwala College immediately.'

411

Hugh expressed his satisfaction.

'I believe you know that an effort is to be made to rescue your sister tonight,' went on His Excellency. 'Rainer brought the – er – man who is going to undertake it to see me, and I must say I feel quite confident of his ability to succeed.'

'So do I, sir,' replied Hugh. 'I don't know why, but I feel perfectly certain he will.'

Rainer laughed.

'It is extraordinary how Abdul Rahim always gives everyone such entire confidence in him,' he remarked. 'And he never fails when he undertakes a task. I am as sure that Miss Shannon will be back tonight as I am certain I am in this room.'

'God grant it!' said His Excellency. 'I have told him to let me know at once, if he effects the rescue, and I shall wait very anxiously until I hear from him.'

'He's a remarkable man for an Indian,' said Miles. 'I feel a new respect for a race that can breed a man with such courage and personality.'

They then devoted themselves to considering the surest way of capturing every man who attended the meeting on Tuesday at Mozang College. All details were discussed and no likely eventuality lost sight of. Hugh, Miles, and Cousins were to make their way into the College by some means or other, which was not apparent at the present, but the two former intended to try if the papers they possessed with the maps of India drawn on them and decorated with the eagles and dragons were passports which would get them through. Cousins had already spent some time examining the place, and he was going there early and would conceal himself above the room where the conference was almost certain to be held. He amazed everyone by relating how he had removed enough of the roof to enable him to crawl on to the rafters beneath and listen through the thin plaster which hid them from the room below. He had covered up the hole he had made so that it would not be noticed by anyone who took it into his head to prowl about on the roof in the meantime.

It was arranged that Rainer and some of his best men were to conceal themselves close to the College and watch, while a strong detachment of armed men would wait some distance away, but within call. As soon as the Deputy Commissioner was sure all the plotters were inside the building he would surround it with his detachment and arrest any man he came across. There were to be two cordons of police, the outer one would remain in a circle round the College and permit nobody to pass in or out, the inner one would wait for three blasts blown on a whistle by Hugh, when the men were to enter and make their way direct to the room where the meeting was being held and arrest every man therein. Absolute secrecy was to be maintained throughout, so that no whisper of alarm could reach the conspirators before they were in the building.

A long time was taken in formulating the plans,

so that there could be no possibility of misunderstanding, but at last the Governor rose and expressed himself as satisfied that they had done all that could be done to ensure the complete success of the raid.

'I feel confident, gentlemen,' he said, 'that, unless something unforeseen happens, the success of your endeavours in bringing to light this conspiracy will be crowned with complete triumph on Tuesday night, and I wish you all the very best of luck.'

They went into dinner after that and Lady Scott was the only lady present. She was a charming woman who still retained a great measure of beauty and had always proved herself a perfect helpmate to her husband. She was tactful, clever and strong-minded and was very popular in Northern India. She gave her visitors a warm welcome and the dinner, being quite an informal affair, was thoroughly enjoyed by all.

Hugh and his two friends left Government House at half past nine and went straight home. In the minds of each of them was the question – 'Will she come?'

They sat in the sitting room or, to be correct, they tried to sit, for every now and again one of them would get up and pace the apartment, a prey to conflicting thoughts and emotions. Time went by on leaden wings; they tried to talk to each other, but hardly knew what they were saying; they smoked an enormous amount of tobacco, and hardly realised that they were smoking. Ten o'clock came and went, half past ten passed slowly by – still no sign. Every unusual sound brought them to their feet with hands clenched in their excitement; once or twice the distant hum of a motor car made them dash to the door. But there was no sign of Joan, and gradually their hearts began to fail them, their hopes to fade away. Cousins was almost as strongly affected as were Hugh and Miles, for he had made no misstatement when he declared that he, too, loved Joan. He loved her as he would have loved a daughter had he ever had one and inside the little man there beat a heart which had the power of a great and lasting affection. Eleven o'clock struck and they began to look at each other grimly, with pale faces and eyes in which the agony of the uncertainty they were suffering was clearly revealed. Minute by minute ticked away and gradually the half hour approached. With a groan Miles dropped his head between his hands, but still the clock ticked on, and the large hand marked half past eleven and moved on in its inexorable way.

'Oh, my God!' burst from Hugh at last, and it was as though his very heart had bared itself. 'He must have failed.'

CHAPTER 30

A TERRIBLE ORDEAL

The rude awakening which Joan had experienced in finding herself lifted from her bed by strange men and carried away to a house she had never seen before, had brought on a mental exhaustion which caused her to sleep, albeit restlessly, for several hours. Her struggles when in the arms of the big Sikh and her efforts to attract attention after being locked in the room also made her physically tired, so that she was not disturbed by the entrance of a Hindu woman at eight o'clock in the morning. The latter brought some native clothes with her and laid them on a chair by the bedside, then gazing curiously at the English girl, without the slightest sign of any emotion on her face, she went out of the room.

Half an hour later Joan awoke, but for a few moments did not recall the events of the night. Then suddenly, after looking round her in astonishment, she remembered and, with a sob of terror, rose and crossing to the door tried it. It was locked.

She returned to the bed and sat down, feeling very weak. She tried to think; to piece together the events which might be expected to produce a reason for this extraordinary happening. She wondered if Novar, to whom Hugh had given such a shock, was responsible. But why should he want her? Surely she would only be an added danger to him while in his possession. She knew she was not in his house, and she had never seen the horrid Jewish-looking man before. She shuddered at the recollection of the leer with which he had favoured her and his coarse words before locking her in. Then suddenly remembering how lightly she was clad, she convulsively and with a new terror, pulled her cloak round her.

Joan had a lot of courage, but she had never experienced a situation like this, and she felt dreadfully frightened and forlorn. Presently when she thought of her brother and Miles and little Cousins, and the terrible state in which they would be over her disappearance, tears began to come. She knelt down and prayed for courage and help and the very act of praying made her feel a little better, so that when she rose she determined that she would face whatever happened with all the bravery she could muster.

She saw the clothes on the chair and wondered who had put them there. They were obviously for her use, but she could not bring herself to put them on until she reflected that anything would be better than being clad in a nightdress especially if – as she thought very likely – she would have to face men. This latter reflection made her cheeks burn and without further hesitation she put on the Indian garments as best she could. She managed all right until she came to the sari, but no amount of ingenuity enabled her to arrange the long veil-like object round her head and body as she knew it should go. She had tried again and again and was about to give it up in despair when the door was unlocked and opened. She shrank away as far as she could, but it was only the Hindu woman who entered carrying a tray. She put this down and seeing that Joan was in difficulties, came to her aid and in a couple of minutes had wound the sari round her and settled it comfortably. Joan plied her with questions, but to each the woman shook her head, and as the English girl knew no Hindustani she was forced to give it up in despair. The other pointed to the tray, then went out and locked the door behind her.

On the tray was tea and toast, an omelette and some fruit. Joan had very little inclination to eat, but after drinking a cup of tea, she decided to make a meal of some sort if only to keep her strength up for whatever ordeal she would have to face.

The morning passed slowly and to Joan in her anxiety the waiting for, she knew not what, was terrible and when, at last, she heard the sound of the key in the lock, it was almost with a sense of relief. Anything was better, she thought, than the awful feeling of suspense. The door opened and Kamper came in. He looked at her in admiration and, although she did not know it, Joan presented a very lovely picture in her Indian garb. She

418

recognised the man who had kidnapped her and clutched the bosom of her dress in an effort to still the tumultuous beating of her heart.

'Good morning, Miss,' said the Jew. 'You look very pretty this morning!'

'How dare you insult me?' she cried. 'Why have you taken me away from my home and why am I here?'

'You vill be told if you come with me.'

Trembling she followed him along a passage, past several rooms, until he stood aside and beckoned her to enter a large apartment which was furnished in a heavy ornate style with valuable carpets spread on the floor. The odour of a strong perfume hung in the air and rather sickened her. On a divan sat two men whom she took to be Parsees from their dress and another stood slightly in the background. At her entrance the latter made a sudden move forward, but was checked by one of the men on the divan who reached up and caught him by the arm. She was given a chair by Kamper and sat down with the strange feeling that she was playing a part in some extraordinary dream and would wake up presently to find herself back in her own home.

One of the men on the divan – the stouter of the two – commenced to speak, and his voice had a strangely familiar ring in it.

'We hope you have not suffered any great inconvenience from your experience, Miss Shannon,' he said. 'Mr Kamper there assures us that he was as gentle as possible.'

Kamper! She knew that name. How often had she heard Hugh mention it. She looked round at the Jew fearfully, who grinned at her in his loathsome way. Then she found her voice.

'What is the meaning of this outrage, and who are you?' she cried hoarsely.

'Don't talk of your adventure as an outrage,' replied the man smoothly. 'I hope you will come to regard it as a very pleasant ordeal later on. And I am sure my friend,' he indicated the man standing by his side, 'hopes so even more than I do. As for who we are,' he went on, 'it is rather a tribute to our disguises that you do not recognise us, but as we have no intention of hiding our personalities from you, allow me to inform you that I am Novar, the gentleman seated by me is Mr Rahtz and our eager friend, who is longing to clasp your hand and say many things to you, is Mr Hudson!'

Joan gasped with terror; she knew now that she was in the gravest peril, but with that thought came the courage which was her heritage from a line of fighting ancestors. She raised her head proudly.

'What do you want with me?' she demanded.

He spread his hands in a deprecating gesture.

'This morning a note went to your brother,' he replied, 'telling him that you would be quite safe so long as he ceased from interfering with us and did not search for you.'

A flicker of hope entered her heart. Apparently she showed it in her eyes, for she smiled.

'Please don't think that your brother, or his

friends, will find out your whereabouts from the messenger. You see we knew that Captain Shannon would have to go to the College and it was hardly likely that Mr Miles and your – er – valet, Cousins, would stop at home doing nothing. Our man had instructions to make sure that nobody was on the premises except the servants, then deliver the note and come away.'

'Are you holding me as a hostage?'

He bowed.

'In a sense, yes. I am sorry it was necessary for you to be brought away in such a hurry without your own clothes. But permit me to remark that you look most charming in the only garments we were able to provide for you.'

'You are brutes,' she said; 'horrible, loathsome brutes, and I despise all of you, as I never thought I could despise anyone! You have me in your power, but that will not prevent my brother doing his duty, and God grant that he will succeed in finding you and punishing you as you deserve!'

'Joan!' cried Hudson in a voice broken by emotion.

'Don't speak to me!' she flashed. 'You showed your character on the ship, and it is only confirmed by your association with these other men. You are a traitor and a coward!'

'Let us have done with these heroics,' said Rahtz with a sneer. 'They only bore me and I dislike being bored. I think that it would be as well for your peace of mind, Miss Shannon, if you told us exactly what knowledge your brother has of our

– er – activities. If you refuse to tell us, there are ways and means of making you speak, and cries of pain can easily be muffled in this building.'

Novar touched him on the arm, and Hudson swore a particularly ugly oath.

'If you dare hurt her, Rahtz,' he shouted, 'you'll have to answer to me.'

Rahtz looked at him contemptuously.

'I'd as soon put a bullet in you as talk to you, Hudson,' he said calmly. 'Your days of usefulness to us are done, and you're nothing but unnecessary lumber now.'

Hudson drew back with an exclamation of fear and hatred. During this sharp passage Joan's mind had been working rapidly. She realised the deadly peril she was in and wondered if she would have the courage not to reveal all she knew if they tortured her. Rahtz's voice roused her from her thoughts.

'Tell us,' he said, 'what your brother has discovered and save yourself a great deal of anguish!'

She actually smiled.

'I have no intention of hiding it,' she replied quietly, though her heart was beating rapidly with anxiety. 'He has found out that you three are in the pay of Russia and are plotting against India. What the plot is he does not know yet, but as I know Hugh, I feel certain that before long he will find out everything and make you pay to the very uttermost.'

Novar gave a sigh of relief, but Rahtz looked at her intently for a second or two as though trying to pierce her inmost soul, and Joan, still with a smile of triumph on her face, waited in dreadful anxiety to know if he were satisfied that she could tell him nothing more. At last he spoke.

'It is lucky for you that you have replied candidly,' he said. She almost gave herself away in her relief. 'I did not want to hurt you, but if you had refused to answer I would not have hesitated.'

'Is that what you meant by writing to my brother to say that I would be quite safe?' she asked contemptuously.

He shrugged his shoulders.

'You are a pawn that has strayed on to the chess board of great events,' he said; 'and to gain my ends I would sweep you aside with as little compunction as I would the ordinary ivory piece.'

'I am quite sure of it,' she said, with an insolence that made him almost admire her.

'You have courage, Miss Shannon,' he remarked. 'I could almost wish that happier events had brought us together and enabled us to be friends.'

'Thank you,' she said bitterly. 'I would rather make friends with a snake.'

He rose and bowed mockingly.

'You honour me,' he said. 'I have a great admiration for the serpent family. A snake knows when to strike and it seldom misses. I flatter myself that I can strike with almost as much success.'

'Satan also associated himself with the snake,' she remarked. 'I have already noticed that you and he have a great deal in common.'

He laughed.

'This is splendid!' he chuckled. 'Miss Shannon, I begin to admire you more and more. You are just the Eve I should love to try my satanic wiles on.'

'Then you would fail,' she retorted.

'I wonder. My apple might have too much delight even for you to resist. Come along, Novar; you too, Kamper; let us leave Miss Shannon with Hudson. He has a lot to say to her I think.'

He bowed to Joan once more and left the apartment with his two companions. She made as though to follow, but Hudson hurried across the room and closed the door.

'At last!' he said hoarsely, but with a note of triumph in his voice. 'This is the first time you and I have been alone since that unfortunate night on the ship when you and your brother misunderstood my intentions.'

'Misunderstood your intentions!' she echoed scornfully. 'In what way were they misunderstood?'

'You both thought I was a rotter; that I intended to harm you, when my only fault was that I loved you and had not strength enough to hide my love.'

'Don't talk to me of love!' she cried. 'Why, such a word on your lips is a desecration of one of the most beautiful gifts of God. You love indeed; with a mind like yours, bestial, filthy, hideous! Please let me go! If my brother and his companions knew that I stood so close to you they would be revolted as I am, and would never rest until they had purged the world of the taint you put upon it.'

An angry frown came upon his face.

'Be careful!' he threatened. 'You are going too far.'

'I could never go far enough in my contempt for a thing like you,' she went on without hesitation. 'There can be nothing worse than a man who takes advantage of a woman and tries to force her into a loathsome compact by threatening danger to those she loves, if she will not bend to his will. And when, in addition to that, he attempts to sell his own country, the country which has given him birth, nourished him, and brought him up as one of her trusted sons and enabled him to enjoy a position of responsibility and honour when he betrays his trust and – oh! I wish I could think of words to tell you what you are – if only I could make you realise the utter depths of degradation to which you have descended, for even you must have been pure once! God grant that there are not many such as you – I am sure there cannot be. Even the companions with whom you have associated yourself are saints compared with you. They are vicious, cruel, unscrupulous, but I cannot think that they can have gone to the very dregs of vice as you have done. You are the worst of traitors, the most contemptible of cowards and are not worthy to associate with the lowest reptile that lives. You—'

'You have said enough,' he said in an ominously calm voice. 'I do not wish to hear any more.'

'Of course you don't! I have tried to make you realise my feelings for you – I only wish I could have put it stronger.'

'Joan, you are cruel!'

'Cruel! To you!' she laughed unsteadily. 'I am beginning to think you must be insane.'

'You'll make me insane if you talk to me in that tone any longer. But hatred is akin to love, and I'll make you love me yet.'

He came towards her.

'Keep away!' she cried. 'I already feel as though your very presence in the same room has made me unclean. Stand aside and let me go!'

'No, I won't! I have listened to you, and now you will have to listen to me.'

'Spare me any further conversation!' she begged.

'Of course, like all women,' he sneered, 'you think you can say anything you like; insult a man to your heart's content and then expect him, poor fool, to bow his head and go away confounded. But I am not such an idiot as that, and so I am going to say a few words. When a man desires a woman he'll get her no matter the price, no matter what either he or she may suffer in the process and—'

'So those are your ideas, are they?' she interrupted, with a greater scorn in her voice than even before.

He raised his hand and went on:

'Yes, they are my ideas and they should be the ideas of any man who calls himself a man. I have wanted several women in my life, but never one as I want you. Although you scoff at my love, it is nevertheless true that I love you with a passion that is eating me away; a passion which is burning my brain and wrecking me physically. You are here now in my power and I assure you that you will never see your brother or your precious American lover again. You are mine!' His voice rose until it became almost shrill. 'Mine until the end of things and nothing you can say will alter it. I am perfectly willing to marry you, if that will give you any satisfaction, although marriage is merely a convention – an excuse for love; but have you I will! Insult me as much as you like; use all the degrading epithets you can think of – nothing will make any difference to the fact that you are in my power!'

He came towards her, the light of an unholy triumph in his eyes. With her breath coming in great sobs of fear, and her heart fluttering wildly, she shrank behind the chair.

'Go away!' she panted. 'Don't dare touch me!'

He laughed and with a bound caught her and dragged her into his arms. She struggled like a wild cat, and beat her fists against his face, but he did not seem to mind.

'I've got you,' he gasped between the blows.

He pressed her to him savagely until all the breath seemed to leave her body, and presently with a great, heartbroken sigh she had no further strength left to fight against his brutality, and hung half-fainting in his arms. He kissed her again and again, and as she felt his loathsome lips press hers with a cruelty that almost brought the blood, she made a feeble effort to resist him; but it was useless, and from sheer horror and fright she fainted dead away.

When he noticed her pallor and felt the lifeless little body hanging in his arms, he became alarmed and, placing her in the chair, tried to revive her. It was some time before she regained consciousness, and when, at last, her eyes opened, and she saw him staring down at her, such a look of contempt came into them that all his savagery was renewed. He stood up and an obscene smile curved his lips.

'You can go to your room now if you like, you little vixen,' he said, 'and you can spend the afternoon making up your mind to be reasonable. At ten o'clock tonight, I'll come to you and offer you marriage. If you agree, we'll be married at once according to the Hindu, Muslim or Sikh rites. If you refuse – well, we'll dispense with a wedding altogether.'

She tottered to her feet and stumbled to the door.

'I'll kill myself before you touch me again,' she said in a voice that could hardly be heard, but which, nevertheless, was full of an undying spirit.

'You won't!' he laughed. 'I'll see to that.'

Opening the door he called to Kamper, who was sitting in a room opposite reading a paper. The Jew strolled out and seeing Joan's condition grinned.

'Miss Shannon desires to go to her room,' said Hudson.

'I don't blame her,' said Kamper insolently. 'This vay, Miss!'

Joan staggered after him down the passage, and once inside the small prison-like apartment gave full vent to her feelings in a flood of tears. Kamper was about to make some coarse remark, but refrained, and going out locked the door.

It was a long time before Joan was composed enough to think clearly, and she still felt weak and very faint. She almost despaired now of anyone coming to her rescue and tried hard, despite her terror, to collect her thoughts sufficiently to prepare for the further and greater ordeal which she knew was before her that night. Her head ached abominably, and it was with difficulty she forced herself to examine the room in the hope that she might find a weapon of some sort with which to defend herself when Hudson made his threatened visit at ten o'clock. But there was nothing in the room except the bed, one chair, and a mat. It was a small bare apartment with one door and no windows, light being admitted through two large ventilators high up. She wondered if by dragging the bed before the door she could keep the scoundrel out and then, to her joy, she saw that the door was furnished with a bolt about halfway up. She was about to shoot it into its socket at once, but reflected that in all probability food would be brought to her, and she knew she would have to eat to keep her strength up and if she drew attention to the bolt by withdrawing it when the Hindu woman came, steps would be taken to render it useless. She determined, therefore, not to touch it until late in the evening and also decided that she would try to pull off one of the legs of the chair to act as a weapon.

The afternoon dragged wearily along, but resting on the bed had enabled Joan to recover all her courage and a lot of confidence. She had hopes now of being able to keep Hudson out, if not all night, at least for a considerable time and perhaps, if he tried to break in the door, which did not look very strong, the others would interfere and make him leave her alone. She had meant what she said when she told him she would kill herself before he touched her again, but she had no means of taking her own life. It had occurred to her that by crushing the glass of the solitary electric bulb in the room and swallowing it she could encompass that end, but her death would be most agonising and probably take such a long time that in the meantime he would be able to have his will with her. If only the meeting at Mozang College was that very night! She knew that Hugh or one of the others would afterwards follow Novar and Rahtz to their haunt and rescue her. As it was she had no hope of rescue at all, unless a miracle happened.

It must have been nearly five when the Hindu woman brought her a meal on a tray. Apparently they had no desire to starve her and as soon as she was left alone again she set to work and forced herself to eat until she could eat no longer. With the food she drank three cups of tea and felt greatly refreshed. Then once more she lay down to wait.

It was quite dark when the woman came back for

the tray, but Joan had not bothered to switch on the light. She had thought of attempting to hide away the only knife with which she had been provided, but it was an old blunt instrument and so bendable that it was utterly useless, so she left it on the tray.

Before departing, the woman turned on the light and made the bed. As she said 'Salaam!' when she was going out, Joan concluded that that was the last time she would visit her that night. The girl waited for another hour or so and then crossing to the door slipped the bolt into place. She next took up the chair and started to wrench off one of the legs. It was a long and difficult task and she hurt her hands considerably and for a long time it resisted all her efforts to move it. At last, however, it began to give and after further pressure came off, and she found herself with quite a serviceable weapon. After that she lay down again and must have dozed off to sleep, for she had little recollection of any time passing before she heard the key being turned in the lock. Instantly she was on the alert and, although her terror returned in full force, she sat up and quietly waited ready to fight till the last. The door was pushed and a voice, which she recognised as Hudson's, uttered an oath.

'Open this door!' he shouted, but she made no reply.

For a considerable time she heard him throwing his weight against it in an effort to break it in, and though it shook ominously it resisted all his attempts, even to the savage kicks he landed on it from time to time. Presently she caught the murmur of other voices and prayed that the newcomers would persuade Hudson to give it up. But no; she heard the latter tell them that she had bolted the door – he having quite forgotten the bolt. There was a laugh and she knew they had gone away for there was no further talking.

'Open the door, Joan,' said Hudson in coaxing tones. 'I just want to speak to you. I won't harm you!'

She took no notice so he redoubled his efforts and after a while she thought the door seemed to be giving a little. She took a firmer grip upon the chair leg and waited. Crash after crash came, then suddenly all was quiet.

'God grant he has gone!' she whispered fervently.

But he had only gone in search of a weapon to smash in the obstacle and after a few minutes he returned with a hatchet, and attacked one of the upper panels. Before such onslaughts the wood-work soon began to give way and a piece came flying into the room accompanied by an oath of satisfaction from the man without. Joan crossed to the side of the door and waited. Two or three minutes later the whole panel gave way; there was a pause and she knew he was looking for her. She made no sign, however, and presently he put his hand through the hole to draw the bolt. Then she brought down the chair leg with all the strength of which she was capable. He gave a howl of pain and the hand was withdrawn. For some minutes he cursed unrestrainedly.

'You hell-cat!' he roared, at last. 'I'll make you suffer for that!'

'You had better go away,' she said quietly, though her whole body was trembling violently.

'I've come to ask you if you'll marry me.'

'I have already given you my answer.'

'Very well, I'm coming in to marry you in my own way, and in spite of yourself.'

'If you put your hand in again you'll receive the same treatment as before.'

For a few moments there was silence, as though he was reflecting, then the head of the hatchet came through the door and moved down to the bolt. Undismayed Joan caught hold of it, and was pulled towards the opening until she could see him leering in at her. Desperately she strove to get the weapon from his grasp, but at last, with a sob, she was compelled to let go. At the same moment his other hand shot through and caught her by the shoulder. Blow after blow she aimed at him, but with a sudden vicious shove he flung her to the floor. In another moment he had drawn the bolt, and was inside the room.

She staggered to her feet, still grasping the leg of the chair, and ran round to the far side of the bed. He stood watching her with mocking eyes and dabbing his left hand, from which the blood was streaming, with a handkerchief.

'Your conquest will be all the sweeter after this,' he said.

Then with a sudden movement he had pushed

the bed towards her and she was pinned to the wall. With fiendish cruelty he continued pushing and she suffered agonies.

'Just a little punishment for your obstinacy,' he chuckled. 'And now perhaps you are ready to come to my arms?'

'Never!' she gasped.

He leapt on to the bed and seized her before she had time to move, and though she fought wildly, hitting at him with all her might, he never let go and gradually dragged her towards him. She caught him one blow on the left side of the head which brought the blood streaming down by his ear, and then he had wrested her weapon from her and flung it away. Holding both her arms he forced her down until she was lying flat on the bed. She kicked and screamed, but he knelt on her legs until at last she lay there powerless to move, in her eyes the fear of worse than death.

For some moments he gloated over her, his eyes shining with a lustful delight.

'My woman!' he said. 'My Joan!'

CHAPTER 31

THE END OF A TRAITOR

Abdul Rahim arrived outside The Retreat somewhere about ten o'clock and, standing in the darkest part of the road, contemplated the entrance gates of the small estate. It was rather a quiet neighbourhood this and, except for an occasional tonga and a few pedestrians, the road was deserted. The gates were in darkness and presently the smartly dressed Mahommedan went up to them and peered through. On the right-hand side was the small lodge and a dim light showed through a window. The drive ran on for about fifty yards and ended in a loop running through a large porch at the entrance of the mansion. The place was well lighted and Rahim saw several vague shadows moving about in front of it, whether of men watching for intruders, or merely servants he had no means of ascertaining. Feeling inside a pocket to make sure that his revolver lay handy, and waiting for two men with a stream of bullocks to pass, he commenced to climb. He scaled the gates rather clumsily yet with occasional glimpses of real agility, and after three or four minutes stood inside the grounds. Approaching the window of the lodge he looked in. The place appeared to consist of a single room, and in one corner of it a woman sat rocking a child to sleep; there was no sign of anyone else.

Rahim stood for a moment rubbing his chin reflectively, then crept to the door and gently pushed it. To his relief it moved quietly open. He knew that the keys of the gate were hung on a nail just inside, for he had seen the gatekeeper place them there the night before by the light of the lantern the man had carried, and Abdul Rahim wanted those keys; the difficulty was to get them without the woman seeing, or hearing him. Gradually he opened the door until there was just room enough to put his hand inside. It was nervy work, for if he were discovered it would probably mean the ruin of his plans. However, his fingers presently touched a key and by slow degrees he gathered the bunch into his hand and lifted it from its nail. A second later he was back at the gate and was trying a key – the largest of four – in the keyhole. As luck would have it, it was the right one and he turned the lock. There were two bolts still to be withdrawn; one worked easily, but the other grated in its socket and it was only by infinite care that he succeeded in drawing it without making a noise. At last it was done and he returned to the lodge. With the loop of the string holding the keys held ready in his hand, he felt for the nail, found it, and hung the bunch back without the slightest suspicion of a sound.

The first part of his task accomplished satisfactorily, Rahim breathed a sigh of relief and set off for the house. He wore rubber-soled shoes and, moving without noise, he took advantage of every bush and tree and, by degrees, drew closer to the building. The porch was lighted up and he realised that it was going to be a difficult matter to get inside without being seen, as there were several men about the grounds, some of whom he had the greatest trouble in avoiding. He crouched behind a large shrub and watched, and presently became aware of a distant knocking which continued intermittently for some time. A few minutes went by, then two men came out of the house laughing loudly. They were both dressed as Parsees and one appeared to be rather weak, as he walked haltingly and leant on the arm of his companion. They strolled away into the grounds and Rahim took a sudden resolve to risk being seen and enter the house at once. He felt an intuition that he must not delay longer. With this decision he rose from his hiding place, strolled across the intervening space and into the house, deeming it safer to walk across slowly, as though he were a member of the household entering on domestic business, rather than dashing across with the obvious intention of avoiding detection.

He found himself in a wide hall with several rooms opening into it and a passage crossing it at right angles at the far end. His revolver, a heavy Army pattern, was in his hand now and he crept quietly towards the passage. The banging had ceased for some time, but there was a confused medley of sounds coming from somewhere in the direction towards which he was going and on his right-hand side. He reached the corner and cautiously looked round. A man was standing within a few feet of him at the door of a room, but his back was turned towards him. The sounds were louder now and it suddenly dawned upon Rahim what they were. At that moment a woman's screams rang out and the man in front of him chuckled. This was no time for ceremony and, grasping his revolver by the barrel, the Indian darted forward and brought it down with sickening force on the head of the fellow before him. Kamper crumpled up with a grunt and slid to the floor senseless. Rahim dragged him into the room – a small bedroom – at the door of which he had been standing, and leaving him just inside, closed the door on him and hurried along to the room from which the sound of screams was issuing. He paused at the door and looked in. The place was in disorder, but the Indian took no notice of the chaos, his horrified gaze was fixed on the bed upon which a girl was lying with a man holding her down by the arms and kneeling on her legs to prevent her struggling.

'My woman! My Joan!' he was saying, and bent to kiss her.

'Mr Hudson, I believe!' said Abdul Rahim quietly.

Hudson spun round as though he had been shot and found himself gazing into a revolver held by a neatly dressed Mahommedan, standing with one hand in a pocket, whose mouth was drawn together so tightly that it looked a mere slit, and in whose eyes the ex-civil servant saw death.

'Who are you?' he asked hoarsely. Even under the painted brown of his face could be seen the pallor of fear.

'Never mind who I am,' was the stern reply. 'It is enough to know that I am here to prevent your doing the dastardly deed you contemplate.'

With a cry in which joy and hope were mingled, Joan rose from the bed and staggered to the side of her deliverer.

'I don't know who you are,' she cried; 'whether you are one of these men or a stranger, but have pity on me! Take me away from him – anywhere; please, please!'

'I am here to take you away, Miss Shannon,' he replied quietly in his peculiar, sibilant English. 'And I do not belong to this gang – I am our brother's friend.'

The sudden relief was too much for the poor girl. She sank on her knees in a revulsion of feeling and, covering her face with her hands, sobbed out her gratitude.

'You are the luckiest man alive, Mr Hudson,' said Rahim still calmly, 'that I did not put a bullet into you at once. However, I doubt not that the pleasure has been reserved for someone else.

Come on, Miss Shannon,' he went on gently, 'let us get away from here!'

'You can't take her from me,' shouted Hudson, in whose eyes the light of madness had reappeared. 'She is mine – mine I tell you!'

Joan rose to her feet and walked shakily to the door. Hudson made a frantic leap towards her, the revolver spun in Rahim's hand like lightning and all in one moment he brought the butt down with a crash on the other man's head. Hudson seemed to stop in mid-air, then with a groan he fell and lay still.

The Mahommedan gazed down at him calmly. 'I was puzzled what to do with you,' he murmured contentedly, 'but you have solved the problem for me. Of course I might have shot you! Now do exactly as I tell you, Miss Shannon,' he added, turning to the girl, who was looking down at Hudson with wide-open eyes, full of horror. 'We may run into others and shall have to go very carefully.'

'Have you killed him?' she asked.

'No; he'll be all right in half an hour. I didn't hit him as hard as the other.' He glanced at his wristwatch. 'It is nearly eleven,' he said, 'your brother will be getting anxious. Come!'

Taking her by the arm he led her down the passage. Looking round the corner to see if there was anybody about, he found the hall empty, and they went on cautiously. Just as they reached the front door, however, he heard the sound of footsteps and bundling Joan unceremoniously into a room nearby, he followed her. The two of them stood behind the door.

'Not a sound!' he hissed.

Watching through the crack he saw the two Parsees slowly enter the house.

'All is silence, my dear Rahtz,' one was saying in English. 'It would appear that Hudson has bent the girl to his will.'

'Not an easy task,' laughed the other.

They passed by and entered a room farther along, and Rahim and Joan breathed freely again. They waited for a few moments, then emerged from their hiding place and, creeping across the hall, made their way out of the house. The lights in the porch had now been switched off and they were thus enabled to reach the shelter of the bushes and trees without danger. By gradual stages Rahim led Joan towards the gates, stopping every now and then to hide as he saw figures moving about in front of them. At last, after a considerable time, they passed the lodge and the Indian tried the gates with anxiety, fearing that the gatekeeper had discovered that they were open and had locked them again. To his relief the one he pulled came towards him and, in a moment, he and Joan were through and hurrying along the road.

'I have a car waiting about a hundred yards away,' he said. 'I hope it has not been stolen.'

'I don't know how to thank you,' she began.

'Don't!' he said shortly. 'What I have done, I have done by the grace of Allah!'

The car had not been stolen, and as he helped her in he saw that she wore no covering to her feet.

'Why you have no shoes!' he said. 'Why did you not tell me? I would have carried you!'

She laughed.

'As though that mattered,' she said.

She settled herself in her seat and he got in beside her.

'Are you comfortable?' he asked.

'Wonderfully!' she murmured.

'Now may I be forgiven and may Mahommed (the blessings of Allah be upon him) intercede for me,' he said suddenly.

'What's the matter?' she asked in quick alarm.

'I have brought no rug to cover you!'

'Never mind that,' she said. 'I had a cloak with me, but I left it behind, and also my—' She stopped and blushed, 'my other garment,' she added hastily.

'I would have brought it if I'd known,' he said.

'Please don't bother! It is not very cold tonight, and I wouldn't mind if I froze now that we are away from that awful place!'

'I know,' he said; 'I'll take off my coat and you can have it.'

She laid her hand on his arm.

'I wouldn't think of it,' she said. 'Really I am quite all right!'

'Are you sure?'

'Perfectly!'

442

'Then we'll make straight for your home,' he said.

He slipped in the clutch and they were off. The word 'home' had brought a great sob of joy from Joan, and he did not speak another word to her until they pulled up near the bungalow.

'Run along in!' he said. 'I'd rather not be present at the reunion.'

Without a word she jumped out of the car and ran into the house. He watched her with a smile until she had disappeared, then turned and drove away.

Hugh had just made his despairing remark that Abdul Rahim must have failed to rescue Joan, when the three men heard the sound of a car apparently approaching the house. They were instantly on their feet, their eyes searching each other's, their faces bloodless, hardly daring to breathe. The front door opened and shut and their burning gaze fixed on the entrance to the room. A figure suddenly appeared there, a little figure whom they did not recognise at first on account of the sari which enveloped her dainty little form. Then, with a wonderful cry which found an echo in every heart, Miles dashed forward and gathered her into his arms.

'Joan! My little Joan!' he cried.

He kissed her, held her from him to gaze hungrily at her, and whisper her name, then kissed her again.

Hugh and Cousins shook hands for a whole

minute, but neither could utter a word. They could not even make a sound, but Hugh's eyes were unnaturally bright and down Cousins' cheeks the tears of joy were streaming without restraint.

Presently Joan gently released herself from her lover's grasp, and flew to Hugh, who took her into a great bear-like hug. Then came Cousins turn and this time she went to him without shyness as though she realised that he had suffered as much as her lover and her brother. The little man put his arms round her with infinite tenderness, like a mother taking into her arms an only child. He was about to kiss her on the forehead, but she raised her lips to his, and he touched them almost reverently.

'I can't say "my Joan",' he said chokingly, 'but I can say, "our Joan"! Thank God you are back safely!'

'Let us go and bring in my rescuer!' she said. 'I want to thank him.'

'Sure,' said Miles. 'We all do!'

'God knows how we're going to do it,' said Hugh. 'But come along!'

They hurried out of the house. Miles, having noticed that Joan wore no shoes, lifted her up and carried her as though she were a baby. Outside nothing but darkness met their searching gaze.

'Oh!' cried Joan, a great disappointment in her voice. 'He has gone!'

The others were almost as disappointed as she, and they stood there sorrowfully until Hugh spoke.

'Never mind,' he said; 'we'll find him, and make him face our gratitude! Rainer will know where to get hold of him.'

They turned and re-entered the house.

'He was wonderful,' sighed Joan, 'just wonderful!'

Twenty minutes after Abdul Rahim had taken Joan away from The Retreat, Hudson sat up and looked round him. There was a fixed intensity in his gaze which was unnatural, and when he noticed the chaotic state of the room he began to chuckle in a low cunning manner. He rose to his feet, crossed over to the bed, and looked at it.

'Where are you, Joan?' he called. 'You're playing a trick on me. Come out of your hiding place!'

He looked under the bed, then straightening himself laughed aloud.

'She's gone! My little bird has flown! I'll find her and I'll kill anyone who has taken her away!'

He staggered to the door and out into the passage. He pushed open another door a little way along and looked in. Kamper was lying on the floor face downwards and Hudson contemplated him for some moments in silence.

'You must be dead, I think,' he said in the tone of one who was entirely unconcerned. 'She killed you I suppose, and she will kill the others, too; I must go and help her.'

He went straight along the passage, passing the hall on his way, and eventually reached the other end where his own rooms were situated. He entered a tiny little sitting room and, closing the door, sat down by a small table on which was a decanter of whisky and two glasses. He stared at the whisky as though he had never seen such a liquor before and, pouring some into a glass smelt it, and drank it. He repeated this process several times until the decanter was almost empty and the more he drank, the more cunning became the look in his eyes. Presently he rose and went into the bedroom. He stood for several minutes in the centre of the room with his hands to his head as though trying to recollect something, but apparently it eluded him, for he sat aimlessly at a writing-table, and picking up a fountain pen played with it in the manner of a child. On the desk in front of him was lying a large writing pad, and he began to write on it as though with no very clear idea of what he was doing. The sight of ink upon paper appeared to please him, for he settled down and wrote at great length covering several sheets with words scrawled in a bewildering jumble. He tired of this at length, and threw his efforts and the writing pad into a waste-paper basket which stood at his feet. One after another he opened the drawers of the desk and presently picked up a revolver. He looked at it and then memory appeared to return to him, for he stood up and made his way back into the passage.

'Must help little Joan,' he muttered.

He reached the hall and wandered along towards the front door. The sound of voices reached him from a room on his right and he paused and listened. Then with a chuckle of satisfaction he turned and entered the room. It was the same apartment in which Joan had faced the three men in the morning. Rahtz and Novar were sitting there smoking, and apparently holding a serious conversation. They looked up as Hudson entered. Rahtz laughed.

'So you have tamed the little Shannon,' he said. 'My word! It must have taken some doing to judge from the state you're in.'

Hudson laughed, a silly, cackling sort of laugh and Novar frowned.

'What's the matter with you, man?' he asked.

'Looking for Joan!' chuckled the ex-civil servant.

Suddenly he stopped laughing and leant towards the other two, his lips curling away from his teeth in a snarl, his eyes bloodshot and staring.

'What have you done with her?' he cried. 'Where have you put her? Why didn't she kill you like the other?'

The two Russians looked at him in amazement.

'What are you talking about?' demanded Rahtz angrily.

'Joan! I want her and you've taken her away.'

Rahtz sprang to his feet.

'Do you mean to say that she has escaped?' he thundered.

Hudson nodded his head.

'You took her away,' he reiterated, 'otherwise she would have killed you, too.'

'Why do you say she would have killed us too?' asked Novar in a shaky voice. 'Has she killed anyone else?'

He rose from his chair and clutched Rahtz by the arm apprehensively. Again Hudson nodded.

'She killed the little man – Kamper. He is dead!' he added in a tone of horrible satisfaction.

Suddenly he gave a scream of maniacal laughter. Peal upon peal rose to the high ceiling and was echoed throughout the room until the place seemed full of laughing, gloating fiends.

'Oh, my God!' cried Novar, and violently. 'He has gone mad!'

Even Rahtz was unnerved for some seconds. Hudson continued to laugh, then as suddenly as he had started he stopped.

'You're devils,' he snarled, 'both of you. You made me give you information from the office, copies of secret letters, and private documents, and now you've taken away Joan from me. But you shan't have her and I won't bring you any more Government secrets, because I'm going to kill you. You won't want anything then.' He laughed again. 'Will you like being dead?' he asked, as though he were asking them if they would like a holiday.

Rahtz pulled himself together and strode forward, but Hudson raised the revolver and pointed it at him.

'Don't move!' he said querulously. 'I'm going to kill you I tell you!'

'We'll talk of that later on,' said Rahtz soothingly. 'At present we've got to find Joan, you know.'

Hudson stared at him doubtfully, then nodded. 'Yes – find Joan,' he said.

'Come along then,' said Rahtz, and took his arm.

But the touch of the arm roused the devil in Hudson. His eyes almost seemed to start from their sockets and he suddenly caught the Russian by the throat with his left arm, with a grip that paralysed his movements. He struggled desperately but it was useless. Hudson was ordinarily a strong man, but now the strength of madness was on him as well and the Russian, in his weak, sickly state, was like a child to him. He swung him backwards and forwards, watching with gloating eyes the while, and uttering insane chuckles of glee. In vain Rahtz croaked out for mercy; the more he tried to speak the harder the madman squeezed his throat. Novar stood helpless, trembling with fear and with beads of perspiration standing out on his forehead. At last, with a desperate effort, he staggered forward and caught Hudson by the right arm. The latter stopped swinging Rahtz about and stared at him.

'Go away!' he said. 'I'll kill you presently.'

'You're acting like a child,' cried Novar in a high-pitched trembling voice. 'We can't find Joan if you do these silly things.'

'Oh,' said the maniac, 'I forgot little Joan!'

He let go of Rahtz, who sank to the floor and crouched there gasping for breath. Novar was more terror-stricken than ever now as he saw that Hudson's left hand was free. He clung hard to the right arm, however, and spoke rapidly, soothingly, in the hope of quieting the man who was looking at him with the burning gaze of the homicidal maniac. His object was to get the revolver from the latter's hand, for he felt certain that sooner or later Hudson would start shooting. He would have been wiser had he let go and spoken to the other from a distance, for the madman presently resented the hold on his arm and tried to shake it off. With a sob of apprehension, Novar clung with all his strength and then Hudson was on him. The two swayed backwards. and forwards and the fat, flabby, out-of-condition Russian soon knew that unless something happened to save him, and that at once, his days were numbered. The lunatic tore his arm from the other's grip – in doing so he dropped the revolver – and his two hands were round Novar's throat. Gradually he forced the latter's head back; the Russian fought desperately, kicking, scratching, trying to bite, but Hudson only laughed horribly, fiendishly. Novar's strength began to go, his lips were turning blue, drops of blood began to ooze from the corners of his eyes.

By this time Rahtz had nearly recovered, and seeing the desperate condition of his friend he picked up Hudson's revolver and got somehow to his feet. He staggered towards the struggling men, and waiting a second until the madman's body was in a line with him, he fired. Hudson let go of

Novar – who dropped groaning to the floor – and slowly turned round. His face wore a look of intense surprise. He uttered no sound, but for a second stood there swaying, then crashed to the floor – dead. Rahtz sank on to a divan and it was nearly ten minutes before either he or Novar moved.

At last Novar raised his head.

'Get me a drink!' he said in a hoarse whisper.

Rahtz poured out a stiff peg of whisky, took it to him, and helped him to drink, after which he returned to the table and gave himself a similar dose. Novar made several attempts to rise, but it was a long time before he eventually got to his feet and then only with the aid of the other. He looked down at the body of their former companion, and shuddered.

'Is he dead?' he asked shakily.

Rahtz nodded.

They sat for some time without moving, gradually recovering from the effects of their ordeal. At length Rahtz drew himself up with a long deep breath.

'We must go and see what has happened,' he muttered. 'If, as he said, the girl has escaped, we are in danger. She is bound to tell where we are hiding.'

'She couldn't get out unless she climbed over the gate,' said Novar.

'That's true,' replied the other, 'and I don't suppose she could do that. You go and organise a search through the grounds, while I look in her room, and see if Kamper really has been killed. If he has somebody else has done it, not she. That girl could never kill anyone.'

Novar took another drink and departed slowly to give orders for a search to be made. Rahtz went along to the room in which Joan had been imprisoned. Of course he found no one there and after glancing round he looked into Kamper's room. The Jew was just beginning to recover. Rahtz helped him up and gave him some water.

'What happened to you?' he asked, when the other was able to rise from the floor and sat on a chair resting his head on his hands.

Kamper looked at him and swore vilely.

'How do I know?' he replied in Russian. 'I was standing in the corridor listening to the noise that was going on in the girl's room, when something hit me on the head.'

'It couldn't have been the girl, I suppose?' queried Rahtz.

'Of course not. She was struggling vith Hudson at the time.'

Rahtz stood biting his lips for a few moments.

'Then somebody must have got in and rescued her,' he said. 'We've been discovered and the sooner we hide the safer for us.'

He told Kamper about Hudson's madness and death, then left him to find Novar. The latter was coming towards him excitedly, followed by three men, when he reached the front door.

'We found the gate open,' cried Novar, 'so

obviously she has got away. The keys were in their place and Babu Lai said that the gate was locked.'

'He lied!' growled Rahtz.

'I don't think so,' replied Novar. 'I kicked him until he groaned for mercy, but he still maintained that he had locked and bolted the gate as usual. Yet it was open.'

'Then whoever got in and rescued the girl had duplicate keys,' said Rahtz. 'She has escaped and someone has rescued her.'

'How do you know that?' asked Novar quickly.

'Because Kamper was standing in the passage listening to the struggle going on between Hudson and the Shannon girl, when he was knocked on the head by someone behind him and lost consciousness. I rather incline to the belief that the same person treated Hudson in a similar manner and the blow helped to bring on his madness. That person is either someone in our employment, who stole the keys of the gate and replaced them, or someone from outside with duplicates.'

'But even if he unlocked the gates from the outside the bolts would have prevented him from opening them.'

'True! He probably climbed over and unlocked and unbolted the gates from the inside. But we can't waste time trying to find out what happened. We are in real danger and the sooner we escape below the better. Luckily only Jai Singh and his brother know of our hiding place so we can't be betrayed.'

The two Russians entered the house – Novar first calling Jai Singh and telling him to gather everyone into the porch as he wanted to speak to them. Kamper was standing in the hall, a rough bandage – which he had fixed himself – on his head.

'What are you going to do?' he asked.

'Gather as few things as possible and get below,' replied Novar tersely, and hurried away to his apartments.

The others followed his example. Ten minutes later Novar came rushing into Rahtz's room, his lips white, and in his eyes a deadly fear.

'Those letters from Bukharin—' he screamed. 'They've gone!'

Rahtz was no less affected and for once in a way even he showed terror.

'My God!' he cried. 'Are you sure?'

'Absolutely! I've searched among all my papers – everywhere – but there is no sign of them.'

'Perhaps you left them behind?'

Novar shook his head.

'No,' he said; 'they were fastened to those drafts you and I made out. The drafts are here, but the letters are gone! I did not examine them before I left the house, but I must have had them then, because they were locked in my safe. They have been stolen from here.'

Rahtz was too overcome to speak for some moments. Then he wiped the perspiration from his forehead.

'One of them was about Germany and the airships, wasn't it?' he asked.

'Yes; and the other telling us to do all we could to damage British prestige in India.'

The Principal of Mozang College glared at his companion.

'You damn fool!' he snapped. 'Oh, you damn fool! This is the end of things. We'll have to urge immediate measures at the meeting on Tuesday night, or we're beaten.'

'Perhaps they even know of the meeting,' said Novar in a voice of abject terror.

'Pull yourself together!' said the other grimly. 'We are on the verge of a catastrophe. Everything now depends upon rapid action and *we shall have to see that it is taken.*'

Novar returned to his room a broken man. Left alone Rahtz buried his face in his hands for some minutes.

'To be checkmated,' he groaned, 'by a schoolmaster is too bitter a pill to swallow.' He stood up and a glint of resolution came into his eyes. 'But we're not beaten yet!' he added aloud, 'not by a very long way.'

Rahtz was a scoundrel, but he was a born fighter and he had the courage of half a dozen Novars.

Ten minutes later the latter stood at the door of the house and spoke to the motley collection of men gathered in front of him. He told them that they must disperse immediately; that the police might raid the premises at any moment and that he suspected one among their number to be a traitor whom he would be certain to discover later on and punish thoroughly. He added that Jai Singh would see that they were all provided with money to keep them for some time and that he would take their addresses so that they could be recalled when they were wanted. He then called Jai Singh to him, took him into his room, and gave him a bundle of notes.

'Distribute those!' he said. 'After that take my car away and hide it for the present, and instruct Mr Rahtz's chauffeur to do the same with his master's car. Leave the other where it is. Mr Hudson has killed himself unfortunately – which reminds me you had better get some men to dig a grave and bury him before they go.'

Jai Singh showed no emotion nor concern of any sort on hearing of Hudson's death. He merely bent his head to show that he understood and hurried from the room.

In less than half an hour there was no one left anywhere on the premises but the three Russians, Jai Singh and his brother. The Sikh had carried out Novar's instructions to the letter, and the five were now preparing to disappear literally into the bowels of the earth.

They entered a small bare room at the back of the house and Jai Singh crossed to a wall and pressed hard against a portion that was rather irregular. Instantly a part of the brick flooring rose and disclosed a flight of steps. At the bottom of the steps were three rooms ventilated by a shaft that ran up through the middle of the house and finished in a group of chimney pots at the top. The underground chambers contained three native beds, a couple of tables and some chairs and enough tinned provisions to last for two weeks at least. One by one the men descended, the trapdoor closed, and there remained no trace whatever of the way to the apartments below.

Hardly had the room resumed its normal appearance than Abdul Rahim entered, still as spick and span as ever. After ringing up the Governor, as he had promised, to report the safety of Joan, he had returned to the scene of his adventures. Hidden opposite the gates he had watched the exodus of about a dozen men with their wives and as many of their household belongings as they could carry; he saw the two cars driven away and the return of one of the drivers. The gates had been locked, and repeating the performance of an earlier hour, he climbed over them into the grounds, followed the driver up to the house, and with the utmost daring crept in after him. By taking the most tremendous risks and at the same time using the greatest caution, he had traced the three Russians and the two Sikhs to the back of the house and watched them disappear below. As soon as the trapdoor had closed all the lights went out and Abdul Rahim concluded that there was a control below. However, he had seen all he desired to see, so retraced his steps to the gates, clambered over them again, and returned to his car, which had been left in the same place as before.

As he took his place at the wheel he smiled softly.

'Now by the blessing of Allah I will return and have a few hours' sleep,' he said.

CHAPTER 32

SHANNON LEAVES THE COLLEGE

An almost boisterously happy young man drove to Sheranwala College the next morning. Shannon's efforts in India promised to be crowned with success; he had received a most complimentary letter from the Chief; no longer would he have to lecture to the young Muslim and mix with colleagues whom he detested; and above all his sister had been restored to him. There was only one fly in the ointment and that was the treatment to which Joan had been subjected at The Retreat. Before going to bed she had related her experiences without keeping back anything, and the grim, set faces of the three men – who had listened to every word in horror – promised that there would be a stern reckoning with the Russians and Hudson when they met. They had nothing but admiration and delighted wonder for Abdul Rahim's great exploit in rescuing her, and Joan had laid stress on the calm, resourceful manner in which the Indian had carried out his self-appointed task. It was a very tired, but a wonderfully happy Joan who eventually went to bed, but she was not a whit happier than Hugh, Miles and Cousins. The little man had surpassed himself in the length and frequency of his quotations, but nobody had tried to stop him and he had taken full advantage of his opportunity.

Hugh reached the College and went straight to Abdullah's office. He was welcomed by a very sorrowful Principal.

'So you are leaving us, Shannon,' he said. 'I am very sorry and I fear my work will become all the heavier for your departure. I feel very disheartened here and am myself almost inclined to resign; however, I will struggle on in the hope that a little success will attend my efforts. But I am speaking selfishly – I must congratulate you on receiving a Government appointment.'

'Thank you,' said Hugh quietly, feeling rather a hypocrite.

'I understand from His Excellency that your work will be confidential, so I will not inquire into its nature, but if, some time in the future, you can reveal it, I shall be most interested to hear all about it. I hope you will not lose touch with me!'

'Of course not,' declared Hugh. 'And I promise to let you know what work I am engaged in as soon as I am at liberty to do so.'

'Thank you! I may tell you that I made a special point of calling on the secretary of the Board and three of the leading members last night to explain to them about your leaving the College. They were rather disposed to raise objections and quote rules but, of course, the Governor's desire was, in its way, a command and that quietened them. A special meeting will be held this afternoon to receive your resignation. It will be accepted with great regret I assure you.'

Hugh laughed a trifle sarcastically.

'Not so long ago,' he said, 'they were anxious to call a special meeting to make me resign.'

'Try not to remember that against them,' said Abdullah. 'They have recently begun to realise that in you they had a man who was worth the rest of the staff put together and actually agree with me that apart from you, and one or two others, we possess the poorest set of professors in the University. It will be a great job to get the right man in your place.'

'Persuade them to pay an adequate salary,' advised Hugh. 'To expect an Englishman to come out to India and work for five hundred rupees a month is absurd. There are no doubt a good many who would do it, because they would not understand the cost of living out here. But it is absolutely impossible to live on that sum, and a man who tries it will only find himself getting into difficulties, and end by being loaded with debt. Of course in that case I can imagine the authorities raising their sanctimonious eyes to heaven and feeling greatly shocked, but they would be morally responsible for the poor fellow's troubles.'

Abdullah laughed.

'You are rather severe, Shannon,' he said.

'I don't think so,' replied Hugh. 'Perhaps I am cynical, but I have divided the people of this country into three divisions – sahibs, snobs, and sinners – and I think the authorities of this college, with the addition of some of the professors, are in their proper place amongst the sinners.'

'You are a dreadful young man,' smiled the Principal. 'Would you like to attend the meeting this afternoon?'

'No, thanks. I might be inclined to tell a few home truths.'

'Well, if you will write your resignation and hand it to me, I will put it before them.'

'I'll go and do it now,' nodded Hugh.

'I understand that you will be leaving India?'

'Probably, but at present I am not sure. Will you come and dine with us on Thursday night? Perhaps I shall be able to give you more information then.'

'I shall be delighted.'

'At eight o'clock then.'

Hugh left the office and strolled round the College bidding farewell to various professors and students. The fat, elderly man with the chins and walrus moustache expressed the greatest regret at his departure and Hugh regarded him with a bland smile. He knew very well that the other was delighted, for always he had been very jealous of Shannon.

'I cannot conceive how we shall get on without you,' he of the chins said ponderously. 'You have become, in the short time you have been with us, a veritable tower of strength. We shall miss you sadly.'

'Very kind of you,' said Hugh. 'I assure you I shall never forget Sheranwala College.'

'That is nice of you.'

But Hugh hardly meant his remark in the way it was taken.

'Are you leaving India?' inquired the ponderous one.

'Very likely.'

'Then you will never have the opportunity of learning our language.'

For answer Hugh broke out into a long oration on the delights of Lahore in fluent Hindustani, and when he presently shook the flabby hand of the fat person, he left behind him one of the most astonished men in India. Doctor Sadiq he found genuinely sorry to say farewell. The ugly little man was full of his own importance as usual and spent some time in trying to persuade Hugh to look out for a post for him in England.

'You see,' he said in explanation, 'I am utterly wasted in this country. People don't appreciate my learning as they should. Of course they are fools and don't realise that in their midst is a man of great ability, probably the best psychologist in India.'

'You're so small, Sadiq,' said Hugh, 'that they miss you because they don't look low enough – they always look up instead of down.'

The eminent psychologist looked at him with a frown.

'Sometimes, Shannon,' he said, 'I think you are pulling my legs.'

Hugh looked reflectively at the other's extremities.

'Are those legs?' he asked with interest.

'Look here,' said Sadiq, 'it's all very well to make fun of me, but I really am eating my heart out in this country. I want to go somewhere where I shall be appreciated at my true worth.'

'And do you think you will be, in England?'

'Of course! Once there I shall settle down and look for a wife.'

'An English girl?'

Sadiq nodded.

'I could have chosen from three or four when I was there in my student days, but like a fool I came back.'

Hugh looked at him as though he would like to shake him, then laughed.

'The trouble with you, Sadiq,' he said, 'is that you were born without a sense of humour.'

He completed his goodbyes and wrote a letter of resignation which he took to the Principal. Then jumping into his car he drove away. A crowd of students was standing at the gates and cheered him as he went by.

In the meantime Miles – who some time before had paid a railway official to watch for the arrival of Oppenheimer – received a telephone message telling him that a man answering to the description of the German had come in on the Calcutta express and had driven to the Punjab Hotel. When Hugh returned home, therefore, he was informed of Oppenheimer's arrival.

'Perhaps it is not he,' he said. 'Why not go along and see?'

'Precisely what I was thinking of doing,' replied Miles. 'I kinder thought the old chap might be glad to see me, especially as he must be worried some because his pals didn't meet him.'

'How do you know they didn't?'

'Not they! I guess they've hidden themselves away as snug as bugs in a rug, and they won't show their faces anywhere till tomorrow night.'

'They might send a message.'

'M'm, they might do that, but I don't think so. I bet Oppenheimer has all the necessary information about the meeting.'

'But they might just send word to let him know that they're in hiding.'

Miles looked at him thoughtfully then nodded.

'Anyhow I'll go right along and look him up. The old guy's pretty cute, but maybe I can get a thoughtless word or two out of him.'

Hugh smiled and shook his head.

'Not much hope of that,' he said. Then suddenly he slapped his thigh. 'By Jove!' he exclaimed. 'I've got the idea of a lifetime.'

'Shoot!' said Miles tersely.

'Let Jerry go! He can speak Russian and explain that he has come from Novar. If he takes one of the papers with the drawings on it, the fact of his having that and speaking Russian may do the trick. And as we are rather vague about the meeting it is just possible he may get some useful information.'

'Gee!' exclaimed Miles in admiration. 'You're the cat's whiskers, Hugh. He can say a messenger was sent with a note in case there was one, and I guess Oppenheimer will fall for it.'

'Where the devil is Cousins?' cried Hugh. 'Jerry!'

At that moment Joan came out of her room.

'Hugh,' she said reprovingly, 'your language is becoming awful. You're a bad example to Oscar.'

Miles grinned.

'I guess he's got nothing on me in that way, Jo,' he chuckled. 'You ought to hear me when I get real sore.'

'I hope I never shall,' she retorted. 'You'll have to reform before I marry you!'

'Sure!' said the American calmly.

Cousins emerged from his bedroom.

'Did I hear someone speak my name in vain?' he inquired.

'Not in vain apparently,' said Hugh. 'Come here! We want to talk to you.'

'Dear! Dear!' murmured the little man, coming along the corridor. 'There is no peace for the wicked. Here have I been pressing my dress suit again and removing sundry strange curves thereon, and you—' He broke off. 'Good gracious!' he exclaimed. 'I believe I have left the hot iron on—'

He rushed back, but reappeared a moment later.

'It is all right,' he said; 'I thought I had left the iron on a part of – of my nether garments "where the wicked cease from troubling, and the weary are at rest". Well, what do you want?'

Hugh explained his plan and Cousins gazed at him in pretended astonishment.

'Who would think,' he said, 'that this bulk of brawn and beef was capable of supporting a brain of such delicate subtlety. Now I know why Mount Everest rears its mighty head so high. It is waiting for your demise, O Hugh, in order that it may remain a perpetual monument of your greatness – "But where the native mountains bare Their foreheads to diviner air, Fit emblem of enduring fame One lofty summit keeps thy name".'

Five minutes later, armed with one of the papers on which the map of India and the eagles and dragons were drawn, Cousins set off for the Punjab Hotel. He was soon there, and entering the reception hall, made his way to the desk. He had not met any of the clerks during his sojourn in the hotel with Joan and Hugh; there was no likelihood, therefore, of his being recognised. He had one difficulty with which to contend, namely, the possibility that the German was staying there under an assumed name, if indeed it was he who had arrived by the Calcutta express. However, his doubts were soon laid at rest for he was informed by the reception clerk that a Mr Oppenheimer had arrived that morning. He asked to see him and five minutes later was shown to suite forty-four.

He found a tallish, fat man with a round, clean-shaven face, fair hair and blue eyes awaiting his advent. The fellow was a German of the most obvious type. He waved Cousins to a chair.

'Oppenheimer I am,' he said in a deep, guttural voice.

Cousins closed the door carefully, and looked searchingly round.

'Are we quite safe from eavesdroppers?' he asked in Russian.

The German started. Then he walked into the bedroom and Cousins could hear him closing the outer door. Presently he returned and shut the bedroom door behind him.

'All is well now,' he said.

'I am from Novar,' said Cousins, still in the same language. 'Did you get his message?'

'Who is this Novar?' asked Oppenheimer, peering cautiously at him.

'Russia, Germany, China!' replied Cousins.

He drew from his pocket the precious paper and held it towards the German. The latter took it and a smile appeared on his face. He returned it, and sank into a deep armchair with a sigh of relief.

'It is enough,' he said. 'I now am sure that you come from our friend Novar. But I speak not the Russian well.'

'My German is not very good,' confessed Cousins.

'Then we will in the English spik,' said Oppenheimer in that tongue. 'It a country I hate is, but the language well I spik.'

'Is it quite safe?' asked Cousins.

'Yes, there no danger is, now that the doors I have locked.'

The other nodded as though satisfied.

'Well,' he said, 'first of all, did you receive the message?'

'Yes! Half an hour ago by a Sikh it came. But, my friend, there some things are I do not understand. Why Novar and Rahtz into hiding have gone?'

'Surely that was explained to you?'

'Yes, yes! But exblanations on baper sometimes vague are.'

'Well, I did not see the letter, but I understood that it would make everything clear to you.'

'But it nodings make clear. Novar simply says, "into hiding we have gone, in order that no shadow of susbicion there can be." Why a shadow of susbicion should there be? I think that if Novar and Rahtz and Hudson out and about as usual went, much safer it would be.'

'The fact is that in Lahore there is an Englishman called Shannon and his valet, whom we think are connected with the British Secret Service—'

Oppenheimer nodded.

'Yes; already of him I know.' Then he looked at Cousins anxiously. 'Do you mean that these Englishmen anything of imbortance have discovered?'

Cousins laughed and shook his head.

'No,' he said, 'they're both absolute fools. But

469

in order to be on the safe side Novar and Rahtz decided that it would be better to give out that they were going away for the Christmas holidays, so that in no way would there be any risk of the meeting being discovered.'

Oppenheimer waved his hand.

'It unnecessary was, mine friend,' he said. 'However, to be too cautious instead of not enough cautious much better is. So!'

He took a well-filled cigar case from his pocket and selected a cigar, then he looked at Cousins and back at the case, and after a second's reflection he sighed and offered his companion one. Cousins helped himself.

'Now, Herr Oppenheimer,' he said, when the cigar was going to his satisfaction, 'I suppose you understand perfectly how to get into the College tomorrow night?'

'But of course. The instructions very clear were.'

'Quite so, but as one of our friends wrote to have them repeated even more clearly, I have been instructed by Novar to call on every – emissary shall I say? – and make sure that there is no shadow of doubt in anyone's mind.'

Cousins waited anxiously for the result of his masterstroke. Oppenheimer waved his hand again – it appeared to be a habit of his when he approved of anything – and nodded solemnly.

'A good brecaution to take it is,' he said. 'But for me no necessity there is – every word in my brain buried has been.'

470

'I am glad to hear that,' smiled Cousins genially. 'Therefore it will be unnecessary for you to repeat the instructions to me in order that I can check you as Rahtz insisted I should. I'm afraid he is very anxious in case anyone makes a mistake.'

The German rubbed his chin reflectively.

'Well, no harm there can be in making quite sure,' he said. 'And berhaps a little detail from my mind has gone. Carefully listen, Mr—' He stopped and looked inquiringly at Cousins.

'Kamper!' said the little man on the spur of the moment.

Oppenheimer stared at him. He began to look a little anxious.

'But Mr Kamper in Bombay I did meet,' he said, 'and—'

'I'm his brother,' said Cousins calmly. 'You met Paul; I am Ivan!'

'Ah! Then it exblained is. You very much like your brother are, but at once I knew the man I met you were not, hein?'

Cousins smiled and nodded, but inwardly he felt very sore at being told that he was like the Russian Jew.

'Now,' went on Oppenheimer, 'my instructions I will like the schoolboy rebeat; so!' He leant forward. 'Into the Mozang College grounds I will enter by the small gate which at the back of the College is. I will a Sikh meet there and to him I will say "Gym". He will to the gymnasium take me. Another Sikh there I will see and he will say,

471

"the moon rises". To him I will answer, "eagles rise higher". I will then my paper to him show and he will to the room in the College take me. So! Have I not every word remembered; no?'

'Exactly!' said Cousins. 'I hope everyone will be as word perfect as you. My brother is sharing the job of going round to everyone with me.'

'Tell him with me to come and talk,' said Oppenheimer.

'Certainly,' replied Cousins, 'but I doubt if he will have time. We are anxious to get back with Novar, Rahtz and Hudson as soon as possible.'

'Our confrères all have arrived, hein?'

'Not all,' smiled. Cousins. 'And now I must go.'

'My friend, I am to see you with pleasure filled. Before you go, there is one question I would ask.'

The little man looked at him, wondering what was coming.

'How that I was really Oppenheimer did you know?' asked the German, 'since you and I before never have met? Surely a great risk you have been taking!'

Cousins shook his head.

'We never take risks, Herr Oppenheimer,' he replied. 'My brother and I watched your arrival and we followed you to this hotel.'

'So!' said the fat man. 'I am answered.'

He shook hands with Cousins.

'Revenge for many years' humiliation draws near, hein?' he said. 'Go, mine friend! Tomorrow the dawn of great things will be!'

As soon as Cousins was out of sight of the hotel, he took a large notebook from his pocket and wrote therein the instructions Oppenheimer had repeated so innocently to him. Then he shut the book and his face creased into a large grin.

'Now may the gods grant that he is not visited by my – er – brother,' he murmured. 'But I don't think he will be, otherwise Novar would not have sent the note by the Sikh.'

Hugh and Miles were greatly pleased with the success of Cousins' interview with the German, and after a lot of discussion it was decided not to change their plans, except to ask the Deputy Commissioner to detail some men specially to watch the gymnasium and the small gate, which they knew to be some distance from the main gates of the College. Shannon and the American intended to disguise themselves slightly in case of recognition and, if no other way of hearing and seeing what went on was possible, to penetrate actually into the room as emissaries. Cousins was to adhere to his original plan of entering the College at an early hour and concealing himself on the roof.

That afternoon Hugh had a long talk with Rainer and told him of Cousins' fresh discovery. The plans for surrounding the College were not materially altered, but Rainer agreed to watch the small gate with his picked men, and to place others in the vicinity of the gymnasium. When the signal came for the main body to enter the grounds and surround the College they were to do so by way of the large gates. If the latter were locked – as in all likelihood they would be – the men would have to clamber over the wall, which was not a very high one.

Hugh asked Rainer where they could find Abdul Rahim, as they were all so anxious to thank him for what he had done for Joan. Rainer smiled.

'I couldn't tell you where he is at present,' he said, 'but you will probably see him in the course of the next few days; in fact, he has definitely stated that he intends on seeing you.'

'That's all right then,' said Hugh, 'but I was afraid that he might disappear as suddenly as he came, and I owe him far more than I shall ever be able to repay.'

'He doesn't need any repayment,' remarked Rainer. 'In fact, he'll probably be very fed-up if you start thanking him.'

'I can't understand the fellow,' said Hugh. 'There is something about him that puzzles me. Who on earth is he?'

Rainer laughed.

'I have already told you,' he replied, 'that he is one of the greatest detectives in the world.'

CHAPTER 33

THE MEETING

Tuesday, December the twenty-first, passed very quietly. Shannon and Miles spent the day in doing nothing, and in the society of Joan the American practically forgot that there were such things as plots and Russians, wars and rumours of wars. Cousins, on the other hand, was very busy. He and his friend Spink, who was now a little in his confidence, took turns in keeping a cautious eye on the movements of Oppenheimer. Between them they noted the arrival of nearly every man who came to the hotel, and compared notes whenever they met. The result was that when Cousins returned to the bungalow at half past five, he was as certain as he could well be that none of the Russians had called on, or sent any further message to, the German.

The little man partook of a kind of high tea and as soon as it was dusk set off for Mozang College. It was dark when he reached the place and, as he expected, the main gates were locked and bolted. Looking round cautiously to see if he were observed, he climbed over the wall and disappeared, feeling certain that nobody had watched

475

his movements. But he was mistaken. A moment after he was lost to view, Abdul Rahim emerged from among the bushes in Rahtz's garden. He, too, glanced round carefully, then followed Cousins over the wall.

Joan had gone to spend the night with Mrs and Miss Rainer, and Hugh and Oscar took a very early dinner. Before she went the girl looked anxiously at the two men.

'Oh, my dears,' she said, the light of unshed tears in her eyes, 'be very, very careful! You two are all I have in the world and if anything happened to you, I would die I think. I shall be terribly anxious until I see you again, but I am so proud of – my men!'

At a quarter to eight a tall Persian and a powerfully built Turk arrived in a car a little distance from Mozang College and left their motor in charge of a sergeant of police, who had been instructed to look out for them by the Deputy Commissioner himself. They walked on down the road and stood close to the gate of a bungalow just beyond Rahtz's, as though wondering if they had reached the right spot. Presently the Persian spoke quietly, and his voice was the voice of Miles.

'Say, Mr Commissioner,' he said, 'have you seen our friends go in yet?'

'No,' came in a whisper from Rainer, who was hidden close behind them. 'We have watched three men enter during the last five minutes, but unless they were disguised none of them was Novar or Rahtz.'

'Good!' murmured the Turk, in the voice of Shannon. 'If we get in first our chances will be increased.'

'Good luck!' whispered the Commissioner.

The two men walked across to the small gate, as though they had decided it was the place they were seeking. It was locked, but they dimly discerned a bearded face looking through at them.

'Gym,' they said almost together.

The gate was unlocked, and as soon as they had entered, locked again. Without a word the man with the beard beckoned to them to follow him. The gymnasium was reached, the door opened, and they were ushered inside. The place was in complete darkness.

'The moon rises,' said a voice in very laboured English.

'Eagles rise higher!' replied Miles and Hugh.

An electric torch was switched right on their faces, causing them to blink owlishly, and they were subjected to a severe scrutiny. They could not see the man who held it, but apparently he was satisfied, for after a moment or two he lowered the torch. They immediately produced their precious passports, which he took and examined with great care, the while their hearts beat rapidly in suspense.

'Come!' he said at length, and gave them back the papers.

Hugh could have cried out his relief, and the American's hand caught his and squeezed it hard.

He returned the pressure. The first part of their job was over, but the most difficult part was to come.

They followed their guide to the other end of the gymnasium where he unlocked another door and leading them through, locked it behind them. They found themselves in the open air and apparently crossing the College grounds towards the main building. Here another locked door barred their way and the precaution was taken again of locking it as soon as they had entered. It occurred to Hugh that extraordinary care was being taken, but he wondered why there were not more men to assist the two Sikhs, as he knew Novar had more than two in his employment and confidence. If all this time was taken over everyone who arrived, the meeting could not commence at eight o'clock.

They were taken along several dark corridors, up a flight of stone steps, then along more corridors. Suddenly their guide stopped at the entrance to a narrow passage which ended in a closed door. This passage like all the rest was in darkness, but a shaft of light shone through a fanlight over the door from the room beyond. The Sikh pointed to the lighted room, and turning went back the way he had come. They waited until his footsteps died away in the distance, then:

'What a bit of Heaven-sent luck!' breathed Hugh. 'I hadn't hoped for this even in my wildest dreams. The very room we guessed at, and left on our own outside! What more could heart of man desire? Oscar, I feel like singing in triumph.'

'Then don't!' said Miles shortly. 'We've got to get busy right now – there isn't too much time, and if we can't squeeze between those blame beams up there, there won't be a whole lot to sing about.'

'We'll get through all right,' said Hugh; 'they're not so close together as that. Give me the rope!'

The American lifted up the long coat he was wearing and unwound a length of stout rope, which Hugh placed over his shoulder.

'Now,' said the latter, 'bend down!'

Miles placed his hands against the wall and bent his back. Shannon climbed on to it as gently as he could and stood up, but although he stretched his arms up as far as he could, his fingers were still several inches from the beams.

'You'll have to straighten yourself and let me get on to your shoulders,' he whispered. 'I can't reach.'

With a suppressed groan his companion gradually raised himself until he was standing straight with Hugh balancing himself on his shoulders. The Englishman could reach a beam easily now and, taking a firm hold on it, he drew himself up. He wriggled through, and in a couple of minutes was lying on the top tying one end of the rope securely to one of the rafters. He let the other end fall to Miles, who was able to hoist himself up with ease. Then Hugh drew up the rope and untied it.

'That's that,' he whispered with satisfaction.

'Now so long as no one takes it into his head to flash a light up in this direction we're all right.'

'All right!' muttered Miles. 'You may be, but I guess I'm not. Gee I think my back's broken. For the love of Mike what is your weight?'

'Only twelve stone and a bit!'

'Only! Golly!'

'S'sh! There's someone coming!'

They heard the sound of footsteps in the distance. It grew louder and presently the Sikh appeared at the end of the passage; with him were three men. As before, he indicated the door of the room and disappeared. The newcomers walked along beneath Shannon and Miles and, entering the apartment, closed the door behind them. Then the two secret agents crawled along the beams until they were lying with their heads against the wall and the fan-light directly beneath them. They found that they had a splendid view of practically the whole room.

It was a large place, brilliantly lighted by half a dozen powerful electric lights. In the centre was a long table covered by a black cloth, with about ten chairs on either side of it, and one at the head. A few large pictures hung on the walls and a sombre-looking durrie covered the floor. On the left-hand side of the room were rows of book-shelves tightly crammed with volumes and, on the other, an enormous cupboard, which probably contained all books and documents relative to the affairs of the College. Unlike most rooms in India, especially on the plains, this one had a plastered ceiling, and it was above this plaster, among the rafters, that Cousins lay.

There were six men already seated at the table, and Hugh and his companion looked at them with interest. Two of them were obviously Chinamen, a third looked like a Turk, while the other three were Persians. The latter were talking to the Turk, but the two Chinamen held themselves aloof. Hugh reached down and pushed the fan-light open a few inches, in order that he and Miles would be able to hear what was being said when presently the conference actually started.

Every few minutes now fresh arrivals were escorted to the room, and took their places by the table. Two stately Afghans were followed shortly afterwards by Oppenheimer, the German, who looked at his companions as though they were rather beneath his notice. Then came two well-dressed Indians with beautifully-wound turbans. After them entered a fussy little white man in evening dress, wearing pince-nez, and with hands glittering with rings.

'Now who can that be?' murmured Hugh.

'I guess he's a representative from Southern Europe somewhere,' whispered Miles; 'probably an Austrian.'

There was an interval of nearly ten minutes and some of the men at the table began to fidget. Then four men arrived together: one was a Turk and joined his compatriot, another was a Chinaman

481

and apparently of some importance, for on seeing him his two countrymen rose to their feet and bowed profoundly. The other two were Indians.

'Four Indians, three Chinese, two Turks, three Persians, two Afghans, one German and one doubtful,' muttered Hugh.

'I'm beginning to wonder when Hudson, Novar, and Rahtz are going to appear,' said Miles. 'I hope those guys didn't get the wind up and beat it after Joan was rescued.'

He was answered almost immediately, for three men came quickly down the passage and, as they entered the room, the watchers saw that two of them were the Russians – the third was a stranger. Novar and Rahtz greeted the company and led their companion to the chair at the head of the table. He was a man with a sallow face, rather long nose, piercing eyes, surmounted by heavy black eyebrows, and a small black beard and moustache. He had very short black hair, turning grey at the temples, and was rather inclined to be stout. He looked round the table and every now and again consulted a paper which he held in his hand. Apparently satisfied, he spoke to Novar, and his deep voice could be plainly heard by Hugh and Miles, but as he spoke in Russian they were at a loss to understand what he said until Novar crossed to the door and locked it. Then returning the Russian took his seat on the right-hand side of the bearded man, Rahtz being already in the chair on his left. Hugh noticed how ill the Principal of Mozang College looked, and it filled him with an unholy joy.

Then proceedings commenced. Novar rose to his feet.

'Gentlemen,' he said, 'as we are of so many nationalities, I think it will be necessary for us to speak in English, a language which, I presume, we all know.' He looked round inquiringly, and then went on. 'As we are shortly going to bring Britain to her knees there is a touch of delightful irony in using the language of that country to lay our plans against her.' There was a short laugh and Novar looked pleased. 'I have great pleasure,' he continued, 'in giving you a very happy surprise! I notice you are all casting inquiring looks at the gentleman who has taken the chair, and it is my privilege to introduce him to you. Gentlemen, allow me to present to you Comrade Bukharin, the Soviet Minister of Foreign Affairs, who has journeyed secretly from Moscow specially to attend this meeting!'

There were cries of excited wonder from the men round the table and somebody started to clap, an effort which was immediately suppressed. Hugh whistled under his breath.

'Gee!' whispered Miles. 'What a coup!'

Bukharin rose and bowed right and left.

'Gentlemen,' he said in slow and careful English, 'it is a very great pleasure to be with you. I arrived only today and I leave again tomorrow. But as this meeting was of such vital importance I felt it would be of assistance to you if I were to be present myself, so that I could place before you certain matters with which my friends, Comrades Novar and Rahtz, are not acquainted. I will have the satisfaction presently of shaking hands with each one of you, and when Comrade Novar has finished I will speak.'

He sat down with an air of great importance, and Novar continued.

'In the first place,' he said, 'you all know that this conference is being held in India, partly because India is the key to the coming situation, but chiefly because it is the most convenient country for at least fourteen of us to reach. A meeting here, in the capital of the Punjab, is not without its dangers, surrounded as we are by our enemies but such precautions have been taken that not a whisper of even the mildest activity has reached the ears of anyone but the company here assembled and one or two of our agents outside.'

'Liar!' murmured Miles.

Oppenheimer rose.

'Mr Chairman,' he said, 'with your bermission, I would one question ask.'

Bukharin nodded.

'Two chairs empty are. Is it that all representatives bresent are not?'

'Those two chairs were placed for Mr Kam and Mr Hudson, whom you know,' replied Novar. 'Alas I Mr Hudson is no more – he died very suddenly the other night—'

'Good Lord!' muttered Hugh, and gripped Miles by the arm.

'Mr Kamper is wandering round the College and on the roof to ensure us against any trespassers.'

'I hope he doesn't butt into Jerry,' said Miles.

'Is there then danger?' asked the fussy little man excitedly.

'Not the least,' replied Novar blandly, 'but we always take every precaution.'

'Goot!' said Oppenheimer, and sat down.

'Now, gentlemen,' went on Novar, taking a sheaf of papers from his pocket, which he consulted occasionally, 'I will present every feature of our plans to you, so that you can convey the whole situation to your respective governments. If I err in any particular I hope the agent interested will put me right. If I am uninterrupted I shall know that no query is to be raised. Before proceeding I may state that China has done us the honour to send no less a personage than Doctor Sun Chien Lung as one of her representatives.'

He smiled at the important-looking Chinaman, who bent his head in acknowledgement.

'The big noise in Southern China,' commented Miles.

'As you know,' Novar continued, 'airships, each capable of carrying a hundred troops are being built at express speed in Bokhara and Samarkand for the invasion of India. Others specially fitted to carry guns and ammunition are also being constructed as well as a fleet of airplanes consisting

485

of both bombing and fighting machines. An army, thoroughly trained and equipped is being gathered secretly in Turkestan and another is gradually collecting in the district of Khorasan in Persia, where a Persian army is already mobilised and training hard. So much for Russia. Persia, besides training the army I have just mentioned, is collecting as many ships as she can which will act as transports to convey the armies in Persia to India. Most of the ships – they are of all sizes – are being gathered in Jask, Bandar Abbas and Mohammerh. Turkey, with the assistance of Germany and Russia, is building airships near Isparta. An army is being gathered together, drilled and equipped in the same district. Austria is doing the same near Maria Zell. Germany has already built an enormous number of airships and airplanes. A great army, almost if not quite equal to the one she put in the field in 1914, is ready now, and it is at present spread over the country in various guises which have so successfully hidden it that its existence is entirely unsuspected; but in the course of a few days it can be united and on the move—'

Oppenheimer nodded his head with great satisfaction.

'Now, gentlemen,' said Novar, 'we come to Afghanistan. Here again an army is being quietly mobilised up in the mountains near Ghazni and Russia is supplying guns, ammunition, and airplanes in order that this army may be as thoroughly equipped as all others. Last, but not least, there is China, and here, gentlemen, a most startling advance is being made. While the whole world is quite assured that nothing but chaos rules in that country; while a small general here and another there is fighting against his neighbour with ill-clad, undisciplined levees and antiquated rifles; while a British fleet and a British army keeps watch and ward from Shanghai to Hankow, and from Peking to Tien-tsing; while the eyes of the world are turned to Eastern China – while all this is happening, a great army drilled on the most modern lines, equipped with up-to-date rifles and machine guns and all the modern appliances of war is being mobilised in the Province of Yun-nan. There is also another great fleet of airships and airplanes being built with the help of German and Russian experts.

'Gentlemen I have given you the outlines of our preparations, which, of course, have been going on for years. On the great day all the allies will strike at practically the same time. Russian airships with troops and airplanes from Samarkand and Bokhara will invade India by way of Afghanistan. One section will land near Lahore, the other in Delhi. Another great army will come by air from China via Burma and, landing in Bengal, will advance to meet the Russian army at Delhi, while a second Chinese force will invade Hong Kong and keep the British troops in the Far East busy. The Afghan army will invade the North-West Province and the Punjab as far as Rawal Pindi.

Persia will confiscate all British ships in her ports, and the combined Persian and Russian armies will sail in the transports to invade India on the western side. Turkey will invade Mesopotamia and Egypt, while the Austrian force will enter Italy and Yugo-Slavia. At the same time Germany with her army, navy, and air force will invade England and France.

'Gentlemen, we cannot fail – it is impossible. But I am convinced that now is the time to strike, or, at least, during the course of the next month. No hint of suspicion or danger has reached our enemies as yet, and that is because we have been flooding the world with Communist propaganda, organising strikes and doing things of that nature to blind England to our real doings. We have succeeded beyond our dreams, but can it go on until September next without the movements of our vast armies becoming known? There is another factor: we have our allies in this country to consider, who are tired of the British rule. Numbers of Indian troops are ready to mutiny, people to rise, but the delay may break their spirit. Am I not right, my friends?'

He looked at the four Indians. One of them nodded.

'The waiting is tedious,' he said. 'Our people are anxiously looking for the deliverance.'

'I knew it,' said Novar; 'therefore, gentlemen, I counsel expediency. A stroke now and the world will shake to its very foundations – a delay until September may make our success infinitely more difficult to obtain.'

He sat down and Bukharin rose. He carefully took a small leather bound book from an inner pocket and laid it open before him.

'Before we discuss the very important date of the commencement of our invasions – which we shall have to do with great consideration and care, before we part tonight – I have figures here which I must put before you. In China there are five hundred thousand men under training; four hundred airships and a thousand airplanes are already built and others are on the way. Afghanistan has an army of twenty thousand men. In Turkestan, Russia has an army waiting of two million, there are six hundred airships and two thousand five hundred airplanes complete – of course you will understand that the airships will have to make several journeys to convey such a large body of troops to India. In Persia there is gathering an army of three hundred thousand Russians and forty thousand Persians. Turkey will put one hundred and fifty thousand men into the field and two hundred airships will be complete early in January. Austria already possesses three hundred and forty airships ready to fly and twelve hundred airplanes and – my figures in this case are not quite complete – the Austrian army now stands at three hundred thousand troops—'

'Tree hondred an' feefty-five tousand,' interrupted the fussy little man.

'Thank you!' said Bukharin. 'Three hundred and fifty-five thousand, gentlemen! As for Germany

– it will amaze you to know that four million men and a thousand airships are ready, besides fifty thousand airplanes. Gentlemen, these figures speak very eloquently for themselves!'

There was a pause while he allowed his information to sink in, then:

'What position will America and France take in the coming struggle?' asked the important Chinaman in perfect English.

'France will be crippled at once by the German invasion. America is too far off to be dangerous, and she will probably keep quiet as soon as she sees what is happening.'

'I'm darned if she will,' muttered Miles. 'I guess you've got another thing coming, my son.'

'And now, gentlemen,' went on the Soviet Foreign Minister, 'it is hardly necessary for me to repeat the various rewards which each of our countries will obtain as the result of the operations, but if you desire it I will do so?'

'No harm in rebeating it there is,' said Oppenheimer.

'Well, Germany will take Alsace and Lorraine, Belgium, and a part of France on a line from Lille, through Rheims and Troyes to Dijon and Besançon, as well as all colonies which she lost in the last war, and a certain number of Britain's to be decided later on. What other terms she will force on England also remains till later. Austria will recover the Trentino, the whole of Czecho Slovakia, Crotia and Bosnia, and possibly Hungary. Turkey will have Iraq, Syria, and Palestine; Persia –

Baluchistan and Sind; and Afghanistan, the North-West Province and the Punjab as far as Rawal Pindi. China will receive—'

He stopped and looked upwards, a startled expression on his face, and everyone in the room followed his example, their faces also expressing uneasy surprise. For a moment Hugh and Miles were unable to understand what had caused this strange conduct, but then they too heard the sound of a muffled struggle going on, apparently above the room.

'Good Lord!' exclaimed Hugh. 'Kamper has discovered Cousins, and I believe they are fighting among the rafters.'

The two men held their breath and listened. In the room everyone sat as though rooted to his seat, with the exception of Bukharin who was standing, his hands clutching the edge of the table. Rahtz and Novar had gone deadly white. Suddenly there was a tearing, cracking sound and showers of plaster fell into the room, hitting some of the men beneath. It seemed to bring them to their senses for they sprang away from the table and crowded together still looking upwards with horror-struck eyes. A second later a leg came clean through the ceiling. Hugh and Miles could not see it, but they saw what happened directly afterwards. There was a great rending, a shout of alarm, and a man's body hurtled through the air and fell with a sickening thud right in the centre of the table where it moved spasmodically for a moment or two, then lay still.

'God grant it's not Jerry!' groaned Miles with white lips.

Hugh closed his eyes involuntarily – a feeling of deadly nausea coming over him. Then he compelled himself to look. The conspirators were still crowded together clutching each other in absolute panic, and apparently almost paralysed by the suddenness of the tragedy. Hugh saw, and a feeling of wonderful relief came over him.

'Thank God!' he cried. 'It's not Jerry – it's Kamper!'

At the same moment Rahtz recovered himself.

'There is someone on the roof,' he cried. 'We've got to get them or—'

He dashed to the door.

'Come on, Oscar!' said Hugh. 'Now's the time!'

He squeezed between the beams and hanging at arms' length, dropped to the floor, followed immediately by Miles. The door was flung open, and Rahtz appeared on the threshold with the rest of the conspirators crowding behind him. As they saw Hugh the whole lot of them stopped dead and a look of malevolent fury and dread came over the Russian's face.

'The last act, Rahtz,' said Hugh quietly. 'Get back all of you!' he added; and they saw the revolvers in the two men's hands.

Hugh blew three blasts on a whistle and from the distance came the sound of running feet. Suddenly with a terrible oath Rahtz threw himself forward, a long knife in his hand. The attack was so sudden that it caught Hugh and Miles unprepared, but there was the sound of a revolver shot from somewhere in the room, the knife dropped from the Russian's uplifted hand, and he groaned with the pain of a bullet through his wrist. Everyone turned with fresh dismay, Hugh and the American looking with the rest in the direction from which the shot had come.

The door of the cupboard was open and standing in the aperture was Abdul Rahim with a grim smile on his lips. His left hand was in the pocket of his coat as usual; in his right was a still smoking revolver.

CHAPTER 34

A GREAT COUP

Cries of horror and dismay came from some of the nineteen men, who had conspired together to throw the world into a holocaust of bloodshed, a few – of whom the Chinamen. were prominent – stood sullenly silent; Bukharin's face was livid and he was crying execrations upon Novar who had collapsed into a chair. All knew that their game was up; that they had been caught in the very act. Hugh and Miles stood grimly facing them, their revolvers held steadily in their hands. On the other side of the room Abdul Rahim lounged carelessly, but no less watchfully, by the door of the cupboard.

Suddenly with shouts of rage some of the bolder spirits among the plotters made an ugly rush at the door. With a grin of delight Hugh pushed his revolver into his companion's left hand and met them with closed fists.

'Back, you bloodthirsty devils!' he roared.

In a moment he was in amongst them striking to right and left with terrific force. Rainer joined Miles at the door; behind him was a crowd of policemen. He stopped in amazement and watched

494

the extraordinary spectacle. Hugh was having some of his own back now, and enjoying himself thoroughly. Man after man went crashing to the floor before his tremendous blows and, in a remarkably short space of time, those who had dared to face him were strewn about the room until it bore the appearance in miniature of a battlefield. Several – and among them Oppenheimer and the little Austrian – had not the courage to stand up to him and these were crushed together in a corner by the bookcase. Bukharin, with a snarl, drew a revolver as he saw the large Englishman bearing down upon him, but Abdul Rahim sent it spinning out of his hand with a well-directed kick, and the next moment the Soviet Foreign Minister felt that a pile-driver had struck him, as a perfect, full-blooded upper-cut caught him on the point of the jaw. The world appeared to whirl round him, he saw more stars than he had ever noticed in the heavens, then he, too, measured his length on the floor.

Hugh stopped and regarded his handiwork with a smile of satisfaction. Novar still sat in a state of collapse, Rahtz was crouching by the wall, holding his wounded wrist in his other hand. But within a few feet of Shannon, standing tall and dignified with his arms folded, and watching him malevolently, was the Chinaman, Sun Chien Lung.

'What is the meaning of this outrage, sir?' he hissed, rather than spoke. 'By what right do you interrupt a meeting in this murderous fashion?'

'By the right of an Englishman who has discovered the whole of your plot against Great Britain.'

The Chinaman's eyes narrowed.

'What plot is that?' he inquired softly.

Hugh was reminded of a serpent hissing and knew this man to be dangerous. He watched him closely, therefore, as he replied.

'The gigantic plot which has been engineered by Russia, and supported by China, Germany, Austria, Persia, Turkey and Afghanistan, against the peace of the world.'

Bukharin staggered to his feet, and clung dizzily to the back of a chair.

'Sir,' he said shakily, 'you are hopelessly mistaken. We were not here on any warlike mission, but were merely in conference over a matter of commercial interest to us all.'

'You lie!' said Hugh sternly. 'My friend and I were concealed on the rafters beneath the roof of the passage outside this room, and heard everything that was said through the open fan-light.'

All eyes were turned to the large square of glass over the door, which was seen to be open several inches. Rahtz swore viciously.

'I also heard every word,' said Abdul Rahim, 'from my position in the cupboard.'

Hugh looked at him curiously, and felt rather piqued. Why had this individual interfered, and how did he know anything about their activities! The secret agent suspected Rainer of divulging more than he had admitted, and resolved to have a few words with that gentleman later on. He turned back to Bukharin.

'We have known what game was going on for a very long time Mr Bukharin, Minister of Russian Foreign Affairs,' he said.

The bearded man went even paler than before, and in his eyes was the gleam of a great fear. Perhaps he thought that he would have been able to keep his name secret.

'I understood you to say that you would have the pleasure of shaking these gentlemen's hands later on,' continued Shannon remorselessly. 'That opportunity may come when you bid them farewell after your trial.'

'Who are you?' gasped Bukharin.

'I am Captain Shannon of the British Intelligence Department and my friend standing by the door' – he did not look round, for he was keeping a careful watch upon the Chinaman – 'is Mr Oscar Miles of the same service of the United States. We, with another member of my department – the gentleman who was probably the cause of your being interrupted' – he nodded at the body of Kamper lying in a grotesque attitude on the table – 'have kept a careful watch for three months, with the result that the British, American and French Governments have known of your activities for some time. In fact, they are only waiting for the result of this meeting to move.'

'How could they know?' asked Novar almost in a whisper.

'From our reports of course. It may be a surprise to you, Novar, to hear that two letters written to you by Bukharin were taken from the safe in your room nearly four weeks ago and sent at one to the Chief of the Intelligence Department!'

With a cry of hopeless anguish Novar fell back in his chair and covered his face with his hands. A shout of fury burst from Bukharin and if he had not been so weak he would probably have attacked his trusted emissary.

Hugh stepped back.

'Come on, Rainer!' he said. 'Collect the bunch!'

Then suddenly Sun Chien Lung drew a vicious-looking knife from under his left arm, and dived forward with incredible swiftness. But Hugh had been expecting something of this nature. He stooped swiftly and catching the Chinaman by the waist put all his power into a heave. The fellow flew over his shoulders and landed on the floor in front of Miles with a crash that shook the room. He lay quite still.

'Another Hercules come to light!' said a quiet voice, and Cousins poked his head between Miles and Rainer.

There was no further attempt at resistance and the Deputy Commissioner entered the room with his men and arrested all the conspirators. Bukharin indeed protested, but he was marched away with the rest. Sun Chien Lung, and two or three others whom Hugh had knocked down, were carried out. Kamper was quite dead, his neck having been broken by the fall, and two policemen removed his body. Presently Hugh, Miles, Rainer, Cousins, and Abdul Rahim were left in the room.

'Say, Jerry,' said the American, 'what happened?'

'I was lying in my little cubby hole trying to hear what was being said below,' replied Cousins, 'when Kamper discovered me and crawled in. We had rather a lengthy argument, and he tried to demonstrate his point of view with a knife. We were right at the height of our little affair, when he slipped from the rafter and as he put his foot through the plaster, I thought it would be as well if he joined his friends below. Were they pleased to see him?'

'Not much,' grinned Hugh. 'And now look here, Rainer, and you too, Rahim, I've a few questions to ask. What was—'

He got no further, for an English police sergeant rushed into the room.

'That man with the wounded hand has got away!' he cried.

'Rahtz!' exclaimed Shannon. 'Damn!'

'I think I know where to find him,' said Abdul Rahim. 'Come with me!'

Gone was the sibilant inflection from his voice and he spoke so commandingly that Hugh and his companions gazed at him curiously and perhaps a trifle resentfully. However, Hugh prepared to follow him.

'Search Rahtz's bungalow, Rainer,' he said; 'perhaps he has gone there!'

They all ran from the room and made their way

out of the building, past the gymnasium, to the small gate. Hugh found that his car had been brought there by the sergeant of police in whose care he had left it. He jumped in and Rahim got in beside him, while Cousins and Miles sprang into the tonneau. With the Mahommedan directing him, Hugh drove to The Retreat and stopped outside the big gates.

'I think you had better go a little farther along and leave the car in a turning I know of,' said Abdul Rahim. 'Probably Rahtz has not arrived here yet, and we may have to wait for him; in that case you don't want to make him suspicious.'

Hugh agreed, and drove the car to the place indicated.

Returning, the four found the gate locked, and were compelled to climb over it. The Indian led them to the house by careful stages. The front door was fastened, but circling round the building they eventually found a small window which had been left open and one by one they squeezed through. With Abdul Rahim still leading the way, carrying an electric torch, they went along a passage whence they turned into another, and stopped by the open door of a room.

'This is where your sister made her heroic fight,' said the Mahommedan to Hugh.

The latter and his companions gazed into the disorderly-looking apartment with very deep emotions, then Hugh turned to Rahim rather abruptly.

'Lead on!' he said curtly.

They came to a small, bare room.

'This is where Rahtz will come, if he hasn't already arrived,' said the smiling Indian. 'Keep away from the centre of the floor!'

He crossed to the wall and pressed hard against a portion which appeared somewhat irregular. At once a trapdoor rose in the centre of the room and they could dimly make out a flight of steps.

'You had better hold your revolvers ready,' said Rahim, and shone his torch on the steps. 'I watched them go down there the night I came for your sister. I returned to see exactly what they would do and was just in time to find out. I'll go first with the light – follow as carefully as you can!'

They reached the bottom without accident and looked round them with interest. They were standing in a small, square chamber containing four chairs and a table on which were a few eating utensils. Opposite them was a door through which they presently passed into another room containing two charpoys (native beds), a chair covered with clothes, and three suitcases. There was another room beyond – this contained one charpoy on which were more clothes, a suitcase and a large worn leather bag. A camp washstand also occupied one corner.

'Well, he's not here yet,' remarked Rahim. 'We'll wait until he does come.'

'How do you know he will?' asked Cousins.

'Because this must be the safest hiding place he

possesses. You see he does not know that I have discovered it. Probably he'll take some time to get here as he will approach the house warily for fear that it is being watched. Now let us discover how to shut the trapdoor from below.'

Somehow the Indian seemed to have fallen quite naturally into the position of leader and, rather to his surprise, Shannon found himself accepting the situation. They returned to the first room and quickly discovered a lever at the bottom of the steps which manipulated the trapdoor. Rahim next searched for an electric-light switch. He discovered two; one apparently controlled the lights upstairs, the other lit all the lamps in the underground rooms.

'That's better,' said Hugh. 'I wonder how long we shall have to wait?'

He had hardly spoken when they heard the sound of stealthy footsteps overhead. In a moment Rahim had switched out the lights again and they were in darkness.

'Back into the next room!' he whispered.

With the aid of his torch, they retreated to the first bedroom and waited in silence. Presently there was a slight creak and they knew that the trapdoor had been raised. Then footsteps were heard descending the steps; a moment later there was a dull boom, followed almost at once by a click as the lights were put on. After that there was silence. A minute or two went by and Hugh cautiously looked into the other room. Rahtz was sitting at the table with his back to him. Nodding to his companions, the young Englishman strode to the Russian's side and taped him on the shoulder. The latter leapt to his feet with such suddenness that he overturned his chair. In a state of absolute amazement he looked at Shannon.

'You!' he gasped. 'You!'

'Yes,' said Hugh, 'and my friends!'

He indicated his three companions, who had followed him. Rahtz shrugged his shoulders and, picking up his chair, sat on it.

'It would appear that I am caught after all,' he said with the utmost coolness.

'You are!' replied Hugh.

'So you even discovered this last refuge,' went on the Russian. 'If I had a hat on I would take it off to you, Shannon. Really you are positively brilliant, and our mistake all along has been in underrating you.'

'It was my friend here who discovered your last refuge, as you call it.' Hugh indicated Abdul Rahim.

'Ah! The person who shot me!' Rahtz held up his right hand, round the wrist of which was a bloodstained handkerchief. 'It was rather undignified to be shot by an Indian,' he added insolently, 'though I must admit it was a good shot.'

'Since you appear to regard Indians with such disdain,' said Hugh hotly, 'it may interest you to know that this gentleman also rescued my sister from your infernal clutches.'

'Indeed!' Rahtz looked at Abdul Rahim with an appearance of bland curiosity. 'But please don't suggest that she was in my – er – clutches. It was Hudson who wanted her so badly. Poor fellow, he died rather suddenly.'

'How?' demanded Hugh.

'I shot him,' was the calm reply.

They stared at him in horror.

'You see,' he went on, 'the poor man went mad, and tried to kill Novar and myself – he very nearly did too, but during the struggle he dropped his revolver; I picked it up and managed to shoot him just as he was strangling Novar. He is buried in the garden somewhere.'

There was silence for a full minute after that, then Hugh roused himself.

'Come on, Rahtz!' he said. 'There's no reason why we should remain here any longer.'

'None at all,' said the Russian. 'Am I to attribute it as a compliment to myself,' he added with an ironical smile, 'or a sign that you are not as brave as you appear, that you have brought three other men to help you to capture me?'

'I think you may congratulate yourself on being treated with consideration at all by Captain Shannon,' said Abdul Rahim quietly.

Rahtz looked at him disdainfully.

'I am not aware that I addressed you,' he said. 'Who are you, anyway?'

'A great admirer of Captain Shannon's,' was the reply.

'You have my sympathy,' murmured the Russian, and rose from his chair. 'Well, I am ready!' he said.

He walked carelessly towards the steps. Then, suddenly, as he passed the electric light switch he put up his hand and the place was plunged into complete darkness. A mocking laugh came from the gloom.

'Gentlemen, I have a revolver in my hand and I am ready to use it,' said Rahtz's voice. 'No doubt one of you has an electric torch. If he switches it on he is a dead man!'

For a moment there was a tense silence, then suddenly Rahim's torch flared out, there was a flash and a terrific concussion followed immediately by another flash and an even greater concussion, a moan, the sound of a body dropping – and silence. The acrid smell of powder filled the close atmosphere.

'Switch on the lights, please,' said Abdul Rahim's quiet voice. 'My torch has fallen, and I fear it is broken.'

Hugh groped along the wall and at last found the switch. A moment and the place was brilliantly illuminated.

On the ground lay Rahtz, stretched on his back. Miles knelt beside him and after examining him stood up.

'I guess his plotting days are over,' he said.

'Dead?' asked Cousins.

The American nodded.

'He was hit clean between he eyes,' he said,

looking at Abdul Rahim with admiration. 'It was a thundering good shot.'

'It's a pity he had to be killed,' said the Indian, 'but it was fate.'

'What did you do?' asked Cousins, with a curious tone in his voice.

'I merely held the torch at arm's length and he fired. Then I fired back.'

'What made you drop it?'

'I think it was hit.' He bent and picked it up. 'Yes,' he said, 'it is quite shattered.'

The others examined it also.

'Look here,' said Cousins, 'I believe you've been hit also. Let me see your left hand!'

The Indian stood smiling at him, his left hand, as ever, stuck in the pocket of his coat.

'Believe me, Mr Cousins,' he said, 'I am perfectly all right.'

The little man turned away with a puzzled frown on his face.

'You're a strange fellow,' he said.

'This business has meant the loss of some lives,' said Hugh regretfully. 'Hudson, Kamper, and now Rahtz. We'll have to get Rainer to send along and have him taken away. Come on! We may as well have a look round before we leave this house.'

They searched the suitcases and the leather bag. The latter was locked, but they forced it open and found inside several important documents relative to Russia's activities, besides large bundles of banknotes and negotiable securities which must have represented a very large amount of money. The suitcases contained very little of interest; a few papers which they stuffed into the bag – as they intended taking it with them – some money and clothes, that was all.

Leaving the underground apartments they ascended the steps and dropped the trapdoor behind them. They went from room to room, but found nothing worthy of notice until they entered a bedroom adjoining a small sitting room which, from evidence left about, they soon concluded was Hudson's. Cousins noticed a writing pad lying in a wastepaper basket. He pulled it out and with it some sheets of paper.

'Wastepaper baskets often contain information worth having,' he said.

He proceeded to study the pad and paper. There was nothing written on the former, but the sheets of paper were covered with words and sentences scrawled about in the utmost confusion. Cousins became very interested and sat down in a chair to read what he could, while the others continued their search of the apartment.

'By Jove!' he exclaimed at last. 'There is something here which the Commissioner will find very interesting, and a few other people as well.'

'What is it?' asked Hugh.

'It is obviously the writing of a madman, for there is no beginning nor end, nor, in fact, any order at all. It consists of sentences and words and Hudson's signature repeated over and over again, but it amounts to this, that he had embezzled over two lacs of rupees from the Government by forged signatures, and that Rahtz discovered it – how, is not stated. Apparently under the threat of exposure the two Russians forced him to act with them and supply them with all kinds of confidential documents. At the end he writes, Joan has gone to kill Novar and Rahtz for my sake – I must help her.'

'Good Lord!' said Hugh. 'Now we know why he was connected with the others. Bring it along, Jerry! There's nothing else worth taking.'

They found the gates open when they reached them, so passed out of the grounds without difficulty. Rainer was waiting for them outside Rahtz's bungalow, and they told him about the Russian's death.

'H'm!' he grunted. 'I suppose I'll have to go and tell his wife. I've already frightened her to death with my searching, but as I warned her something might happen to him if he resisted, I hope it won't come as too great a shock. Every triumph has its drawbacks,' he added. 'Poor woman!'

He came back in ten minutes wiping his brow with a handkerchief.

'She took it very badly,' he growled. 'I've left her in a dead faint. Luckily there's a woman friend of hers there who'll look after her.' He called to a sergeant of police who was standing near by. 'Harris,' he said, 'take two or three men to The Retreat on Shadrah Road, and bring the body of

Rahtz home. Mr Rahim will tell you how to enter the room where it is lying.'

The Indian gave careful instructions and even drew a diagram, so that the sergeant went away fully posted with directions about getting into the underground chambers.

'Now,' said Rainer, 'you fellows will want to get back. Miss Shannon will be getting anxious. I hope you've room in your car for me.'

'Sure!' said Miles heartily, then added with a grin, 'Sorry, Hugh, I forgot it was your automobile.'

Shannon laughed maliciously.

'I've almost forgotten that fact myself,' he said. 'Jump in everybody You too, Rahim – I've a bone to pick with you and the D.C. Besides we want to thank you for what you did the other night, and my sister will be hurt if you don't come.'

Abdul Rahim smiled.

'I'll come,' he said, 'but I'd rather face the bone than the thanks. I've a car of my own hidden a little way away, so I'll follow you in that. Rainer's bungalow I presume?'

Hugh nodded and as the Indian strolled away, turned to the Deputy Commissioner with a grin.

'Our friend is a trifle familiar,' he remarked.

'I like it,' said the other.

On the way, Cousins told Rainer about the sheets of paper found in Hudson's waste-paper basket and what they contained. Rainer was vastly interested and took them into his own possession.

'These will make a lot of people sit up and think,'

he said. 'I'll hand them over to the Governor. By the way, you fellows, His Excellency is very gratified over the wonderful success that has attended your efforts. I found time to ring him up from Rahtz's bungalow and he desire's me to bring you all to see him at eleven tomorrow morning.'

They stopped at the telegraph office on the way and Hugh kept the rest of the party waiting nearly half an hour while he wrote out a long cable and despatched it. He had brought his small code book with him in his breast pocket in order to prevent delay and now, with a sigh of relief and satisfaction, he sent away the news to England, which would prove to be the forerunner of a great sensation.

Abdul Rahim had arrived at Rainer's bungalow some time before them, and he was chatting with the ladies when they entered. Joan ran to meet them her eyes shining with a great happiness.

'Oh, Hugh,' she cried, 'isn't it wonderful? Mr Rahim has been telling us of your great success. Won't Sir Leonard Wallace be delighted?'

'I hope so,' replied Hugh. 'Have you thanked Rahim for rescuing you?'

'I've tried to, but he wouldn't let me.'

'Well, I guess I'll have a go,' said Miles.

'If you do,' said the Indian, 'I'll depart at once, and I understand that Captain Shannon has a bone to pick with me and Mr Rainer!'

'A bone to pick with—!' exclaimed Joan. 'How absurd!'

'Nevertheless I have,' said Hugh obstinately, 'and quite a large one. I want to know how Rahim knew anything about the meeting and raid tonight and how, in fact, he knew anything about the activities of the Russians at all! And, as he is a friend of Mr Rainer's, who knew everything, I have been forced to the conclusion that Rainer must have told him.'

Abdul Rahim stood in the centre of the room and smiled. His left hand still reposed in his coat pocket and he looked anything but annoyed or embarrassed by Hugh's words.

'Rainer,' he said, turning to the Commissioner, 'I am going to give you away.'

'Go ahead!' said the other, who looked thoroughly pleased with himself.

'Well, I called here the other morning,' went on Rahim and his voice was perfectly clear and resonant, with no trace of a sibilant inflection whatever, 'and Rainer, I am delighted to say, was so pleased to see me that he told me everything where you imagined the meeting would take place and I resolved to be present myself in case of accidents. I arrived at Mozang College about half past six this evening, had the pleasure of seeing Mr Cousins climb over the wall and followed him. After a great deal of trouble I got into the College, and found my way to the room in question. Of course, the door was locked, but I possess a little instrument which will open most doors. It opened that one and I entered and locked it behind me, then looked about for a hiding place. The large cupboard was the only possible place, and I unlocked the door as I had done the other. It was lined with shelves, but each one was long enough and wide enough to contain me if I cleared off the papers and books. I chose one of the lowest and piled all its litter on to the others. Time passed very slowly and I began to wonder if I was in the wrong room after all, but the orderly position of the chairs around the table reassured me and, at last, I heard a sound and scrambled into the cupboard and pulled the doors to, just as the key turned in the lock and someone entered. I could not see, but I heard everything that went on – well, you know the rest!'

'The Secret Service could do with a man like you,' said Hugh, 'and besides thanking you for rescuing my sister I have also to thank you for saving my life when Rahtz—'

'I hardly saved your life,' interrupted Rahim hastily. 'I am sure you would have avoided his knife.'

'I doubt it,' replied Hugh. He turned to the Deputy Commissioner. 'But really, Rainer,' he began, 'you should never have broken a confidence which—'

He was interrupted by a great burst of laughter from Cousins. Everyone turned in amazement to look at the little man, who was lying back in his chair and emitting peal after peal while tears of merriment ran down his cheeks. The sight of that face creased up into its thousand wrinkles of mirth set the rest of the company laughing too. Presently Miles went over to him and patted him on the back.

'Steady on, Jerry,' he said. 'I guess the events of the day have made you hysterical.'

'Hysterical be blowed!' gasped the ideal valet. 'I was laughing at Shannon's remark that the Secret Service could do with a man like – like – er – Rahim!'

'Well, what's funny in that? Pull yourself together, you boob!'

But Rainer also seemed to see the humour of it. He rocked in his chair.

'Now I know why – why Mr Abdul Rahim always keeps his left hand in his pocket,' went on Cousins. 'Don't you see—' He roared with laughter again, then rose to his feet and looked at Abdul Rahim. 'Forgive me, sir,' he said, 'but I couldn't help it. Shannon, you ass, this is *Sir Leonard Wallace*!'

'What!' shouted Hugh.

'Holy Mike!' murmured Miles.

He sat down but, missing the chair, landed on the floor, from where he continued to stare with his mouth open at the Chief of the British Secret Service.

'Cousins is right,' said Sir Leonard, smiling round at the astonished company. 'Just before the aeroplane left with my despatches, I decided to come out myself. I thought I might be of some use and I also wanted to be on the spot to watch the final stages of your triumph, Shannon, and congratulate you, Cousins and Miles on a magnificent achievement. As soon as I arrived I disguised myself in this get up. It occurred to me that by keeping in the background and not making myself known I would be of more help to you than if I divulged my presence in Lahore. I watched your visit to Novar with the three Indians and later rode on the luggage carrier of his car, when he went to The Retreat. The following morning I made myself known to Rainer and he told me everything. I have thoroughly enjoyed your curiosity about me. It only remains for me to change my garb and resume my normal appearance. Then I shall try to tell you what Great Britain and in fact, the whole world owes to you three men.'

His left hand was not in his pocket now. On it was a brown kid glove and as Miles looked he remembered hearing that the famous Chief of the British Intelligence Department had lost his left arm in the service of his country. The substitute was a good one, but it was only an artificial arm after all.

In the midst of the excited exclamations that greeted Sir Leonard's remarks, he turned to Rainer.

'Can I have that bath, Rainer?' he said. 'I should like to attend the supper party, you promised us, as myself.'

'Come along now, Sir Leonard,' said Rainer.

'By the way, sir,' said Shannon, 'I cabled my report to you tonight.'

'That's all right,' said the Chief. 'I left a note for Major Brien to hand it to the Prime Minister as soon as it arrived.'

He and Rainer excused themselves, and left the room.

'By Jove!' exclaimed Hugh, with a broad grin on his face and eyes sparkling with delight. 'By Jove!'

'Say, Hugh,' said Miles, rising from the floor, 'this is sure the third greatest day of my life.'

'What were the first and second, Oscar?' asked Joan.

'The second greatest day was when I discovered you loved me, little girl,' said the American. 'The first and greatest of all days hasn't arrived yet, but I guess it will soon. And that will be the day we are married.'

'You darling!' whispered Joan.

'"There is a tide in the affairs of men, which, taken at the flood leads on to fortune",' said Cousins.

Hugh had seated himself close to Helen Rainer and was talking earnestly to her. Suddenly she smiled and nodded very shyly, a heightened colour in her cheeks. Mrs Rainer noticed the glance her daughter gave to Hugh and her eyes opened wide, but a look of pleased surprise came into her face. Cousins also seemed to find something significant in the attitudes of Miss Rainer and Hugh.

'"Here will I dwell, for Heaven is in these lips And all is dross that is not Helena",' quoted the little man.

'Shut up, Cousins!' growled Hugh.

Cousins shut up.

EPILOGUE

A great sensation shook the world during the course of the next few days, when it became known by means of the press of Great Britain, the United States and France, how Russia, Germany and their many satellites had conspired to plunge the world once again into a terrible war, and that the three nations had sent a joint ultimatum to those bloodthirsty countries demanding the instant demobilisation of all warlike forces and dismantling of all aircraft except those built for commercial purposes. At the same time a mighty British fleet sailed up the Baltic, another combined British and French fleet patrolled the North Sea and the British Mediterranean squadron entered the Dardanelles and, sailing across the Sea of Marmora, anchored close to Constantinople.

The German inhabitants of the Rhine woke up one morning to find a great British and French army almost encamped at their doors, the army in India was mobilised and stood ready in the Punjab and the North-West Province and also in Bengal. Persian ports were surprised at the appearance of British cruisers, and a great American fleet was known to be halfway across the Pacific on its way to China.

Excitement knew no bounds when it was officially reported that the agents of the aggressive powers had actually been arrested whilst holding a meeting in Lahore, and that amongst them was Bukharin himself – the Soviet Minister for Foreign Affairs. British newspapers came out with a verbatim report of the proceedings, and a great storm of indignation spread throughout France, Italy, and the English-speaking countries. A rush of able-bodied men for enlistment took place in Great Britain and the Dominions, an almost unprecedented wave of patriotism came over the Empire, and there was such an intensity of feeling against Communism that the British, Colonial, and American representatives of that doctrine went in danger of their lives, or, at least, of very rough handling, and therefore conceived it wiser to disappear from view.

The world throbbed with suspense for two days, extraordinary rumours were afloat one minute and contradicted the next, a situation of extreme gravity arose on the money markets, business was at a standstill – everyone waited for the first shot that would plunge creation into a war more terrible than the last. Then there came a terse official statement, which sent the world hysterical with joy, which made strong men run about the streets laughing childishly, and crying the news to each other as they went.

Russia and Germany with their many dupes had climbed down. The ultimatum was accepted without reservation.

At once, Great Britain, the United States, the British Dominions, France, Italy, Belgium – all the powers loyal to the gospel of peace and goodwill – were *en fête*. Armistice Day of 1918 was quite overshadowed by the joy of this wonderful day of all days. London went mad with delight, a wonderful crowd gathered before Buckingham Palace and demonstrated its loyalty to the throne as never before. New York, Paris, Brussels, Rome were no whit behind in displaying their enthusiasm.

International commissions were appointed to see that the terms of the ultimatum were thoroughly carried out. They did their work completely and well, and until they reported 'All's well', the three great nations, which had acted with such firm and dramatic suddenness, remained under arms.

Bolshevism had received a blow from which it would probably never recover.

Hugh Shannon, Oscar Miles and Cousins were received by the British Cabinet, and the Prime Minister thanked them on behalf of the Empire for their great services. His Majesty the King commanded their presence at the Palace, where he himself expressed his gratitude to them and honoured them with the decorations they so thoroughly deserved. In spite of attempts to keep their identity secret they soon became known and time after time were almost mobbed by

518

enthusiastic crowds. As Cousins remarked, their use as secret agents was entirely destroyed, but he and Shannon were given posts which would keep them at home for the future.

The French Government invited them to Paris where they were given a truly royal welcome and fêted in magnificent style, and the United States, not to be outdone, demanded their presence and would take no refusal.

Before they went, however, a pleasing ceremony took place in London, and that was a double wedding between Joan and Miles, and Helen Rainer and Hugh. Every effort was made to keep the event secret, but somehow it leaked out, and when the happy couples left the church, they were greeted by a vast crowd which lined the whole route to Sir Leonard Wallace's house – where the reception took place – and cheered them to the echo.

Many notabilities were present at the reception, and not the least amongst them was the Lieutenant-Governor of the Punjab, Sir Reginald Scott.

Soon after the wedding, both couples left for the United States attended by Cousins. The warm-hearted people of the great American Republic outdid even England and France in the magnificence` of their welcome, with a little extra enthusiasm for Oscar Miles and his shy little bride, whose beauty and sweetness instantly charmed them, and whom they took to their hearts as only the people of the United States can.

Miles found himself appointed as Chief of the

Intelligence Department in succession to a predecessor, who in his great delight at the exploits of his junior, had voluntarily resigned to make way for him.

As Cousins remarked, hoping that the shades of Dryden would forgive him:

'Heaven that but once was prodigal before,
To Oscar gave so much, she could not give him more.'